SILENT WILD

a novel by

LLOYD RICE

Pine Publishing, Inc.

Published by
PINE PUBLISHING, INC.

This is a novel of fiction. Other than certain historical figures and places, identified in *Author's Note*, all characters, places and incidents are products of the author's imagination or are used fictitiously. Any resemblance to actual persons, living or dead, is entirely coincidental.

Copyright © 2002 by Pine Publishing, Inc.

All rights reserved. No part of this book may be used or reproduced in any manner whatsoever without written permission, except in the case of brief quotations, with attribution, in articles and reviews. For information address: Pine Publishing, Inc. P.O. Box 999 Pine Island, MN 55963.

Library of Congress Control Number: 2002091886

ISBN: 0-9720550-0-2

First paperback printing August 2002

Printed in the United States of America

Pine Publishing, Inc. has the mission of fostering awareness and preservation of the wonders of nature by presenting stories of people's lives, as they relate to these fragile treasures. Inquiries are invited from those who want to publish stories or verse that contribute to this awareness and preservation.

PROLOGUE

Glaciers scraped and ground over the solid rock lying under northeastern Minnesota and the Province of Ontario. Melting glacier ice filled millions of basins and joining streams that became a chain of lakes along the United States/Canada border.

Tens of thousands of years later, inhabitants hunted, fished, and fashioned birch bark canoes to traverse this water highway.

Hardy, vigorous Voyageurs in the 1700's canoed and portaged the lake-highway lifeline to trade with the Indian Nations of the far west, and then returned east. Lake Voyageurs, from Montreal, paddled their larger canoes through the Great Lakes chain to Lake Superior and Grand Portage. The rendezvous at Grand Portage, between the Inland Voyageurs and the Lake Voyageurs, has been said to be indescribable in its spirit, ethos, and exuberance.

The boundary waters area remained silent and wild, as adjacent lands were developed by people who came to harvest timber, minerals, and fish...and some who came just to be a part of the wilderness life.

Newly married Buck and Casey Ryker, along with Buck's ex-SEAL Teammate, George Heudak, left Colorado in 1993 to establish their lives and livelihoods in the north. Their beloved Boundary Waters Canoe Area, along with their chosen way of life, was challenged, as never before, on June 14, 1999.

1

A patched and rusted flatbed truck raced along a northern Minnesota county road. It turned abruptly onto a gravel lane, billowing dust as it neared a richly painted sign bearing the words Ryker Log Homes. The barreling behemoth lurched into the narrow driveway and on into a twelve-acre construction yard, shattering the northwoods silence. It skidded to a stop in front of the yard tool shack. The brawny driver jumped out of the truck marked Heudak Hauling.

"You tree-huggers will go off your nut at this story," George Heudak shouted at his ex-SEAL buddy, Buck Ryker.

"What story?" Buck said. He continued stashing the tools left by his recently departed four-man construction crew.

"Charlie's got the dope. He just called me at home. Says he wants to give us both the story first hand. He's at the Sawbill—sounded like he was about ready to piss his pants. Let's go."

"Can't make it. I've got homework tonight," Buck hollered from inside the shack.

"You mean you think you'll get lucky? Casey will probably eighty-six that plan," George said."

"I *mean* Casey and I have to go over finances to see if we're going to lose our ass in this log home business."

"Like I say, you'd better hear this," George insisted. "Charlie says it's the worst boundary waters news yet."

"Got to lock up first," Buck growled. "See you there in twenty minutes—but damned if I'll stay long."

George slammed into his more-or-less-red flatbed and spun wheels out of the driveway.

Buck wondered about Charlie's *bad news*. The "tree-hugger" jibe was wilderness preservation talk. It usually amounted to a cynical slam at tourists who wanted to see no change in the wild and silent boundary waters area. The barb was aimed especially at city visitors who were enthralled about "experiencing" the area for a few weeks, as opposed to the locals who viewed the wild as their own playground, and who made their lives in it.

George was gung-ho for the wilderness, but Buck's interest in Voyageur history and his participation in the environment controversy had begun George's half-serious razzing.

Buck turned off all power to the yard, except for the sensor alarm system, fingered the electronic keypad numbers, and slammed the steel door shut. He took one long look around the twelve-acre construction yard—the mammoth piles of forty-foot logs, the half-erected log home in progress, the giant log-handling machines. *A lot of sweat and not enough equity*, he thought.

* * *

Over the six years of their marriage and partnership, he and Casey had made a marginal go of the business. The last three years, her part-time nursing job at the Cascade Clinic had helped pull them through. Most days, she returned from work with a satisfaction born out of giving real service to the local folks who were comfortable with her realistic, knowledgeable and empathetic handling of their medical concerns.

Casey and Buck had originally attended the twelve-week Boundary Log Home School to learn the basics. Development of their design and manufacturing skills began with their own place and continued with major help from other log home builders (friendly competitors) in the area. Their own story-and-a-half log home had been a work-in-progress for several years, but now was nearly complete.

Ryker Log Homes was now custom-designing, building and delivering to owners in Minnesota, Wisconsin, and Iowa. A good summer and the business might get solidly in the black. They hoped Casey could quit her job at the clinic.

Buck's 200-yard walk to the house usually gave him a swell of satisfaction. The mix of pungent pine aroma and clean-earth smell of the aspens greeted his senses. The brisk, clear mid-June air stirred whatever he had for a soul. But today, something else was in the air.

* * *

Casey padded out of the upstairs shower, toweling off as Buck banged in the back door. She stopped at the top of the heavy-timbered stairway that overlooked the ruggedly comfortable living room.

"What was the truck noise," she hollered toward the kitchen.

Buck strode through the kitchen door to the bottom of the stairs. His sudden appearance aroused her into an instinctive flurry of cover-up. Buck's instinct was also aroused. Her tall, lithe form had helped make her a standout near-pro volleyball athlete. Her black hair, enhanced by too-blue eyes, gave her a countenance that would draw the gods down from Mount Olympus. After six years, it was still like seeing her for the first time, he thought. He smiled and knew that she sensed the moment.

"Oh, that was George," he said.

"Detach that stare and I'll get dressed," she said. "You can tell me all about it over a beer."

"Casey, George has some urgent problem he wants to tell me about. I have to head over to the Sawbill for a very short meeting." Silence hung in the air like a black-yellow sky waiting for a tornado.

"That's the first time I've heard 'urgent' and 'George' in the same sentence," Casey finally said. "We had an evening planned. I've got a roast in the oven. We need to get at the projections. We have—you have—been putting it off for two weeks."

"I know, but I've got to do this. I'll get back quick."

"We'll see," Casey said and retreated into the bedroom. There was no joy in Rykerville.

* * *

Dual rear wheels spewed gravel as Buck gunned the Chev Silverado pickup out of the driveway. *This was a helluva way to end a day!* He didn't need any more problems, but he had to admit, he was causing this one. He raced the two rough miles out to the county road as if he were bulldozing through the trees. There were three homes on his RR 37, but he rarely saw a human on the narrow gravel road. Anyone driving in these parts needed to know the territory. The turnoff to an individual property was barely discernible. Casey had finally designed, built and painted the "Ryker Log Homes" sign to guide clients and suppliers—a three by four-foot carved piece, painted with a dark green background and red and ochre highlighted letters.

He headed southeast on County Road 18 to The Sawbill Bar and Grill—the local hangout, pig-out, take-out, and make-out place. The strip of paved county road waved and weaved over the boggy tundra. This should have been a visceral delight, cruising the narrow two-laner, through the poplars and fir that he could almost touch with his arm out the window. But George's warning sounded ominous: another challenge to the Boundary Waters Canoe Area.

Since the end of World War II, millions had enjoyed the unique wilderness experience. But there had been constant pressure from many sides to make the BWCA more accessible to logging, mining and motorized traffic. The challenges had been pretty much kept at bay by environmental groups, tri-county residents who wanted to preserve the BWCA and lawmakers who were interested in maintaining, for future generations, one of the nation's few remaining wilderness areas. Now, was a dispute going to be a problem for him? In fact, it already was!

Solving problems in the SEALS had been simpler. Either kill or be killed. Teammates did the job together, acting as one unit. No problems could be allowed among them. Only one adversary: the enemy. Life in the northwoods was simple at times. But there were factions, people complications. Even he and George did not see eye-to-eye on some issues these days.

They had plenty of grab-ass fights during SEAL training, but the bouts were quickly over. The competition had begun their first day in the rookies' chow line. George's six-three/240 was immediately a challenge to Buck's six-one/190. They had enough salt in their verbal shoves to flavor the five pounds of food each had on his tray. Whether on the rifle range, obstacle course or in the weight room, neither man needed any other motive to give his all. "Big George" could dead-lift 460 pounds, fifty pounds more than Buck, but in the 225-pound bench-press, Buck's sleek toughness won. After straining through forty-five reps, George quit. "I gotta go to the can. Get yourself a hernia," he mumbled. The other trainees could see the competitive tension building and were waiting for the "I'm-better-than-you" pot to boil over. However, by the end of the applied physical torture of "Hell Week," mutual respect and focus on surviving the final weeks took over. Even when Buck was designated Squad Leader, their friendship held. George simply became Buck's main man. They finally realized they were not going to die right there on the beach of Coronado Island Naval Amphibious Base. Continued training was a slightly lesser degree of hell. Hours and hours in cold water until a few trainees chose to ring the "I quit" bell.

As the remaining candidates proved that they could exceed basic human endurance, the training became more instructional. They learned to treat the M60 machine gun, the M16 rifle and the grenade launcher as personal best friends.

Initially, maneuvers in the 24-foot Hurricane "black boats" were relatively fun and games – 200HP Volvo marine diesels driving them through waves at 30 knots or more. Breathtaking! Then the exercises required the Hurricanes to roar around at full speed, picking up trainee swimmers in full gear with an arm catch. Even during the fiercest jungle firefights, the cardinal rule was: leave no Teammate behind, alive, wounded or dead.

After their parachute training, finals and graduation, they proudly wore the Navy Special Warfare Command "Trident" insignia. Their requests for "action" sent them to Central America and preparation for operations in Panama at the end of 1989. That action and the subsequent months did not inspire them to re-up. They agreed that there was more to life than being submerged in cold, dark water, slogging through infested marches and being dropped out of helicopters into the sea, to swim five miles into the beach.

Fortunately, George's uncle in Colorado Springs offered to take on a "couple strong backs" in his house-building business. George and Buck began a riotous life of twelve-hour workdays and serious woman-chasing between C.S. and Denver. George was in his element. Buck had enough after a year.

Then he met Casey.

* * *

Buck quickly covered the nine miles on County 18, at seventy-five. The brilliant orange sun angled fiercely into his rear view mirror as he attacked the Sawbill parking lot. The gravel dust from his six tires joined that of the last pickup-maniacs to get there. He could barely see the two paneled entrance doors as he got out. The doors were newly painted red, covering the dents and gouges from being the targets in late night bottle-throwing events. Buck pushed through the left-hand door to the bar. The other went to the dining area—not really necessary since there was no wall between the two inside.

The decor was basically early Schmidt's, Miller and Leinenkugel. If you didn't care much for ducks, bear and moose, the art adorning the walls would not be your cup of schnapps. The tables and chairs were the originals, installed in the late seventies. The styles of some, however, pre-dated that. The chrome legs and laminate tops with chrome edges had stood up to a lot of abuse. Diners were treated to place mats, provided years ago by various beer and booze distributors. The menu had stayed about the same over the years. A few more burgers and fries were served now, along with the Sawbill's historic hot beef, pork or turkey sandwiches that heaped more mashed potatoes and gravy than most anyone could eat. Locals and some travelers rated the Sawbill food above anything out on the North Shore highway.

Buck walked up to the long bar where George and Charlie Henstead were stooled. He ordered a bottle of Leinenkugel Red and paid the big blonde who served beer and booze and took no shit. The three men moved immediately to a table on the fringe of the eating area.

"Thanks for coming, Buck," Charlie said with sincerity. He looked like he would rather not be there.

"It's OK, Charlie. What's up?"

George interrupted, "Charlie can give you the whys and wherefores. I'll just say that he's heard that some big outfit is trying to change the law to allow them to put tourist lodges near some of the BWCA portages."

Charlie winced and took a deep breath. "Buck, let me tell you everything I know about this."

Buck nodded and kept his disbelief in check. Charlie Henstead was the chairman of the Nordland County citizen's group. It included representatives from a section of northeastern Minnesota bordering the Boundary Waters Canoe Area. Charlie and his wife, Lillian, were retired and tried to make ends meet by taking turns keeping the doors open at the Tourist Information Center. The Center, located out on the North Shore highway, was financed by fees paid by local commercial businesses. Charlie and Lillian lived in an old logging lodge that Charlie kept patching against the weather.

"It started with a phone call from my nephew in Washington, D.C.," Charlie continued. His earlier pallid countenance became ruddy as the adrenaline and the beer took effect. George, recognizing the probable need for liquid support, eased to the bar and returned with three bottles of Leinie Red. The world stopped momentarily while the three took long drinks of the local favorite.

"He just called me this afternoon," Charlie went on. "He's an aide to Congressman Wayneson, you know. He usually sees most of the Congressman's paperwork but doesn't hear any of the discussions. Last evening he was working late. He's a real hard worker, David is. He couldn't help overhearing a phone conversation that the Congressman was having. David was about to leave but he heard Boundary Waters Canoe Area mentioned. He perked up his ears and listened for a few minutes—as long as he dared—outside the Congressman's private office."

"You guys OK here?" Big Blonde interrupted.

"Bring us a round, willya honey," George said with a swipe at her backside.

"Well," Charlie said, "the gist of it is that the phone call concerned a proposal for a bill to allow commercial establishments near the portages between some of the restricted BWCA lakes. The Congressman seemed reluctant but did agree to meet with representatives from the big corporation. David didn't know if he would be able to find out much more about it, but said he thought I should know. He did say he heard Heron Lake mentioned."

"It can't be," Buck said.

George added, "Hard to believe."

"Can you call your nephew to find out the name of the corporation?" Buck asked.

"I can call David at home tonight, but I don't know what he can do," Charlie said. "I think I should call a meeting of the citizen's group.

"Hold off until we hear more facts," Buck said.

"Yeah, no use getting everyone's dong in a wringer at

this stage," George said. "Buck, can they build something on the Heron portage?"

"It's big enough, but who knows how crazy it would be to try to build there. Anyone going through all this must have checked it out." Buck paused and then continued, "I'd better get out there and take a look. I'll go out tomorrow early and come back the next day."

"When will I hear from you, Buck?" Charlie was pale again.

"Squeeze what you can out of your nephew," Buck directed. "If you think you've got enough info, call the group together...let's see, today's Monday...schedule it for Wednesday about seven. I should be back by then." Buck felt like he was back leading the platoon into a battle zone.

* * *

"This could be a problem," cautioned LeYan Syn. Her perfect forehead was furrowed as she held the complete attention of the two men at the huge mahogany boardroom table. "My research on this boundary waters area tells me that the locals and the environmentalists are about as likely to agree as the Arabs and the Jews." The distracting beauty was executive vice-president for Alactra, an international conglomerate. She paused in her presentation to the president, Alasam Alactra, and Bill Anderson, token American and head of operations for Boundary Lodges, a subsidiary of Alactra.

"Assuming that we can successfully lobby in the U.S. Congress to introduce a bill allowing development in this BWCA," LeYan continued, "we might still have what they call 'tree-huggers' to deal with."

When Alasam Alactra spoke, it was as if the stone gates of history opened and the wisdom of the ages came forth. There was no question that he was the soul and patriarch of his company. He gazed out of the floor-to-ceiling windows toward the Chicago Loop. The sumptuous fortieth floor office suite of the Alactra Building commanded a view northward to the curve of Lake Michigan.

"What do you recommend?" Alasam said with a quiet consideration that pleased LeYan, even though he was facing away from her.

Moving from her chair, on the far side of the large table, she walked slowly toward her mentor, pausing to answer. "I recommend that we learn everything we can about the local situation, starting with the first portage site. I would send Luther and Benny to scope the area. I have booked them on a flight today to Duluth, Minnesota. When they get there, they will take a floatplane to the proposed construction area. They will be equipped with a raft to reach the portage by water. After returning to Duluth, they will use a rental car to drive back to the BWCA and begin surveillance and inquiry. With your approval, I will give them their instructions immediately."

She glided slowly to stand alongside Alasam's chair. Her thigh pressed against the soft leather arm, displaying a toned and tan bare leg through the long slit in the fashionably designed, Asian style dress.

It was a scene not lost on Anderson. He struggled to re-establish that he was still in the room. "Do you think those two guys can handle this kind of thing discreetly?" he asked.

Luther and Benny were long-time loyal grunts that Mr. Alactra had hired to do some heavy persuading, when he first came to America. The two cousins had a deep and abiding affection for the Blues Brothers of the seventies. They had adopted the black suit, black hat, black sunglasses look, but were on a different planet from John Belushi and Dan Ackroyd. Their corporate moniker had become "The Cousins."

"They will do what I tell them," LeYan said sharply, barely turning her head toward Anderson. "They won't use a heavy hand until I approve."

The meeting was over. Anderson was dismissed.

2

Buck and Charlie left the Sawbill, squeezing past two local logger hard hats that burst in like linebackers on a blitz.

"Charlie, it was good to get this early clue," Buck said. "I hope we can take advantage of it."

"I hope so too," was all Charlie could muster. He got into his 1992 Buick LeSabre and waved at a departing Buck.

The evening sky had darkened like an eclipse of the sun, moon and stars. The trees whirred by as Buck headed home. The poplars, aspens and even the friendly firs seemed to be thrusting fingers at him, instead of welcoming him as they had on the trip to the Sawbill. He was already late. No use thinking about Casey. He'd already torn that. He would explain. She'd be OK.

In the past, they had always been able to work things out—like the time a month ago when Casey's brother, John, had called. Buck had not seen John since their wedding, a fact for which he was grateful.

Casey was the firstborn. John's arrival two years later was considered a blessed event, nigh onto the immaculate. Emily and Floyd Brown insisted on no "Jack"—only John, as in *Chapter three, verse sixteen.* Buck always used "Jack."

The doting parents had enough time to get Casey started in life so that they could focus on their main man. After providing for his pampered and precious teen scene, they could hardly wait to get John enrolled in pre-med. His big guy good looks and campus cool kept the coeds standing in line. He squeaked through Family Practice, but never really got around to practice. Life with a 1990

Porsche, a cabin on the edge of Olympia Park and technically MD credentials, was too good to interrupt with regular working hours. He did some occasional clinic work to keep his hand in and pay some of the cabin rent. Emily and Floyd became less and less thrilled about their continuing financial subsidy.

Buck remembered in detail the conversation when John had called. Casey rang the tool shack intercom and said, "Buck, it's John on the line."

"Do I have to?"

"Buck!"

"Oh, OK. Put him on."

"Hello, Jack. This is Buck."

"Hi guy. How you doing?" With no answer forthcoming, John continued, "Need to ask your advice," John smoothed. Still no answer. "You there, Buck?"

"I'm here."

"How are chances of giving you a hand in the log home business this summer?"

"That is about the last thing I would expect you to be interested in. What's wrong with the doctor business?"

"I've been reading a lot about the environment, wilderness, trees and all that. Just thought I'd like to get next to it."

"Next to what?"

"Oh, you know, the lakes, trees and all that."

Buck paused, wondering if Brother John had malpracticed, been served with a paternity suit or had his subsidy cut off.

"That certainly is an interesting thought. Why don't you let Casey and me think about it and we will get back to you, OK? Later then."

After Buck had explained the conversation to Casey, she was at first almost excited to be able to help. However, the more she remembered all those years as a runner-up sibling and recalled John's disinterest in gainful employment, compared with his major motivation as a playboy, the more she questioned. He was the last thing they needed at Ryker Homes. That had been consensus.

* * *

A few deep breaths and Buck started to review the situation. To begin with, he was surprised that George did not seem more concerned about the portage challenge. In his first few years in the area, George could not wait to splash his canoe into a boundary waters lake. He would sometimes be out there for three or four days with only some food and a sleeping bag. He would come back visibly inspired and raring to go. In the last couple of years, however, his one-man log-hauling business occupied most of his interest; even exceeded his dedicated interest in the Local Ladies. And that *was* different. He had begun to favor the idea of extending the rights of loggers to cut more acreage, wherever it could be found.

"That tree-hugger talk won't rattle my cage," George had said. "When loggers have logs to haul, I'm their man!"

But all that was George's problem, Buck thought. He had decided he would leave home early and get to the Spit Lake landing about daybreak; should take him about twelve hours to get out to High Portage. After some investigation, he would pitch his two-person tent for the night.

Damn! He wished Casey would go with him. In their first years in northern Minnesota, they had thrilled at canoeing into the silent wilderness at least a few days a month, when weather permitted. They enjoyed each other, the exercise and the solitude. They often wondered if the wildlife was disturbed by their nocturnal thrashing.

Pull yourself together, he thought as he entered their driveway. *Think positive. This is something that no one anticipated, but it's something I have to deal with.* He left the pickup outside the rustic extra-large two-car garage. He considered that he would load the canoe and other gear later, ready to shove off at 3:30 in the morning. He walked up to the back screen door and saw the note:

"Betty called from the clinic...asked if I could help her with insurance claims tonight 'till about eleven. Since our business concerns are apparently on hold, I'm there," Casey had written.

Buck slowly entered their home. After studying many, many log home plans, he and Casey had designed this place to be their perfect example of a warm and wonderful northwoods cabin, including hand-crafted windows, doors and carved beams. The fieldstone fireplace longed for a North Shore blizzard to fully demonstrate its soul-satisfying effusion. Casey had decorated some walls with abstract prints and her own oils that were not great but they were hers. She set one rule: no walls gimmicked with prints of ducks, bears and deer. He left a note on the refrigerator: "Rumor of a threat to BWCA portage. Need to check it out. Back Wednesday night."

It would be a cold, dark ride to the landing. He didn't expect the Wednesday night homecoming to be much better. He opened the door to the guest bedroom to begin a short night.

* * *

"This sure as hell ain't no northwoods." Luther grumbled in his window seat as the Northwest D9S descended into Duluth International Airport. "Looks more like Syracuse."

"Course it ain't. We gotta fly a hunnert more miles north of here," Benny said without looking up from a Dean Koontz paperback. He had grabbed it in the O'Hare airport because it looked violent and sexy. It was.

Four business suits and a plumpish middle-age lady, quieting a two- or three-year-old, deplaned first. The Cousins usually waited to leave last. The process of squeezing their wide hulks down the aisle could cause near panic if they tried to battle for exit position. They plodded into the terminal and claimed their only luggage:

a longish black imitation leather case. Airport security became very interested, until they saw it contained only some shaving gear and a couple of pairs of huge shorts. They never felt the need to change from their black suit/hat/shades uniform, regardless of their destination or objective.

"Where's Modern Airlift?" Benny demanded of a little girl behind the car rental counter. Before she could answer, he leaned forward and said, "What-a-ya-got? We gotta reservation for some kind of car."

The little girl, who seemed hardly old enough to purchase second hand smoke or drive herself to work, was visibly shaken by Benny's assault.

"Well, we've got a Taurus sedan and an Escort," she wavered.

"No Cadillac?" Luther grumped.

"No sir. We've only got the two."

"We'll take the Taurus," said Benny. "And where's Modern Airlift?"

"The office is out on Haines Road," she said quickly. "May I please have your driver's license?" Benny tapped his fingers erratically while she did the paper work.

Benny opened the driver door and stooped over the front seat, holding the electric seat operator until the seat was as far back as it would go. He raised the steering wheel and eased in. Luther squeezed into the passenger seat, struggling with the manual seat lever to get the seat back to the max. Benny gunned out of the rental parking area and headed through the gate with an abandon that appeared to shock the guard at the checkout shack.

The Modern Airlift office was visible about 200 yards further along Airport Road. Benny turned in the chain link gate and started a beeline course directly across the field to the office. Then he abruptly lurched to the right as a taxiing Piper Cub came at them, as if to remind him that the area was part of an airstrip, not a drag strip.

"I thought flying in one of these model planes was going to be scary," growled Luther-the-passenger. "Can't be any worse than your horseshit driving." Recovering, he continued, "You know, we shoulda been a little sweeter to that blonde. She mighta wanted to show us around town or somethin'."

"Get real!" Benny rasped. "If she hadn't been behind that counter, she would have run her little ass off the other way. If you're gonna get anything, you're gonna have to pay for it—like always."

"I suppose you're gettin' so much," Luther countered.

The Taurus screeched up in front of the glass door marked *Modern Airlift*, ignoring the area to the left of the hangar boldly signed "Customer Parking."

"We ain't customers yet," Benny explained to Luther's look.

Halfway in the door, Benny eyed the two men talking at the counter and interrupted, "You got a reservation for Smith and Smith Meterists?" Benny always had trouble saying "mete-or-olo-gist" in spite of LeYan's training.

"Yes sir, are you Mr. Smith?" asked the taller of the two men. He sported the standard issue leather flight jacket with the Modern Airlift logo above the left pocket.

"Ya, I'm Smith and this is Smith," he thumbed toward Luther.

LeYan directed the meteorological scam, hoping that the two could pull it off. It would give them a reason to convince a pilot to fly into the restricted BWCA—that reason plus a couple other offers that smacked of the Godfather.

"Your secretary said that you want to fly into the area near the boundary waters. Is that correct?" the pilot asked.

Benny seemed to have a little trouble getting past the concept of LeYan as his secretary. Perhaps a tad of fantasy arose. Reviving, he answered, "That's right. We came from an emergency meeting of the society. There's a possibility of unusual weather imminent (LeYan told him to practice that word) in the area. We have to do some surveyance (almost got it) to check it out. We'll just want you to drop us off, wait a few hours while we investigate and then bring us back. We'll need an inflated raft with a battery motor and food for lunch."

"When do you want to go?" the pilot asked.

"No use leaving too early," Luther hoped, already dreaming about a late night on the town.

"We'll want to leave at sunrise," Benny said, ignoring the cousin's disappointment. "How long does it take to Heron Lake and how much moolah?"

"It's about an hour flight in there and the charge is $500 plus $200 for the raft and chow. In advance. No flights over the BWCA without special authorization."

"We'll see," said Benny quietly, handing the pilot seven C's. "Sunrise then. Be sure to have the gear."

"And plenty of food," added Luther. "And where's the North Star Motel?"

"This is a map to our takeoff point," the pilot responded. "North Star Motel you'll have to find yourself. I've never heard of it."

"Let's move," directed Benny and they banged out the door. "We've got to find the motel, but first we have to stop and buy something to put in that big case of yours."

* * *

The reveille alarm shrieked Buck alive at 3:30 AM in the guest bedroom. He had gotten used to the morning classical music station that Casey had set for six on their clock radio: Beethoven, followed by "pork chops at $1.99" hawked by Highway Superette. She was probably right though—the calm musical eye opener no doubt would add years to their lives.

It was good to have the truck loaded. He grabbed the food box, some coffee to go and headed out the back door. He glanced at his note on the refrigerator, remembered Casey's and shook his head. *Get over it,* he thought. *You've got a job to do.*

3

The waters of the lake rippled quietly, below shrouds of rising early morning mist. Suddenly, a rock promontory loomed like the prow of an enemy ship piercing through the peaceful fog. Buck stopped paddling and rested his manual *motor* across the width of his canoe. Even though he was not yet within the official BWCA, the sensations engulfed him.

Listen to the silence...

Feel the mist rising from the glassy surface...

Glide...

Breathe the moist, pure air...

Slit the water with the paddle...pull...

Hear the quiet...

Glide...

Watch the shoreline come alive, the rising sun warming the world.

In a flash, a flurry of action jumped toward him from the shore brush. He grabbed for his M-16—but it wasn't there. Then he realized that the sudden "enemy" was a Drake and Mrs. Mallard, roused from an early morning feed. Buck shook his head and smiled at his instinctive adrenaline rush. The jungles of South America—some things stay with you, no matter how long ago or far.

Buck realized that his problems were not life-threatening. The danger he was in was different. Maybe more difficult in some ways. He could not just grab the situation and take action. More like a jungle sinkhole—nothing you could do but struggle. People problems were tougher—tough to change minds, motives. At some point a person might just say "to hell with it." But he was not going to quit this one.

* * *

The Taurus growled out of the motel parking lot and lurched recklessly out to highway. The streetlights punched holes in the early morning black sky, but a sliver of yellow/blue was building out on the endless Lake Superior horizon.

"The pilot don't want to fly into this boundary lake thing," Luther said, breaking ten minutes of silence. He had occupied most of the time wolfing down much of the motel's doughnut/roll "Continental Breakfast" set out the night before.

"So what?" Benny replied.

"So we're supposed to get out to this nowhere lake spot with our raft. I don't want to paddle that raft forever."

"We'll get out to where we want. If an extra couple C's won't do it for the pilot, he may find himself without a plane."

"Whadaya mean—you'd fly the plane?" Luther was now fully awake.

"No problem, I've done it."

* * *

The lights were shining through the small, clouded windows of the floatplane, reprising a noir scene that could have been described by Spillane or Le Carré.

"Good morning," Benny said to the waiting pilot, with uncharacteristic friendliness. "Are we ready to rumble?"

"A few more minutes to get the gear aboard and we're

set. I don't mind saying that it took some doing to get that raft you asked for."

"But you got it," Benny pressed while trying a pleasant smile.

"Four-man inflatable raft. We just barely got it through the cabin door. Two paddles, no electric motor. A ton of food and drink. But you didn't mention fishing gear," the pilot said.

"We won't be fishing, just testing. We have our instruments here in this case." Benny nodded at the long black case Luther was holding to his chest like someone was going to grab it from him.

At seven o'clock, the odd gang of three lifted off and headed NNE.

* * *

Buck's half-mile paddle to the first portage was a good warm-up. He eased the canoe between the entry boulders. At this time of year, with higher water levels, he could paddle part of the portage. When he got to the shallow rapids, he jumped out and slogged along the shoreline, using a rope to pull the canoe through to deeper water. An easy twenty minutes and he was out of Spit Lake portage and paddling in Knob Lake.

He continued a half-mile around the point to the Pebble River portage entrance. In order to reach the open part of the Pebble River, he had to do some work. He stepped out from the middle of the canoe into a foot of the water that looked so clear he could drink it. Now for the loading trick he had not done for a while: hoist the Duluth pack onto his back with arms through the straps. Then pull the canoe up farther on the shore and turn it over. He lifted one end and walked his hands on both sides toward the middle of the canoe. With a flex of the knees and an arm-press, he heaved the sixty-pound hulk aloft for a moment before he let it settle back, with the padded carrying yoke resting on his shoulders.

The quarter-mile portage was not going to be too

tough. Some dead tree trunks, mostly birch, were strewn across the two-or-three-foot-wide path, which alternated muddy stretches and welcome higher and dryer ground.

The portage path was a thoroughfare for every living thing: moose, deer, 'coons, rabbits, beaver and once in a while humans. In this world, the attributes of humans often became indistinct and questionable, certainly not superior. The animals were here in their natural homes. The humans were merely tourists—sometimes the "ugly Americans."

After a few dozen yards, his unaccustomed shoulders were beginning to feel the weight. He imagined the early Voyageurs, lugging even more weight over much longer portages, sometimes for eighteen-hour days. In Buck's case, the strain of his hundred-pound load would be compensated shortly by the relief of unloading.

He soon reached the shore of the open water, reversed his canoe-hoisting action, loaded the pack into the canoe and shoved off into the navigable stretch of Pebble River. He was now truly in the Boundary Waters Canoe Area Wilderness. As he paddled, the quiet settled in on him again.

This was the other side of the world, both in place and in aura, from paddling the inlets and rivers of Central America, during the SEAL active duty that he and George lived ten years before. The quiet happened then also: enemy positions were stealthily approached; a Team, supremely trained to perform an operation, joined at the soul, with the knowledge that one misstep could jeopardize each person or the whole Team.

He was doing well on time—paddling toward the next portage at about 5:30AM. The slit of sun gave promise of a clear day and the blue and yellow band at the horizon was expanding. The Pebble River ended where it ran into the small Pebble Lake. Then there would be a portage to the Heron Lake entrance.

Three miles to go, he thought, and he would reach that big water. He actually could have made better time, but the pleasure of the silence and the tree-lined passage held him in awe. He rested his paddle for a minute and just let the world stop.

*　*　*

"S-p-l-a-s-h! Splash. Splash. Splash."

Buck knew, even before he saw the source of the noise, that the sounds were natural—from one of the inhabitants of this special world.

The mother moose had crashed through the young trees by the river's edge into the water just behind him. She was now thrashing and swimming twenty feet from shore. She looked at him and then toward the shore. Buck, following her gaze, could barely make out her baby, testing its footing among the rocks and driftwood that created a regular pattern along the shoreline. The baby nibbled nervously at some early-greening vegetation. Mother was even more nervous, but probably had the instinct that the intruder would be no match for her. Buck waited, with paddle poised in mid-stroke, to avoid riling mama. She took her time wading back into shore and then nudged the youngster into the safety of the birch and poplar thicket, away from the human interloper.

Released from the minor drama, Buck pulled a stroke on the left and then on the right—enough to get him back into an active part of the river current. He breathed deeply. It was life-giving. Why didn't he figure out a way to live right here?

"Dumb!" he said loud enough to create a small echo against the tree walls on either side of Pebble River. If he lived here, so could thousands of others. He could no more capture and tie-down a piece of this wilderness than he could buy a piece of the moon.

He thought again of the Voyageurs of the 1700's. They didn't think about owning. They were happy to traverse the passages and leave them unchanged. They might have used the very route he would be canoeing. They slogged through these same portages. They sang their songs and smoked their pipes to keep themselves sane when the mosquitoes descended upon them. They reached inland territories, inhabited by Chippewa and Dakota, with whom they traded pots, pans, and hardware for the wondrous beaver and other furs that the tribes had skillfully gathered.

The "pork-eaters," as the inland Voyageurs were called because pork fat provided their basic relief from dried peas and lyed corn, then retraced their unbelievably arduous treks back to Grand Portage on Lake Superior. The singing, eating, drinking, dancing, carousing spectacle that ensued at Grand Portage, when they met up with the big-canoe lake Voyageurs, that would take the furs to Montreal over the Great Lakes, was a testimony to the energy and vigor needed to survive the life.

The rising sun nearly blinded Buck as he reached the entrance to Pebble Lake. A short paddle through the small body of water brought him to another portage. One more time—unload the Duluth pack, strap it onto the shoulders, hoist the canoe and trudge into the portage path.

He was, on this June day, one of the early portagers of the season. Later on, much of the tree litter would have been kicked away, the path beaten down. This one was a challenge—160 rods—nearly a half-mile of rough stepping through twisted branches, wading through muddy depressions and some higher ground sprinkled with the leavings of the rightful land owners. But once there he would have clear sailing on Heron Lake.

After struggling with their heavy packs nine horrendous miles from lake level up 500 feet, along the Pigeon River from Grand Portage, the little-giant inland-Voyageurs would have had a sense of relief as they encountered the broad expanse of the first leg of the water highway westward. They would break into song and enjoy the independence that was their life.

Buck thought about the independence of those early paddlers in the wilderness. He could now conjure up the feeling that they might have had. Their minds were free. Their goals were clear and honest, their challenges ever-changing. He knew that his challenges were just beginning. They would test his integrity.

* * *

Buck gazed at the expanse of Heron Lake. It was part of the route of explorers and voyageurs used two hundred years before. It was a mile or so across to the Ontario shore. He would hug the south shoreline on his three-mile burst to High Portage. He thought it would be pure pleasure, but after nearly a mile of strong paddling, he realized he had guessed too soon.

"Damn shoulders," Buck said aloud. Twelve-hour working days did not always equate with muscle maintenance. Now he felt every pull of the paddle. The canoe life exacts a price for experiencing its exhilaration. Like so many endeavors, there is no gain without some degree of pain. With an hour or so of paddling to go, a small motor would have eased the strain. He thought about a tourist lodge within a few miles of where he was—disgorging multi-people in motorboats; people who had very little concept of the value of quiet.

He had not eaten since he left home. Time to take a break. He remembered that a Forest Service campsite would soon be appearing on the southern shore, to his left. The only maintained campsite on Heron, it offered canoe access and an iron fire grate.

After about fifteen minutes, he steered carefully between the entrance boulders and beached the bow in a muddy spot that appeared to have been used a number of times already this spring. No need for the whole pack, he just grabbed the food bag with care because he had six eggs well-packed in there. The thermos coffee should still be hot enough. He now wished he had taken time to troll for a walleye or trout. But the eggs and bacon would be quicker. He got the fire started and his pan produced the heaven-to-a-hungry-man aroma of sizzling bacon.

If canoeing in silent waters is a maximum pleasure, sitting by a fireside, gazing out into the wilderness lake is a close second, he thought. After relishing his shore lunch, he rinsed his pan in the lake and returned with water to douse the small fire. While he waited for every ember to die, he inhaled some of the world's most refreshing air—an elixir that had the power to transport him away from concerns.

But only for a moment.

The droning noise was obviously a motor. A second later it was obviously a plane engine. But it seemed to be a distance south. Maybe it had not yet penetrated into the BWCA. The engine sounds sputtered—almost like the plane was going down. Then the full-throttle sounds returned. It sounded like the plane was heading in his direction.

* * *

The pontoon plane was flapping in the air like a kite in heavy wind. Benny had drawn his newly purchased Colt .45 and was holding it in the pilot's ear.

"Ya shoulda done what I asked and we wouldn't have to go through this. Now get in the back seat. I'll take over this plane. Your horseshit attitude is a breach of contract. Besides, we're not too happy that you had to land at the marina and waste all that time with the rudder. Now Luther, tie him up." The pilot's eyes opened even wider.

"With what?" Luther was in near panic.

"With your damn shorts, if you have to," Benny shouted. There should be rope back there off the raft."

Luther grabbed the rope and began winding it around the pilot like he was embalming a mummy.

"I'm going to fly around a little to get used to these controls," Benny said after a cautious look at the mummy.

"I hope so," Luther said, eagerly opening the liter of Jack Daniel's that he had placed in the long black case, along with a Remington deer rifle. The local gun dealer had wondered about the cousins' hunting attire, but didn't press the matter.

"How in hell are we gonna get out of here again?" Luther asked, the Jack D. warming his cockles.

"The same way we're going in. We got a three mile runway to get in, then up and out."

After fifteen minutes of in-flight practice, Benny penciled a mark on the flight map and handed it to Luther.

"See the X. That's where we are," Benny said. "We're going to land by a little island near that narrow strip between Heron Lake and West Heron. See if you can find it."

Luther looked at the map like the instructions to reprogram his VCR. He kept at it and soon his finger found the island, just off the northern shoreline.

"I guess if you follow the north shoreline of Heron Lake, you get to that island," Luther said. The pilot was attempting to peer through the ropes to see where his plane was taking him.

"Cousin," Benny smiled, "sometimes you amaze me. I hope you're as good at paddling the raft."

* * *

Buck could hear the engine sounds, but could not see anything. *It's got to be Forest Service*, he thought and dismissed the intrusion. It was time to leave the shore paradise and move on to High Portage. He poured a cup of coffee, drank it and served the last cup in the thermos to the gray embers of the spent fire. Not a sizzle resulted. He picked up his small amount of gear, including a few plastic and paper packaging items. *Take out whatever you bring in*. He eased his way down the slippery path to the rocky shore. The canoe launch was automatic. He was soon making good time, under the perfection of the high cirrus clouds and within the ethereal realm of the freshest air and all-encompassing silence.

The approach to the portage at the west end of Heron Lake looked much the same as it had when he was there the previous fall. However, nature has a way of healing the wounds made by trespassers—there had been brush growth this spring. The portage path up the hill was barely visible. As he edged in the boulder-strewn labyrinth, a six-inch green turtle disdainfully gave up its perch on a sunny rock and slipped into the clear water. Buck looked ahead to an almost impenetrable thicket of brush, leading to small then larger birch and pines. He pulled the canoe well up on shore.

The portage trail, from his landing, was a tough quarter mile, abruptly uphill to an elevation about fifty feet above Heron Lake. He hauled the full Duluth pack, tent roll and water jug through the thicket, brushing aside small downed trees as he went. Soon, the birch and poplar would vie for position as they closed in farther on the trail. *Imagine tourist families lugging their stuff up this grade? I suppose this "trail" would become an asphalt driveway, with golf carts zooming back and forth.* At that moment, squirrels were zooming back and forth freely, as the hermit thrushes and white throats greeted the season with song.

Buck selected a high point on the portage and stopped. He looked farther to the west, over the four miles of West Heron Lake. He knew that the sunset would be spectacular. Certainly, if someone were to build a lodge, this would be the spot. "Two bedroom, bath and living room with fireplace and spa," he could imagine the sales brochure proclaiming. They would probably try to get $1,000 a week. Eighty such units, occupied forty weeks a year, would gross over three million dollars—a substantial motive for raping the wilderness.

But now there was work to be done. This was bear country. He was reminded of the old saying, "Sometimes you gits da bear and sometimes da bear gits you." Buck knew that the surest way to attract the bear was to give her access to (or even a smell of) your food pack. So he took the fishing gear and water bottle out of the big pack and began to secure it.

He tied a separate thirty-foot length of rope to each of the two straps of his big pack and threw one length over a twelve-foot high branch of a nearby tree. He let that loose end hang and threw the other rope over a similar height branch of a tree twenty feet away, temporarily tying the end of the rope on that trunk. Returning to the first rope, he hoisted the pack up about ten feet and tied the rope on that trunk. Then he went back to the second rope and elevated the pack until it was suspended about ten feet off the ground and halfway between the two trees. Simply hoisting a pack up in one tree branch would be nothing more than an invitation. Bear would be up that trunk in a minute, enjoying your goodies. That was that, but he would have to get the pack down again to get his tent and gear ready for the night.

But now it was what he called "the cream of the day" for wetting the line. He unsheathed his St. Croix rod and the old Shakespeare reel his dad had given him on their first trip to the BWCA. Al (John Allan Ryker) had told him it would be the only reel he would ever need. For almost fifteen years, that prophecy had been true. He had packed two beat-up daredevils: red/white and black/white stripers, plus two each of his trusty spinner/dragonfly combo. With his gear assembled, he grabbed the water bottle and climbed his way down to the water. The spot he picked was at the west end of the portage, looking toward West Heron Lake. *Should be a trout lurking, or at least passing by.*

The yellow ball of sun was undergoing an orange transfusion as it gave advance notice of an impending drop below the darkening horizon. At its present angle, it was creating a super-shine reflection on the rippling water.

The high ground and thick growth of trees behind him muffled the sound from the east, but Buck was sure he heard a plane engine. The roar was diminishing as if a plane were descending. *Who could be landing out here on the edge of the wilderness?* The sounds faded then stopped like a flowing water spout being rudely cranked to "off". *Must have turned north toward Ontario.*

Piercing spears of white/yellow/orange fired at Buck's eyes as he squinted to find the blue-green area where he wanted to drop his lure. The perfect spot he was aiming at appeared to have endless depth. But when his spinner and hook splashed down among the shards of light, the upper world was separated from the dark under world. A few more casts and he felt the exquisite thrill of the line pulling taut and then streaming away, knifing a surgeon's cut in the mirroring surface. He gave the trout its due diligence and reeled in a two-pound beauty—just right for the pan.

Buck climbed rapidly up the rough trail to his campsite. He had to reverse his hoist trick to get his two-person tent, fire tools and cooking gear down. He built a small fire for cooking that he knew would soon feel plenty good. No big fire was necessary. He believed in the old adage, probably never uttered by an Indian: "White man build big fire, stand far off. Indian build small fire, sit close." The dry birch branches provided enthusiastic flames.

He let the exuberance die down to two-inch ember rods while he filleted the trout and sliced some raw potatoes. He poured from a small bottle of Casey's olive oil into one pan and got the fries going. The fish would take only a few minutes in the other pan.

He ladled plenty of coffee grounds into his generously dented aluminum pot and positioned it carefully on the small grill he had brought. A thick crust had been allowed to build inside the coffee pot. When the pot wouldn't hold enough anymore—he had to start another one. They were becoming a rare item—hard to find in an old hardware store. The encrusted pot boiled a rich flavor that mostly he and George appreciated. He never tried using the pot at home, reserving it for the tool shack in the yard (mostly for him—the crew seemed to have been weaned on Mountain Dew) and for camping. Casey had even admitted that the flavor was surprisingly good, but said "ick" when shown the pot.

Buck sat back and breathed deeply as nature closed in around him. He ate slowly, reveling in the silence.

Gradually the complete paradisian mood began to fade like the twilight, replaced in the same measure by a mental load he had been trying to ignore. Casey would be home by now. He wondered what she was thinking. *Could she come closer to his interest in protecting the silent wild environment; or should he distance himself from the BWCA cause?* She was only twenty crow-miles away; but it might as well have been a thousand. Was this an irreconcilable difference? Would it drive a wedge between them?

4

Bill Anderson said to his wife over breakfast, "Finally! I'm going to get somewhere in this Alactra organization. The lodge project in northern Minnesota will give me a chance to really be in charge. It can set me up for five years or more."

It was sometimes difficult to explain to his wife the role he played in the company. She had given up a good job with a leading New York computer firm to stay home and do family—to help establish a secure life.

Anderson's experience was varied—sometimes of questionable loyalty to his employer. Alasom Alactra had picked him, through the headhunter routine, for exactly the characteristics of capability but usability. The concept of vice-president, operating manager, Boundary Lodges, had thrilled him when Alasom and LeYan had interviewed him and offered a compensation package that was beyond his expectations.

"But listen, honey, I have to go. Have to meet the dragon lady first thing. We can celebrate a little tonight. OK?"

* * *

Anderson studied the wall-size map of northeastern Minnesota and northwestern Wisconsin, projected on the conference room screen. The detailed maps, available from W.A. Fisher Company, gave a mile-by-mile picture of the boundary area.

LeYan entered and lounged at the table, near Anderson. She waited for him to speak. She had easily won the pecking order battle with Anderson, the blond, blue-eyed WASP. She had given plenty in her twenty-nine years to be in this position of control. She was obviously enjoying it.

LeYan Syn was born in the Malaysian sultanate of Brunei. Her father, Sibu, was one of the major businessmen who used influence in the government to advance his own profitable interests. While he had waded through rice fields during the first ten years of his life, his quick wit and charisma soon disarmed the elders and thrust him into an unusual position of top gun. He married LeMay, the only Malaysian beauty he could not totally overwhelm. She was more than a mother to LeYan. Along with her street smarts and intelligence, LeMay provided the role of advisor, coach, devil's advocate, promoter, and strategist.

With all that support and her inherited dark, slender beauty, LeYan charmed Malaysian society. While many local young men had attempted to climb the mountain of her composure, she had made up her mind to escrow her most personal assets until she was able to achieve the highest bidder. This discipline, however, did not even slightly diminish her appetite for enjoying the life among the bright social vistas of Malaysia. She met Alasom Alactra, owner of a multi-conglomerate, when she was twenty. She saw an entry into the international life she dreamed about. While Alactra was willing to give up a great deal to have her, she was able to steer their relationship toward business. He agreed that she could have a major impact upon many of the people he would regularly need to influence.

"So you think that by now the Cousins are close to our first construction site?" Anderson said.

"By now they should be moving toward the portage at Heron Lake. That is our first objective," LeYan answered.

"What do you think they can do?" Anderson clearly was not convinced.

"They will make a non-technical analysis of the approach to the potential lodge site and snap a few pictures. They will then go to the nearby towns to evaluate local attitudes. I expect a report from Benny shortly."

"Well, they are non-technical enough," Anderson said.

"Listen, Anderson, I would not send you out to accomplish what I expect them to do," LeYan said as she headed for the door.

"Thank you for that," he said. They both knew that she *could* have. Such an assignment would not at all fit his preferred image.

LeYan stopped at the conference room doorway. "Please have your complete development proposal ready for presentation by tomorrow. I will need to review it before we recommend it to Mr. Alactra. We will soon have to use it to convince others, including the tree-huggers, that the plan is sound."

5

Jonas Thacher, MD, drove slowly into the Ryker Homes driveway as if he were looking to buy the place. He sauntered up to the heavy wood front door, greeting but holding at bay the big gray malamute that might have defended the Ryker household but was a bit too friendly. A slim, well-built six-footer, Thacher played some pick-up B-Ball at the local high school and had signed up to run in the "Grandma's" marathon in Duluth. The event attracted seasoned runners from Nairobi to New Zealand. His blond, smooth good looks had fluttered most of the nurses at Cascade Clinic where he was the chief physician.

A knock at the castle-like door brought Casey bounding down the stairs. She was still buttoning the top button of her short denim running shorts as she unlatched and opened the door. Her cut-off T-shirt shouted, "Grandma's—1997". She had taken women's eighteenth place two years before.

"Don't get dressed on my account," Thacher smiled.

"I was just going for a run," she said, ignoring his leer. "What are you doing in these parts?"

"Oh, just driving. It's not far."

"I know how far it is. I drive it three days a week. What can I do for you?"

"Just wanted to thank you for helping Betty with the insurance paper work last night," he said. "You mentioned to the girls that you would be eating dinner alone tonight—thought I'd ask you out for a bite."

"Sounds good, but I've really got a lot of computer work to do after I run."

"Computer work?"

"Yes, I keep the finances and do the accounting for our log home company."

"Is there no end to your talents? Have you entered Grandma's?"

"No way. Too much to do," she said.

"Need I mention, 'All work and no play—'" he said with a mock frown.

"No, you need not..." Her answer was cut off by the sound of an engine roaring and gravel spitting. An oldie-but-goodie double-axle red flatbed truck barreled into the driveway, past Thacher's SUV and out to the huge log loader sitting near a half-built log home. The ten-inch peeled pine logs of the home were notched to mesh at the corners and grooved to fit closely on top of each other, making a solid, almost white-looking structure.

"Who's that?" Thacher asked.

"That's George."

"What does he do?"

"Right now he's checking out the log loader. It was just repaired today. He owns a log-trucking business about five miles from here."

They watched as George made a quick study of the gaping "clam" mechanism that was used to grab huge logs off a truck and later lift them into place as a structure was being assembled. In minutes, he was back in his truck heading toward them. It slid to a halt in front of the house.

"Loader looks OK," he hollered from the truck window.

"George, this is Doctor Thacher from the Clinic," Casey hollered back as she and Thacher moved toward the noisy vehicle.

"Hello, George," the doctor offered, looking pleased that George wasn't staying.

"Hiya, Doc. Making house calls?"

"Not exactly."

"Live around here?" George said.

"Lease a place on the Superior shore, near the Clinic."

"Good for you. Casey, I've got to be going. See ya."

As George roared off, Casey and doc moved back toward the front door.

"Man of few words. Is he a friend?"

"Friend of my husband's—of ours."

"Well, Casey, let's go to dinner."

"I'd have to change and all that."

"You look fine. In fact, you look…"

"Doctor," Casey broke in, "I've got to do my run and then work. I've got the nine to five tomorrow, and then there's that six o'clock staff meeting you scheduled. So I'll see you tomorrow."

"I'd say that's a sign-off," the doctor said.

"I'd say so," Casey replied and put her hand on the wrought iron door latch. "Hope you have a good evening, driving around." Her smile warmed an otherwise chilly exchange.

"Think about a drink after the meeting tomorrow," Doc said. On the way to his white Lexus 4WD he wrestled a bit with the malamute. He looked back to the house to see if Casey was watching. Disappointed, he jogged out to the SUV and threaded his way out through the pines.

* * *

George drove from Ryker Homes out to County Road 18 and on to the Sawbill Bar & Grill. The Tuesday night crowd was there in strength. More were still arriving, to add to the hard hats who had been there since 4:30. George was well acquainted with nearly everyone—especially the big-hair, jeans-clad girls and the loggers at the bar. A mix of young and older couples had settled down in the dozen-and-a-half back tables, eager to tie-into what was agreed to be "pretty damn close to home cookin'." He joined three men at a table by the bar. Charlie Henstead looked serious, but talked in an animated fashion to Mac Smalle, owner of the Amoco station and Jake Sharker, a local canoe outfitter.

"Charlie," George greeted, "how's it going? Hi, Mac. Jake."

"Have you seen Buck?" Charlie answered, side-stepping any extraneous conversation.

"He was planning to drive to the landing for a trip out to Heron Lake and the portage. Gonna be back tomorrow," George said.

"That's a helluva ambitious trip for two days," Jake said. As a major boundary waters enthusiast, he knew the nearby lakes like he had drawn the map.

"Well, Buck was not exactly going for the fun of it. After he heard about this flap last night, he wanted to check out the portage to eyeball how someone might have come up with this crazy idea to develop near boundary portages," George said.

Mac Smalle was incredulous: "Who's going to build near portages? It's got to be illegal. Can't the sheriff stop 'em?"

"Nobody knows for sure about anything right now, but there is this rumor about laws being changed," Charlie tried to explain.

"When are we going to find out?" Jake Sharker demanded.

"Gents, we're going to have a meeting of our county group and decide how to proceed, Charlie said.

"I'll see Buck at the landing tomorrow afternoon to tell him about this meeting. We'll go right to the Lodge," George said.

George stood up, moved to the bar and bought a bottle of Leinie Red, hipping a couple of the smiling girls on the way. They each gave him a punch in the shoulder, along with an exaggerated, "Hello, George."

When he returned to the table, George inquired, "Any of you guys know this Doc Thacher from the Cascade Clinic?"

Jake Sharker said, "My wife was in there last month. She thought he was quite a dude. Nurses seem to like his tan—and who knows what else. They say he's brown all winter. Has quite a pad on the Superior shore. Why do you ask?"

"Oh, I just heard about him being around," George said. "Shouldn't think he'd have much business out here in the sticks."

"Maybe he's got a girl up here," Mac offered.

George nodded toward the hard hats and loggers at the bar. "Don't think he'd last long if he did. The boys would discourage him."

* * *

"I'd like to see that 'tons of food' you were talking about, pilot," Luther complained. "This stuff would go better at a Ladies Aid lunch. If it wasn't for this whole salami, we'd starve. Benny, hand me that Jack D."

"Before you get too far into that Jack D, you better get your bed ready for tonight. It will get dark fast," Benny said with a nod toward the inflatable raft.

"What do you mean, 'my bed'?" Luther lurched around to look.

"Unless you want to sleep on a log, the raft is it. I have to stay here in the plane to keep our friend company," Benny explained. "I don't think you want to stay half awake all night to watch him. Now start getting the raft out of here. We're going to need it in the morning anyway."

The pilot had been freed from his mummy ropes and was now simply tethered to a rear seat. Benny had explained to him that as soon as they would get back near the plane base, they would tie him up, leave and then call Modern Airlift to let them know where he was.

Luther and Benny wrestled the raft out on the shore near the plane and both got ready for a long, dark night on Heron Lake.

* * *

The setting sun made a final dramatic flaming thrust below the lake horizon. Buck felt the temperature easing down. A mild breeze stirred the fir branches, wafting a piney smell to mix with the fire's pungent smoke. The overhead sky was black, pressing down on the cobalt blue band just above the water surface, as if the starry night were pushing the remainder of the day into the depths.

The half-hearted embers still warmed him and let the night settle in a little closer. In one respect, his head could not be clearer, in this peaceful and refreshing setting. On the other hand, many thoughts juxtaposed, competing for his concentration: Casey, the business, good buddy George, Charlie Henstead and the over-riding unknown of the potential wilderness invaders. At the moment he simply could not condone the sound of motors shattering the pure, natural silence. That fact was clear, instinctive and definite. The broader concept of commercial lodging and accompanying intrusions, he could not even visualize.

He imagined that it was the same shock to the soul's senses that galvanized men of vision in the early nineteen hundreds, when faced with similar challenges to the wilderness. In 1903, Edward Backus, a northern industrialist, strove for approval to install hydro-electric dams at boundary waters portages to facilitate his lumbering and paper-production industry. He would have cut the tall pines and raised lake levels eighty feet, flooding shorelines, rapids and waterfalls. It took a quarter century for men like Ernest Oberholtzer and Walton League's Howard Selover and Secretary of Agriculture William Jardine to stave off the insult. They convinced legislatures and citizen groups of the immeasurable value of a wilderness. Buck remembered some of the words in the legislation: "...untrammeled by mankind, where man himself is a visitor who does not remain." Buck felt that his personal interests and needs had to be secondary to his part in preserving what he was now experiencing on this trip.

The day's efforts, the food and the mood now sent him to his tent, with the fire stoked as a signal to the night and whatever might be out there.

* * *

The crash sounded like two oak branches ripping off and falling to the ground, followed by a thrashing about that could only mean one thing out here in the woods: the black bear had decided to visit...and was very, very hungry.

Buck unzipped the tent door quickly and saw the bear halfway up the tree, not huge but plenty ominous in the pre-dawn darkness. What had attracted her? The food pack was still out of reach. Then he realized his mistake—his human error. He had left the two fry pans on a rock near the cooking grate. So, she smelled the pans then saw the pack in the tree.

The bear was lurching toward the suspended pack in total frustration. How long would it be before she decided to take out her frustration on his tent and him?

Buck grabbed the two fry pans and began banging them together. The bear's determination sagged a bit, but she was by no means deterred. He picked up a burned out fire log and threw it at the bear's head. It was boxed away like it was part of a game. The second log scored on the bear's head, and she got mad as hell. The growl and open-mouth teeth-baring were convincing.

Missus was about Buck's same 200 pounds but was far more motivated. Add her long claws and arm strength that went well beyond human, and he knew he was no match. They were both scared. The human brain had to be the difference, no matter how devious.

He picked up one of the pans and aimed it just past missus and out a ways into the woods. She maybe smelled it going by and paid attention. When he threw the second pan a little farther out, she was convinced. With interested grunts, instead of growls, she stomped out toward the pans, in the thicket of firs. Her aggressive nature turned to loud licking of the pans.

After a few minutes, the bear looked back to Buck and the fire. She whirled and took several long strides toward him. His adrenalin level went over the top and survival mode took over. His only other ammunition was a group of softball size rocks near the fire. No time for slow-pitch. He overhanded one and another at the bear. He was more accurate with this weapon and the tide of battle began to turn against the bear, in spite of her roaring and pawing the air like a heavyweight. This was fortunate because he knew that his only alternative was to run for the canoe. As the black bear lumbered back into the woods, Buck realized that he was the intruder here, not the bear.

Buck looked at his watch—*too late to sleep now*. The lake depths were returning the favor of sunset and forcing a slim band of pale yellow, ahead of the soon-to-be-rising sun, back up into the black sky. *Might as well have a quick breakfast and hit the trail*. He started a fire among the last night's coals, and put some water on for coffee. After lowering his pack and retrieving the pans, he took down the tent and secured his gear in the pack. He pushed the remaining fire apart, stomped out each ember with his heavy boots and sizzled some coffee and water on for good measure. He lifted the pack and tent roll onto his back, checked the fire one last time, and climbed down to his canoe at the shoreline. It was good to push off and welcome the sun winking at water level as if to mark his route east. He had departed the portage leaving virtually no sign that he had been there.

* * *

A mile to the east of Buck, Benny faced a quandary about his hostage.

"No use trying to tie you up back at the plane," Benny said to the pilot who was wide-eyed with apprehension. "You'll just have to go along with us."

Luther helped Benny launch the four-man raft between the pontoon of the plane and the muddy shoreline. "Ahhh—shit!" from Luther signaled his misjudgment of the distance from a shoreline log to the raft. His black wingtips and rayon socks would never be the same.

He more-or-less fell into the raft and got ready to load on the gear. First some food and the Jack D. Then the instrument case and the camera. Benny pushed the pilot ahead of him, Luther assisting since the pilot's hands were tied. Benny followed and shoved off with the paddle. They now could have used that electric motor the pilot couldn't supply.

"Well, Luther, it looks like you get to paddle. Just what you always wanted, right?" Benny encouraged.

"I'm not doin' nuttin' 'til I get the water out of my shoes and socks."

"I suppose I could row," the pilot said.

"Not a chance. You stay in the front with your hands at your sides. Besides, we need the lightest guy up there," Benny said.

After some trial-and-error paddling, splashing and cursing, the group started to make some progress toward the point of the small island. As they came around the point, they could see the west end of Heron Lake.

"That's where the start of the portage is supposed to be," Benny said. "You're doing fine, Luther, keep up the good work."

Luther's expression said, better than words, what he thought Benny could do with this whole trip. Knowing that it was inevitable, he simply had to "relax" and hate it. "I better get some damn good R&R after all this is over," he said.

Benny didn't push it. Suddenly he put his saluting hand above his eyes and leaned forward, as if the additional foot would improve his vision.

"Look, Luther! Do you see that speck right by the start of the portage? Looks like a boat!"

"Damn it, I can't see in that direction. I'm rowing, remember."

"Well stop rowing. We don't want anyone to see us. Pull closer to shore so he can't make us out. I'd hate to have to make a noise with that Remington. I'd either have to waste him or put a hole in his boat."

The raft nestled in behind a big birch that had fallen into the water from its shoreline perch. The three sat there incongruously: two men in black suits, ties and hats (one barefoot with trouser legs rolled up) and a leather-jacketed slender captive with wild eyes. Finally, Benny spoke:

"We'll just have to wait here until he gets farther away. It looks like he's heading toward the far shoreline. Then we'll slip in, take some pictures, get back to the plane and get out of here."

* * *

Buck took one last look along the northern shore before he headed back southeast, on Heron Lake. He was about to turn when he thought he saw some movement near the small island. He looked straight east and then back to the island. This time whatever he saw was gone. He checked his map and took a deep pull to the right. He would make good time along the south shore, if an east wind did not start to blow. But he would still have to hump to make it to the landing before sunset. No leisurely shore lunch. No drifting and dreaming. If he were about to dream about anything now, it would be to get home and have a nice dinner and evening with Casey—like he blew Monday night.

He wondered how the night work went for her. At least he didn't think she would have the problems she had when she was a new RN at Olympia General near Denver. They recently had laughed about their second date. Casey had suggested that Buck come over to her apartment to give her a few of the self-defense tips that he had been telling about.

The Sunday afternoon session had gone well, starting with the basic arm-throw, the eye-gouge, the Adam's apple chop (assuming that the opponent is an Adam) and the groin kick (demonstrated very carefully). Casey put a curfew on the date, after a half hour of lip-to-lip combat. She won that round, but the die was cast and they both knew it.

During her first few months at the hospital, when she was still a gung ho nurse, she viewed anyone wearing a white coat and a stethoscope as next to godliness. There were a few in the white coat category, however, that she found did not warrant that degree of reverence. Admittedly she was hard to resist as a target of opportunity, so she soon learned to sort out the healers from the wheeler-dealers. A young doctor grabbed her from behind one evening in the supply room and immediately regretted it. She had learned her SEAL lesson well. Her instinctive turn and knee action sent him away bent over and groaning non-medical terms. Her disclosure of the event did not match with his; and the potential for administrative ugliness was only avoided by the timeliness of Buck's proposal and their departure for Minnesota.

Now he had the county meeting to think about. If there was a meeting tonight, he would be late getting home. But one thing was clear to him. He needed this trip to help remind him of the sanctity of the wilderness and its vulnerability. No question, a lodge could be built on the portage, if people let it happen. He couldn't let it happen. It was too easy to get caught up in just living and forget the timeless gifts of nature. He was now ready for the meeting. He knew, though, that they might not be ready for *him*.

6

Benny was stressed. "I need to talk to LeYan Syn," he announced to Paulette, at the Alactra office. "I mean I need to talk to her now."

"All right, Benny, hold on. She's in a meeting. I will bring in a message. Wait."

"Make it quick. I'm standing in the middle of Lake Superior! Call me back. She has my number."

He had convinced the pilot to land in a small bay ten miles up the shore from the original takeoff point. Luther was keeping an eye open while gathering their few take-along possessions. The cell phone buzzed in a few minutes.

"Benny here."

"How did it go?" LeYan said calmly.

"Went OK. Had to push the pilot some. Landed the plane myself at the lake. We took some pictures of a bunch of trees. Good view from the top where this guy camped. Got out of there a couple hours ago. Rough night. Luther is ready to put in for hazardous duty pay."

"What guy was camping there?"

"Some guy. Took off in his canoe as we were getting there—still a couple miles off."

"Did he see you?"

"Naw. We stayed back until he got a couple miles east along the far shore. If he had seen us, I would have plugged him."

"Where are you?"

"About ten miles northeast of Duluth, pulled up at some cabin dock. We'll go in and find out the address. If you could have someone head out here to pick us up we'd be much obliged. He can call me on the way and I'll give him directions."

"I have already contacted someone to do that. I will let him know that you are there. He will be calling you within thirty minutes. Will there be any problem with the pilot?"

"I doubt it. I gave him plenty money. I don't think he'll want to spill the beans to his buddies—or anyone else—about being hijacked. Not good for business."

"Give him an extra five hundred and tell him we know his home address and where his kids go to school."

"Gotcha."

"Now Benny, here is the next part of your project. We have managed to find one of the locals who would enjoy the benefits of being helpful to us. He implied that there is one guy who could become a problem—a real tree-hugger. Benny, that is someone who is more interested in coddling all those lakes and trees you flew over than using them to full advantage. We are going to invite him here to the office to talk sensibly, but it would be better if we scared him away from the issue. Understand?"

"I get your message, but who is he?"

"After you get picked up, the car will be turned over to you. Register at the North Star Motel in Duluth. Get settled in and call me—either here or on my mobile number. I will give you the details then."

"OK. But one question. What's a metologist?"

"You don't need to know. Call me."

* * *

"Hooyah!"

Buck heard the SEAL greeting before he could see him. Then in a second or two he could confirm that it was the only voice that it could be.

"Hooyah." Buck hollered back to George who was standing on the shore at Spit Lake.

The trip back on Wednesday afternoon had been an absolute pleasure. Pure air, nothing but wild to look at, occasional glimpses of the animal inhabitants doing their things. He had paddled smoothly, stroking deep into the calm waters. The silent surroundings were interrupted once at the west end of Pebble River. A pair of loons was not immediately willing to give way and he had to steer around them.

What was George doing at the landing? Probably something to do with the meeting. It was a kick just seeing him there waiting. But, of course, the "Hooyah" was nothing but the standard SEAL's greeting—didn't mean anything really—just loud.

"Hey, get your ass moving. You got a boat of Sandinista guerrillas on your tail," George hollered, still 300 feet away.

That sounded like old George.

"Lob 'em a couple grenades," Buck answered and aimed at the landing.

"We've got a date with the clan," George said as Buck pulled his packs and paddles out of the canoe.

They each grabbed an end and hoisted the canoe up on the pickup rack Buck had built to cradle the craft.

"What clan are you talking about?" Buck asked.

"Charlie wants to cover the issues with a couple of us before he alerts the whole group. You know them. Sharker and Smalle. That's all he could get."

"Where? When?"

"At the Township school—because it's close. He said seven o'clock. We should be able to make it. How was it out there"

"Great trip as usual," Buck said. "Wish I could get out there more often. A little excitement this time."

"What happened?"

"Bear came looking for food. Found me. Luckily she lost interest." Buck opened his cab and stowed the pack and tent roll. "They sure could build something on High Portage, but it would be over me."

"Sounds like you have an opinion," George said.

"George, just go out there. No way should anyone take over that wilderness with buildings, motors, or chain saws."

"Oh, you decided that did you?"

"Yeah. You got a problem with that?"

"Only if you're trying to tell me that this whole boundary area is off limits."

"Well, that's what I'm telling you," Buck said calmly.

"Well, who are you?"

"Nothing but me—but that's enough." Buck's tone became raw.

"Oh, yeah, maybe I'm enough to change that!" George said.

"I doubt it." Buck turned back to his truck.

"Listen, Bud, do you want to check it out right here?"

"Wouldn't that be great—you and me duking it out here in the mud," Buck smiled. Whoever beat or got beat, it would be an ugly scene."

"Yeah, I guess I haven't had a good brawl for a couple years. No use practicing on you," George grinned.

"See you at the Township Hall. No beer there I suppose. You got any?" Buck looked enthusiastic.

"Do sharks shit in the sea?" George reached in the cab of his truck, grabbed two cans of Millers, and tossed them to Buck. "Oh, by the way, how are things at home?"

"Nothing real good. Nothing real bad. Why do you ask"

"You said Casey would be a little pissed about your running off to the lakes instead of taking care of business."

"We'll get to it. She'll be OK."

"What do you know about this doc at the Clinic? George asked. I came by to look at the loader last night about suppertime. He was there."

"Beats me," Buck answered casually, but inside he was thinking, *why in hell would the doc come out to the house?*

"See you at the hall." George ground his truck slowly through the rutted driveway and out to the county road.

Buck shook his head slowly. He sure as hell didn't need the doc to worry about. He checked the canoe tiedowns and followed George out. He remembered Casey's reaction after the doc had first started at the clinic. She came home one day threatening to use one of her SEAL moves on the white-coat wonder if he didn't cool his jets. Buck offered to go and *visit* with him, but she said she would just ignore him. *Maybe Doc had become more difficult to ignore.* He might still have to pay an office call when he could find time. But now he was ten minutes from the Township Hall. Right or wrong, it was time to tackle some issues head on.

* * *

Charlie Henstead looked deep in thought as he drove his LeSabre to Township Hall. He also looked depressed and said aloud, "I don't like it, but I have got to do it." He had been laid off for ten years. The taconite plant on Lake Superior's shoreline had to cut costs. His assistant bookkeeper job had to go. He and his wife of forty years had to move away from their cozy mortgage in East Beaver. He found the old logging lodge out on County 18 that he could buy for a song. Viewed through squinted eyes and colored glasses, it could be exaggerated as charming. An eyes-wide-open examination, however, revealed deteriorated window frames, moss-grown log exterior, wood plank floor that cracked open enough to occasionally accommodate a few uninvited guests. The electric system was a patchwork and of questionable dependability. He had told Lillian that he would repair and refurbish—"fix it up like new." But after a few years, money was too tight to buy materials and his energy had drained along with his bank balance.

When Lillian's arthritis and heart problems got worse, they had all they could do to hang onto their part time jobs at the Tourist Information Center. Their scant wages, added to the small Social Security check, barely paid for food and Lillian's medicine. Fortunately, their two fieldstone fireplaces and an old pot-belly stove were wood-burning. While downed trees and other scrub wood were plentiful, it was getting tougher for him to get enough chain-sawed and split to keep them warm. He had become reconciled to their living out their years in this fashion. All he hoped for was to keep the peaceful look in Lillian's eyes. He knew that without the drugs, the pained look would return.

When his nephew, David, had first called on Monday, Charlie was excited to become a part of a big thing, whatever it was. He did not expect that it might become an opportunity for him.

Now, today, a lady by the name of "Lee Ann" had called him at the Information Center a couple hours before. She said she was working with a group that was trying to bring economic recovery to the region—including the people who had been laid off from mining and lumber jobs. She said she knew Congressman Wayneson. In fact, she said, she would be lunching with him soon. "Mr. Henstead, your expertise can be very valuable to us. Your fee can be either in the form of a large payment after the project is underway, or it can be in the form of an annuity that would give you a nice amount each month," she had said. Those words were now burned into his memory. He immediately fantasized about how much these amounts might be. A part of him worried about what the deal might involve, but then he thought about Frank. The government had taken away his only child, Frank, to die in Vietnam. Maybe the world owed him this chance...a way to get partly paid back. So far it seemed like a simple thing that he had to do; but, what did this "Lee Ann" lady mean when she said, "Just keep us informed so that we can do the right thing for your area." Then the scary part: "Charlie, remember, it would destroy the whole opportunity if you said anything to anybody about our arrangement." Then she told him that she was interested in the Buck Ryker he had mentioned as being kind of a group leader and fan of the wilderness. She said, "Tell Ryker that it is in the group's best interest to have him come to our office in Chicago. We'll have a ticket, at the Northwest counter in Duluth, for the seven o'clock flight tomorrow morning. We will meet him at the gate when he lands at O'Hare."

"Holy Mackerel!" Charlie had exclaimed to himself as he put down the phone. "That lady means business!" He had then called George on the Heudak Hauling cell phone to set up the Township Hall meeting and brief him about Buck's trip: "Maybe you can start Buck thinking positively about the importance of going to Chicago." George had answered, "I'll tell him, but he does his own thinking."

* * *

Buck pulled into the Township Hall yard alongside George's red truck. He was leaning against the blue replacement door, sipping a Millers.

"No Charlie?" Buck asked.

"Not yet. He drives pretty slow in that old LeSabre. Figures he'll get better mileage at thirty miles an hour. There's one other thing he said to me when he called and yanked me away from a paying customer."

"What's that?" Buck could now understand why George was not in the best of spirits at the landing.

"He's really nervous about this portage deal," George said. "His nephew keeps calling him. And he's got the idea that the company wants a representative of this area to come to Chicago to talk about it. Charlie thinks you should be the point man and make the trip."

"No way! Why me?"

"Well, ask him. Here he comes."

Charlie parked beside Buck's truck and eased out of the Buick slowly. Once out of the door, he stopped for a minute, holding onto the open door while he slowly straightened his torso.

"How's the back, Charlie?" Buck asked quietly.

"Not too bad. Just have to take it a little easy. Can't move too fast right away. It kind of stiffens when I sit for a while in the car."

"Thanks for coming, fellas," Charlie continued. "Let's go in. Mac and Jake should be along shortly."

"What's new?" Buck asked.

"I've got news," Charlie said.

"Charlie," George interrupted. "Do you really think anything is going to come of this tourist lodge deal? I can't believe it's possible. The environmental groups would go crazy."

"Oh, something will come of it all right—if they get the right people involved," Charlie said with unusual conviction. "The question is, do *we* want to get involved or just let it happen to us."

"So what's the news?" Buck urged.

"Just this. I've heard that the company wants to meet with a representative from the county citizens."

Mac Smalle and Jake Sharker drove up and they all entered the building together. The Township School had been built in 1898 to serve a population of mainly miners and loggers in the county. When these two economic mainstays had either evaporated or consolidated themselves closer to the North Shore, the building became as neglected as an orphaned urchin. In order to reduce vandalism and provide for an occasional gathering, a county group had maintained it reasonably well. The large sign above the double doorway proclaimed it officially: "Township Hall." "Government Property," printed in smaller letters below the other, did not dissuade all pranksters; but, through the years the principal damage had been from the weather. The two four-panel doors were painted white on the outside, like the entire exterior. The insides of the doors were varnished over a yellow-tan stain, revealing the straight-grain pine. The twenty-four by thirty-six foot single room belied the possibility of educating the twenty-plus rough-dressed, first through eighth grade boys and girls. Those days, the eighteen-or-nineteen-year-old teacher had the splendid career opportunity to not only instruct the broad curriculum but to prepare noon meals, stoke the potbelly stove, treat minor sickness and get the little ones bundled up for a multi-mile walk home along barely defined roads. But, after all, she *was* earning room, board and possibly an extra twenty dollars a month.

The bright yellow-painted plaster walls tried to enliven the old, forgotten image of the public servant centenarian. The three, tall, slender, double-hung windows on each side wall grudgingly admitted a meager portion of the failing twilight. Charlie twisted the knob on the ancient ceramic light switch. He turned it carefully, ninety degrees to the ON position. It worked! The two, one-hundred watt bulbs, suspended from the twelve-foot ceiling improved the illumination marginally. One of them had a frosted glass shade that made it substantially less dismal than the other.

The five men eschewed the eight historic wood and iron, folded-seat student desks that were basically on display, not meant for adults of substantial girth. They circled five of the ubiquitous steel folding chairs lined up against both walls.

"Charlie, you shouldn't have gone to all this trouble. Just a plain meeting room would have been OK," George opened.

"Yeah, Charlie, this sure is a lot better than the Sawbill where we'd have to drink beer and watch the girls," Sharker added.

"Gents, this is a serious matter. I didn't want to noise it all over. I just want to quickly cover a couple of issues and then you can go and drink as much beer as you want," Charlie said.

"Quick sounds good. I've been gone for two days. Got to get home while I still have one," Buck urged.

"Buck, that's the first issue. How was your trip to the portage?" Charlie asked.

"Well, you don't need the travelogue. The fact is that the portage between Heron and West Heron could be a location for some kind of tourist lodge or group of buildings. Depending on Ontario or Minnesota's decision, power could be brought in overland. Otherwise, they would need fuel-powered generators. Sewer and water might be a problem, but could probably be solved at considerable expense. Of course, it's a beautiful spot. Great for tenting, but I'll be damned if there should be a permanent structure. I'm ready to hit that head on," Buck stated.

"Now back to this request from the company," Charlie said.

"By the way, what is the name of this company?" Jake Sharker questioned with a frown that put more deep furrows in his already fissured, leathery face. Fifty-two years, lived mostly in the wild outdoors, had given him the look of a Voyageur, only about a foot taller.

"David wasn't sure of the spelling, but it's something like Alactra. Guess that's the name of the head man—the owner," Charlie said. "Anyway, they want to talk to us. I thought you would be the best one to go, Buck."

"Charlie, I'm already in too deep from being gone from the business for two days," Buck said.

"Remember," George said with a grin, "you always wanted to be the team leader."

Not knowing exactly why he wanted to acknowledge that, Buck said, "You know that the chiefs picked me. I didn't volunteer."

"It looks like we're picking you again, Buck," Mac Smalle summed it up.

"What does it involve?" Buck resigned himself.

"They say there will be a ticket waiting for you at the Northwest counter tomorrow for the seven o'clock flight to Minneapolis and then to Chicago. They made a reservation at North Star Motel near the Duluth airport, in case you want to stay there tonight. You can call the motel to confirm and arrange for your arrival time. The company will meet you at O'Hare airport in Chicago. You can either stay over or come back tomorrow night," Charlie promised with a look of relief.

"Tomorrow morning! Yeah, I'll have to go to Duluth tonight. Otherwise I'd have to get up in the middle of the night to make that seven o'clock flight."

"Look at it this way, Buck, you can't get in much

more trouble at home than you are now." George seemed to be enjoying this.

"Screw you, George!"

"Aw hell, your world isn't going to end. Never saw you turn down a sticky situation in Panama."

"Who's turning anything down? You smooth talkers got me sold. But I'm telling you one thing: when I get the full picture here, I will sure as hell be telling you what I think should be done. You damn well better back me up!"

"Charlie, it strikes me that you are more than a little bit interested in this whole idea," George said, cooling the rhetoric and avoiding a direct answer to Buck's challenge.

Charlie rebutted immediately, "Someone's got to get involved. If I had not gotten the message, we all would have sooner or later. And Buck, you have always presented yourself well at our meetings. Remember when we had to consider the proposal to log off that section of virgin pines?"

"Oh yeah, he did great," George interrupted. "He and a few other tree-huggers cost me twenty thousand bucks. I had a contract to cut and haul tons of pine logs from that section. I guess my loss was somebody's gain—whatever that was."

"That decision was supported by the whole county. You can't put that on Buck," Jake said.

"Well, I'm not, but he was point-man," George said.

"I'm out of here," Buck said, heading for the door. "I'll talk to you sometime Friday, Charlie. I'll probably stop off in Milwaukee to see my dad tomorrow night."

"Buck, beware of those city ladies," Mac Smalle cautioned with a smile. "Last time I was in Chicago for an Amoco meeting, some of us just about got ourselves in trouble."

* * *

LeYan lounged in her high-rise living room. Her president, Alasom Alactra, had insisted that her supreme comfort was important to the company. While she knew he had a key, it had so far remained unused. The gas fireplace crackled, warming the conditioned air and flecking bits of light randomly over the deep buff carpeting and soft caramel leather sofa. Indirect lighting, coved around the room's perimeter, bathed the ceiling subtly. A prince's trove of Indonesian sculpture adorned exotic wood tables and modernistic stainless steel and wood etageres. High style floor lamps focused upon a few framed Japanese etchings on the walls. She chose this often as a place from which to conduct her business. It gave her a sense of peace and was a symbol of status in her young life. She had "broken through the glass ceiling" that for her was never even there.

"Sir, I need to reach Mr. Benny Smith. It is of utmost importance." LeYan was firm with the North Star Motel manager on duty, who was as much a "sir" as Benny was a "Mr."

After a pause, the manager explained, "Lady, I just called room 108, where they're registered, and there is no answer. If I see 'em or even smell 'em, I'll give them a message to call you pronto."

"Thank you, sir. I will suggest to Mr. Smith that he provide you with a substantial gratuity."

"That would be great. I heard what a gratuity is. By the way, are you ever coming here?"

"Why, thank you for asking. I certainly hope to be seeing you soon."

* * *

While the Chicago-Duluth dialogue was becoming more pleasant, the line between Washington, D.C. and Fall River in northern Minnesota was heating up.

"Listen, Rebelde, I told you I can pull it off if you can get your act together. I need the details from your drilling tests in the boundary area before I talk to Alactra," political fixer, Jim Bob Akkre, demanded on the phone from his D.C. office. "We both know that there's probably oil or copper out there. If you guys know how to find it, we'll have something to talk about. I'm sure I can slip the exploration rights into the same Congress bill that would allow those chicken shit tourist cabins on portages."

Ramon Rebelde anxiously agreed, from his room at the Lumberman Hotel.

"OK, then," Akkre said. "Let's get it done, and we'll both get rich."

7

Casey steered her old Subaru into the tree-lined Ryker Log Homes driveway, turned right toward the rustic one- and one-half story house and parked in front of the oversize log-style garage. She and Buck had decided that they did not need automatic openers. Either could handle the doors without strain. *Good cross-training.* She walked thirty feet from the garage to the house and unlocked the heavy wooden back door, then returned to the branch-scraped 4WD "good runner" to grab the two bags of groceries she usually brought home on her Wednesday work day. *Actually, I could shop once every two weeks, with all the meat, fish and vegetables we've got in the freezer*, she thought.

Their shrinking bank balance came to mind. *Damn! We should have received the thirty thousand from the Iowa log home sale by now! It was due a month ago.* Buck was supposed to lay on some heavy pressure for payment. *Unfortunately, he can't call from the canoe.* Right now they really needed her weekly check from the clinic. The extra pay from Monday night's filing work would be welcome. The atmosphere at the clinic had recently become uncomfortable...as if some of the staff resented her part time freedom and full time attention from the doctor. His appearance at the house yesterday afternoon was a shock. *Why is he after me? He's got plenty of little local girls to hit on.* What a relief, she thought—to get home—away from all the personal crap—and back to her real world.

Just walking in the door was a pleasure. She and Buck had designed their log home over the six months that they had lived in a rented log cabin with only a wood stove to warm them and an outhouse to accommodate them. The room heat was really only necessary when they had to get out from under the covers. Drawings and information sheets had been spread out over the rough table near the stove so they could dive into them every spare moment. It helped to be attending the log home training school at the same time. They got many practical tips that resulted in a sound structure. Their life was fun, exciting, loving and productive.

Why is this insidious division creeping into our life? OK, the wilderness is great. OK, Buck needs to feel it. But how much? Why don't I? Maybe I do, but we have to deal with what we need now. If we could only discuss things, as we have at other times. Why is this deal so frantic? Why can't we be ourselves and just love through it?

Casey changed from her nurses uniform into her denim shorts and tank top, drew up to the computer in the den and brought up the Quicken program for their business. *This is the real fun of it, she thought. If I could only spend enough hours per day, instead of taking an hour to get up to speed, a couple hours of work and a half hour to close down. I could work six hours solidly—design, research and keep the accounts.* Of course, the immediate cash flow benefit of the weekly clinic check was hard to ignore—as was Doctor Thacher.

* * *

Buck felt lousy as he drove home from the meeting. He had always shied away from activists. Now he felt like one. But he knew that something had to be done. No matter which way he turned, he had the opportunity to fail. A deep breath and he said aloud, "No big deal! Leave home tonight by ten, get to the motel by midnight. New day at six, go to Chicago and eyeball the bears in their den." He realized he had been talking to himself a lot lately.

The sight of the Subaru in the driveway excited him more than he could account for. *At least she is home.*

He walked quietly through the back door, but realized that he should not appear suddenly. He banged the door, for a start.

"Hi, Casey, it's me," he hollered. He walked over to the CD player and selected Willie Nelson's song that tells mothers to beware of cowboys. He felt like a cowboy. Maybe there is something in the song that would help the situation. Maybe the song would make it worse. When he turned, he saw her in the den, at the computer.

The meeting of eyes, as Buck walked toward Casey, could have been a cinematic challenge for a silent movie. Joy, pain, anger, disappointment, hope—all welled up in one long look. So much was said to both of them in that one visual encounter that words were secondary. Neither wanted to gamble on saying the right or wrong first words. But Buck had to break the ice.

"I have missed you, Casey."

"It has seemed like a long time."

"How was work today?"

"Not too bad. How was your trip?"

"It was good—did what I thought I had to do. He paused before continuing: "But now the bad news—for me at least. I have to leave again tonight for Chicago."

Casey's eyes changed from soft, limpid blue to razor ice.

Buck, anticipating the reaction, hastened to say, "We just had this short meeting at the Township Hall. They asked me to represent the area and talk to the company that is stirring up all this trouble."

"And you have to leave tonight? You just know that you have to solve all the problems yourself?" She turned away.

"I think you know that I don't want to do this, but I'm in it," Buck said. "I'll fly out of Duluth at seven tomorrow morning, get to their meeting, fly to Milwaukee, stay over with dad and be back Friday afternoon."

"The best thing I can say about this is that it's good you can see your dad," Casey said softly.

Buck swallowed and said, "That's very nice of you to put it that way."

After a second, Casey said, "Buck, if you don't hold me, I'll break." Their embrace was so total that it seemed to engulf their entire life together. Reluctantly, Casey broke it off.

"We'd better not start something we can't finish," she said.

"I guess you're right. I'll go and grab a cold shower," he said as he retreated, and then turned back toward her. "You know, Saturday we should be able to spend the day on business."

Casey's look could not be mistaken for enthusiasm. Her eyes blinked and her tone became cautious. "Well, I'll be gone a good part of the day. Some of us at the clinic have planned to be at the Marathon."

Buck had forgotten that the famous Grandma's Marathon from Two Harbors to Duluth was to be held Saturday. He had thought about entering, but didn't take the time to pursue it. Casey entered two years ago and placed eighteenth out of a field of hundreds of women from all over the world. He knew she would have liked to enter this year.

"Oh, that's great!" he said with obvious disappointment. "I suppose Doc is in this group."

"He's running—expects to finish, at least," she said with growing defensiveness.

"It seems he is getting harder and harder to ignore," Buck said.

Casey's smooth countenance was quickly overtaken by a deepening color that began to blend with her rust tank top. "What does that mean?"

"I don't know what it means. I just don't know." He walked slowly up the stairs to the bath and into a shower that no longer needed to be cold. *My God*, he thought, *first we argue about priorities, now I'm acting like a jealous husband. We just don't seem to be able to get it right.* After the shower, he pulled on a navy polo shirt and light gray chinos. The gray herringbone sport coat should work—even in Chicago. He packed a few items in a small case and walked down the steps, knowing that the parting would not be sweet.

"I'll be back Friday, early afternoon," he said as he walked toward the back door. "I've asked George to look in on the crew tomorrow morning to get them going."

"I suppose I might as well put in another day at the clinic," Casey said, with her attention focused on the computer.

"Whatever turns you on," Buck said. He realized too late how ironic and snide that sounded. He quietly closed the back door and immediately addressed the fact that he had to unload the canoe off the pickup rack before he could leave.

Casey watched him leave and thought, *there we go again. Our feelings and our brains are not working together at all.* Suddenly, the atmosphere at the clinic didn't seem that bad.

* * *

Charlie left the Township Hall meeting and thought about Mac Smalle's comment to Buck about getting in trouble in Chicago. In six years, he had never known Buck to cat around. Well, after all, why would he, with Casey to go home to…but some guys…? But there was other kind of trouble. He would hate to get Buck hurt because of his deal with the big company. *Can't worry about it now*, he thought. He drove slowly to the Information Center.

The Shady Lady, as he called her to himself, said she would call at nine o'clock. He couldn't remember being there at this time of night before. He looked at his Westclox pocket watch—a reliable relic he had bought in Duluth so many years ago for two dollars. That was when he had been assistant bookkeeper at the bustling taconite plant. *Oh, if the plant was still going! I might be head bookkeeper. Things would be different.* It was ten minutes to nine, give or take five minutes. He didn't require his timepiece to be exact. He was never late to anything. *"Better a half hour early than five minutes late,"* he always said. Charlie took out his ring of ten keys—not all currently in use, *but you can never tell when you might need that old padlock key.* He selected one and eased it into the worn brass cylinder lock on the forest-green-painted paneled door. The one-inch deadbolt responded like an old friend to his careful touch, and he stepped over the oak threshold.

The Center had been built by a volunteer group, with a donated double-wide mobile home as its base. Knotty pine paneling had been installed on the walls that were now glorified with maps and aerial photos of the Boundary Waters Canoe Area.

LeYan had asked him where she could contact him after his meeting with Buck Ryker. Charlie told her to call the same Information Center number she called before. He did not want his wife, Lillian, to know he was dealing with the Chicago company. She wouldn't understand and it would likely upset her. He promised LeYan he would be there when she called at nine. The old-fashioned "party-line" vintage telephone rang loudly at exactly that time.

"Hello, this is Charlie Henstead."

"Hello Charlie. How are you tonight?" Her soft, calm voice was so reassuring that Charlie wondered why he had been concerned.

"Oh, I'm fine, I guess."

"Well, I'm sure you are, Charlie. Does this hour inconvenience you? We will have to talk often, you and I. In fact, we may have to meet one of these days. By the way, did you have your meeting with Mr. Ryker?"

"Yes we did. I told him how important it was to meet with you. He's very busy but he agreed to go to your office in Chicago tomorrow morning. He's very concerned about the development project, you know."

"Did you tell him about the ticket at the Northwest counter and the reservation at the Duluth North Star Motel?" LeYan began a slightly more authoritative tone.

"Yes, Ma'am," Charlie answered quickly. "He'll go there tonight. Should be there about midnight."

LeYan, recognizing that she had turned up the heat a little, turned it down again, "We will look forward to meeting your Mr. Ryker...it's Buck, you say?"

"Yes. Buck. He and his wife have a business constructing and selling log homes. Real nice ones too."

"Charlie, as a little advance on our financial arrangement, I am sending you a nice check. We do appreciate your help. And, as you know, more will be coming your way when we get the project started."

"Thank you. Should I call you Lee Ann?"

"Please do. It's spelled funny: L, e, capital Y, a, n. Oh, one other thing, Charlie. I would like to speak to you again soon. Could I call you at your home in the evening and just take a second to set a time to call again at this number? I know you prefer not to talk at home."

"I guess that would work." He gave her his home number.

"All right then Charlie. We'll be talking. Have a pleasant evening."

* * *

Two seconds later, LeYan dialed the North Star Motel in Duluth, Minnesota, and got an answer on the fourth ring.

"Good evening, North Star Motel," the night manager said after hoisting himself out of the back room recliner, that was functionally related to the nineteen-inch color TV. "Oh, hello, Miss Lee Ann. It is really good to hear from you. By the way, do you spell your name with one word or two?" He smiled proudly at how smoothly he asked the question. "Oh, one word: L, e, capital Y, a, n. That sounds interesting. I hope to see you soon. Yes, I'll put you through to Mr. Benny Smith."

Benny grabbed the phone on the first ring. The TV was boring and Luther was snoring.

"Benny, this is LeYan. How did things go with the pilot and the new car transfer?"

"First rate. We won't hear from the pilot again unless we want him. He said he's ready to take us anywhere we want to go. We've got the car—another Taurus, like the one we had, only brown. Luther, of course, wanted a Cadillac." Hearing his name in his sleep, Luther rolled over heavily. His insides followed him reluctantly, but not without an unbelievably loud protest. Benny moved his chair over by the window.

"OK, Benny, here is the new plan. A guy named Buck Ryker—no not Buck Rogers, Buck Ryker—will check into your motel about midnight. Watch for him and be sure you know what room he checks into. It can't be too hard. I put you in the smallest motel in town. You didn't mention our company name to the desk clerk did you? And you paid cash in advance. Good. He thinks I'm your secretary and therefore made your reservation. I told him we were from the Bombardier snowmobile distributor.

"After you see Ryker get there, wait for about four hours and then give him a visit. I don't care how you do it, but scare the hell out of him! Oh, if you used anything from the room mini-bar, be sure you go down *now* and pay for it in cash. Ring the bell a few times. The clerk will probably be asleep. But, be nice to him. He is on our side—thinks I'm going to show up and rub against him."

"Then what?" Benny asked eagerly.

"Then call me on my mobile number at seven o'clock."

"I'll handle it. I've got a few items here that should send our Buckie to the moon...oh, Miss LeYan?"

"Yes?"

"What does it take to get someone thinking that you're going to rub up against him?" Benny asked in an unusual voice.

"Forget about it, Benny. Just call me at seven."

Benny stepped out of North Star room 108 and was surprised at how good the night air felt at eleven-thirty. He took some unaccustomed deep breaths and said to himself, "This ain't Chicago"—and after a refreshing pause, "I don't know this guy, but I've got to waste him. That's my job."

* * *

The silence in Benny's motel room matched the quiet in Jim Bob Akkre's Washington, D.C. office—but they were worlds apart. He liked to call himself a "political facilitator." Many in the *Beltway* had other names for him. He sat at a mahogany desk nearly as large as a pool table. The expansive top was meant to hold a few well-organized evidences of executive deliberation, when it wasn't completely cleared of all but the leather-framed blotter. In Akkre's care, however, the top was filled with stacks of files, several used coffee mugs and the June issue of *Playboy*. The oak parquet floor, around the desk, served as a repository for more papers and two file boxes into which brown-covered documents and budget reports had been dumped. The expensive-looking oriental rug was rumpled by the legs of the two sumptuous navy blue leather chairs that had been shoved closer to the desk. One side of the large room held floor-to-ceiling shelves, enclosed with glass front doors, encasing a standard array of formally bound legal volumes. Akkre's only contribution to the prestigious collection was a stack of *Playboy* and *Mercenary World* back issues. The other side of the 700 square foot office accommodated a room-length mahogany counter with cabinets below. The grass cloth walls above the counter were adorned with large, gold-framed original oils depicting red-coated horsemen in English hunt scenes. Except for the cluttered desk and well-stocked wet bar in the center of the long counter, the incongruity of Akkre and the opulent room was striking. He had assumed the paid-up lease from a recently defamed attorney, for whom he had been of dubious assistance. He had taken the office in payment. The attorney would not be needing it for five to seven years.

Akkre sipped his first Dewar's on the rocks since his late dinner at The Bombay Club. He thought about the telephone call he was about to make. It could mean hundreds of thousands of dollars to him. It was late to make a call to such an important man as Alasom Alactra, but he had received the e-mail message that the president of Alactra International would be available from 10:30 to eleven o'clock Chicago time. The digital clock, near the wet bar, showed ll:45 EDT. He walked over to the bar, freshened his drink and dialed the unlisted number.

"Good evening," Mr. Alactra answered. He never conducted business conversations in his home, regardless of the hour. His mansion in Highland Park was sacrosanct. Also, the telephone recording system in his office was very effective.

"Mr. Alactra, this is Jim Bob Akkre."

"Yes?"

"Have you had a chance to read my proposal?"

"Yes, it arrived by Federal Express this morning. My vice-president for operations and my executive vice-president have both reviewed it thoroughly."

"Don't you agree, Mr. Alactra, that we have a vast potential for mineral production in that northern area of Minnesota? And then, the unique opportunity to transport to eastern markets over the Great Lakes?" Akkre asked eagerly.

"Do you know that minerals exist there in quantity?" Alactra questioned.

"I am in contact with an exploration company whose preliminary tests are very promising. They have further sample tests being taken today. Mr. Ramon Rebelde heads an experienced exploration company. His staff and crew are absolutely discreet. No one will know that they are in the area," Akkre said.

"Are the tests being conducted with U.S. government approval?" Alactra asked.

Of course they are not and you know it, Akkre thought. "Well, of course, Mr. Alactra, we cannot risk anyone's awareness of these tests until we are ready to proceed. I submit," Akkre said carefully, "that the situation is similar to your quest for approval to build commercial establishments in currently development-free areas."

"We are proceeding entirely within the jurisdiction of the United States Congress," Alactra answered adamantly.

"A process with which I may be able to offer assistance. As I am sure you know, I have, over the years, gained the confidence of a majority of representatives on both sides of the aisle," Akkre said.

"I am aware," Alactra acknowledged.

The Beltway bigwig followed immediately, now more sure of his ground, "I suggest that, in addition to my assistance in gaining passage of the bill that allows your development, I can help craft the language that will authorize a mining or drilling project."

Ignoring Akkre's offer, Alactra said, "And you are proposing that this development and marketing be accomplished within the structure of Alactra International, with the actual operation to be leased to your friend's company?"

"Yes sir, that is what we propose," Akkre said brightly.

"My executive vice-president is making arrangements to meet two Congressmen in your city. If your test results tomorrow are favorable, you may want to join them. I would suggest, however, that the matter not be discussed until we develop some consensus on the basic bill."

"I would be happy to meet him prior to the meeting, if you wish," Akkre said with a smile, already fingering his bottle of scotch in anticipation of a minor celebration.

"My executive vice-president is LeYan Syn," Alactra said abruptly. "*She* will contact your office Monday morning to advise you of *her* plans."

Akkre had never heard of a female EVP at this level.

"Thank you for your time, sir. I look forward to a mutually profitable association."

"Miss Syn will have the authority to represent Alactra International in any matters."

Jim Bob found himself listening to a dial tone.

In his twenty-eight years in the Washington D.C. political scene, Akkre had learned to brush off mild affronts such as being hung up on. Actually, it had been a good day for him. He had assisted a lobbyist for a national association in convincing two Senators that a new amendment ran counter to industry progress. It would have put more teeth in broad safety regulations. The dinner lasted well into the third after-dinner drink. The lobbyist had paid the check and further showed his appreciation by writing a very special unlisted phone number and "Miss Sally" on the inside of a match book.

* * *

"Hello," Alasom Alactra answered his second call of the late Wednesday night. He smiled as he recognized the voice that he expected.

"Alasom, is that you?" LeYan did not usually use the first name except on especially friendly occasions. In this case, it was more of a code word to be certain that it was he.

"Yes, LeYan. How are you?"

"I am very good."

"Oh, I know you are." Alasom made a rare joke.

"I have been trying to reach you for a half hour," she chided mildly.

"I have been listening to a Mr. Jim Bob Akkre from Washington, Dallas and other places of infamy. You know, he is the one who sent that exploration proposal. I will relate that conversation to you in due time. But first, you must tell me about your evening."

"Thank you, sir. I believe the local situation in Minnesota is under control. If, indeed, the local man we have invited chooses to accept, I am sure his composure will have been shaken and stirred."

"Good," Alactra commented. It was customary for LeYan to spare him the details, although he always listened attentively to whatever she deemed appropriate for him to hear. "Do you plan to meet with your Congress friends soon?"

"Yes. I would like to set up a lunch on Monday. I will try to leave word with the two Congressmen tomorrow. I know that they are both in Washington at this time. Then I will confirm a one-thirty or two o'clock reservation."

"You might want to consider inviting Mr. Akkre to your lunch. He has many years of experience in Washington and no doubt knows your Congressmen. He seemed anxious to assist our cause and would be available to meet you before the lunch," Alactra paused and then continued. "Of course he also has his own agenda."

"I try not to spend any more time with the so-called political fixers than I have to," LeYan said, "but I will ask your secretary to leave a message at Akkre's office, alerting him to my call."

Alactra briefly reviewed Akkre's conversation. "By the time you speak to him, he will no doubt have the results of today's exploratory testing," he concluded.

"I will certainly ask him to join us at lunch Monday. Goodnight, Alasom. Please call if you need me for anything."

"Thank you, LeYan. Oh—one other thing—the more I think about Akkre, the more I think we have to watch him carefully. He is not like any *lobbyist* that I have ever observed."

* * *

Jim Bob Akkre reached the operator at the Lumberman Hotel in Fall River, Minnesota, and asked her to page Ramon Rebelde. He was certain his man would be in the bar at 11:30.

"Hello Rebelde. You still alive? Sounds like a revolution going on in there," Akkre said, trying to shake the oil man back to business.

"Hell yes, I'm alive. Who wants to know?"

"This is J.B. Akkre—the guy who's going to make you rich. What did you do today?"

"First off, who's going to make who rich? We took thirty-one sample readings and they all look good. It's like Oklahoma in the twenties. The nickel and copper also look promising."

"How do you prove that? Of course I believe every word you tell me, Ramon, but I have to convince some very skeptical people."

"The way we do it is with photos of each sample. They have been sent to our people in Fort Worth. They will be developed, enlarged and put on poster board for you skeptics."

"I will need them in D.C. before noon Monday," Akkre urged.

"Our office will get the film early tomorrow. The finished charts will go out by afternoon. You should have them in D.C. by ten Monday morning."

"Be sure you include your detailed rationale with each chart. Remember, we're not dealing with experts.

"It'll be like A - B - C."

"You have any problems out in the sticks?" Akkre asked.

"Not really, except my guys are a little nervous—keep hearing sounds like footsteps on brush and crap. When they look around, no one's there. Must be their imagination."

"Well, keep your eyes open. I'm sure you know how to discourage any intruders.

"You know, I have to come back to Dallas tomorrow anyway," Akkre continued. "Why don't we have a late lunch at the Derrick Club on Friday. You can hand me the photo charts, we can make plans and count our money in advance." Jim Bob always kept the money out front.

"Money is good! Call my office Friday morning to see if I'll make it back," Rebelde said. "Otherwise, you can lay the Derrick Club on me Saturday. I'll have all day to abuse your credit card. Hey, I gotta go. This lady has been eyeing me all night. She's the youngest one in this bar—probably not a day over sixty-two."

8

County Road 18, on this late Wednesday night, was one long, black hole. Buck's halogen high beams pierced the tunnel of ink like two white lasers. He thought, *if a deer decides to cross, it would just be me against him. No way could I stop unless I inch along under forty, and that's not going to happen!*

He had spent so much time thinking the past two days, he was tired of headwork. He plugged a Bruce Springsteen cassette into the player and turned it up loud enough to scare away the deer and moose for two miles. Springsteen was what he needed. *Ain't Got You* came on, followed by *Tougher Than the Rest*, and more of the same. The driving beat helped him unthink. In 1975, he had heard the older boys talk about attending the first concert "The Boss" ever held in Milwaukee. He had been a fan ever since—on the rare occasions that he had time to think about it. Casey liked bluegrass music when she was relaxing, but deferred to Mozart and his friends when she wanted "peace and quiet" for work background.

The only warnings of nearing the North Shore highway were the vehicle lights, flashing like fireflies between the trees. The descent to the near lake-level highway was a minor surprise. There had been no rise in the past several miles; but now there was a sharp decline, as if he were going to pitch right into the *shining big sea water* of Lake Superior.

As he approached the intersection, he saw the sharp beads of red from the reflective STOP sign. He turned sharply to the right to proceed southwest along the lake to Duluth. The visibility was better on the state route, but the black strand of asphalt, divided either by a broken or solid yellow stripe, was still like following a curving tightrope in the dark. Instead of offering a nearby guiding effect, the intermittent sounds and the fluorescence of the roaring surf were distracting at night. Half the time the lake effect was there and other times the tightrope got squeezed between forty- to sixty-foot fir and scrub poplar trees.

    Springsteen deserted him so he turned on KDAL FM from Duluth and again volumed it loud enough to blow away most thoughts. He stopped at the Two Harbors convenience store, twenty-six miles from Duluth, topped off his gas tank and re-filled his driving cup. Experiencing the luxury of a freeway for the rest of the trip, he eased up over the speed limit, but then realized that this was no time to get a ticket.

    He reached the outskirts of Duluth, turned right on Arrowhead Road and found the North Star Motel—an appropriate name, it would be *One Star* in anyone's tour book. The sign promised "A Memorable Lodging Experience."

    The faded tan stucco building stretched out, one unit deep. There were thirty units on each of two levels. The lower level rooms were entered off the concrete sidewalk. The upper units were reached by a building-long expanded metal catwalk. There was a partly rusted black iron stairway near the office end and another at the far end. *A great setup for fishermen, snowmobilers, hookers or local terrorists*, he thought. He shook his head at his latent SEAL edginess. Sixty parking spaces were about half filled...mostly pickups, a couple station wagons and a brown Taurus.

    When Buck had called to confirm the reservation, the motel guy said he would be in the office all night. "I sleep in a recliner in the back room. Just ring the buzzer," the clerk promised. True to his word, he hopped to the door when Buck rang. He told Buck that one night was all paid for. He could leave anytime in the morning he wanted. Just drop the key in the room. He gave him the key to room 229. "Second floor, second from the end," the clerk said. Buck parked his Silverado near the far end and squeaked his way up the metal stairway. It reminded him of scaling the precarious metal ladder up the side of a deep sea oil rig during SEAL training.

The room was unremarkable but looked clean. After seven hours sleep over the past two nights, Buck was ready. He set his travel alarm for 5:30 AM. Sleep came immediately.

* * *

The leeches seemed to go on forever. U.S. Navy SEAL Buck Ryker finally gave up trying to pick them off his exposed parts and fell into an exhausted sleep sitting against a tree. Then SNAP! The fine steel cable, attached to a tree across the jungle path, yanked a branch he had tucked under his leg. He opened his eyes, without making a move or sound, and tightened his grip on the M-16.

Buck had dreamed these encounters many times over the past seven years, but they had returned more often over the last few days. He usually turned over and went back to a more peaceful sleep. His main method for encouraging sleep was to review his current log home in progress—much better than the sheep bit. His crew had used the special calipers to carefully mark the notches required at the ends of logs, to allow them to cross properly at the corners. Precise sawing and chiseling created the matching joints. They were working on the top row of the wall logs. Next would be tagging each log with an identifying number to make re-assembly possible at the owner's site. He was about to drift off when another dream recurred—climbing up the ladder of the oil rig—except the sound was not a dream!

Buck mentally lurched but held fast physically as he again heard the squeak that could only be the metal stairway that he had climbed a few hours earlier.

He listened.

A few more squeaks and there were sounds like footsteps, softly setting down on the catwalk.

He remembered that his door was only about twelve feet from the top of the stairs.

The footsteps stopped. There was an eerie silence.

Thoughts raced through Buck's mind. *Another motel customer who had been given a 229 key by mistake? Or some drunk who didn't know where he was?*

During the eternity of silence, Buck eased out of bed and into the bathroom for a better defensive position. The mercury vapor yard light, out in the parking area near the office, cast angular streaks of light through the window's partly closed horizontal blinds. His vision, now totally accustomed to the dark, gave him a clear picture of the room—*hell of a lot better than the green night-scopes he had used in blackout stealth operations.*

He waited. No more footsteps. *Must be right outside the door.* Then, a touch of metal at the door knob. The hair on his body lifted like a cat's.

Buck saw the knob barely turn back and forth. *Did the guy actually have a key?* The key was not working. The knob turned quietly back and forth again—perhaps out of momentary frustration. *What could the guy do now?* Then Buck knew!

An almost noiseless thump on the window glass confirmed Buck's guess. A scratching sound followed, from back of the flimsy drapes that were pulled to the sides of the window.

Had he been in a sound sleep, Buck knew that he would not have heard any of these sounds. The intruder was good, very good—probably had a professional glass-cutter kit. *What next?* He waited again. *If this clown doesn't make a move in the next two seconds—attack mode.*

At first, Buck heard a different thump. Then a sizzle. He didn't have to use SEAL experience to tell what had been dropped through the neat round hole in the window glass.

It was a stick of dynamite—probably with a short fuse, judging by the hurried clatter he heard on the stairs.

Two bounds brought Buck to the red stick with the sparkling three-inch string at the end. He could have tried to pinch off the fire, but he knew that doesn't always work the first time and there would not be a second chance.

One more move to the door and it was open—he was on the catwalk. A dark figure in what appeared to be a black suit and hat was running out to the middle of the parking lot. Buck looped the dynamite out as far away from his truck below as he could.

That particular section of Duluth had probably never experienced a 4:30 AM. wake-up call like this one. The dynamite exploded while it was still fifteen feet in the air. The black suit guy pitched forward onto the gravel of the parking area and slid about five feet forward. Buck thought he saw the heavy hitter get up and stagger into one of the first level units.

Buck quickly dressed, grabbed his gear and got out of there. He was not going to hang around for the police and others to start asking questions. He drove out of the parking lot, in the opposite direction from the motel office.

The North Star was certainly a "Memorable Lodging Experience."

* * *

Benny's hands were bleeding. His nose was scuffed, but the front of the black hat had cushioned the impact of his head hitting the gravel. His black trousers would never be the same. There were large tears in the knees that would have been the pride of a cool fifteen-year-old punk rocker in jeans.

Luther woke with a start as Benny lurched in the door.

"Benny, what have you been doing?" he asked with suitable concern.

"Our job, you no-good!" Benny was not happy. "I just missed blowing up the tree-hugger guy."

Luther, recognizing that this was no time to be testy

with Benny, said, "Why don't you go in and take a nice shower. I'll try to fix your suit."

The shower did bring Benny back to his usual degree of self-confidence. "Well, the guy was just lucky—like he was waiting for me. I'll just tell LeYan that I'll get him when he comes back. With that big black Silverado, we'll be able to find him at the airport."

"Your hands are still bleeding. What are you going to do?"

"They'll be OK for a while. We'll head north and find some kind of a clinic that won't be nosey. I don't want to show up at no hospital around here. Now we have to get our ass outta here before the cops come. Just grab our stuff and go out like nothing happened. Just act natural."

"Well, we may *act* natural, but you ain't exactly going to *look* natural. I couldn't do much with your suit and hat."

"Never mind, we'll find a store—maybe at this Two Harbors—and get me some new stuff and fix up my hands."

* * *

Buck drove the speed limit out Haines Road, past the county jail and took a left before reaching the National Guard airfield. The large sign proclaimed "Air National Guard—Global Power For America." Two F-16's were warming up outside the two-story operations building. Buck thought he would like to expand their "routine patrols" to include defense against invaders of the wilderness. He continued another mile to the Duluth International Airport. The terminal sloped toward the front parking area, relating it to the ground more than the sky. He parked in a space under one of the towering lights, grabbed his carryon and locked the doors. The big 6.5HP, dual-rear diesel was a tempting target if he parked it in the dark.

The interior of the terminal gave the impression of a modern white-painted A-frame. He noticed the Airport Security office opposite the Northwest Airlines ticket counter. *Glad to see that security*, he thought, looking out the floor-to-ceiling windows at his pride and joy Silverado.

Northwest had his ticket waiting for him: One-way flight to Minneapolis and a change of planes to Chicago. There was also an open ticket for his trip home. He walked past the "Afterburner Lounge and Dining Room" and into the small coffee shop. Several cups of coffee would be welcome after the past two hours of action. The outside wall of the shop was all window and lined with two-person booths. The first booth was occupied by a pert young woman dressed in a conservative business suit. It was conservative except that the short skirt was barely visible under the suit jacket. Her blond hair had not completely recovered from last night. She was sleepily sipping coffee and was probably unaware of her interesting display. The sight served as an effective eye-opener. She noticed his look and smiled. Why was he already wondering if she would be sitting near him on the plane? *Cool it, fella*, he sneered at himself. *You've got to get out more.* He busied himself with his ticket while he tossed down a roll and coffee.

The twelve passengers boarded and the blond wriggled into the outside seat across the aisle from his window seat. A two-week-old *Time* helped him focus away, contrary to all the other passengers within craning position. When the plane had come to a stop in Minneapolis, the guy in the window seat by the blond helped her with her bag. They chatted amiably as they moved to the door. *Forget about it*, Buck thought. *You weren't even close.*

* * *

Benny rarely let Luther drive; but this was one time. His hands were still bleeding into the North Star Motel towels wrapped bulkily, halfway to his elbows.

"Luther, we are not in a funeral procession here. It is possible to drive over forty. This is a freeway," Benny urged.

"OK, OK, you haven't done so damn good. I'm, doing what I think is right. We sure as hell don't want a ticket!"

The Taurus continued along the freeway like a Slow Moving Vehicle, in spite of the early morning traffic average of one vehicle per mile. The only danger came from the propensity of locals to lurch onto the highway without any concern about on-coming targets.

"Stop here," Benny said, eyeing the general store/gas station in Two Harbors. "They'll probably have a pair of pants that I can use. And pick up some paper towels so I can get rid of this bloody stuff."

"OK. We can get something to eat."

"Yeah but go in and get the pants first. Get dark—black if they've got 'em. Forty-six waist. Whatever. Just get 'em."

Luther emerged with frosted doughnuts holed on a thumb and little finger of one hand. The other held a pair of indigo jeans. "It's all they had," Luther said. "They've got sandwiches you can heat up in the microwave. I'm going back in."

"Gimme the pants. I'll put 'em on while you fill up with gas. Then ask 'em if there's a clinic or something further up north."

As they started to exit the scene, Benny said, "I have to call LeYan." He walked over to the outside pay phone and dialed her at home.

"LeYan? Benny."

"Did you get him?" LeYan was not interested in small talk.

"LeYan," Benny said out of desperation, "I saw this sign in the gun store where we got the dynamite and guns. It said 'sometimes you gits da bear and sometimes da bear gits you.'"

"What the hell does that mean?" She had gone beyond cool or neutral to agitated. "You must have really screwed up!"

"Listen, LeYan. This guy ain't no ordinary local. And I tell you this: he's coming!"

9

Twin Cities International Airport loomed large, as the Northwest Airlink flight from Duluth touched down. Buck knew that he had nearly a mile hike to his departure gate. It would give him a chance to stretch his legs and get into a serious frame of mind about the Chicago meeting. *They will try to sell me*, he thought. *Why else would they haul me into their office?*

The telephone kiosks reminded him: *Call dad! It's nearly eight. He should be up by now.* He had to wait for an open phone. The suits were busy calling their clients and offices.

"Hello, dad, this is Buck. Happy birthday tomorrow. I'm in Minneapolis, on the way to Chicago…no, not a log home deal. I've got a meeting with a company. I hope to be done by late afternoon. How'd you like a guest tonight? OK, I'll call you from O'Hare after the meeting. Maybe you could pick me up at the Milwaukee airport."

Buck smiled as he hung up. *It will be great to see Al again.* It had been last Christmas since they were together. Casey and Buck had met Al in Duluth for a long, festive dinner at the Pickwick restaurant.

Recalling for a moment his BWCA trips with his dad, he didn't need any more conviction about the portage threat. He knew what Al would do.

* * *

The Northwest Flight Attendant in the First Class section did her best to make sure that Buck had a pleasant 80-minute trip to O'Hare. Deplaning, he felt the interesting sensation of hundreds of inquiring eyes focused on him momentarily and then moving to the next passenger emerging from the disembarkation tunnel. He stared back.

First, the "Mr. Ryker" sign, held by a blond man in a suit, attracted him. But only for a split second. The exotic-looking beauty standing next to the sign not only grabbed his attention, but was receiving celebrity-type notice from at least half of the large crowd waiting in the gate area.

"I'm Ryker," Buck announced. He held out his hand to the sign-man, who started to shift the sign in order to shake Buck's hand.

"Hello, Mr. Ryker. I'm LeYan Syn." She beat the blond guy to the shake. "This is Bill Anderson, our vice-president for operations." LeYan, having covered all the bases, left only a nod necessary between the two men.

Since Buck had nothing but his carryon, they proceeded to a white limo, parked illegally, in front of the automatic terminal doors. They sat together on the wide, pearl gray leather back seat, with Anderson in the middle. It was clear that the scene was not the proper place for serious topics. The weather subject was covered thoroughly. LeYan spoke very little, but her looks at Buck contained an unusual mixture of challenge and vulnerability.

* * *

Buck avoided the classic tourist gawk as they stepped out of the limo, in front of the *got-to-be-fifty-stories* Alactra building. The lobby was equally impressive, with enough marble and terrazzo to redo the U.S. Capitol rotunda. Alactra International looked like it was there to stay.

LeYan smiled at the uniformed guard seated behind the desk. "Please inform Mr. Alactra's secretary that Bill and I and our guest are on our way up."

"Yes, Ms. Syn," he said, simultaneously dialing a number and pressing a button to demand the express elevator.

Inside the elevator, Anderson selected "Forty" in the panel designated "Express to Floors Forty and Above."

The softly lighted elevator moved soundlessly for what seemed to be no more than a minute and eased to a stop at Forty. There were numbers on the panel for floors forty through forty-six plus one selection square that did not have a number.

* * *

The doors parted and the three occupants stepped into a small lobby that was at once serene, luxurious and businesslike. A two-inch thick marble slab atop an expertly crafted zebra wood desk was the station for a young broad-chested Asian man in a tasteful blue suit, white shirt and subtly striped tie. The suit, shirt and tie seemed to be identical to Anderson's. *Uniforms?* The Asian's initial look, as he raised his head slowly, was calmly fierce. Then it became a slight smile. Well behind him was a larger, wood-topped desk, centered in a fifteen-by-twenty-foot area. The focal point, however, was the ten-foot-high expanse of glass that allowed a spectacular view of a good share of Chicago and the Lake Michigan shoreline. The woman sitting in the executive chair behind the desk could have been anyone's idea of a perfectly groomed, youngish-looking matron. She formed a Mona Lisa smile as she looked up from her desk. Both she and the Asian man rose as the visitors stepped onto the deep plush of the entry-area rug that partially covered the bamboo wood floor.

"Good morning Paulette," LeYan said. "Good morning Ling."

"Good morning LeYan, Bill, and welcome, Mr. Ryker," Paulette said without leaving her desk area. Ling simply smiled again and gave a small nod. Buck noticed that Ling's well-tailored suit did not hide a trim but heavily muscled torso. He could have been cast in a martial arts movie with no augmentation required.

"I will inform Mr. Alactra that you are here. Do you wish to use the conference room, LeYan? He can meet you there," Paulette continued.

"Thank you, Paulette," LeYan smiled. The attitude between the two women seemed to be obvious total respect, or more. Bill Anderson was merely there.

The bamboo floor continued into the hallway and into the conference room on the other side of the reception/work station wall. Upon opening the ceiling-height door, the eye was instantly directed to the same window panorama as in the previous room. Vying for attention, the huge mahogany, slightly oval table then became the focus. It was ensconced on a rug of the same design and soft rust color as the one in the entry area. Mildly abstract paintings of a somewhat Oriental nature were hung on the two side walls. The interior end wall was paneled inconspicuously but no doubt was the business end of the room. A barely perceptible scent of sandalwood challenged expectations.

"Won't you sit down, Mr. Ryker?" LeYan said. "Would you care for a soft drink or coffee or tea?" *Or me?* Buck finished to himself. He stepped onto the enveloping plush and sank into one of the rosewood-framed leather chairs.

"Black coffee would be just fine," he said. LeYan leaned out of the conference room door toward Ling's marble desk and passed along the request, as well as exhibiting an unnecessarily provocative pose.

A door in the end wall, that blended almost completely into the woodwork, opened, and a silver-haired man of medium stature stepped silently into the room.

"Mr. Ryker, may I present Alasom Alactra, Chairman and President of Alactra International," LeYan announced with obvious pride. Alactra walked over and extended his hand as Buck stood. All four then sat into the comfortable chairs.

"Mr. Ryker, thank you for journeying all this way to be our guest. We felt it was important for you to visit our office in order to become acquainted with our people and our proposal," Alactra said in a smooth, low voice. "Now, as you might imagine, I have not become personally involved with the details of the proposal, but I do fully support the concept and the plans that LeYan and Bill have developed. While Ms. Syn, as my executive vice-president, will be my personal liaison, Bill here is vice-president of operations and has the most complete involvement with the project that we envision."

The monologue continued: "What we propose is to provide a means for thousands of Americans to experience the wonders of your wilderness. We are aware of its value and wish to treat the area with the respect that it deserves. As a by-product of this objective, we are certain that you and the residents of northern Minnesota will also benefit. The project will be creating jobs immediately and the ongoing service requirements will continue to profit many in your area."

My God, Buck thought, *this man talks like he is the best thing that has ever happened to northern Minnesota—maybe America.*

"Mr. Alactra, I know that you have to leave now," LeYan said. "Thank you for taking time to give us your vision. Bill and I will review the entire project with Mr. Ryker and answer any questions that he might have. Also, Mr. Alactra, thank you for offering your penthouse for our lunch and continued discussion."

"Mr. Ryker, again, thank you for visiting us. I am sorry I cannot stay. Perhaps we can have a good chat the next time you are in Chicago." The silver-haired smoothie rose and disappeared as silently as he had come.

"Well, Mr. Ryker," Anderson finally opened his mouth. "What do you think of Mr. Alactra?" LeYan winced slightly.

"He should run for office," Buck said.

"Well, he is already president," Anderson attempted a joke.

LeYan, trying to minimize the conversational gaffes, stood and walked toward the huge window. While she proceeded to briefly review the background and current activities of Alactra International, she accomplished her main objective by standing in front of the sunlit glass wall. She then walked over to within an arm's length of Buck's chair, which he had turned to face the window, and said, "Is there anything I can do for you before Bill begins his presentation?"

Buck gave the offer a moment's thought, meeting her gaze steadily, and said, "No…can't think of a thing." She immediately backed off, showing a slight puzzle, and glanced at Anderson. He started opening the paneled doors, to reveal a rear projection screen on the left, balanced by a similar size whiteboard on the right. He turned some dials and picked up a remote device.

LeYan, now looking all business, checked her watch. "We can get started on the presentation and then break for lunch. It's now nearly eleven. How would 12:30 be for lunch in the penthouse?"

Buck nodded and thought, *I wonder what's going to be on the menu in the penthouse. I have already been offered the specialty of the house.*

10

Luther eased out of the convenience store lot onto the North Shore highway. "What did you find out about a clinic?" Benny demanded.

"They said there was a hospital here in Two Harbors and then a smaller clinic about forty-five miles farther."

"I don't want no big hospital," Benny said. "We'll head for that clinic. What did they call it?"

"Cascade Clinic. They said you can't miss it. It's on the main highway. They do a lot of ski and snowmobile injuries in the winter and hiking and worker stuff otherwise."

The hour to the Cascade Clinic, at an uninspired forty-eight miles per hour, had lulled Benny to a short nap. He awoke with a minor panic.

"You OK there, Luther? Not sleepy are you?" Benny asked, gazing apprehensively at the narrow-shoulder asphalt double lane through the trees. He opened the window and got his face partway out. "Good air in these parts. I can smell the pines. Why don't you open yours?"

There was no action or comment from Luther until he finally said, "There it is, on the left. The Cascade Clinic." The one-story tan brick building was an outpost, situated on about two acres carved out of an almost solid mass of pines and birch. A ten-foot ring of rough grass was all that kept the back and both sides out of the forest. A crescent-shaped gravel patch in front served both as driveway and parking area. Luther drove to a spot immediately blocking the glass-front entry door. Cascade Clinic and Jonas Thacher, MD were painted on the glass.

Benny gingerly opened the car door with his still-wrapped hands and then used his shoulder, elbow and foot to get the clinic door open. He gave an oblivious Luther a spiteful stare for not offering to help. Luther stayed in the car with his cigarette for company.

"Good morning, sir," the lady in white said pleasantly, as Benny walked up to the four-foot high counter.

"Can I get someone to fix my hands?" Benny asked.

"Have you been in an accident?" asked the lady whose name tag said simply Betty Rhodes.

"Sort of. I fell and slid on the gravel."

"Do you have any other injuries—any bruises or internal discomfort?"

"No I don't, Betty. I would appreciate it if someone would just clean up my hands and put on some smaller bandages," he said, holding up his two bundled mitts. "My friend and I are in a hurry to get going. We have an appointment up north."

"I will ask the nurse if she can treat you right away. Will you please fill out the admittance form, listing your medical insurance information?"

"Betty, I can't fill out no form with these hands. And I'll be paying in cash." Betty checked the small glass window in the door and then retreated to the back room.

In a minute, a tall, black-haired nurse, in a white uniform that seemed to enhance her attractiveness, walked through the swinging door. Her name tag read Casey Ryker.

"Hello," Casey said with what some would call a wry smile. "I understand you need some care for your hands. Have you been fighting again?" She made a mock frown.

Benny said seriously, "I fell on the gravel this morning and I need some new bandages."

"I won't argue that," Casey said, eyeing the bloody wads of paper towels. She led him into the sterile-looking room that appeared to be a mini-hospital all in one well-equipped area. In spite of Benny's protests, she took his blood pressure, peered in his eyeballs, but stopped short of forcing him onto the scale.

"You probably don't need to know your weight," she said.

"You got that right, lady…er, nurse."

She bathed his skinned-up hands, nose and forehead. The wrapping she put on his hands allowed his fingers and thumbs to operate freely. Finishing, she said, "Well now, I think you'll live. I will ask Dr. Thacher to come in."

"That won't be necessary," he said, starting to raise one hand in protest.

"It will only take a minute," she said, walking out and not acknowledging Benny's objection.

Dr. Thacher looked to be right out of *Chicago Hope*, only taller than the average TV actor. He peered at Benny from a number of angles and, apparently satisfied, ended the examination with, "Are you heading further up north?"

"Yes."

"If you have any pain or discomfort, you can stop in at the hospital in Fall River, just north of town."

"OK. Thanks, Doc."

The doctor held the door to the lobby and nodded to Betty at the desk. "You can check out with Mrs. Rhodes."

"We don't have many people paying cash," Mrs. Rhodes said as she handed Benny the receipt.

"Right," he said as he walked out of the Cascade Clinic.

Betty, Casey and Jonas had gathered at the front desk.

"I don't expect we'll see him again," Thacher said.

"With any luck…" Casey said, rolling her blue eyes.

"How'd it go?" Luther asked, when Benny returned to the car.

Benny spoke, but only to himself, "That smart-ass nurse has got to be Ryker's squeeze. Wait 'till LeYan hears this one."

11

The words spilled forth as Bill Anderson warmed to his subject. He even commanded *LeYan's* attention. Aerial footage of boundary water lakes glittered on the screen. The blue sky and the blue water, interspersed with hundreds of forested islands and shorelines, were breathtaking. Buck had lived and breathed this wilderness many times, but he had never seen an extended aerial view this beautiful. There was not a building, not a cabin, not a boat, not a person to be seen, even at very close inspection. He got up and examined the screen, as if with a magnifying glass, when he saw a spot he recognized. Anderson smiled with pride at the obvious emotion that was caused by his presentation.

He has just proved to me that this land and water should not be touched, Buck confirmed to himself.

The presentation continued, even more enthusiastically. The visual showed a camera shot zooming in, to a spot between two lakes. The action became an artist's rendering of the beginning of a trail, at the shoreline of a lake. However, the trail was neatly paved with stones and had rustic handrails on both sides. The trail scene dissolved to art of a building, barely visible through large pines, sprinkled with birches. Another visual fade showed a medium distance vista of the front of a three-story log building. The forest green painted trim, gabled windows and rustic details gave the appearance of a huge upscale lake lodge. It reminded Buck of the picture he had seen glorifying the early 1900's home that Teddy Roosevelt built in the Adirondacks.

Beautiful, but out of place in the boundary country, Buck grimaced.

"Welcome to Boundary Lodges!" the token American said dramatically, apparently concluding the canned pitch.

Buck said nothing.

After an uncomfortable moment, during which Anderson stood like a statue with his eyes opened wide and his mouth slightly ajar, LeYan spoke.

"It *is* impressive, isn't it? I'm sure you have some questions, Mr. Ryker."

Buck looked first at Anderson and then LeYan. "I'm not sure I know where to start."

"Well, while you are thinking, let me say that this project would include as many as ten or twelve of these lodges over the next five to eight years. The benefits to your entire area would be immeasurable."

Just like the devastation, Buck thought.

LeYan continued quickly, "Bill, of course, would coordinate the project from this office. But we would need a uniquely knowledgeable and qualified manager for the development at each site. At the moment, we can think of no one better qualified for this important responsibility than you, Buck." The more personal reference came with the same look of determination that LeYan had first shown during the quiet limo ride from the airport.

With no immediate response from Buck, LeYan said, "Bill, we have given Mr. Ryker an awful lot to think about. Why don't we break for lunch? We can talk there in more comfortable surroundings." She left very little more to say. They walked out to the outer office and approached the elevator.

"LeYan, may I speak with you for a moment?" Paulette said, rising to meet her. Continuing in a whisper, Paulette spoke to LeYan's ears only, "Benny has been trying to reach you."

"Call him back in ten minutes, please, and buzz me in the penthouse. I can take it in the bath area," LeYan requested.

In a second, the threesome was on its way, closer to heaven, or to whatever LeYan's strategy would propose.

* * *

A world of sophisticated luxury greeted them as they stepped out of the elevator at the hallowed forty-sixth floor onto the somewhat darker shade of bamboo flooring than below. The living room was large, by any standard. However, because of the different ceiling heights and treatments, various moods were created. Quiet intimacy was pervasive. Equally imposing, as in the office suites, was the expansive view of Chicago and Lake Michigan, now sparkling in the early afternoon sun. The main room blended into the dining area to the left. The floor-to-ceiling window wall continued around to present a nearly 180-degree vista. The scene was undeniably impressive. Buck knew he had to say something to return to reality.

"This sure beats the Sawbill Bar and Grill," he said.

LeYan smiled and said, "We may as well sit in the dining room. We will be served before long. Buck—may I call you Buck?—I have ordered a simple filet of beef with béarnaise, asparagus and new potatoes. Is that satisfactory?" A nearby device, bearing no resemblance to a telephone, rang twice, precluding Buck's answer. She said, "Please excuse me. I believe that is a call for me." She walked into the distant hallway. Anderson gestured to the carved wood and zebra skin dining room chairs. He turned on his pitch again, from where he had stopped in the conference room.

* * *

The penthouse master bath had as many square feet as a small house. Tile, glass and marble were brought together into one feeling by the subtle lighting. LeYan lifted the receiver of the decorative phone on the marble lavatory counter.

"This is LeYan."

"This is Benny. I know you don't have a job for me right now, but I've got some news you might want."

"Go ahead, Benny."

"You know I had a little accident in the motel parking lot—got skinned up some. We drove north, actually east as they call it here, to get up to Fall River. We stopped at a small clinic about seventy-five miles up from Duluth. I went in to get some bandages on my hands. Didn't give my right name. Paid cash. Guess who was there?"

"Benny, I don't have time for riddles!"

"It was a nurse called Casey Ryker. She seemed to be pretty cozy with this stud doctor they got there. I looked in the phone book and there's only one Ryker, and that's B.A. Ryker. She's got to be his squeeze…er, his wife."

LeYan answered quickly. "Here's what you do. Stay in the area. Take turns keeping an eye on her. Follow her home or wherever she goes. Got it? Then call me tonight. You know, if you keep up the good work, you might get on my good list."

Excitedly Benny asked, "Does that mean…"

"It means," she interrupted, "that you might get on my good list. I have to run. Call me."

* * *

She resumed control as she glided back into the dining room. "Why Bill, didn't you offer our guest a drink?"

"Well, we were waiting for you," Bill said weakly.

"Buck, would you like a drink? Champagne? A beer?" she asked, placing her hand on his shoulder.

"Whatever you are having," Buck said, meeting her gaze.

"Oh, good. Let's have champagne." Anderson took his cue and opened the under-counter refrigerator by the wet bar.

Buck checked his watch: 1:15; champagne; no substitute for food; better ease off. The hosts showed no sign of slowing their ongoing pitch. His hunger focused on the filet.

"Why don't you tell us about your log home business," Anderson said.

"Pretty simple really. We peel and cut the logs, lay

them out to fit the custom design, haul them to the buyer's location and erect the log shell. We then help the buyer contract to have everything else installed and finished."

Having heard enough about that, LeYan said, "I believe Mr. Henstead said you are married."

"Yes, I am."

"Is your wife involved in your business?" she asked.

"Yes, very involved—as much as she can be."

"Oh, does she have other interests?"

"Right now she works three days a week as a nurse at a clinic."

"That must keep her very busy. How long have you been married?"

"About six years." The inquisition continued with Buck answering as briefly as possible. As a defense against more questions, Buck asked a few of his own about construction and feasibility. Anderson answered with few details, but great conviction.

The catered lunch was as outstanding as the view. Buck thought about how he and Casey could use a long weekend in a place like this.

"Let's get back to you, Buck," Anderson said, trying to reassert himself. "What are your impressions at this point?"

"Bill, LeYan, it is about time I lay it on the line. Number one, my purpose here is to get information. I will report what you have presented back to the Nordland County group. That's twenty-five to thirty citizens that generally represent the thinking of the majority in the county."

Eager for some positive sign, Bill asked, "How about the possibility of your taking over as construction manager?"

"That is my second point," Buck said. "I believe that would be a conflict of interest. Also, I have a full-time responsibility with my log home business."

"I think we should give Buck a chance to think these matters over, Bill," LeYan said, walking to the bar. She poured a half glass of champagne for herself and eased back to Buck's chair without breaking direct eye contact. She filled his glass and held hers forward in a silent "cheers." She also shot a look at Anderson that did not fit the conversation. If it was some kind of signal, he certainly responded. He pulled back from the table and said, "If you will excuse me, Buck, Mr. Alactra has asked me to develop some information that he needs by three o'clock. I need to call him with a report. We hope you can be our guest here tonight in the penthouse. My wife and I would like to join you for dinner. Paulette will be happy to arrange a flight for you in the morning. We can have the limo available to bring you to O'Hare. You will be returning to Duluth, I presume." Anderson moved through the living room toward the elevator. "We will plan to see you this evening then."

That's doubtful, Billy, Buck thought as he and LeYan adjourned to the living room. The Dragon Lady, as he now thought of LeYan, lounged herself in one corner of the curved leather sofa that faced Lake Michigan. He retreated toward the matching chair.

"It appears, Buck, that we have some time to talk. You could sit over here. The view is better."

When he walked over near her, she placed her hand on his mid-section and said, "Marvelous abs. You must work out a lot."

"Just enough," he said, and continued, "actually, I think a short trip would be timely—all that champagne."

"Through the dining room and into the hallway," she said and gave him a playful wave.

Nature's function could wait. Buck saw what he assumed would be available in the bathroom and grabbed the fancy phone. He took out his ticket and dialed for reservations. "What flights do you have this afternoon from O'Hare to Milwaukee?" After a pause, he acknowledged, "7:15 would be fine. Arrival at five after eight. Great! The name is Ryker: R-Y-K-E-R. I'll pick up the ticket at about 5:15."

* * *

Buck walked down the hall to a now-darkened dining room. The bamboo shades had been drawn and were partially obscuring the sunlight that had been streaming in the wall of windows. Only a view straight north to the lake remained. The effect was an instant twilight mood that she had enhanced by switching on the gas fireplace. She had obviously done something with her dress. It seemed to be shorter on both ends. She rose as he came near the curved sofa and took his hand, easing them both back down into the leather softness.

"Now here's your champagne—or would you prefer brandy?"

"This is fine," Buck said.

"It was nice of Bill to plan a dinner for tonight," she said. "Of course, we could have dinner here in the penthouse. We should really take plenty of time to discuss the opportunities you would have here with Alactra."

"LeYan, you and Bill have certainly made this a pleasant and interesting day. As I mentioned before, my job is to get information back to the citizens so that they can evaluate your proposal." For a moment, the only sounds in the twilight room were the fluttering of the gas flame and some other soft whirring that Buck could not place. The faint motor noise seemed to emanate from a metal grid above the windows, across from the sofa. Then her voice covered the sound again.

"I really believe that, if you and I spent some time together, you would see the Boundary Lodges in a very positive light." She leaned toward him, put her hand on his knee and joined her eyes with his. He knew that in a minute he would have to get physical—either in rejection or acceptance.

He rose slowly and moved toward the window. As if to examine the lake in the distance, his gaze went to the top of the glass, with his eyes actually rolling upward to encompass the air conditioning vent above the window frame. The motor noise again became apparent and a small metal cylinder was barely visible.

He and LeYan were not alone after all. Another eye was observing what might be happening in the Dragon Lady's den. It was time, he decided.

"LeYan, I made a call when I was in the bathroom. I don't get a chance to see my dad in Milwaukee very often. I was able to get a late flight this afternoon. So I should head for O'Hare shortly." Her face changed abruptly from soft loveliness to surprise to disappointment to barely-suppressed anger and scorn.

"Well, aren't you the little surprise package. We had no idea that you planned to rush off," she spit out like a pneumatic nailer.

"Should I talk to Paulette about a ride to the airport?" he asked. She was up and on her way back through the dining room to the hall.

"Call yourself a cab," she said in a voice he had not heard before.

The Dragon Lady called Paulette from the phone in the bathroom. "Paulette, get that yokel out of here. Put him in a cab, or let him walk for that matter. Also, get Anderson up here immediately, and get a call into Congressman Wayneson. I need to confirm the Monday lunch."

Buck rode the elevator down six floors and stepped out to see Paulette alone at her desk. "I understand that you are leaving, Mr. Ryker," she said with a smile.

"Yes, could you call me a cab?"

"It should be waiting at the curb by the time you get down there. By the way, congratulations."

"For what?" Buck turned back to the attractive silver-blond lady as he moved to the elevator.

"For escaping the web. *LeYan* is usually the one who decides when to end an interview. Oh, there is one more thing I want you to know. Alasom Alactra is truly a good man."

"I certainly hope so," he said, and stepped into the softly lighted quiet of the Alactra Express. Delicate Oriental music seemed to exude from the walls and ceiling.

* * *

Bill Anderson entered the penthouse. "Where is Buck?"

"He's gone back home," LeYan said with a frown. "He had to see his father or someone in Milwaukee. He's a loser! And he sure as hell is going to lose this one! I'm going to take him out of the action, one way or another!"

* * *

Buck's immediate action was a pleasant cab ride to O'Hare International and a phone call to Milwaukee.

"Hello, Dad, this is Buck. I'm at O'Hare. I am due to leave at 7:15 and arrive shortly after eight. How does that work for you? Good. Maybe we could zip into town and have dinner at the German place. We haven't eaten together there for years. Too late, Buck realized that he should have avoided the last part since the previous time was a solemn dinner, two days after the funeral of his mother, Helen. He was just leaving his dad alone for the first time. He hung up slowly, hoping that the memory would not sadden his dad as well.

12

John Allan Ryker backed his ten-year-old Ford station wagon out of the single car garage, attached to his colonial house in the Blue Mound section of Milwaukee. *Colonial* was an exaggeration for the smallish two-story, but that is what the real estate agent called it three years before. Al had thought about selling it. It was shortly after Helen had died. He decided he did not need "that much house." Fortunately, no one rushed to buy it. The twenty-five years of memories were too strong and the neighbors had become like family. He stayed.

* * *

Al joined the U.S. Navy in 1963 to become a Frogman, soon to be designated a SEAL. His time in the jungles of Vietnam was shortened when a gook mortar hit his platoon riverboat. His shattered left leg brought a medical discharge. Returning that early in the ugly conflict was a grave disappointment, until he became re-acquainted with a high school girl friend. He and Helen were married in June of 1966. Hard work, intelligence and the motivation of a son (he hoped) on the way got him through tech school. His credentials got him a pick of electrician jobs. Buckminster Allan Ryker was born in November of 1967. The name Buckminster was controversial with Helen, but derived from Al's early interest in the designs and creative brilliance of Buckminster Fuller, a modern-day Leonardo da Vinci. No one minded when the sturdy little guy became forever, *Buck*.

Al was devoting most of his time to gaining advancement where he worked. He was offered overtime and took it. Popular and athletic, Buck knocked around with his rough-and-ready pals. Helen recognized that he needed some very strong male direction to balance the influence of his buddies. Al agreed and began encouraging his son to enjoy hunting and fishing. The fall of Buck's thirteenth birthday, they hunted partridges along the Brule River in the northern tip of Wisconsin. The proximity to the canoe routes of the Voyageurs elicited stories that Buck found fascinating. The next year they returned to the Brule and took a short trip to the Lake Superior south shore. Al pointed across the vast expanse in the direction of Grand Portage. The decision was made. They must adventure into the canoe wilderness territory.

The trips kept Buck's interests directed most of the time. But by his sophomore year, Buck's sturdy good looks opened up temptations that kept him on the edge. Anticipating a precarious relationship the summer before Buck's junior year, Al took charge again. Father and son left the first day of school vacation for five days camping and canoeing in the wilderness. Buck was less than delighted to be away from his wild world of fun and females, but the bragging rights would be some compensation.

It was no piece of cake—canoeing, portaging, making camp, building fires, cleaning and cooking fish. But even through a few days of harsh weather, a stronger bond developed. Buck saw his dad's SEAL pride, training and endurance put to the test. Without declaring, Buck came to his own conclusion: after graduation, he would join the Navy and try out for the SEAL Special Forces.

With his future thus planned, Buck knew that he had to dedicate the next two years to discipline and physical training in order to stand a chance to make the grade as a SEAL.

* * *

Casey studied a patient's computerized record and insurance information. Cascade Clinic was closed and the lobby was dark. Two fluorescent desk lights illuminated the main nurses station where Casey worked after hours.

"We'll have to give you a bonus..." Dr. Jonas Thacher began, but stopped abruptly.

"My God, you scared me!" Casey said. "I didn't know you were still here."

"Actually, I must admit...I had gone home but was heading back past the clinic to the Bergen House for dinner when I saw your white bomber out in front. I had to see what you were up to. Came in the back door. What *are* you up to?"

"I told Betty that I would help her get the insurance work done. I didn't need to get home right away. But I'm getting ready to leave now. It's nearly seven."

"Since you have some time, why don't we have dinner at the Bergen and I'll bring you back here to pick up your car?"

"You don't want to go to dinner at the Bergen House with a lady in a white uniform."

"This particular lady I would be proud to be with in whatever she wore. Besides, I bet you've got some casual outfit here that would do fine."

"I'd have to be back early."

"As long as you stay for an after-dinner drink, anytime is OK."

Casey changed into a pair of Bermuda shorts and a loose top. *How'd he know I had this?* They left through the heavy steel door at the rear of the clinic and got into Doc's crouching Jaguar. *The car even looks eager!* She thought.

* * *

"Benny, wake up, she's leaving!" Luther slurred. The Jack D had been his best companion during their vigil since two-thirty that afternoon. They had gambled that the nurse Ryker would not leave before she had completed a shift. But they had not planned on an over-four-hour wait. At about four o'clock, Luther had actually jogged five hundred yards to a roadside grocery for life sustenance.

"Damn it Luther, her car's still there!" Benny cursed.

"Cool it, cousin, I saw this Jag go 'round the back about a half hour ago. Now they just left together. Probably was the doc. See, I told you—there's action there. You suppose she's going to shack up while the honcho's away?"

"Forget it. Which way'd they go?" Benny demanded.

"South...or to the right anyway. You can't miss 'em—probably the only Jag in this part of the state."

"We'll find 'em," Benny said with a conviction born out of LeYan's latest directive.

"Whataya gonna do with 'em?" Luther asked.

"We'll see where she goes, then we'll decide—after I call LeYan. Probably push 'em off the edge into the lake." Benny liked to scare Luther once in a while.

* * *

Al took the east-west freeway and turned onto U.S. 43 and Howell Avenue south to General Mitchell International Airport. As agreed, Al met Buck at the curb, outside the baggage area. Al got out and they had an unabashed hug before they both piled into the wagon.

"Well, big guy, what were you doing in Chicago?" Al said.

"That's a long story, Dad. We better save it until we've tossed back a couple Dortmunders. I'd rather hear about what you have been doing."

"Oh, I keep busy. I finally got this old wagon dinged up after the winter...running good now...after, let's see..." he looked down at the odometer..."ninety-six thousand, four hundred and fifty-two miles. Should make it to 150 easy."

"Have you had any more consulting jobs?" Buck knew that Al had enough money to live on with a small pension, severance pay and Social Security to come. He had taken the early retirement offered to him so that he could be home to take care of Helen. Her heart gave out only ten months later.

"With all the construction going on, I could work full time on residential—but that's for young guys. They are giving me quite a few commercial and industrial jobs—mostly laying out electrical systems. It's really been pretty good. Haven't even had time to plan a trip to your north country."

"Dad, we've got to do that—get out in the canoe country. It's beautiful—no change from when you and I took our trips fifteen years ago."

* * *

The issue of lodges on the portages arose as Buck and Al sat down at the table in the old world Hanzhaus.

"I just cannot believe that anyone would seriously consider it," Al said. "Of course, I have never been able to justify the expanded use of motorboats on BWCA lakes either," Al said.

"Dad, I don't want the portage subject to screw up our evening, but I will explain my involvement. First a mug of Dortmunder Union beer and a menu." When the waiter came, Buck ordered the smoked pork chops and red cabbage. Al said, "Make that two."

"I heard about this thing on Monday," Buck explained. "Tuesday I put the canoe in at Spit Lake landing and took the route to the portage between Heron and West Heron. That's what seemed to me to be a likely spot. Later it turned out to be right."

"How did it look?"

"Great spot for camping—high on a bluff. Of course it would be good for a cabin or lodge also. It would be difficult handling the utilities. Could be done, though. But I'll be damned if I'll let them do it."

"What are you up against with this Chicago company? What was the name again? It sounded familiar."

"Alactra International."

"I have heard of them," Al said, furrowing his forehead in thought. "We did some work for them a couple years ago. They didn't want a Chicago company to know what they were doing. I wasn't involved but heard about it. Wired-in some very special lighting in their penthouse and unusual installations of microphones and cameras."

"In the ductwork?" Buck asked.

"Could be. I think so. How did you know?"

"I got the tour."

"I think they have a reputation for some shady deals. Legal, but questionable," Al said.

"I can believe it."

"You sure you want to get involved with them?"

"Oh, I'll just see what happens," Buck said. "They made me a couple offers that I was able to refuse. I'll see what the county group has to say tomorrow night. If we have any kind of agreement, we should be able to talk to our representatives and get some political support."

"You know, one of our Wisconsin Senators is a BWCA fan. I read where he goes up there as often as he can. He has also been active in protecting those areas near Superior, where we used to hunt. His name is Arthur Wood. He's usually quite accessible—lives here in Milwaukee. He might be of some help."

"Sounds good," Buck said. "I'd like to get him to a county meeting."

"I think Tom Lacey would help. You know Tom—the owner and my boss at work. Well, he used to be my boss. Now, nobody's my boss," Al smiled. "Anyway, he knows the Senator well from political activities. I can ask him to make a connection so you can call the Senator."

"Great, Dad. Now that we have all the world's problems settled, we can get down to some serious eating. Here comes the food."

* * *

"LeYan, this is Benny," he said from the Bergen House lobby pay phone. "Nurse Ryker is rubbing kneesies with the doctor at a fancy place called the Bergen House. They've been here for a couple hours—since about seven."

LeYan spoke from her apartment phone, "OK, let's think...the main thing I want you to do is nail that bastard Buck Ryker. He will be getting into the Duluth airport sometime tomorrow morning. Find him there and rattle his cage good. I want him to know that he had better get back to his tree house and stay there. It is too late to do anything about his wife...maybe later. Get back to Duluth. Check the flights from Milwaukee and watch for him in the morning."

"Will do," Benny said. "I'll check in with you in the morning, after we do him."

"Oh, one thing occurs to me," she said. "Since you are right there, you might as well do your tire trick on their car. Do it and get out of there!"

"They'll play hell getting four Jag tires around here," Benny said, after telling Luther the plan.

* * *

"You have to tell me how you and Casey are doing," Al said, as they were finishing their meal. Buck did not sound very convincing—even to himself—as he told Al how great everything was between them. Al could see something in Buck's eyes.

"You wouldn't be smoothing it over for me, would you?" Al asked. Buck realized that he had been smoothing it over for himself. They cautiously explored the troubles in paradise until they got back to the *colonial* in Blue Mound.

"It's not quite eleven. I think I'll give Casey a call," Buck said. The phone rang four times, until the message came on. The disappointment drained him momentarily. He tried the number again with the same result. Nothing he could do—no use re-dialing over and over again like an idiot, he thought. Al, getting a glass of water in the kitchen, realized what had happened and how Buck felt.

"Give it a rest, Buck. You two are still in love. Give her a chance to show it."

13

Where in the hell was Casey, filled his mind. He knew that Al could tell that all was not right at home. Bad enough that *he* was worried, without burdening his dad. Buck passed on the early flight to the Twin Cities. No point in rustling Dad out that early. He caught the 8:30 and settled down to coffee and rolls, in first class. *Unlikely that Alactra would be treating him this well again.*

He remembered Al's words when they discussed their early days together in the boundary waters: he said he could not believe that motorboats would ever be allowed in the BWCA lakes. Buck thought back to the mediation meetings that were held in 1997 to seek a compromise between environmentalists, who stood fast for no motors, and the local groups. The citizens who lived and worked adjacent to the restricted areas wanted to be able to move more freely through the chain of lakes, including the use of Jeeps or trucks to assist transport on portages. Mediation accomplished nothing. Finally, a compromise bill was passed into law. The issue cooled, but he knew that the controversy would continue.

Buck was pleased about the possibility of involving the Wisconsin Senator. He could be an interested voice of support in Washington. Buck was certain that Al would get the necessary information to contact Senator Wood ASAP. He could possibly be reached before the county meeting tonight!

The plane barely got to full altitude before it began its descent into the Twin Cities. After landing, he grabbed his carryon and walked nearly a mile to the gate for Mesaba, Northwest's Air Link to Duluth. Since he had about an hour wait, he dialed home. *Of course she was supposed to be at the clinic. Why even try? Would have been better to call the clinic.* But he had made it a practice to never try to call her there, or even drop in. As he expected, he got their machine message.

* * *

The Mesaba flight left on time and in about forty minutes, Lake Superior spread out on the right. The familiar landscape was a welcome sight. He was anxious to get behind the wheel of the Silverado and head north—it would be calm reality compared with the Chicago rat race.

Halfway out into the parking lot, the hair on the back of his neck bristled. Everything was too quiet—especially for this midday hour—like a jungle under siege, when even the birds shut down, waiting, waiting. *You're crazy*, he thought, *this is Duluth, what can happen?*

As he walked to his truck, his peripheral caught movement in the next lane over. A guy in a black hat was getting out of a brown Taurus.

The guy immediately crouched down behind another car. A second black hat exited from the Taurus and Buck made a decision. *I'm not going to let some goons shoot up my truck.* He made a beeline back to the terminal and ran over to the Security Desk.

"Help, help! Some goons are breaking into my truck!" he shouted. "Right now! I need help out there, right now!" He figured the out-of-control, frantic action would get the most attention. He was right.

The two uniformed Security Guards dropped their sandwiches and wheeled around from back of the counter to follow Buck. A Duluth Police squad car, parked in front of the terminal, screeched a U-ee and followed them as they ran toward the Silverado.

"Holy shit!" Benny screamed at Luther. "Get your ass in the car. He's got the whole cop club coming." The Cousins were in the Taurus in a second, but Benny restrained himself and exited the parking lot at normal speed. "That guy is a lost cause," Benny growled. "He's always one jump ahead of us. What are we going to tell LeYan?"

"We? *Bullshit, We! You're* the one who's screwing up," Luther shouted and looked out to the rear. They're not following us. Get us the hell out of here!"

Benny got out to the Air National Guard Field, turned toward the North Shore and said with strangely calm determination, "We're going to get that son-of-a-bitch yet. We know that he'll be heading up north through Fall River and then out on some local road. We'll wait and catch him out in the sticks. Luther, how much dynamite we got left?"

* * *

They're after me, all right!" Buck said aloud. He left the airport with a relief similar to escaping the enemy by submerging in the swamp. *When will the 'gators get here?*

Anxiety faded as he entered the freeway to Two Harbors. Now the surroundings were familiar to him, the day clear and warm. He had completed his mission. He would report tonight to the county meeting and it would be over. He could get back to work—and Casey. He would get as far as the clinic in about an hour. He wondered if he should stop. The one time he ever showed up there was to deliver some Valentine flowers. Betty and the other two staff ladies had clustered around. He would never do *that* again. But now he had to find out how she was, *where* she was and *why* she wasn't home last night.

He didn't need Springsteen today. The sight of black, rocky cliffs and mammoth shoreline boulders, buffeted by the frothing surf, filled his senses. He passed the entrance to a popular northern ski area and thought of the time he and Casey had enjoyed a short visit there, when their log yard was snowed in. The slopes were no Rockies runs, like Casey had been used to, but fun. That was three years ago, when they last had taken out time for winter *fun*. In recent years, it had been winter *work*. At least he should take Casey to a leisurely dinner at Bergen House.

Eight more miles to Cascade Clinic. *Would she be there?*

* * *

"Hot damn! There's his big truck now!" Benny exclaimed. "I knew he'd stop here to check in with the broad."

"What are you going to do about it?" Luther asked. "It's total daylight. You can't shoot him up here."

"'Course not! We'll wait until he leaves, follow him 'til he gets off the highway, into the boondocks."

"Then what?"

"There's prackly no traffic on those back roads," Benny explained. "We'll catch up to him and give him something to remember us by—so he won't throw any more monkey wrenches into LeYan's plans."

* * *

Buck stepped into the Cascade Clinic as wary as if the entry were booby-trapped. Betty was at the front desk, as usual. She looked up and broke into an open-mouth grin.

"Buck, good to see ya!"

"Hi, Betty. Casey around?" He was surprised at his casual tone of voice.

"I believe she is in the lounge. Late lunch, you know. I'll tell her you're here."

"No problem, Betty. I'll just go in." Betty's instinct brought about a frown as Buck pushed through the swinging door. The scene was incongruity itself: Casey, her brother John and Dr. Jonas Thacher having a large laugh. They greeted Buck's appearance as if the Pope had walked in—naked.

Casey, recovering first, said, "Buck, what are you doing here?"

"Casey what are *you* doing here?" Buck replied.

"I'm working today," her answer was as bloody obvious as his question was dumb.

"Nice job," Buck said, eyeing the scene.

"You know John, and this is Dr. Jonas Thacher," Casey said.

"I've heard of you, Doc. Hello, Jack."

"Good to meet you, Buck." Doc stood to greet him eye-to-eye. They shook hands, sort of.

Buck looked at Casey as if there were no one else in the room, "Since I couldn't reach you by phone last night or this morning, just thought I would chance it here since I was driving right by."

"Well, you were gone today and they need help here," Casey said.

"There was an unusual workload this morning..." Doc began.

"I can see how busy you are," Buck cut in. The two other nurses on staff had been talking with two girls who were obviously their visiting daughters. Sensing the workload controversy, they got up abruptly and retreated to the front lobby.

"You know, Doc," Buck said firmly, "it would be fine with me if would honor us with your absence. Casey and I have to talk." Doc looked at Casey and John, who now looked a little pale and strained. Exit Doc.

"There's no need for you to get pushy," Casey said with a flush building in her face.

"What are you doing here, Jack?" Buck asked, ignoring Casey's comment.

"The doctor and I were just talking. He's got a job for me, he thinks."

"How did that come about?" Buck asked.

"I knew Casey worked here so I called Doctor Thacher and talked to him about a position.

"Casey, I think we need to talk. I'm heading home. Will you come?" Buck said.

"This is my job. I have a responsibility. I'll be home at my usual time."

"I'm afraid I don't know what your *usual* time is. Apparently last night's *usual* time was plenty late; or were you so busy that you had to sleep here at the clinic?" He turned toward the door and said, "I've got the county meeting tonight—maybe I'll see you later."

Betty did not try to conceal a grim look on her face, as Buck got through the door. There was still some gravel left in the clinic driveway after Buck roared out, but it was widely rearranged.

"You stupid ass!" Buck said aloud, and then thought, *Ya got emotional and said just the opposite of what you wanted to say!* He knew that it was the complete surprise of seeing brother John and the doc schmoozing around with Casey that pulled his ripcord. "Sonofabitch!!!" he hollered.

* * *

While Benny and Luther were lying in wait, Claude Tremayne answered the phone in his office in Grand Portage, near the Canada border. He had asked for only one thing when he became a designated counselor for the Chippewa reservation. He wanted to always have the "great lake" in his view.

"Tremayne here. You say what? Sinking pipes? Like a sand point pipe for a well? Where? That's crazy! They have got to be trouble—no right to be there. Watch 'em close. Good work, Brightcloud. Talk to you later." He walked to his full-wall map and inserted a pin marker on the south shore of Marsh Lake. He then placed a telephone call to Charlie Henstead.

* * *

Charlie Henstead jumped when the Information Center telephone rang. He and Lillian did not get many calls during their hours in the Center. He was afraid it might be LeYan, and he was not ready to talk to her yet. "Charlie here," he answered. "Oh, hello, Claude, how are you?" "It's Claude Tremayne," Charlie whispered to Lillian, with his hand over the black speaker cup on the old-fashioned phone.

"What do you think they are doing out there?" Charlie

asked Claude, his eyes opening wider. Lillian watched him with concern.

"Well, OK. I'll see you there in about an hour." Charlie hung up and turned to his wife, "Claude's boys have seen some unusual activity out by Marsh Lake. He wants to talk to George and me before tonight's county meeting. He said three o'clock at the Sawbill."

"Are you sure that you need to get involved in this, Charlie?" Lillian asked.

"Lil, there is no problem. It's just talk. I'll leave about a quarter to three and will be back by four-thirty. You should be able to handle all the customers." Charlie smiled grimly at the irony. There had not been a visitor in the Center all day. But he was concerned about Claude's warning: another serious threat to everyone in the boundary waters region.

14

The Derrick Club in Fort Worth was not exactly Dallas' Oilman's Club, but it *did* have character. Walnut trim, red leather booths and dimmed lights gave the place an "anything-can-happen" look. Red and black figured carpeting muffled the clodding of patrons' *cowboy* boots. In view of the transitory nature of the predominantly oil industry customers, Derrick did not have yearly club dues. "Members" were registered but did have to pay the twenty-dollar cover charge to enter. That policy and the exorbitant prices for food and drink restricted off-the-street drop-in trade. Guests were charged the cover also.

Jim Bob Akkre, a long-time member, was on his second scotch when he saw Ramon Rebelde enter. He slid out of the large red booth, stood and stuck his hand out to the swarthy oilman.

"You look like you just got off the rig," Akkre said. "What are you drinking?"

"You guessed right, buddy. We've got a boomer just north of here. Had to whip the crew into shape. I'll take a Heineken. Don't suppose they've got Leinenkugel here. I got kind of used to that up north."

"Never heard of it. How'd you make out that night I called you in Fall River? You sounded a little loose in the joints."

"Oh, the boys had a good time entertaining the barmaid with Cajun jokes. Each one thought he had it made with her. At one o'clock, she closed the bar and they found out she was the manager's wife. Like, they were nowhere, man."

"How 'bout you?"

"Just terrific! The little lady I mentioned was eyeing

me took me home with her, to meet her sister it turned out. The sister was in a wheelchair and didn't get out much. The little lady just wanted her sister to meet someone from Texas. We had tea."

"I hope your luck is better at finding oil or copper or nickel or something," Akkre said.

"Gotta be! Actually we scored some damn good traces. I left the boys out there to keep testing. I'll go back Tuesday. Then that should be it."

"Tuesday is late! I need proof Monday."

"Don't get excited. I've got photos here that are plenty good enough to sell anybody. The Tuesday stuff will just be frosting on the cake."

"OK, let's have another bump and go over to my office in Dallas. I want to get this story down to the fine hairs."

"I thought we were going to eat. I could use a good Texas steak."

"You couldn't afford to eat here," Akkre said. "There's a good rib place near my office. We can pick some up and eat while we go over your stuff."

"No one ever accused you of being a big spender," Rebelde mumbled.

"I'll be a big spender when you find something we can tell the boys of Colombia about," Akkre said. "In the meantime I've got to convince a smart-ass girlie and two or three Congressmen that what you have here is the greatest thing since soft money. I've got to jump back on the plane to D.C. yet this afternoon late."

* * *

Buck's anger at Thacher, at Casey's brother and at himself poured straight through to the accelerator. In ten minutes from the clinic he was at the outskirts of Fall River. He geared down from overdrive to drive to second to slow from seventy to thirty-five. A brown vehicle that he had been watching in his rear view, not seeing a brake light flash, made up the block interval in seconds. He saw the car swerve wildly as it braked hard on some loose sand near the edge of the asphalt. He couldn't be certain, but it looked familiar. The pursuer pulled over to the curb and slowed to a near stop.

The town was bustling. The public parking lot fronting on the harbor was filled. Two pickups, towing RV's, were stretched along the curb across from the angled single vehicle slots. Kids were standing on the top of the two-foot-wide rock-faced breakwater edge—scaring their parents. Sailboats were bobbing just outside the calm water of the inner harbor. Gulls were going crazy with the tourist-aided feeding frenzy. The functioning lighthouse, on a spit of land pointing out to the vastness of Lake Superior, completed the North Shore scene. If Grandma Moses had done harbor scenes, she could have depicted this active serenity. It would have been the equal of her New England village skating vistas.

One of the few positive thoughts that broke through Buck's fast and angry drive from the clinic was his dad's comment about Senator Wood. He was sure that Al would have started his contacts this morning. Al had given him the Senator's Milwaukee office number from the phone book. He eyed his watch—*five to three, might as well give it a try.* He stopped in front of the Lumberman Hotel, near the end of the harbor drive. Its bar was one of his favorite but infrequent watering holes. The cozy lobby was a welcoming sight. He went to the pay phone and began the credit card process.

"This is the office of Senator Wood," the lady said pleasantly.

"This is Buck Ryker. I believe that Mr. Tom Lacey may have advised the Senator that I would be calling."

"Yes, Mr. Ryker, I have a note here to put you through," she said.

"This is Art Wood," a solid voice said. "How are you doing, Mr. Ryker? Are you back home already? Tom Lacey just got through to me after lunch."

"I have just arrived in Fall River and will be going

home from here," Buck answered. "I appreciate your taking time to talk."

"Buck, I am vitally interested in preserving the northland wilderness areas, whether it's Minnesota, Wisconsin, Michigan or wherever. As they say, 'When they are used up, we can't get any more.' What is the situation that you are concerned about?" Buck outlined the challenge and the action to date as concisely as possible.

"That's one hell of a wild idea," the Senator said. "But I suppose a case could be made for it, if all the right buttons were pushed. The problem might be the possibility of a regional issue like that being attached to a larger bill. It could ride through unless a big fuss were made. Are you prepared to make a big fuss, Buck?"

"Big as I have to," Buck answered, realizing that he was extending himself into an unknown area of commitment. "Citizens in our area are meeting tonight to discuss the issue. I have the feeling that some of them might be on the fence because of economic advantages that they think might result."

"You can't blame local citizens for being concerned about their own welfare. I run up against that all the time. It's real and valid," Wood said. "But, at the same time, we have to strive for the longer term big picture, don't we? There is not an easy solution."

"I am finding that out. It would certainly help if you could attend our meeting. We don't really want to officially involve our own members of Congress at this time."

"Well, of course I can't make it tonight, but maybe next week, if you have another gathering. Why don't you check back with me Monday or Tuesday?"

"Will do, Senator. Thanks again for your time and interest.

Score one for the home team, Buck thought.

Another fifteen miles on the state highway and Buck took a left near Nordland Bay Lodge and drove inland. In three hours, he would have to be back at Nordland Lodge for the county meeting, but he needed to check in with his crew. About a mile in from the highway, he stopped where he had a good view of the intersection.

After a few minutes, he saw it! The brown Taurus made the turn! *No question about it. He's following and it's not for the fun of it.*

He accelerated and knew that the Taurus had seen him!

Fifty-five—sixty—sixty-five and the Taurus kept pace!

He got it up to seventy. Taurus crept closer! It was obvious that it would soon be on his bumper.

Buck remembered a curve in the road about half a mile up. The instant he was out of a direct line of sight, he jammed on the brakes and screeched to a momentary standstill! He knew that the Taurus would be only a hundred yards back—maybe less.

As soon as the Taurus came into view in his rearview mirror, he accelerated slowly in reverse. The distance between the two vehicles rapidly diminished.

At first, Buck could see the driver whipping his steering wheel one way and the other, not knowing which way to turn. The Taurus was braking madly. The passenger seemed to be trying to light a red stick.

"Dynamite!" Buck said aloud.

The Taurus jockey continued to brake and turned into the left lane of the narrow road ... and then wildly careened back, as a car came from the other direction.

The separation was now zero! The passenger was bouncing around and could not light the stick.

The custom-wide, wrecker-type, heavy steel rear bumper on the Silverado mashed into the front of the Taurus, instantly halting its forward progress!

But the Silverado didn't stop. It ground in reverse, pushing the attenuated auto back until its rear wheels were off the right side of the road.

The truck's six wheels spun, then held traction and drove the wrecked Ford down into the watery ditch—and farther, until its rear was hung up on several broken-off poplar tree trunks.

"End of the line, boys," Buck smiled as he grabbed

forward gear and plowed back onto the tar road. All he could see in the car were two white bags filling the entire front seat.

All was quiet at the wreck, except for a steady hiss from the radiator and an indistinguishable steady clicking. Then the driver door creaked open slowly. After two minutes, Benny stuck one leg out—into a foot of water. He squeezed his hulk out from behind the air bag. Leaning against the door for a few minutes, he ignored the muddy water rising nearly to his knees. He waded around the front to the passenger side and struggled to open that door. Luther had his head back all the way against the headrest and was blinking his eyes erratically.

"You OK?" Benny asked.

"Yeah," Luther groaned. He punched the air bag with no effect and squirmed out into the swampy ditch.

"We better dump that dynamite and hide the gun back in the trees," Benny said. "We're gonna have to hitch a ride with someone back to the town."

"Yeah," Luther said. "You do that."

"You know something, Luther, I'm gonna kill that bastard!"

* * *

"Yeah, this guy in a big truck just creamed us head-on. Coulda killed us," Benny explained to a propane delivery truck driver who was heading out to the highway. "My friend here didn't do too bad but I got all cut up on the hands and arms. Already put some bandages on myself. Can you get us back to Fall River?"

"That's where I'm going," the driver said. "Do you want me to drop you off up at the county hospital?"

"Naw, just leave us at a motel. We'll get cleaned up and take it from there," Benny said. They drove in crowded silence. The truck cab was not designed for two ruffled turkeys and a heavy duty good 'ole boy.

"What are you going to do for a car?" Luther asked one of his better questions.

Benny's eyes opened like he had just had the idea himself. "Do you know any place we could rent a car for a day or so?" he asked the driver.

"There is an auto repair shop that sometimes has cars for rent, but they would be closed now for the weekend."

"That's the shits," Benny said with supreme discouragement.

"Well, I've got an old Dodge Dart that I could rent you for a couple days. It runs, is about all I can say for it. You could probably buy it for what you'd pay for regular car rental."

"What'll you take for it?" Benny slipped into his negotiator mode, a role he could not forego, regardless of the circumstances. "How about a couple hunnert—two big C-notes?" The driver's eyes brightened. Benny had met his match.

"Two-seventy-five and you got a deal," the driver said. "I'll throw in a couple extra spares."

"OK, man. Take us to the car first. We'll get to the motel from there," Benny concluded.

* * *

The driver was right. The Dodge ran and that was about all. Luther was very uncomfortable. "I wish we'd get away from this lousy town and all this crap."

"Nothing wrong with the town, Luther. It's this *Buck Rogers* that's the problem—the one I'm gonna waste. Now look out for a motel." They drove toward the water from the highway and saw the sign for the Lumberman Hotel.

"How about that hotel," Luther said.

"We don't want no hotel—just a plain motel where we can slip in and out. There's one. The Lakeside. Good enough!" Benny pulled up to the door marked "Office" and left the motor running. He rolled his window down, reached the outside handle and opened his creaking door. "Amazing that our boy kept this wreck this long," he growled.

"Better let me get the room, Benny," Luther said. "You look like death heated up." Benny saw the sense in that and soon Luther came out with the key to room 102. After some clean up, they hit the Lumberman Bar like waves breaking on the rocks.

"We're back in business, cousin," Benny said, raising his shot glass. "Can't have many of these, though. We've got work to do tonight, as soon as it gets dark."

15

If those goons are still alive, they're not going to give up, Buck thought. He now realized that they were the ones who had tried to get him at the motel and then the airport parking lot. And now, more dynamite! Apparently that is their chosen weapon. They could do some serious damage in the yard, or to the house. *Better talk to the crew about posting a guard for the next few nights.*

The radio in the tool shack was loud, even as he first turned off RR37 into his driveway. *Couldn't even hear the dynamite above that noise*, he smiled. He reached into the shack and stopped the decibels. The immediate silence got attention. Four sets of eyes jerked toward him as he approached the building area.

"Hi, Buck, how was Chicago? See any sights?" one of the crew asked.

"No sights. Just some tall buildings. Stayed with my dad in Milwaukee last night. How's the schedule? Are we going to get it finished by Tuesday night? I have to get some money so I can pay you guys."

"We'll get it done all right," was the enthusiastic answer.

"Would anyone like some overtime?" Buck asked.

"You mean this weekend?"

"Well, here's the deal," Buck explained. "There are a couple guys in the area that I am suspicious of. You might call them spies. I heard that they are interested in checking out our building system—maybe damaging it. I'll probably talk to them in a couple days, but in the meantime, I don't want them nosing around. I'll be here most of the time, but I may have to be gone some. I don't want Casey here alone. I'd like to be able to call a couple of you to kind of baby-sit the place for a few hours. OK, thanks, Joe. I'll leave a message for you if I can't reach anyone. Now it's four o'clock; why don't you all take off for the day. Give my regards to the Sawbill."

Buck stowed all the tools in the shack and turned on all the security systems. He drove to the house, entered the front door and walked directly to the office area. He would have to leave for the county meeting soon, but could at least try to make one positive move: he called his customer in Spirit Lake, Iowa. After three rings, his quarry actually answered the telephone. With a mild apology, the man said that the check for $30,000 was in the mail—sent yesterday. Buck smiled to think how that news would please Casey. Then a frown. He had made an ass of himself at the clinic. They would no doubt have it out all over again when he came home tonight after the county meeting. He wondered if he should leave a note now. *Maybe just about the check.* He wrote: "Called Johnson in Spirit Lake. He said he put $30,000 in the mail yesterday. We'll hope—Buck." He stuck the note to the back screen door.

"We'll hope, all right," he talked to himself again—and remembered that old song: *Talkin' to Myself About You.*

* * *

This will be the test, he thought. Buck had decided to pick up George and give him a lift to the Nordland Bay Lodge for the county meeting. It would be a chance to give his thoughts a trial run with his buddy. Maybe they wouldn't be buddies by the time they got to the meeting.

The stenciled sign for Heudak Hauling was barely visible. It was a small white marker, alongside the tire tracks that entered through a nearly solid evergreen wall. Weeds grew down to the well-worn tracks, but the upper tree branches showed the effects of wide loads whapping their way through in both directions.

His cabin was two hundred yards back in the trees.

The two-acre clearing was a scene of organized mess. No trash piles, but many varieties of logs and sliced-off slabs were stacked randomly. A small mountain of cut and split firewood waited to be piled in rows for drying. The smell of cut pine and cedar, mixed with the forest freshness was a wonder of nature. The twenty-four-foot-square cabin had a new-looking green asphalt shingle roof, with a cement block chimney sticking up in the center of the back. George had owned the place for six years. Two years before, during a slow-down in hauling, he re-sided the outside with four-by-eight sheets of rough cedar plywood. The lower half of the unpainted sheets was streaked by rain and sun, where it was not protected by the roof overhang. In a fit of civilized living, he had a well and inside plumbing installed. It didn't mean much to him, but his occasional sleep-over friends appreciated it. The inside featured a concrete block fireplace alongside a pot belly wood stove. A small outside propane tank fired a gas cooking stove. An ancient Westinghouse refrigerator cooled the Miller and a few other essentials.

George sat in an old wood rocker on the front stoop, but got up when Buck pulled in.

"Great breathing out here today. Shouldn't leave," he said with great sincerity. He got in Buck's truck.

"Yeah, it's a pain in the ass to leave what you want to do to chase someone else's wild idea," Buck said as he drove through the trees out to the country road.

"What part do you think is a wild idea—what they're doing or your trying to stop 'em?" George asked.

"That depends. This afternoon it looked like a wild idea to try to stop 'em."

"What's that mean?"

"In a mile or so, I'll show you. When I landed at noon, I saw a couple guys sneaking toward the truck. We scared them away, but they followed me to Fall River and then out here. After I rounded a curve, I did a panic stop and backed up as they came up on me—rammed the goons' car into the ditch. That's it, up there on the left." Buck slowed as he passed the wreck and said, "They'll be out of commission for a while."

"Why you little devil. I didn't think you had it in you anymore. Any damage to your truck?"

"Oh, the bumper won't ever be the same, but nothing serious.

"How was Chicago?"

"They're determined all right," Buck said. Got propositioned three ways from Sunday. The EVP of this company is a sultry siren you would die for."

"No way, buddy, no way." George had no feeling for city girls.

"Anyway, they offered me a big job, managing the log project on the building sites. Might be eight or ten."

George looked straight ahead. "Maybe you should have taken it."

Buck gave him a look like his buddy had just reverted to SEAL language and called him a "Puke". He gave no answer.

"What does all this intelligence tell you to do now?" George asked.

"I'm going to tell the members what I know and what I think. Then there will have to be some kind of decision. I'm expecting that *some* people will have opinions."

"Cool the snide, Buster," George's eyes narrowed. "I've got opinions about a lot of things that I don't always haul out in front of everybody. I can see both sides. I don't want to see the wilderness chopped up, but a little development might be good for the people around here."

This was about what Buck expected from George, but he wondered how he would really vote in a showdown, and said, "Remember in 1997, when everyone was up in arms about allowing motors on more boundary lakes, and putting trucks on portages to haul the boats and people. As I recall, you were dead set against any change in the law to let that happen."

George looked out his window. "They got a compromise. A couple more lakes were motorized, a couple more portages with trucks."

"That's just it, George. If those compromises keep up, the BWCA will be nibbled to death. And this crazy portage development would be worse. After ten years or so, the area would look like Disneyland."

George turned to Buck. "In the last two years, I have talked to a lot more people who make their lives here and need to see development to survive. The loggers I haul for need more area to log. If they can't get into some of the restricted areas, they'll be out of business."

"If they get in there and cut," Buck said, "then that source will be gone. They'll have to move anyway. And the wilderness areas will be screwed up for a hundred years."

Buck turned left at the highway and drove two miles to Nordland Bay Lodge. The parking lot was nearly filled on the June Friday evening. Instead of the Sawbill group, there were expensive SUV's, sports cars, a few big shiny pickups and even a limo.

As they got out of the truck, George said, as if he were confessing a secret, "Oh, now there is a new wrinkle. I met Charlie and Claude this afternoon and they told me. We're early. Let's hit the bar. I'll tell you about it."

Buck always enjoyed entering the Nordland Bay Lodge. An institution on the North Shore, it drew locals and tourists all the way from Duluth, as well as down from Thunder Bay. In addition to the Lodge, which offered hotel rooms, restaurant, bar, and meeting rooms, a dozen twin-unit cabins were spaced out along the craggy shoreline. Today, he barely noticed the lobby's massive fieldstone fireplace, pine paneling, and shellacked foot-thick pine log corner posts. They entered the bar and each grabbed a red-leather-topped heavy pine stool.

"Tell me," Buck said.

George reported the news that Claude Tremayne's boys had told him: that it appeared like a crew was taking samples near Marsh Lake. George thought that the portage talk was just a feint to keep attention away from the prospecting. Buck wondered if Alactra was in on both deals. Then Charlie walked up.

"Hello, Buck. How was your trip?"

"I'll tell you all about it in the meeting. Isn't it about time?" The three men left the bar and descended the broad stairway with highly polished peeled pine handrails and huge half-round logs as steps. They entered the large meeting room. Six eight-foot tables had been placed together to form one unit, which was now covered with heavy red felt cloths. There were twenty-two chairs, of which a dozen were already occupied. Four more men followed Buck, George and Charlie. All eyes looked toward the door when Claude Tremayne entered, accompanied by two young men. Claude always came to the meetings in a good-looking sport coat outfit with a string tie at his shirt collar. He was not about flash. He wanted to look business-like, he had said when complimented. His two companions wore short-sleeve shirts, neat Docker slacks, and small turquoise rings holding their black, combed-back hair. They looked shy but had a resolve to their expressions.

Charlie wasted no time getting to business. He was always nervous about presiding at these meetings, but summoned courage by staying with facts rather than giving opinions. "Let's get going, boys," he said with the knowledge that he was senior in the group. "I expect a couple more, but they will catch up. Many of you have a clue about the reason for this special meeting. I will just review the facts to date and anyone can ask for clarification." He outlined the conversations, phone calls and activities that had taken place during the week. No mention was made, however, of a LeYan Syn.

"Now for information that I do not even have yet, I will ask Buck Ryker to tell us about his canoe trip out to High Portage on Tuesday *and* his trip to Chicago yesterday, at the invitation of the Alactra company that I just referred to. And I must offer our appreciation to Buck for spending the past four days gathering information for our consideration."

Buck stood and acknowledged some short but solid applause, with one palm held up modestly but ironically, in the classic American Indian "How" position. He related the motel attack and the session at Alactra. The two Alactra offers made but refused were withheld. He passed on the airport scene and made no mention of the wreck on the country road that only he and George knew about. His story was complete enough to forestall continuing questions, but two hands were raised. He acknowledged Mac Smalle.

"Buck, who do you think tried to get you at the motel?"

"I can't say exactly," Buck answered, "but they followed me again today. They must be trying to tell me something. I have reason to believe that they may be gone now." He nodded at Jake Sharker.

"Do you think that this lodge project on portages would benefit our area economically?" Jake asked.

The big question, well put, Buck thought, then said, "If I would answer like a politician, I'd say that it depends on what you mean by 'benefit'." A few members laughed along with Buck's smile. "But to give you a better answer, which of course is just my opinion, I would say that there would certainly be short-term benefits. From what I have seen of the buildings planned, they would use about as much lumber and concrete work as this building here for each of their lodges. They might buy that locally, but at low, contract prices. They would likely tell the supplier what they would pay rather than asking. My guess is that most of the other building materials and furnishings would be trucked in from Chicago, Milwaukee or Twin Cities. They would hire some local construction labor on a project basis. Then the short-term benefit would be over. The only continuing benefit I can see would be the local service help they would need—probably as many as fifty women and men for maintenance and serving positions."

"We've hardly got enough of those around here right now, during the tourist season," interjected Tim Licter, owner of a sizable lake resort.

"As far as rub-off business from the additional tourist traffic, that might be balanced by the loss of lodging that would normally go to our traditional hotel-motel and resort businesses. I am sure you can see that I am not trying to paint a bright picture, but it isn't what I think that counts. My advice is that we all consider the pros and cons for a week and get back together next Friday. I have spoken to Senator Art Wood from Wisconsin. He is of course knowledgeable about how Congress works and would be willing to attend our session next Friday. Charlie may want to ask for a vote on whether he should come. Also, Charlie has another separate issue to bring up." Buck sat and Charlie rose.

"We can talk more about Buck's information later, but first I would like you to hear what Claude Tremayne has to say."

Claude did not rise. He sat near the center of one side of the table with a young man on each side. He looked the part of the reservation leader that he had become through the years. His full head of black hair was trimmed but long enough to reach his back collar. Silver streaks at the sides and one bold swipe on top looked like it could have been accomplished by a painter of primitive portraits.

"These young men were fishing in Marsh Lake Wednesday. They saw four men in two canoes go ashore about three miles west of the portage on the lake. The men carried lengths of pipe and other equipment. Brightcloud and Strongbird here went ashore a distance away and approached carefully, after the men had made camp. You tell them, Brightcloud."

"They walked about a thousand yards into the woods and began sinking pipes. They all kept looking around as if they were afraid. Strongbird and I thought they might have seen us, so we went back to our canoe and came home."

The back door opened and one of the girls from the front desk tiptoed in to where Buck was sitting and handed him a note. The note stated: "Telephone call—urgent."

* * *

"Buck Ryker," he said at the front desk phone.
"This is *Casey Ryker*. I'm your wife! We just had a fire in the yard! I thought you might like to know."
"What…" Buck started to ask, but the line was dead.

* * *

Buck knew that what was going bad before, just got worse. He walked quickly back to the room and told Charlie he was leaving. He stopped by George and asked if he could find a ride home…that the goons had struck again. He had a twenty-minute drive to come to terms with himself. His overt reaction to the BWCA challenge now seemed almost foolish, but he knew that he would take the same action again. He hated the way he and Casey were on opposite sides of the issue. Now there was the DANGER TO HER. He hadn't really thought about that before. If she had been hurt, he would have turned himself into a *terminator*. Maybe he still would. He had come close to it in the afternoon—close enough to get himself in real trouble if the goons had any way to accuse him without incriminating themselves. He felt that all of his reasons would come up lame with Casey. But they were his reasons, his beliefs, his principles. *If I don't hang in there—if I don't tough it out—what am I?*

16

Friday night at the bar in the Lumberman Hotel may well have been the major hit-on and be-hit-on spot in Fall River. There were only about thirty tables and a dozen stools at the bar, but the crowd usually exceeded the accommodations. Benny and Luther enjoyed just squeezing through the SRO bodies, when a couple stools opened up at the bar. "Hey, I think fell in love a couple times just getting through all that perfume," Luther said.

"Maybe you did, but I don't see any of them following you," Benny remarked. After what was to them an exasperating wait of several minutes, Benny got through to the busy bar brunette, "Whataya got that's large?"

"We got anything you want. What do you want?" the brunette answered firmly. It was obvious that she could have taken Benny three out of three falls. The Cousins settled for double Jack Daniel's with Bud chasers. She slapped the two JD's down and grabbed two Buds before the boys could waste her time.

"Heavy stuff, that one," Luther observed.

"Luther, I think we've done it," Benny said, ignoring his cousin's comment. "That fire should send that local jerk a signal that he should just stay home."

"But that wasn't much of a fire. Funny that other guy should show up just as we were getting a good blaze going," Luther said.

"Yeah, maybe he was a neighbor, but there was no use pushing it when we could get away clean," Benny rationalized. "I'm going to call LeYan and tell her we got the job done. Let's have a round first."

Benny waved Ms. Barkeep over and was about to speak when she beat him to the words, "What'll you two beauties have this time? Same? Say, are you two undertakers or do you think you're the poor man's Blues Brothers? I'll give you this, you're the only weirdos that sit in this place with dark glasses on. You don't have to drink yourselves blind. You've got a head start."

"I think she likes us," Luther said with enthusiasm, after she left.

The Cousins were at first unaware of the arrival of four men who managed to force their way into a corner table. One of them might have been a six-foot-plus blond local but the other three transmission-oil-pony-tails jerked all but the blind to attention. They were loud but soon blended into the high-decibel crowd.

"You see those guys?" Luther finally said, with a head nod that was noticed by a dozen nearby patrons.

"Yeah, so what. I gotta call LeYan," Benny said as he slumped off the stool. His steadying hand, on the shoulder of the closest party lady, was at first rejected but then shrugged off. He wavered his way to the pay phone on the far side of the lobby. After much fumbling with his credit card and three misdials, the process actually resulted in a solid ring.

"Yes," LeYan answered.

"Hell-o-o, LeYan. This is your pal, Benny."

"Benny, are you drunk?"

"Oh, no-o-o. Luther and I are doing fine. We really nailed that Ryker guy. Set a fire in his big log yard."

"What about him?"

"Well, he wasn't around but some other hick showed up so we left. Nobody saw...us..."

"Benny, are you there?"

"Oh...we're...here, all right."

"Benny, now listen to me closely. I don't want to talk to you when you are like this. Do you think you can do one more thing—and do it right? OK, then call me tomorrow morning."

Luther, feeling in charge with Benny gone, had

pushed his way over to the four men at the corner table. He stood there, wavering.

"So what in hell are you guys doing here?" he said.

"Who in hell are you?" growled one of the crankcase-swarthies. He rose to nearly touch noses with Luther. Mr. Blond smoothie put out a hand to return swarthy to his chair.

Blond said, "My friend here rightly asks the question, 'Why should you want to know who we are?' Who are *you*, may we ask? You look like you just got off the boat ... from Chicago."

"Thas' right…Chicago…but we flew," Luther more or less said. Consciousness partially returned as he saw Benny approach. They grabbed two chairs from nearby tables and crowded in with the four.

"Where are you guys from?" Benny asked.

"I'm from Dallas. These men are from Baton Rouge," Blond said.

Loose Luther said, "Where's that?"

"Where's lousy Chicago, you idiot? Baton Rouge is the capital of Louisiana," asserted swarthy.

Benny was suddenly calming, "What do you do there?"

"We're oil experts. We know how to find the black stuff." Swarthy was feeling no pain.

Blond to the rescue, "He means he does that in Texas and out in the Gulf."

"What are you doing around here?" Luther was interested.

The blond was becoming irritated with the badgering. "You're pretty nosey. Why don't you tell us what you're doing? You look like you're dressed for a funeral."

"We're on a mission…to check out some tree-huggers…you know those nerds who are crazy for forests and lakes," Benny answered.

"We'll drink to that," Blond said—and they did. "This country up here could use some development. Look at this town. With its location—right on the big lake—no reason it couldn't be another New Orleans. Or at least a Gulfport or Biloxi—ten or twenty times what they've got here."

"You think they've got oil around here?" Benny asked.

"You never know. Now, what are you guys doing?" Luther and the swarthies had lost interest and were standing at the bar, being put down by the bar lady.

"We might just get some of that development going, if we can keep the tree-huggers off our back," Benny concluded.

"Who are these people you're after?"

"Oh, there's a character out north about twenty miles. Drives a big Silverado pickup. Thinks he owns the lakes and trees in the boundary canoe area."

"Boundary waters—yeah, we heard that you're supposed to get a permit to go in there," Blond said.

Swarthy, staggering back from the bar, added his foggy point of view, "We didn't need any permit...just went in. Nobody better not try to give us any shit about it either."

"We flew into one of those lakes right on the border a couple days ago. Didn't see you," Benny said.

The talkative swarthy was swelling with importance as Blond was looking nervous. "We were in Marsh Lake. Set up a camp. Thought we heard a plane. Other than that, didn't hear a thing except some bushes cracking. Saw a big moose but couldn't shoot it—too much noise."

Without the usual *last call*, the attractive brunette, who at this hour seemed to be the only sober person in the place, cleaned up the bar, raised the hinged counter section that had been keeping her captive and said, "Lights out in ten minutes folks. And I'm not foolin'!"

The oil men challenged gravity by pouring themselves up to rooms at the hotel. The blond observed, "They get some strange ones in here. Those two are throwbacks from Al Capone!"

"How long we stay in this crazy town?" one of the oil crew asked.

"Rebelde will get here Tuesday to look at the site. Then we all go back together, Wednesday early," Blond said.

"How many more times do we have to go out to the bayou?" another swarthy asked. He could have been wishing he were gliding silently in his musky version of these northern lakes—the fabled Louisiana bayous.

Blond guy, turned cheerleader and tour guide, answered, "Tomorrow we'll take you guys out on the big lake and catch you some trout that you wouldn't believe. Sunday, we'll rest up. No doubt you will want to attend Mass. We'll finish up our work on Monday and Tuesday. That should give us plenty time to punch some holes and fake some more samples from that impossible ground."

Benny and Luther stumbled their way out to their dandy Dodge Dart. "I've got to call LeYan in the morning," Benny said. "She'll be interested in what those oil guys were doing."

It had been a heavy day and a heavier night. Luther was already asleep.

* * *

The goons had not disabled the electrical system. The big lights were still flooding most of the yard. Buck could smell the acrid stink of some dead fire. He pulled ahead to the log home under construction. One corner was charred. It would have to be replaced. *Four hours time lost. Damn it!* This was all a result of his getting involved with the crazy idea that someone would disturb the wilderness. This fire and the previous harassment were supposed to scare him.

No way! Buck thought. *Now the next hurdle*, he thought. Laurel and Hardy came to mind: "A fine mess you've gotten into."

He parked the truck in front of the garage and walked to the back door of the house. He was surprised for a moment. The door was locked. Then common sense worked and he realized that Casey would certainly lock the door during all that had happened. He unlocked the door and walked in.

"It's me," he announced. There was no reply.

"Casey, do you hear me?"

"I hear you."

He walked into the living room, toward the office area. Casey sat in front of the computer with arms folded. "What the hell is going on?" she demanded.

"Well, a lot is going on, but first, are you OK?"

"I've been better," she said.

"Tell me what happened."

"Joe called me from the Sawbill. Said he was just having a brew and would be back. Apparently you had asked him to check the place. Believe me, I did not enjoy the feeling, but thought you would be home soon. By the time he got back, a fire had started. I called 911. It was about burned out by the time they got here."

"I know I should have called you. I got the word from the Iowa deal and then called George about picking him up. We had a pretty heated discussion on the way to the meeting. Then I thought you would be on the way from the clinic. We got there and I went right into the meeting."

"You seem to be having a lot of second thoughts lately. I'd like to know what your first thoughts are."

"OK, you're on," Buck said as he moved to the stove to brew a cup of coffee. "Want a cup?"

"I'll take a tea," Casey answered.

Even the thought of tea seemed to ease the pain. "First thought number one," he said. "I don't want you to be here alone at night any more. If I have to be gone, I want someone here with you."

"Oh, a babysitter. That's great. Also you are getting pretty heavy on the 'I want' statements."

Buck answered, "You know it's for you. I don't know who could be here. Maybe someone from the clinic. Maybe your doc friend could show up! I understand that he came by the other evening."

"Oh, good old George filled you in on that did he"

"Why not? It's a little different."

"Yes, it would have been if I had let him stay. If good buddy George had stuck around for another three minutes, he would have seen the doc leave. But so what, anyway. He was in the area, he just stopped in to thank me for helping Betty Monday night."

"Maybe that isn't *different*—maybe just unusual. But back to the point, I really hope you will agree to have someone here. Maybe Lillian. Charlie wouldn't mind."

"Assuming that you are serious, as much as I like Lillian, do you really see her as a protector?"

"It's something we can think about. I'm certain the goons won't be back tonight, but I'm going to stake 'em out anyway. I'll grab some chow and a sleeping bag. I'll be in the tool shack tonight."

"No big deal," Casey said. "I haven't seen much of you lately anyway. I'll be leaving early for the marathon. Whatever marathon you are on, I wish you luck."

17

Mozart awakened Casey at five o'clock. If it had been anyone else, she would have yanked out the radio cord. At the moment, the idea of driving two hours to watch a marathon seemed idiotic. She showered and squinted at the mirror. She looked OK, under the circumstances. First choice out of her closet was her running gear—running shorts and Grandma's T-shirt. *Too brief,* she thought. She had to consider the other girls who would be there from the clinic. It seemed that they liked their doughnuts more than she did. She put on the same Bermudas and loose top that she had worn last night for dinner with the doc. *No use getting him turned on.* It had been tough enough holding him off in the Bergen House parking lot, until he noticed that all four tires on his Jaguar had been slashed. She had called a cab to get back to her Subaru at the clinic. It seemed to take forever. She had thought of calling Buck at his father's house in Milwaukee, but didn't want to call from The Bergen. Then it seemed too late. She shook her head and realized that, *if I had made the call and talked to him last night, this day would have dawned a lot brighter.* Now explanations would be as limp as her spirits.

She left the house at five-twenty and drove by the tool shack with only a pause. *He might be sleeping,* she copped-out. She picked up a coffee in Fall River and opened the window to let fresh lake air keep her company for the ninety miles to Two Harbors. She remembered the experience of running Grandma's Marathon in 1997:

Eighteenth place among women, Casey recalled with a smile. *Not too bad!* She passed the entrance to Split Rock Lighthouse State Park. It was almost exactly two years since she and Buck had made the Marathon trip together. *I wish he were here right now and we could do the past two years over again!*

She eyed her watch. *Ten to seven—should make the twenty-five miles before Jonas starts the race.* Then it occurred to her: *Why the Jonas? What happened to the Dr. Thacher?* She turned KDAL-FM up loud to dump that thought.

Traffic at Two Harbors was backed up at the semaphore. The start of the race was at the south end of town. Every vehicle was headed there. Casey tensed at the delay and did bumper-to-bumper until she pulled off on a side street and got out. She jogged the last few blocks.

The race area resembled a state fair midway. Venders, police, spectators, media, race volunteers and officials were all focused on the thousands of runners who were all ganged up awaiting a starting gun.

She jumped when she felt a hand on her arm.

It was Betty Rhodes from the clinic.

"Hi, Casey," Betty said breathlessly. "Isn't this a mess? Where'd you park?"

"Hi. I'm back toward town, about six blocks. Any sign of the doc?"

"I saw him a few minutes ago, about in the middle of that gang of runners. He's got a red bandanna on his head—looks quite rakish—there he is—look where I'm pointing."

Casey saw the doc and had a sensation that surprised her. She turned back toward Betty and said, "This is such a mob, where do you think we should go to catch the runners going by?"

"I thought about that and asked my husband. He said a good place would be south on the freeway halfway to Ryan Road. Park there and walk across to the racecourse. I'm right close. I'll give you a ride to your car."

* * *

Buck didn't sleep much, laid out in the sleeping bag on the wood slab floor of the tool shack. Every wind or animal noise alerted his senses like an electric shock. Even the breeze that often made the pines sing, played an unnerving tune. But, he realized, *no more gooks or goons.* He heard Casey drive up, pause and continue out the driveway. He thought that it was just as well. Five-thirty is no time to meet and greet. He got up at six-thirty, hauled in his sleeping bag and did bacon and eggs for breakfast. One of his crew arrived early to help with the cleanup. The fire had been superficial. They could lightly sand the logs that had been singed. Couple hours work and they would be back to new. The real damage had been to the security of Ryker Homes and the relationship of the two owners. He knifed off some of the char and spent a few hours cleaning up the yard.

The tool shack phone rang loud enough to be heard for 500 feet.

"Ryker's."

"Hi, Buck."

"George, what's new?"

"You up for lunch today?"

"Guess so. I'm batching it."

"Pick you up in an hour or so—about 11:30."

"I'll be here."

George's double-axle flatbed roared to a stop at the tool shack. He hopped out to survey the fire damage. "Not too bad," he said.

"Not a problem—couple hours work. But what really pisses me is that they got to us," Buck let it all hang out. "Guess I'll have to fence and floodlight the place like the Navy base."

"Don't get paranoid. This may never happen again, but I agree: there are some folks that need watching. If we get any more hassles, I think we know how to handle 'em, don't we, buddy."

* * *

The twelve-mile spectator spot worked. Betty and Casey each parked out by the freeway on the side road and walked to the racecourse along Lake Superior. They pushed through the three-deep spectators and after ten minutes saw the doc. His bandanna was bobbing and he was grasping his water bottle. But he was in there fighting. He glanced over to his gallery of two waving nurses. His step perked up perceptibly.

"Where now, o leader?" Casey asked Betty.

"Might as well go to the finish at Grandma's Restaurant. We may still be able to wedge in. My guess is the other guys will have grabbed a table."

* * *

The crowds filled the area leading to Lake Avenue and the end of the racecourse. Casey found a parking place up the hill from the lakefront. She couldn't see where Betty parked, but pushed her way to the restaurant and soon saw the two techs and the intern. They had been perched at an outdoor table since the race began. Betty arrived from another direction

"Gen, Howard, Patsy—you guys are really race fans!" Betty said.

"Had to grab the table," Howard said. "When it comes to enforced drinking, we can handle it."

The leaders were projected to cross the finish line shortly after 9:30. The best time in this marathon's history was two hours, nine minutes plus, run by Dick Beardsley in 1981.

Betty ordered a Coke and Casey said, "Make it two." After ten minutes, the fans saw the leader plodding toward the finish line. The PA system blared:

"Patrick Muturi wins the 1999 Grandma's Marathon. Patrick Muturi from Kenya, with a time of two hours, fifteen minutes and forty-four seconds. Congratulations, Patrick."

Minutes later, Irena Bogacheva from Kyrgyzstan placed first for women, with a time of two hours, thirty-eight minutes and forty-four seconds.

"Where's Doc?" they all said.

* * *

Many runners and forty-five minutes later, Howard shouted, "There he is!" The red bandanna was askew, but he looked OK. He was not pressing—just trying to get through it. Howard got down to the finish line to "catch" him. The two made their way back to the table and the gallery of fans.

"Congratulations," they unisoned.

"Thanks, buddies. Thanks for coming," Doc Thacher exhaled and then collapsed into a chair. "How was it?" and other inane comments were tossed out to no response. The Doctor was plainly exhausted—for the moment. Casey excused herself to make a run at the very popular ladies restroom.

Noticing that she left, Thacher seemed to revive surprisingly fast. "Now that I have my breath, I repeat, I really appreciate your support. I'll save the champagne for Monday, after work."

They watched the "also-rans" and Casey returned. Howard and the two med techs left about 11:30. Betty and Casey basked in the sports euphoria for another half hour. Betty then eased out, professing the need to get her son to soccer practice.

"Well, here we are," Doc said.

"Yes, I'm here. And you are almost here—is that right"

"Oh, I'm in good shape…probably be able to do another…half mile…maybe." They laughed. He continued, "While you were out, I asked the group to join me for a little bubbly at my place. They all accepted. I hope you will also. It's on the way."

"I suppose it *is* on the way. I guess I could make a short stop," Casey said.

"It is just about three miles past the clinic. Turn in at the Harbor Point sign on the highway. Can't miss it. I'm going to leave now—get home and get the body relaxed. I may be in the sauna or shower when you get there. Just make yourself at home."

"What are you driving today?" Casey smiled as she remembered the doc's disabled pride-and-joy at the Bergen House parking lot, after the Thursday night dinner.

"I took the SUV. It will be a week before I can get tires for the Jag," he grimaced. "What kind of weirdos would slash all my tires?"

"Maybe a jealous husband," Casey offered.

"Haven't seen one of those in weeks," he said. "I arranged with a B-Ball buddy to get me back to my car at Two Harbors. I see him over there now, so I'll cut out. See you at the Thacher shack." The tall, blond runner whipped off his bandanna and walked to his buddy. The two of them slouched away with arms around each other's shoulders, feigning severe ambulatory difficulties.

Casey sat for a few minutes finishing her Coke and then relinquished her table as runners and observers continued to throng into the area. After acknowledging some fellow runners from two years previous, she hiked three blocks back to Superior Street. At that point, Duluth looked like a miniature San Francisco. With the waterfront, teeming with ocean-going and smaller craft, at her back, she began the climb to her trusty vehicle. A cable car would have been helpful on the substantial incline. She had read that early Duluth used a cable-drawn car to carry people from the main waterfront streets up to the skyline parks. The cable car served the citizens for sixty years until just before World War Two.

By the time she reached the Subaru, she felt like *she* had run the Marathon. Once in the car, she skirted the lower congested areas by following Skyline Boulevard and then angling down to the highway north. It would be after one o'clock by the time she reached Two Harbors—then another hour and a half to the clinic. *Should make Jonas's—Dr. Thacher's—place by three-thirty. Strange that none of the clinic crew mentioned stopping at Doc's—especially Betty.*

Hunger was setting in. *Better grab a sandwich in*

Silver Bay. The idea of calling home from Silver Bay occurred to her. It was not a happy thought. *Not a good way to start a mending process. Maybe give him a call when I leave the Thacher "shack."*

* * *

The Sawbill Bar & Grill was in a major thrust on this Saturday in June. George and Buck got the last open table at about 11:45. Couples and family groups mostly filled the tables. The bar-stool shift had changed from the weekday hard hats to the weekend fishermen returning from their dawn-to-eleven lake adventures.

George dominated the subject of lumber acreage. "If these cutters don't find more timber, I'm going to have to find other hauling jobs."

Buck reassured him, as they enjoyed their first Leinie, "George, the way houses are going up all over the area, the demand for lumber will stay strong. You'll just have to expand your contacts. You can't depend on finding all your customers at the Sawbill."

"So where is Casey today?" George finally got off the subject.

"She joined a group from the clinic to watch the marathon."

"Surprised she felt like it after all that ruckus last night. Do you think you are rid of whoever who is harassing you?" George said.

"Joe is working today to keep an eye on the place while I'm gone; but, I can't imagine that the goons will be back. They have done about everything they could to give me the message—short of taking me out."

"Buck, I've got to say that all this crap you've been getting is way beyond reason. Pushing their opportunity is one thing, but if they will do all this, who knows what they would do to the wilderness. Now this oil exploration maneuver—got to think it's connected to the lodge deal. After you left the meeting last night, Tremayne's boys told again what they saw. Can you believe it, not everyone in that group was totally against the development in the BWCA."

"I can believe it," Buck said. "Some of those guys haven't been out in the real restricted areas for years. But they would go if someone would pull their fishing boats out there and then back again in the evening. And they think the economy might benefit from this development."

"So they're like I was—live for today and forget the future," George said.

"I hope we can remind them that once the wilderness is gone, it's over. You don't get it back," Buck said. "What did they think about the Senator coming to our meeting?"

"Oh, a few are leery of any politician, but the vote Charlie took was definitely a 'yes'."

"I will call his office today and leave word for him to come Friday."

"How are you and Casey doing?" George tried to make it casual.

"It has been a little tough. I am hoping for the best today when she gets back. I might ask you for some help. I would like to make an over-night trip Monday, out to Marsh Lake, and take Casey along, if we're still speaking. Suppose you could get the yard crew started in the morning? Maybe stay at the house one night—to keep an eye on things?"

"No problem. What days?"

"Monday, if I can get the permit squared away in time and if Casey is willing and can take the day off."

"Charlie should be able to get you the permit all right. Even if he doesn't, you're going on official business," George said. "But that's out where those prospectors have been seen on the south shore."

"I know. I'll have to keep a look out. But we'll be on the north side. I am guessing that they will use that one Forest Service campsite on the south shore. We will be beyond that."

As they pushed their chairs back and walked out

together, George said, "I don't think they will have any welcoming committee out for you!"

* * *

Jim Bob Akkre sat in his fourth floor Washington, D.C. office at two on a beautiful but warm Saturday afternoon. He pondered an e-mail that he had just received from Ramon Rebelde, his Friday's lunch partner. The phone rang.

"Akkre here."

"Mr. Akkre, this is LeYan Syn from Alactra International."

"Hello, LeYan. How nice to hear from you."

"I am hearing that you have people digging around in the boundary waters area. That could get to be a substantial problem for our relationship! Just what is going on? What are they doing? They could undermine this whole project, if they are seen!"

"Chill, baby! In the first place, my project could make your tourist cabins look like peanuts by comparison. At the very least, it will add value to your proposition."

"I am not so certain that the Congressmen will be enthusiastic about mining or drilling out there in the wilderness," LeYan said.

"Not a big deal—a couple hundred pumps out where no one can see them anyway. My oil contact said that his people ran into two strange characters dressed in black who were talking about development on portages," Akkre said. "I don't want your hit men making waves for my exploration team."

"I do have two men in the Fall River area, but they should not be involved with your people at all. Besides, they will be out of there by Monday," LeYan said.

"Shouldn't be a problem then. My guys will be leaving Wednesday morning. The supervisor is going there on Tuesday to finish it."

LeYan said in a calmer voice, "I spoke to my man this morning. When he told me about meeting your people, I directed him to avoid any further contact. We must be careful of too much talk. We can't afford to rile the locals. I have a local informant who tells me that they had a meeting last night to discuss the Boundary Lodges. They will meet again next Friday. It seems there is no problem now, but there is one pain in the ass among them who could be trouble. I believe we have cooled his jets. I doubt if your people would run into him, but he does get out in the wild in his canoe."

"I'm sure my guys will know how to take care of him if he shows up," Akkre said.

* * *

Harbor Point was one of the premier locations on the North Shore. The developer had wiped out dozens of small houses built on many acres in the early nineteen hundreds. The Norwegian fishermen and their families who settled there had arrived in the roadless territory by boat. Only the seagulls and the rocky shoreline remained. The handout-wise gulls now swooped and pooped the decks of the spanking-new, gray-shingled luxury pads, stacked along the craggy coast.

Casey was expecting some kind of rustic cabin. Her expectations were blown away as she approached a modern structure that could have been inspired by Frank Lloyd Wright. She parked and walked slowly into a stone-paved, covered entrance leading to a four-foot wooden door, accented with wrought iron straps. She paused, gazing at the large pines that framed the building. *No other cars yet*, she thought. *They must have stopped for lunch.*

Surprisingly, smoke poured out of the huge stone chimney centered in the structure. She stepped inside and was greeted by a rugged, stonewalled entry. The fire crackled in the fieldstone fireplace that extended to at least a sixteen-foot ceiling. The expansive fireplace opening could easily handle four-foot logs. In this mild season, two glowing logs fought the central air conditioning for dominance. Heavy leather upholstery and cherry framing characterized the ten-foot sofa. It was centered on a deep plush modern figured rug that partially covered the polished, irregular slate floor. A few modern color-slashed paintings were positioned for dramatic effect, but during the day lost out to the broad Lake Superior view through the windows.

"Anybody home?" Casey hollered.

A voice from the nearby master suite answered, "Just got out of the shower. Be out in a minute."

Dr. Jonas Thacher M.D. stepped down the one step from the bedroom hallway to the great room level. He paused, near the fireplace, almost posing, in his cargo shorts and "Grandma's Marathon 1999" T-shirt.

"What can I get you?" he asked.

"Well, I'll wait for the others."

"They should be here by now," he said. "Maybe they got lost. Let's have a wine and make ourselves comfortable." He waved her over to the leather sofa in front of the fireplace.

"You know, Jonas, I can't stay long," she said as she sat tentatively.

"Ah, first name. That's a start."

"Doctor Thacher, let me ask you a question. Did you actually issue any other invitations to this little party? You know I will find out tomorrow or Monday."

"My how inquisitive she is. So what if you were the only one I invited? I think the others were all busy anyway. I told them that we would have a little bubbly Monday, after hours." His admission was accompanied by a demonstration of affection.

Casey brushed his hand off of her knee, stood, and walked to the panoramic window. The view of the waves rushing against the rocky shorelines vied with her mixed emotions. She could not believe her indecision. Her emotion became more severe when Thacher walked up behind her and placed his hands on her bare upper arms.

"Don't, Jonas," she said with a wavering voice.

"You know what that kind of 'don't' does to a man," he said softly, with a hoarseness that signaled his intent.

Before she could answer, she felt him turning her slowly toward him. She breathed deeply and tried to avoid his intense gaze and smile.

Lightening did not flash.

Thunder did not clap.

However, the pager did buzz.

"I can't believe it," Thacher said disgustedly, as he walked to the pager he had left on the fireplace mantle. "I'm on emergency call for the Fall River Hospital today and tomorrow. I made the dumb move to check in when I got home from the marathon.

"You're just a dedicated medical servant, that's all there is to it," Casey said, as the doc dialed the hospital. She moved steadily toward the door, waved, and said, "I have to head home now. Nice place you have here, Dr. Thacher."

She strode out of the door with a feeling of relief and freshness that matched the breeze wafting through the pines. After a look back to the Thacher "shack," she wound the old Subaru up through the trees to the highway.

* * *

The deserted clinic did not welcome her like the many mornings when she was the first to arrive and open the door. She went to her locker and desk drawer. Everything fit in the canvas Grandma's Marathon tote bag she had bought from a vendor on the way back to her car. Her watch showed four-twenty as the Ryker Homes number rang the third time. *One more time and I'll get the recorded message. Please, no.*

"Ryker Homes," Buck answered with a loud voice that was slightly out of breath.

"Buck, hello." Casey's voice held a softness that he barely recognized. It moved him with such a feeling that he had to swallow before answering.

Finally he said, "It's good to hear you. Where are you?"

"I stopped at the clinic to call you. I don't want to be here. Can you meet me someplace? Soon?"

"That's a big 10-4," Buck blurted out, realizing that it was one of the dumber things he had said recently. He hadn't used the old trucker's CB sign-off for years.

"Are you drunk?"

"No. I was just a little surprised by your call. Hell yes, I'll meet you. How about The Landing? If you drive very carefully and I crank it up to ninety, we should get there about the same time."

"I can hardly wait," she said.

"That's a big 10-4," he said, and they both laughed.

* * *

Saturday was a busy day at the Information Center. Charlie had all the tourists he could handle in the morning and through the noon hour. Lillian was feeling "a little down" so Charlie insisted she stay home. He had called an informal "coffee meeting" at the Center for three o'clock. Neither George nor Buck could make it, but Mac Smalle and Jake Sharker were due any minute. Charlie gave his present customers somewhat short shrift so that he would be available when the boys got there. The pine-paneled area where the round table sat was an appropriate spot. The large BWCA maps on the wall would put them right in the wilderness mood. The half dozen powdered sugar doughnuts Charlie brought from home would ensure a pleasant atmosphere. The two guests arrived and Charlie poured.

"Called George and Buck, but they couldn't make it," Charlie opened. "What did you think of the meeting last night?"

"Well, it was what we had to do—get all the facts and thoughts out on the table," Jake Sharker said.

"Unless you're real close to that wilderness feeling, you can see some value in the development," Mac said. "I see more traffic, more activity, more cars and more need for gas, oil and service at my station. I might have to expand my convenience section—get a couple refrigerator cases and a larger coffee machine."

"Is that really what we want?" Jake asked. "More traffic, junk on the roads, noise—won't be any different than a big city."

"But won't it be more business for you?" Mac asked.

"I suppose I might get some more business outfitting canoes and camping groups, but I am about booked up on trips now. I'd have to hire some guys to be guides. I don't know anyone I could trust to do the job right. All the young guys are tied up with jet skis and SUV's. They don't hardly know how to canoe anymore."

"You paint an ugly picture, Jake," Charlie said.

"Yeah, it was a bit of an exaggeration," Jake said. "But you know how the edges of National Parks, like Yellowstone, have gotten. If you would let them, the developers would have a fast food joint on both sides of Old Faithful."

"Maybe the three of us could get a McDonald's franchise at Spit Lake boat landing," Mac said.

"Sure, call it McWilderness!" Jake added.

"You guys are crazy," Charlie said. "Let's get serious. What do you think of the story that Tremayne's boys told?"

"Gotta admit, I'd hate to see oil derricks and pumps on the shore of Marsh Lake," Mac said.

"No telling what would happen to the plants, birds and animals," Jake said.

"I've tried to keep an open mind on this," Charlie said, "but talking to some of the members, a number of them think that the development would help our economy. They say that the lumber industry can only carry us so far. With the mining petering out, tourists are about all we have left. But, except for some of the service businesses, I don't know if the oil or the lodges would help us or hurt us."

"I doubt if tourists want to come up here to see oil rigs, mining, or the trucks and such that goes along with it," Jake said.

"How about the trouble that Buck has been having?" Mac asked.

"Well, one thing, if anyone can handle it, Buck can. But it sure shouldn't continue!" Jake said.

"It's got to be that corporation that's after him, trying to scare him off—it seemed to start about the same time we heard about them," Mac said.

"Do you really think so?" Charlie looked very concerned. "Why would they want to hassle him?"

"One reason would be that we made him the point man and we all know how he thinks. He wouldn't want anything to change the wilderness," Jake said.

"He loves that quiet canoeing," Mac said.

"Can't blame him," Jake said. "Nothing like it anyplace else."

Mac stood up and said, "Well, gents, I have to get back to the station—plan that expansion, you know." He laughed and waved his palm back and forth as if to say, "cancel last message."

Jake got up and moved to the door. "Needs some thinking time."

"Needs some thinking time, all right," Charlie said, half to himself. He walked to the telephone and dialed his home number.

"Lil, I am locking up a little early today. How are you? Oh...well, I'll be home soon." He hung up and began closing up the Information Center. He heard two car doors that sounded like more customers.

The door burst open. Two heavyweights in black suits and hats thrust in. Combined, they out-weighed Charlie about four to one. Their beady eyes matched their hats.

"You Charlie?" Benny drilled.

"Why yes."

"You been talking to LeYan?"

"Do you mean LeYan Syn from Alactra International?"

"Who else? She gave me a message for you. You better listen:

"Get that Buck Ryker off our ass! He's not going to do you or anybody else any good, dead!" For emphasis, Benny banged the top of the glass-enclosed display case that contained a selection of Chippewa arrowheads and a stone-bowl peace pipe. As stridently as they had clamored in, the two black suits wheeled and stomped out the door.

* * *

"We gave that Charlie something to think about," Luther said. The new bottle of Jack D. looked well used.

"Yeah, he's not going to give us any trouble. But I don't know if he can push that Ryker guy around," Benny said as he sprawled on the twin bed in the Lakeside Motel in Fall River. "Wake me for supper."

"I need a big steak," Luther said with determination. "It's four o'clock. I'll set this radio thing for five and we can make happy hour. I saw in the book that a place called The Landing has got huge steaks!"

Benny was already snoring.

* * *

Casey drove resolutely toward The Landing, their favorite dinner restaurant in Fall River. She imagined Buck barreling along at top speed. She recalled a Shakespeare line from her English Lit class—maybe it was from Romeo and Juliet: *Love goes toward love, as schoolboys from their books, but love from love, towards school with heavy looks.* She hoped that they were through with the heavy looks.

She felt tacky in her Bermuda shorts and Grandma's tee shirt—especially after twelve hours of driving, pushing, shoving and defending her honor. She realized that she could have refreshed at the clinic, but she was too eager to leave. *Buck won't be here for ten minutes. I'll just use the ladies room*, she thought as she walked up the broad stone steps to The Landing.

* * *

Buck pushed the Silverado to an anxious limit, forcing a rush of pine-scented air through open windows. The local C&W station blasted a continuum of rhythm at nearly sonic boom volume. He sang along, nearly as loud, using words that would have confounded the composer.

* * *

As Casey walked to the hostess desk, the crisply uniformed serving people were just completing the set-up for dinner. The dining room had been a very large living room of a late 1920's house. It exuded comfort rather than flash. A separate cocktail lounge had been added down the hall from the dining room. The vast horseshoe-shaped polished wood bar would support twenty or more in a few hours. There were also booths for four on both sides. The walls on one side and the end were total windowscapes, allowing appetizing views of Lake Superior.

She considered the separate "Wharf" cocktail lounge, but chose the dining room. The hostess guided her to the corner table-for-four that they had asked for in the past.

"My husband will be joining me soon," Casey said. Will you bring me a vodka gimlet?" The hostess smiled and nodded in a way to indicate her doubt. In her experience, it was unusual for a married couple to have a tryst at five o'clock.

At about 5:15, Buck turned off Falls Road onto the side street that led to The Landing parking lot. He parked, walked around to the front of the restaurant and started up the stone steps that looked like they were carved out of the solid rock upon which the seventy-year-old structure was built.

An old, light blue car careened along Falls Road and attempted a 180-degree power-turn to grab a spot directly in front of the brick walkway. The Dodge Dart only made it about 100 degrees, had to reverse and jockey back and forth several times to accomplish a parking exhibition typical of a first-time driver. Never-mind that the spot was clearly signed "No Parking – Loading Zone."

Buck paused as he entered the front door, recognizing the black suits and hats squeezing their bulks out of the narrow car doors. *That's got to be the goons and that's got to be the Dart belonging to Sam-the-propane-man*, he thought. He walked into the entry and then stepped back into the alcove leading to the restrooms.

Benny and Luther lurched up the stone steps with Luther in the lead by five. He burst in through the entrance door, slamming it nearly shut in Benny's face. They bungled in and made an urgent veer to the right, away from Buck, in the direction of The Wharf cocktail lounge. A 22 x 28 sign in a chrome frame proclaimed "Happy Hour – 5 to 7 – Hors d'oeuvres!"

"This is more like it," Luther said, as if they had been discussing other options, which they had not.

After watching the twosome stagger into The Wharf, Buck approached the Dining Room hostess stand and saw Casey sitting at their table. He waved, moved to the pay phone in the restroom hall and dialed the Nordland County Sheriff. "Hello, Dan, this is Buck Ryker. Glad to catch you on a Saturday afternoon—thought you required your criminals to take the weekend off."

"Oh yeah, you're 24/7 all right," Buck continued after Dan's response. "For you that means seven hours a day, twenty-four days a month. But since you're there today, I've got a funny one for you. There are a couple of weirdos in black suits that have been following me around for the past two days. That's *my* problem, but Casey and I were going to have an early dinner at The Landing and who shows up but these goons. I mean they are feeling no pain . But this is the main thing—they are driving a light blue Dodge Dart. How many of those do you know of around town...yeah, right, Sam-the-propane-man. Got to be his."

"Well, right now they are up to their elbows in The Wharf's horses duvers...doubt if they could make a defensive move without five or ten minutes consideration."

"Thanks, Dan. I think these jokers could use a good

lock-up—if only to protect them from themselves." Buck hung up, thinking that some days things do go right. He walked into the dining room to face Casey waiting for him. It wasn't quite like the lovers running toward each other through the field of flowers, but close. He ventured a real kiss before he sat down. The venture was well worth it. He quickly told her about the goons and calling Dan.

It was unusual, on a Saturday afternoon at The Landing, to experience a large-scale disturbance. First came the shouting…"We're from Chicago…where's your badge…whaddaya mean, we *bought* that car…whaddaya mean *title*, we just bought it yesterday…well, OK, you don't need to pull a gun on us. OK, OK, we're coming. Just give us a minute here…damn booths are too small."

Buck kissed Casey on the ear and said, "Do you want another drink, or do you want to race me home?"

"Why don't you give me a ten minute head start," she said. Her eyes had never been bluer, or softer.

* * *

The Ryker Log Home sign welcomed Casey as seldom before. The burgeoning birch blended with the pines to form an almost-arbor over the driveway. She drove into the construction yard, noticing Joe's truck. Pulling alongside, she said, "Thanks, Joe. We'll be home now. Appreciate your coming over." She drove to the house, parked the Subaru in front of one garage door, raced to the back door and then inside. Whenever she stopped to think of it, the comfort and easy style of their house gave her a deep sense of peace and tranquility. She would not trade it for a mansion—or a cantilevered cottage on the coastline. After a speedy shower, she heard the back door open and footsteps start. *Got to be Buck*, she thought. *Did I lock that back door?*

She ventured out, apprehensively, at the top of the stairway, surrounded by an L.L. Bean extra large towel.

Suddenly, it seemed, Buck appeared at the bottom of the stairway. Casey Brown Ryker and Buck Allan Ryker reprised the scene of nearly a week before...as if life were beginning again.

This time, there was no call from George, no conflict of interest, no hesitation, no holds barred—only "love goes toward love."

* * *

Charlie and Lillian sat in their living room. The word "eclectic" would have done them a favor. The fact is, it was early-everything. But, it was home, and on this fine day, it was bearable. It could have been an appealing hunting lodge style, with cement-chinked rugged pine walls and beamed ceilings. However, the chinks had, by and large, become un-chinked. The spring humidity cast a dank aura as they sat on the mohair sofa, circa 1958, that they had moved from their bright little cottage in East Beaver.

"Lil, you know that I have been talking to this big company in Chicago. They have offered me some money—you might say, an annuity—to give them information about the boundary waters issue." Lil started to speak, but Charlie held up his hand.

"But I have decided to stop talking to them. I don't want to scare you, but they have been getting after Buck, and this afternoon, two strange-looking guys came into the Center and told me that the company—Alactra—wanted me to tell Buck to back off. I can't...I won't do that. I'm just not going to get involved any more. From now on, if the phone rings, we don't answer."

* * *

"Representative Wayneson, this is LeYan Syn from Alactra International. Thank you for answering today. I apologize for bothering you on the weekend...Oh, I know what you mean. These days, a Saturday or Sunday is just like any other day.

"I just wanted to confirm our lunch at The Cloak Room Monday...Yes, 1:30. It will be an honor to meet you. I understand that Representative Saguaro will join us…good!

"I have also taken the liberty of inviting a man whom I believe you know…Jim Bob Akkre…Oh, you do…that is fine. We should be able to have a very…let's say, *productive discussion*, as I have heard used by the press," Le Yan said and continued, "I will have your usual table reserved for one o'clock. If I am a few minutes past 1:30 it will be as a result of my plane from Chicago being a bit late. I am certain that Mr. Akkre will be there by 1:30. Again, thank you sir."

LeYan pushed the key that directly rang the private home phone of Alasom Alactra.

"Hello," the voice answered without identification.

"Alasom, this is LeYan."

"I was hoping that you would call," he said.

"I have just confirmed my lunch with the two representatives."

"We should probably discuss our strategy further," he said with exaggerated seriousness. "Perhaps you could drive out. Unfortunately, Mrs. Alactra has to be gone for the weekend and the servants are gone, but no doubt we can manage."

"I will be there in about an hour. Can I bring anything?"

"Your smiling face is all that is required." Thus spake Alasom Alactra at six o'clock on Saturday, June 19, 1999.

18

It was nearly nine o'clock when the Rykers came to life. Their evening had been all-consuming—a total release of desire and emotion. Buck rolled out of bed first, walked toward the bath, and turned back to Casey.

As if it had just been a long interruption since they first met at The Landing, Buck said, "By the way, how was the Marathon?"

"I think we just had one," Casey answered with a sideways smile and eyes slanted in his direction.

"OK, wise guy—I mean, how did the race go?"

"I won," she said. "Otherwise, not worth mentioning."

"All right, mystery lady. So be it. After a shower, I'm making scrambled eggs and bacon. You want some?"

"You cooking? We've got to do this more often."

"If you've got the money, honey, I got the time," he said and disappeared into the bathroom.

* * *

The eggs, bacon, toast, tea and strong coffee, balanced by a background of bluegrass, let reality soak slowly back into their kitchen table togetherness.

"I saw your note about the check from the Iowa buyer," Casey said softly. "That is good news."

"Yes, that *was* good news. Now we can start the financials with a plus at the top of the column. Do you feel like diving into the business details today?" he asked, pouring himself another cup of his thick coffee. Casey, as usual, turned up her nose at the encrusted aluminum pot. He had brought it in from the shack for the special occasion.

"That's fine, but there is one other thing I thought of,"

she said. "It has been a while since we have attended services. I feel like I would like to go. What do you think?" Her head was inclined toward the plate, but her eyes turned up to him.

"You know that when you give me that big-eye Colorado nurse look, you got me. I think that Princess Di imported her look from you."

"Buck! Princess Diana was killed in an accident nearly two years ago!"

"I know, but I can remember the look."

"We can make it to the eleven o'clock service," she concluded.

The bright, sunny morning brought a wave of pleasure to Buck, as he made a quick inspection of the yard. He saw that Joe had cleaned up the rest of the fire damage to the home under construction. He was certain that the crew would have smooth sailing to finish the home and get it ready to load by the coming Tuesday night.

* * *

The congregation at Portage Devotional Church was well turned-out on the warm June day. Most of the men were in short sleeves—the women in print dresses or slack outfits. As usual, the young girls vied for who could wear the shortest skirts. The boys pretended not to notice, but their straight forward heads fought with their roving eyes. Buck realized that it was a good idea to go to church. It put a number of things into proper perspective. It did, however, bring him a moment of nostalgia, remembering his mother making church attendance a rite of passage for a young boy.

"Hello, Buck...and Casey. Good to see you here." Claude Tremayne walked over to shake their hands, as the service was letting out. "Heard you had a fire."

"Not much. Couple of goons apparently did it. But I think we have them under control. Sheriff Dan picked them up last night. He will search their car. If he finds any evidence, they will have a vacation at county expense." He wanted to avoid discussing, in front of Casey, the sighting of the oil exploration crew.

"Well, good to see you, Claude," he blurted out and took Casey by the arm.

"You seem to be in a rush," she said.

"Can't wait to get at those financials," he said and gave her a hand up into the Silverado cab. For the first time in a week, Buck kept his speed under the limit.

"The last time I had a chance to talk to Claude...for more than hello," she paused for effect, "he told me about a lady who has lived in a cabin overlooking Pigeon River Canyon. What an historic place to live—right there where the Voyageurs portaged up from Superior to start their trip west on the Grand Portage Trail and the Pigeon River."

"Yes, I have heard about her. She lives on the Chippewa reservation, mostly writing I guess. She can live there for the rest of her life, if she wants to. When she dies or moves, the Grand Portage Band will take away her cabins and the place will revert to the wilderness." Buck thought, *Now is the time.* "We could hike up that nine-mile trail sometime. It would be tough going, but fun." He turned off the North Shore highway onto the paved county road.

"You know," he continued, "the boys are doing well on their schedule to get the log home done. We could slip away for a little canoe trip for a couple days—one night. Could you take a day off from the clinic?"

Casey smiled. "I think that sounds like fun. Now I have a little surprise for you. Are you in a relaxed state of mind?"

"If I were more relaxed, I couldn't hang onto the steering wheel. What is it, oh mystery woman?"

"When I left the clinic yesterday, I left the clinic!"

"Was that an echo I heard?"

"Seriously, I put a note on Betty's desk that told her I might not be returning to work there. I said I would call her tomorrow night to explain."

"What will the doc say?"

"Frankly, my dear—I could not care less!"

"That bad, eh?"

"I think it's over! I hope you don't mind. At least I won't be going back this week."

"Other than your phone call yesterday afternoon, I haven't heard anything that good for a long time!" Buck said.

"You know, sailor, I could get to like you." She ruffled his short-cropped hair, like she used to.

"Careful, babe, you might start an incident," Buck said with considerable pleasure. "Now about the trip...I think we could take off tomorrow morning early. I can call Joe tonight to fill him in on the work plan for the next two days. I might ask George to sleep over tomorrow night. What do you think?"

"Let's do it!" Casey answered.

The sense of euphoria extended until Buck parked by the garage, approached the back door and saw the note. Casey was examining the pansies and petunias bursting along the sunny east side of the house.

The note was printed in large black capitals on one-half of a manila file folder:

> BUCK –
> TRIED TO CATCH YOU THIS MORNING.
> ALACTRA PEOPLE ARE GETTING ROUGH.
> I THINK WE SHOULD LET THE POLS
> FIGURE IT OUT. I'M SCARED FOR LIL
> AND ME—AND YOU.
> CHARLIE

* * *

The Sunday noon crowd had filled the Sawbill Bar & Grill parking lot. As Buck drove by on the way to the Amoco station, he recalled their Family Dinner that drew people from three counties—roast chicken, dressing, mashed potatoes, gravy, green beans and pie: $5.95. Coffee, tea, milk extra. When he and Casey had first arrived in the area, the price was $3.95; but the Scallia family still had to really hustle to make a go of it, even at the increased prices. The evening booze trade created the profit.

Mac Smalle's Amoco station, down County 18 from the Sawbill, looked busy but actually had only two customers—a Ranger pickup, pulling a Starline camper, and a Toyota SUV towing a fourteen-foot Lund fishing boat. Between the two, the gas pumps were blocked. Buck pulled up behind the travel camper and walked into the station to buy a Dr Pepper. He thought some of driving out to Charlie's house to find out more about the note that he had quickly stuck in his pocket. But he did not want to concern Lillian any more than she probably was already. He would give Charlie a quick call after supper—or maybe have Mac check in with him.

Mac finished with the camper people from North Dakota and nodded to Buck. He walked into the station to charge the SUV driver's credit card. Buck went back out to move his truck up to the pump, after the Ranger and camper left. He filled his tank and returned to the station desk.

"Hello, Buck. How's it going? Did you hear from Charlie? He was out at your place this morning."

"He left a note. Seems he's a little upset."

Mac related Charlie's story about the visit from the two thugs in black suits. "Yeah, he's scared all right," Mac said.

"I think the sheriff and I took care of the goons last night. They are either in the slammer or on their way out of town. I don't think there is any reason to worry. Mac, could you call Charlie at the Center tomorrow and calm him down? Casey and I are going to leave early tomorrow for a two-day to Marsh Lake. I would rather not call Charlie at home tonight, and risk disturbing Lillian."

"I'll do it. Now let me tell you a strange one. Just after Charlie came by, a big four-door, dual-wheel job pulled in. They had a couple 55-gallon drums in the back and some lengths of pipe tied onto a rack over the box. They didn't buy anything—just asked me if I knew anyone 'round here with a black Silverado. They looked weird to me so I told 'em I didn't. Big blond guy gave me a real fish-eye and pulled out like he was mad. They headed out toward your turnoff. You got any other enemies you haven't told us about?"

"Not that I know of, but I seem to be in-season. Maybe they're friends of the goons. Thanks for steering them away. I'll talk to you Tuesday, when we get back."

* * *

Sunday was usually George's *day of rest*—unless he had a Saturday night sleepover. Today, Buck could hear some TV noise as soon as he entered George's long driveway. As he got closer, he could see the small set, out on the 4 x 4 entry deck. It was blasting a Minnesota Twins game, to no audience. The broadcast sound and static were of about equal volume.

"Hooyah," Buck hollered to get a rise out of the resident ex-SEAL. After a couple of minutes, he got a response.

"Yeah, I'm here." *Big George* appeared, walking around the side of his small house from the shed in the back. He carried a basket of clothes as far as some lines he had strung up between two poplar trees. He was a vision in his GI shorts, no shirt—only a pair of ankle-high boots, no socks.

"I see you're ready for company," Buck opened.

"Anyone who finds his way out here takes what he gets. I was just washing out everything I have, in the pump house—good day for drying. What's up?"

"Couple things: I think I've got the goons in the lock-up—and Casey quit the clinic. Oh, and we're going to wet the canoe in Marsh Lake tomorrow—early."

"Leave you alone for a day and you lose your head altogether," George said. He began hanging up some well-used skivvies, shirts and jeans. "Marsh Lake—right out with those oil freaks. I thought I had talked you out of that."

"Marsh is the closest real boundary waters lake and I'm not going to let a blond guy and some ponytails keep me away," Buck replied. Mac said they were around looking for me this morning. If I see 'em out there, I see 'em. That's all."

"You just can't leave it alone, can you? *I* should be going out there with you—*not Casey*!" George shook his head.

"We'll be camping on the north side. They were seen working on the south side."

"Yeah, that's what you said yesterday, but it's only a half mile or less across. You will probably be the only canoe out there. They'll see you!"

"They may not even be there. From what Mac said they are *here* now. If you are looking to tangle with them, you might see them at the yard—if you were there."

"You mean you want me to baby-sit your place? I already said I would."

"It would be good for you—could even take a real shower instead of that hose you've got in the pump house—could cook some real food."

"Nothing wrong with my food, or my shower either," George growled. "But if you want me to save your ass again, I suppose I can do it."

"Joe's got the work program. If you could show up around five or so tomorrow afternoon, that would be great," Buck said. He got back in his truck and then hollered, "Take it easy on the wild parties, though. Neighbors, you know."

"What neighbors? The raccoons won't give a damn."

* * *

LeYan dialed "The Big Man on the Beltway" using the cell phone number on the business card that Jim Bob Akkre had sent her. The outrageous claim was followed by an unbelievable BMOB in parenthesis. After two rings, the connection was apparently made, but there was no answer—just some mumbling and, it seemed, giggling.

"Jim Bob here," finally came over the wire, along with some harsh muffled words and more giggling.

"This is LeYan Syn. Is this Mr. Akkre?"

"Ah, LeYan. How are you this Sunday?"

"Mr. Akkre, I am calling to confirm our lunch tomorrow with Congressmen Wayneson and Saguaro. I have made a reservation at The Cloak Room for one o'clock. However, I told them that we would actually schedule the meeting for 1:30. I might be there a few minutes after that, if my plane is delayed. It would be beneficial if you could be there at least by 1:30 to meet them."

"Consider it done, doll." BMOB downed the last swallow of scotch in his glass.

"Mr. Akkre, I'm sure you agree that it is essential for us to show a united front tomorrow."

"Sure thing, honey. United it is…and that reminds me…maybe we could continue our discussion after lunch." Akkre waited, with anticipation, for a pleasant response, but strangely, he had been cut off.

Jim Bob rolled out of bed and wrote himself a note: *Call Alactra. Get LeYan's flight number.*

"Sally, how'd you like to be my secretary tomorrow morning?"

"If you got the money, honey, I've got the time. Wherever you want it, the rate's the same." She lit her cigarette with the hotel matches.

"Not that," Akkre said. "I mean pick up someone at the airport—the babe I just talked to on the phone. You could hire a limo and then meet her at the gate. That would impress her right out of her tiny little outfit."

"I'll do it, but…"

"Yeah, I know," he interrupted, "the rate's the same."

* * *

Buck thought about the back-and-forth with George. He realized that it is true that Ryker Homes is isolated, but until this past week, there had never been a concern. In the future, he would question leaving Casey alone at night. Maybe get a younger dog, or two. Rocky, the old malamute, had gotten too fat and friendly to provide much security. Maybe a Rottweiler—or a pair of Dobermans or German Shepherds—whatever Casey would feel comfortable with.

He announced his arrival home with a door bang and a "Casey, it's me."

"I'm at the computer," she answered in a loud voice, over a Sunday symphony. As he entered, she continued, "I am glad it's you and no one else."

"Sounds good, but what does that mean?"

"We had visitors while you were gone," she said quietly.

Shivers on a warm June day were unusual. So was his sudden sense of vulnerability. *Can't I even leave the place on a Sunday afternoon*, he thought. "Did you get a look at them?"

"Rocky barked a couple times so I looked out and saw a big pickup pull in as far as the "T" in the driveway. It was one of those four-door jobs with a short box on the back. There seemed to be four guys. They all looked back and forth, but did not turn toward the house. They drove into the yard fifty feet or so, paused to look, turned around and left. Strange for a Sunday."

"Probably had the wrong address," he said, but thought, *Damn right, it's strange!*

"I guess so," she said and turned back to her computer.

"What did Rocky do after he barked?"

"Oh," she laughed, "he walked slowly toward their truck with his tail wagging."

"You know," Buck said, "I think it is time we get Rocky a couple of buddies."

* * *

One of the Baton Rouge ponytails spoke through a swallow of beer, "One thing for sure—we would not get trouble from that furry old mutt they had. We could have torched that place this afternoon. There wasn't no Silverado around."

The big blond guy answered in a way that settled the subject, "We could have, but we wouldn't have. That would have been dumb. We get no bonus for doing a job for those Chicago thugs. This trip was just for Rebelde's information. Our job is to get back out to Marsh Lake tomorrow and finish the project. We don't want anything interfering. Rebelde will meet us out there Tuesday morning to check our work and then we're through! In spite of what that black-suit guy said the other night, I don't believe we'll see anything of the Silverado local and his canoe. If we do, we've got some anti-canoe medicine that will take care of him." Blond paused to shift gears. "Now, we've got to eat and turn in early so we can get out to the camp before sunrise. We need to develop enough evidence, out of that loon shit we're digging in, to make it look like there is oil there—or copper—or something.

19

Buck's alarm jarred him awake. He had decided that Mozart would not do the job at 3 AM. He looked at Casey and wished they did not have to go anywhere.

"Is it morning already?" she groaned.

"Barely, but unfortunately it is, for us." He went to the bath for a shower-fix.

After a large breakfast and coffee to go, the two got into the already loaded dual-wheel Silverado.

"You know, I don't think I have ever seen you at 3:30 in the morning before," Buck said.

"With any luck, you won't ever again." Casey grabbed a pillow and put her head back against the headrest and side pillar. "Wake me when it's over—or when it starts—whatever."

He felt exhilarated. For three years, he had wanted to get out in the wild with Casey ... to share the peace, the pureness. There was an edge to this trip, but chances of bumping into the oil guys were slight.

* * *

The boat landing area showed signs of some visitors already this season. The evidence of human incursion was in dramatic contrast with the silent, natural view across the boundary waters lake. But he was resigned to that diversity—no visitors were going to bring their canoes and packs in here on moccasin feet. The surprise to Buck was that there were fresh, dual-wheel tire tracks leading down to the water's edge and then straight back out of the landing area. He didn't think Casey noticed. The other thing that caught his attention was a loose pile of Styrofoam take-out containers about twelve feet into the trees. The way that they were perched on the low brush convinced him that they had not been subjected to last night's rain.

They are here! Look out! he thought.

Casey was busy assembling the gear at the water's edge. Buck smiled as he saw her hoist the heavy Duluth pack and lug it to the shore. Without a word, they each grabbed an end of the canoe and hauled it to the launch point.

"You play your cards right and I might hire you," he said.

"You couldn't afford me, Buster," was the immediate reply.

As Buck had planned, they reached the portage to Marsh Lake before sunrise. They were able to walk the shallow stream and "line" the canoe, with pack aboard, by towing it with ropes until they reached the access to Marsh Lake. Once underway in the misty, rippling waters, Buck set a moderate pace. He knew that Casey would be using muscles unaccustomed to this action, but he knew that she would want to do some paddling.

"How are you doing?" Buck finally broke an hour's silence.

"I could go on forever. I love it!" she said.

"How about another hour and we'll be at the halfway campsite. We can stop and check it out."

"You're on!"

The sun rose behind their shoulders, the mist with it. The atmosphere, after the night's light rain, was cool and damp. It would soon dry when the sun did its thing.

"Should be a bluebird sky today," Buck said.

"The silence and the scenery just make it a paradise," she said.

In another half hour, the sky was almost cloudless and the sun had warmed the two voyageurs to their T-shirts.

"Isn't it surprising that no one else is out here enjoying this?"

"Yes, but the season has just begun and the weekend

paddlers are through. Some parties have already gone through today before us. They are one lake ahead by now. When I was out on Heron Lake last week, there were several motorboats zipping around. There are no motors allowed on this lake. Not yet anyway."

"If I heard a motor, I would want to get the hell out of here," Casey said with a vehemence that surprised him. "Talk about your bull in a china shop..."

"I guess that's what we are trying to do—keep the bulls out of the wilderness 'china shop'," he said.

"I took my Sigurd Olson book out last night—you know, *The Singing Wilderness*. I brought it along. He wrote it over forty years ago, but his thoughts still are true today. Do you want to hear a small part of it?" she asked.

"You're the tour director," he said, with a deep satisfaction that his partner was enjoying herself.

"OK, here goes—right off, the first page tells the reader how valuable this place is—right where we are now. Well, I won't read it. It just beautifully describes the great silence, the loons, the simple joys where travel is still by pack and canoe.

Casey paused to sense Buck's reaction. He was quietly slitting the mirror-like water on one side and the other, gazing straight ahead. "Then in another place, he writes about the need we have to be closer to lakes, rivers, mountains, meadows, and forests."

Buck had stopped paddling and for an unmeasured time the two sat in a drifting canoe, observing exactly the sensations about which Sigurd Olson had written.

Finally, Casey said, "Do you think we could ever have a life with those simple joys and avoid the busyness?"

"Case, I have had some simple joys in the past twenty-four hours; but, I don't expect to avoid more challenges, or the busyness that they will require. Ironically, we have to work hard to keep it simple."

* * *

"It is time," Alasom Alactra said, "to make the ultimate

decision. We have information. We have research. We have opinions. But we have not done our company's usual due diligence for the Boundary Lodges project. The press of other business has precluded my full attention. Do we have consensus that Boundary Lodges will succeed?"

In addition to LeYan Syn and Bill Anderson, two other members of "the cabinet" sat in the eight o'clock Monday morning meeting. One was a physically imposing, leather-faced mountain-of-a-man, known by the name of "Hands." He could have been given a number of other body-oriented names, such as "The Giant," but one look at his massive, gnarled palms and fingers, made other possibilities irrelevant. At the urging of one of his pick-up B-Ball buddies, he once tried out as a rookie for the Bulls. However, he moved his 6-11, 295 pounds more like a middle linebacker than a flashing forward. The Bull's coach carefully eased Hands out of the lineup before the rookie could maim any of the high-priced help.

Hands was LeYan's chief of security. He controlled a number of full time and freelance persuaders—including Benny and Luther. They were all ready and able to carry out any assignment from "enforcement" to guarding LeYan's body. At times, LeYan would take over tactical direction of Benny, Luther and one or two others. Hands only spoke when asked a direct question. It was invariably a low-bass "yes" or "no."

The other man in attendance would likely not speak at all. He was an unusually cerebral young Orthodox Jew, who had simultaneously mastered business law and oriental studies at Harvard. His name was Mr. Chron. He was mainly occupied by absorbing everything said (and probably expressed by body language and facial attitude). This would go into his laptop and ultimately be summarized for Mr. Alactra.

The question Alasom proposed was too basic, too profound for anyone less secure than LeYan to consider.

"There is consensus, Mr. Alactra. We can, we will make it a success. Bill will expand on that."

Anderson, recognizing the need for precise statements, said, "The major parts of the strategy are these: Congressional approval, facilities development, marketing and continuing promotion. In view of our recent concerns about local attitudes, it may be that public relations is the first order of business. Of course, LeYan has the best handle on that." He nodded in her direction.

"Since PR on this project is somewhat of a moving target—even to the point of coinciding with the need for Congressional approval," LeYan began, "I have not attempted to lay out my exact strategy." Alasom nodded in approval, as he always did to her statements—at least in front of others.

"Thursday we met with this Ryker from the local group. As we might expect, he was unable to comprehend the overall values. We are certain that his credibility will soon vanish, even with his own people."

"Thank you, LeYan," Alactra said. "I believe you are working with government people to obtain necessary approvals."

"Yes sir, I leave shortly for a lunch meeting with two influential Congressmen and that D.C. person that, I believe, spoke to you, Mr. Alactra."

"He is a representative of some business contacts we have in Dallas and South America," Alactra explained. "We have not totally determined their interests, but we know that they have major influence in Washington. LeYan, perhaps you will obtain some further insight when you meet with him."

"I will try. Frankly, I was not impressed with his knowledge or manner the two times I have spoken to him. I would not want him blundering into any of our plans."

Mr. Alactra rose to conclude the meeting. He, Anderson and Chron left. LeYan put her hand on Hands' forearm and asked him to remain. She usually referred to him as Mr. Hands. His Croatian name was too sinister and difficult to pronounce. "Mr. Hands, will you please stay for a few minutes?" she said softly. Her reaction to

Hands was not nearly as obvious as virtually every other woman (including Paulette) whom he encountered. However, it was believed by a few that LeYan and Hands had a warm relationship. The barrier to a more frequent association was his often impassive nature and the absolute loyalty they both maintained for Alasom Alactra. Hands had been involved in a South Chicago brawl five years ago that resulted in his being charged with manslaughter for a single blow. Alactra's attorney became aware of Hands' problem and potential value to Alactra International. The attorneys were able to obtain an acquittal on the basis of "self-defense." While a prison term for thirty-year-old Hands would not likely involve the usual abuse to a new convict, the caged confinement would have affected him psychologically—and he knew it. His freedom was repaid to Alactra with unassailable, lifelong allegiance.

"How have you been getting along? It has been a long time since we have had a chance to talk," she said. Hands nodded with the hint of a smile. "I have a favor to ask," she continued. "It is in connection with the boundary waters tree-hugger. Benny and Luther have been harassing him, but have not accomplished much. I am concerned that this Ryker can make trouble for us. Could you go there today and convince him to back off? We have given him enough trouble already that one more confrontation with him and his wife should do it."

"Yes," he said.

"If you stop back here about 12:30, Paulette will have your tickets for a 2 PM flight, along with some background information and suggestions." She moved against his huge frame and his right hand nearly covered the silky firmness of her buttocks. He placed his left arm around her shoulders and they stood for a moment.

"LeYan," he said with warmth and finality. He turned and walked out. She grasped the arm of the conference room chair and then eased into the seat, fanning her face with a manila folder.

Hands had almost the same impact on Paulette when he waved to her on his way to the elevator. Ling did not look up. Hands ignored Alactra's other protector.

* * *

The warm morning sun made Hands remove his blue blazer and hold it over his left shoulder with his left index finger. Tree-limb-like hairy arms were exposed below the rolled-up sleeves of a blue summer-weight shirt. He wore no watch. He loosened his navy blue tie. On the way to his two-room apartment six blocks distant, he stopped for coffee at his regular lunch counter. He put his blazer back on, in the air-conditioned café, and sat at a stool. A neat, five-foot-two-eyes-of-blue waitress immediately brought him a cup of coffee and a large cinnamon roll. "How are you today?" she asked with an encouraging smile. Standing there in front of him, her eyes looked almost directly into his, in his sitting position.

"Horny," he said.

She took a deep breath and said, steadily, "Any time you say."

Hands finished his coffee and roll. He rose slowly as the petite miss moved to the cash register. It sat on top of the glass counter that contained a variety of enticements. He paid his bill, while her eyes did not leave his. He turned and took one step toward the door. She did not move a muscle, after closing the cash register drawer. Hands stopped and took a step back, facing her. He slowly reached both arms over the counter and grasped her elbows in his grappling-hook hands. She did not make a sound. Fred, the café manager, standing in back of the serving counter, and the four people sitting at stools, stared silently at the unfolding drama.

Hands began lifting her straight up in the air. When her feet were about thirty-six inches off the floor, she drew her legs up tight under her short uniform skirt. In one move, Hands boosted her up another twelve inches and toward him, stepping back from the counter. He set the waitress back down in front of the counter and took her small hand in his mitt. As they walked out the door, she turned and projected back to the manager, "Fred, I believe I'll take a little time off. See you later."

* * *

Suddenly Buck's line strung out like a guy-wire on a telephone pole. Then it veered strongly to the left and Buck reeled to keep the tension on the hook. He had let Casey do most of the paddling for the past half hour while he trolled for a lake trout or walleye. He was in luck—this one felt like it would give them a meal. In a few minutes of man-against-fish, he netted a two-pound walleye. Casey stopped paddling and applauded his accomplishment, but razzed, "That's kind of small, isn't it?"

By the time he had it on the stringer, Casey had maneuvered the canoe close to the landing for the campsite. Buck squinted across the half mile of Marsh Lake toward the only campsite that the oil boys were likely to use. He was having second thoughts about spending the evening so close.

"Now that I think of it, the next campsite is a better spot. It's only about a mile farther," he said, thinking that he didn't want their evening campfire to be visible to anyone who might be across the lake.

* * *

The first rifle shot was low and outside. It skipped into the water like a hell-bent dragonfly. Buck could not believe that they were being fired at.

The second shot was closer—zinged off a boulder, not three feet from the canoe. Now, they both knew!

"What was that?" Casey gasped.

"Get down in the canoe—behind the pack." Casey crouched down while Buck attempted to move closer into the shore.

The third shot, that Buck knew was from a high-powered deer rifle, probably a Winchester 30-06, drilled a three-fourths inch hole through both sides of the bow of the canoe. The force began a tipping motion that Buck added to by leaning in the direction of the tip.

"We're going over. Get under the canoe," he hollered.

Once they were under the canoe, the trapped air space gave them nearly a foot of headroom—as long as it lasted.

He spoke directly into her ear as they hung on to the gunnels on each side of the overturned canoe. "We'll just stay here for five minutes until they think we're done for."

"Buck, who..."

"Let's save our breath 'til we're out of this." After ten minutes and no more shots, Buck took a deep breath, submerged under the side facing the shore and came up alongside. He did a hand-over-hand out to the end and cautiously peered at the opposite shoreline. The sun was making shadows of every boulder or rock point. He could not see any activity. He gulped a breath, ducking his head under the canoe, and came up next to Casey in the breathing space.

"I want you to take a deep breath, duck under the and come up outside. Then swim and crawl between the boulders until you climb up onto the shore. When you get on shore, you will be behind the rocky point. It will shield you from across the lake."

"Who do you think it was?"

"Just some weirdos—they won't be back. I'm going to gradually pull the canoe to shore and grab our pack of gear. Then I'll crawl up the bank to where you are."

Casey was accustomed to water but this water was cold—not a place to hang around. In a few minutes, she clambered up on the rocky, muddy shore and grabbed her way up to the campsite. She sat on the large log that had been placed about four feet from the fire grate. There was a similar log across on the other side. Although the air temperature was probably over sixty, she felt cold from being totally wet. She shivered and looked hopefully at where the fire would be. With any luck, the Duluth pack would keep most of their food and gear at least partially dry. She sat there shivering and shivering.

A large hand suddenly covered Casey's mouth. It held her head firm. An arm encircled her waist from the back. She was entrapped as if with steel cables.

She jammed both hands against the arm that held her waist. It was solid and immovable. Her breath came in gasps of air that had the smell similar to Buck returning from canoeing or walking in the woods—fresh, but with a twang of water and brush. She tried wildly to think of the SEAL moves that Buck had taught her, but, then ...

"Please, Mrs. Ryker. I do you no harm. Please don't yell. I let you go now." The dark-haired young man released her and quickly stepped around in front of her, allowing a two-arms-length distance between them.

"Who are you?" Casey demanded, with a hoarse voice.

"I am Brightcloud, a friend of Claude Tremayne. I had to grab you like that so that you would not cry out. I am truly sorry to have frightened you. My brother, Strongbird, and I are here because of the people across the lake." At that, Strongbird stepped soundlessly out of the trees, twenty feet away.

"Brightcloud, Strongbird, good to see you," Buck smiled as he dragged the wet pack in one hand and two Thermos jugs in the other.

"It damn well wasn't so good when he first got here!" Casey growled, still shaken from shock and visions of unlimited attack.

"Mrs. Ryker, I apologize again. Buck, I felt I had to keep her from crying out in surprise. Maybe I wouldn't have had to be so rough," Brightcloud said.

"It's over," Buck said. "Casey, I am sorry too. I hope you are OK." Casey nodded "Yes."

After a discussion of what had happened, the three men concluded that it must have been the oil crew, just trying to scare away any visitors.

"Buck, did you know about these guys?" Casey asked.

"Brightcloud and Strongbird saw them last week, but no one knew they were here—or where they might be." Casey turned away with no further comment.

Claude Tremayne's boys hauled the canoe to a dry place on the shore while Buck started a fire. Casey opened the pack and found some mostly dry clothes for a change behind a dense fir tree. The three men determined that the hole in the canoe would need to be plugged. Strongbird offered to boil some birch to produce a resin that would patch the hole.

"Thanks, boys, I have some caulk in the pack that should take care of it. The hole is just above the waterline. If we keep the weight in the stern and the bow riding high, it will be OK. If the caulk doesn't take, I'll have to do what you suggest. I've done that before." Handshakes and thanks went around among the three. Casey managed a wave, as the brothers left.

The campsite was quiet. Buck took a deep breath, found his caulk and was about to descend to the canoe to begin the repair job.

Casey said, "I am disappointed that you didn't tell me about the oil crew."

Buck slowly set down his caulking gear where he was standing and from that distance looked at Casey.

"I know now that I made a mistake. I agree that I should have told you. I just thought that there would be almost zero chance of their being aware of us—especially since we got here so early. I thought about it a lot but decided that I shouldn't worry you about something that was not likely to happen." He walked toward her and continued, "I probably should not have asked you to come. Damn it, Casey, I just wanted to be with you out here! Pretty dumb, huh?"

She turned to him with soft eyes, "No, not dumb—but as you said, 'It's over.' Now, I'm getting hungry." His still wet clothes dried more than somewhat against her dry clothes, in an embrace that was seldom expressed at high noon in a boundary waters campsite.

"Looks like we'll have to spend the night. The caulk needs at least eight hours to dry," he said, still holding her.

"I've heard of running out of gas on a date, but having to plug a hole in your canoe is a new one," she said.

"We should really get out early. Maybe you will get off easy tonight."

"What's the matter, sailor?" she asked. "Remember, no guts, no glory."

"You'll be sorry you said that."

"I don't *think* so," Casey said and playfully pushed him away.

He had tied the walleye to a small boulder at the shoreline. It would be a welcome lunch, along with some fried potatoes, that never achieve, on a stove, the same flavor as being cooked over a fire. He and the boys had pulled the canoe up and in back of a rocky outcropping so that it would not be visible from the opposite shore. After a careful caulk job, he returned to the campsite to see Casey starting the pan of potatoes. He laid out the walleye on a flat rock and began filleting.

"We can pitch the tent right in that flat area over there," Buck indicated with a nod in the direction of a clearing that looked like it had been used many times before. "I'll get some boulders and make a small fire-circle back farther in the clearing for tonight. We probably won't need the fire very long anyway."

"You seem to have a plan," she said.

20

Washington, D.C. means one thing: greed. Greed for power and greed for money. That is no longer a surprise.

But it is the name of the game for the politicos, the lawyers and hangers-on who go with the flow and make the flow. A grassroots issue may begin as a matter of extreme economic need or a remedy for social injustice. By the time it becomes one of the few that are considered worthy of our elected officials' time or interest, the original issue may not be recognizable. Basic legislation often gets barnacled with so many non-relevant appendages that the major need is obscured and lost in the shuffle of amendments.

Jim Bob Akkre was one of those who had expertise in attaching barnacles. His part of the greed was to charge heavy doses of cash for pleasing and squeezing pols in the House and Senate. You want a ten million dollar bridge over your county trout stream? Jim Bob can get it for you. Simple. Just inform influential members of the right committee that, if the bridge isn't approved, someone's rural-community thirty-mile stretch of four-lane paved highway will be cut off in mid-appropriation.

But as Jim Bob would say, "It ain't pretty, but somebody's got to do it."

There is a dichotomy that relates to the Capital City of the United States: for all the leadership disappointments, it is one of the world's most interesting, beautiful, and inspiring cities. But, not necessarily the most pleasant in summer.

Magnolia trees do their best to soften the sun's force, but locals know that the rising heat and humidity will often make the city nearly unbearable. Unbearable, that is, to the majority who do not feed directly off of the political frenzy. Sweat is a minor problem for those who move in air-conditioned comfort from Georgetown, McLean and $400-per-night hotels to the taxpayer-provided government edifices.

Jim Bob had a free morning before his lunch date with LeYan Syn and the Congressmen. Years ago, he would have spent some time prepping: what was the history of the boundary waters area, what has been the involvement of local, state, federal government? He had heard of a man named Sigurd Olson who had stirred many with his writings about the wilderness. He remembered the wrangles in 1978, when laws were passed that put some new restrictions on the 1,075,000 acre Boundary Waters Canoe Area. But that was more than a generation ago. Jim Bob and his sponsors now had agendas that they considered much more important.

He made a tactical error this Monday morning. He decided to *walk* the three blocks from his "Miss Sally" tryst to the protection of his air-conditioned office. His claimed weight of 190 pounds was a dream, compared with his actual lumpy 230. Under the right conditions, he could pour it all into a well-tailored midnight blue suit. Today was something else. The sweat started within one block of his tryst site. His blue blazer, light blue button-down Oxford cloth shirt and rep tie had been ill chosen. In one block, the tie came off. Next block, the blazer had to go. By the time he lurched into the oasis of his office building lobby, he looked like he had just dropped out of a marathon at the halfway point.

The refreshing blast of cool air brought Jim Bob back to pleasant realities—a fantastic night— a paying customer for today's lunch—maybe something after—life is sweet! His thoughts went back to the 1978 BWCA law. From virtually the moment of passage, local area citizens had begun a drumbeat of agitation to reduce the effect of the law. But then, a court ruling specified further restrictions to start in 1999. The controversy began to escalate in late 1996. Polemic discussions, media frenzy, letters-to-the-editors, political posturing and federal mediation continued until adroit and timely moves were made by Minnesota Congressmen. A compromise bill was passed into law in 1998, allowing boat-hauling vehicles on two portages and extending the use of boat motors on some lakes. The *quid pro quo* was additional forest land to be placed under existing use-regulations.

Akkre now had no involvement with these non-interest-bearing issues. He had other spheres to influence.

* * *

Alasom Alactra kissed LeYan's hand in the luxury of his limo. They had departed the Alactra International building after the morning meeting, to be driven to O'Hare International. The elixir of their weekend had quickened his pace and sharpened his perceptions.

"LeYan, as you know, you have made me very happy. I wish I could see that happiness in your face."

"I *am* very happy, Alasom. I am afraid that my thoughts stray to our project and all its complications."

"We have many projects worthy of your attention," he said softly, as his chauffeur waited to open the limo door and assist LeYan's exit. "You know that there are some aspects of the Boundary Lodges that we have pursued more—let's say—casually than usual. But, whatever the outcome, I know that you will have done the right thing."

LeYan looked at the father-like figure with an emotion closer to devotion and admiration than love. She spoke softly to herself as she proceeded into the terminal, "I must succeed. I *will* succeed!"

* * *

The cab ride from the J.B. Akkre's office building to The Cloak Room Restaurant gave him enough time to gain total composure. After years of practice, he knew exactly how long it would take him to get into gear for some serious moneymaking.

The Cloak Room did not strike a person immediately as a glamorous eating establishment. It was a watering hole for the political fraternity. Therefore, it was the hangout for the hangers-on whose expense accounts could afford the six-dollar drinks and forty-dollar entrees.

Jim Bob arrived well before the appointed one-thirty. He always made it a practice to arrive early. It gave him a chance to ease up, partake of a couple scotches, and establish a modicum of one-upmanship—if only in his own mind. The place was comfortably classy.

The Cloak Room had prospered through ten administrations. A veteran of World War Two, Antonio Olare figured that if a haberdasher could be President, he could start a restaurant. His instincts and dedication to quality were derived from a restaurant heritage. His bistro became the place to go for some of the thousands moving into D.C. government work, when "smaller government" had not yet been invented. He realized that if he raised his prices gradually, he would make the same money with fewer customers to serve. The by-product was that the clientele was forced into a higher income (or at least, expense) bracket. His early specialties (i.e., Revolutionary Reuben) gave way to Veal Antonio and Sole de Olare. His martinis were stout and carried a hundred-proof price.

Jim Bob was in friendly territory, sitting at the long bar, overlooking the step-down dining room. "Sam, my man," he projected to the red-coated barman, "how are the nation's heroes treating you today?"

"Not too bad, J.B. What'll you have? Usual?"

"Why not—my first double of the day," he confided.

"What's going down today?" Sam asked.

"Got to meet a couple Congressmen and very likely the most exotic woman you have seen all week. Haven't seen her yet myself, but I just know we're in for a vision."

"Out of your class then?" Sam laughed.

"Don't underestimate Slick Jimmy. I have observed a lot of presidents, you know."

Slick Jimmy kept an eye on the Maitre d'. The dining room was a field of fifty or so tables, two steps down from the bar. The tables were fastidiously fitted-out with crisp white cloths, fanned napkins, highly polished silver and cut glass goblets. Portraits of presidents from George Washington on, except for some who were not Antonio's favorites, hung on the walls. There was no mistaking the audience to which The Cloak Room catered. Of course, the reality was that there had not yet been a president inside these walls in the past forty years. It was a den—sometimes of iniquity, sometimes of thieves, sometimes just of schmoozing: influential people leaning on other influential people. Members of Congress met each other. Chairpeople met adversaries and cronies. Lawyers met everybody. A few of D.C.'s "beautiful people" and celebrities were often in attendance.

Andre, the Maitre d', suddenly came to attention. His body language shouted that VIP's had arrived. Representatives Wayneson and Saguaro entered and were escorted to the corner table for six usually requested by Wayneson. The conversation of the would-be sophisticates at nearby tables slowed only slightly, but their eyeballs were attentive to the well-known members of Congress. Jim Bob checked his watch at 1:25. When he looked up, Andre was on "tilt" again—and for good reason.

Diners at The Cloak Room had trained themselves to refrain from outward expressions of interest in, or even apparent awareness of, notables or remarkables that made their entrances. All the training went for naught when LeYan descended the two steps into the dining room on Andre's arm. Her svelte, well-proportioned figure was a perfect complement for her medium height. Her light-olive, sculpted face would easily have taken a Miss Malaysia title. Her clinging, almost-mini, summer print dress, hinted at an Asian style only by its closed collar. Most of the well-trained diners recovered and tried to forget. But one man, seated at a table of two lawyers and their two clients gasped, "My God, did you see that?" Except for a few sidelong glances, most of the staring ceased after LeYan and the Congressmen began talking.

"Well, Ms. Syn..." Wayneson started.

"Please, make it LeYan," she interrupted.

"OK, LeYan, this is indeed a pleasure. I am sure we are the envy of the assembly here."

Congressman Saguaro nodded and said, "Right."

"I expect my associate to join us shortly," she said. "He is maybe someone you know, since he has been active in Washington for many years. He is Mr. Akkre...I believe *Jim Bob* Akkre...a consultant for Texas oil companies."

"Oh, J.B. Akkre. I didn't know he used his high-priced time on anything north of Mississippi," Saguaro said and smiled.

LeYan wanted first impressions to be as positive as possible and quickly asserted, "His people have vast interests all over North and South America. I believe you will find that they coincide with the country's interests that you represent. I have not actually met him, but I believe that is Akkre now."

J.B. Akkre wove his way between the tables, toward them, with eyes fixed as if he were looking though binoculars. His 230 pounds were propelled in a determined manner that would have bowled over anything that got in the way. A man at a close-by table seemed to think J.B. was aiming at him and started to rise, but then sat down with slight embarrassment.

"Congressman Wayneson, Congressman Saguaro (J.B. knew how to pronounce Sa-whar-o), so good to see you. LeYan, you are looking more fabulous than I expected."

"Hello J.B," Saguaro warmed. "Last time we met you were pushing for casinos in Mississippi. How did things work out there?"

"Great, just great. They're now getting millions of visitors to the area. Completely changed the county. Now it's an important vacation destination."

"Has the employment of blacks improved during this period of economic growth?" Wayneson asked.

"Hasn't hurt it a bit. Not at all," J.B. danced.

LeYan was not only bored out of her tawny skin by this exchange but getting leery of J.B.'s ability to handle it.

"Mr. Akkre, I think these gentlemen would like to know what interests you and your people have in the wilderness area," LeYan said. Her look at him unmistakably said "cut to the chase."

"LeYan, Congressmen, that is the issue, isn't it? Can't say that we're thinking 'non-profit', but we have a strong principle of doing good." LeYan turned her head so that her guests could not see her eyes rolling at the bully bullshit. "The issue (J.B. liked the word 'issue') is progress. These wilderness areas have been dormant, like an old log ready to decay into the ground. Why, we're talking over a million acres in Minnesota alone. Who knows how much in Canada? During the past fifty years that these areas have been dead, the United States has nearly doubled in population. Why should the wilderness areas be denied the progress enjoyed by the rest of the country?"

Congressman Wayneson said softly, "I will say that the people I talk to in these northern areas do not feel that they are being depressed by their current state of, as you say, 'underdevelopment'. On the contrary, they pretty much enjoy the *lack* of development."

LeYan moved just enough to command attention and to signal her intention to forestall further foot-in-mouth by J.B. Akkre.

"Mr. Wayneson—may I call you 'Mister' ..." she smiled.

"You may call me John—and this is Frank, as in Congressman Saguaro."

"Thank you, gentlemen. John and Frank it shall be. Now..." she continued quickly before J.B. could blunder in, "I am sure that I speak for my exuberant friend here...our interests do not presume to intrude on the nature of the wilderness. We propose to *enhance* the natural setting by providing architecturally considerate lodges that will allow more U.S. citizens to experience the wonders of the wild." She continued to pre-empt Jim Bob's intrusions and introduced the Alactra proposal in a manner that was difficult to refuse. She gave John and Frank each a copy of the proposal, written by Alactra attorneys, in a fashion that would allow immediate incorporation into legislative consideration. The lunch came to a close with handshakes all around. John and Frank left together through the labyrinth of tables, acknowledging cronies all the way to the maitre d' stand. LeYan and Jim Bob did not speak until the Congressmen were gone.

"Why'd you cut me off like that?" Jim Bob complained.

"Listen, Akkre, if you don't understand how intricate these proposals have to be, I don't want your involvement. I believe Mr. Alactra made it clear that the matter of oil rights should not surface until we have the lodge approvals more or less agreed upon."

"Well, OK, I guess he did mention that. I'll hold off for a while, but I've got people pushing me too. And I'm spending a fortune on the prospecting crew out in the boonies, doing testing. I had some proof along today. Bet they would have been impressed. By the way," Slick Jimmy tried a smooth segue, "Were you surprised to be met at the Dulles gate?"

"I was. It helped."

"You know—I thought we might discuss a little strategy this afternoon. You know, have a few drinks and the like."

"No way, Akkre. I'm out of here."

"I'll give you a rain check, then," Jim Bob said.

LeYan breezed out of The Cloak Room so fast that Jim Bob was left bumbling his way between the tables and up to the bar.

"How'd it go then, Slick?" Sam, the bartender, asked.

"Mark my words, Samuel, she's mine. It's just a matter of time."

21

LeYan cabbed to Dulles, glad to be rid of Akkre. After arriving at her departure gate, she went to a kiosk and called Bill Anderson at the Alactra office. "Bill, I tell you that this Jim Bob Akkre is a loose cannon. Besides that, he's dumb! Left alone with the Congressmen, he could screw up the whole deal. I think that Mr. Alactra should contact his old buddies in Dallas and arrange to put him in the corral. I had a good session with the Congressmen, after I got Akkre shut up; but one thing is sure—I have to get that Ryker eliminated before he influences anyone in D.C."

"I got a call from your local contact, Charlie," Bill Anderson said. "LeYan, he is as nervous as a cat on top of this conference table. I'm not sure how long we can depend on him."

"Money talks with him. Call him and tell him that you are sending him a grand for investigative expenses. We'll have him by the short hairs."

"OK, will do."

"Also, you know that I sent Hands to the area today to put the fear into Ryker and his nurse," Le Yan said. "We could have Hands pay a visit to Charlie as well, if he doesn't take kindly to your bonus. I'll be back in Chicago tonight. See you at the office in the morning—not very early.

* * *

Hands was a picture of contentment, asleep in the large, First Class seat on the Northwest flight from O'Hare to the Twin Cities. Two flight attendants watched him closely and giggled behind shielded mouths. He had to be awakened to fasten his seat belt when the plane started its descent into the airport. The lucky lady chose to run the back of her fingers along his bare forearm to arouse him. He thanked her with a wink.

Having negotiated distant gates and long hikes with his carryon bag before, Hands elected to save his energy for later. He jumped on a patrolling electric cart and proceeded to the gate for the flight to Duluth—the beginning of his assignment in the far north. He glanced at the new wrist watch that LeYan had left with his ticket. It was just past three.

* * *

Jim Bob took a leisurely cab ride from The Cloak Room back to his office. He smiled at his good fortune. The lunch had been an exciting experience, in spite of a slight rebuff from LeYan. "She needs me, she'll come around," he said.

The cabby said, "What you say?"

J.B. said, "Just thinking out loud."

Every now and then, he took time out to think, instead of react. He sat at his huge desk. He pushed away enough files and papers to make room for a list, that he inked on the back of a 9x12 mailing envelope:

- Alactra needs my influence
- I know who to influence
- Colombia cartel pushing/results
- Don't trust Rebelde
- Not sure about Senate
- Is Ryker dangerous?
- If so, I'll get him!
- Make LeYan an offer she can't refuse!!

After the exhausting thought process, he moved to his commodious side bar for refreshment. Then, taking the issues in order of their importance, he put a check beside the last item on the list and called to his secretary. Miss Hilda Kaski knocked on his door. He had recently been careful to acknowledge her courtesy, instead of roaring, "Come in, damn it!"

Hilda had come with the office, and had been the *right hand* of her unfortunate attorney boss, who never wrote her from his white-collar incarceration. Jim Bob initially had dreamed about a young, voluptuous Mickey Spillane type secretary, but faced with the efficiency of Miss Kaski, he realized he should get his jollies elsewhere.

"Please, (oh, he was nothing, if not polite) send flowers to this person." He handed her LeYan's card. "The message should say, 'Looking forward to our next meeting! – J.B.'" He smiled, at the subtle nature of the message, as Hilda departed to do his bidding.

"Next issue, Rebelde," he said to himself. Then—

"Hilda," he bayed, forgetting the polite approach. She trotted back in. "Get me Ramon Rebelde. By now he should be at the Lumberman Hotel in Fall River, Minnesota."

While he waited, he ruminated about his situation: the Colombian cartel expected a lot from him. Whatever this wilderness oil cause was all about, there were laws and factions dead-set against making any disturbance in the wild. Was this a project for him? For twenty years, he had worked in D.C. and Dallas to get favorable laws passed for his oil industry clients. This boundary waters involvement, that both Alactra and the cartel were paying him for, might not be more than a pittance, compared with his regular projects in the Gulf, but who knows—the access through the Great Lakes to eastern markets was certainly an unusual opportunity. The intercom buzzed. "Mr. Rebelde is on," Hilda announced.

"Ramon, how's it going?"

"No problem, if I didn't have your dumb locals to deal with!" Rebelde growled.

This was not the response that Akkre expected. After all he was (or, would be) *paying* Rebelde. "So what happened—" he started to ask.

"Just got a call from my lead guy in the bush. He says he had to waste a guy in a canoe. It got too close—they had to take him out."

"They *killed* him?"

"Who knows, but we gave him major trouble. He won't be moving for a while."

"Well, that's *your* problem," Akkre said. "What's the answer with the oil or copper findings?"

"That's a good question. Another damn good question is 'When do we get paid?'"

Faced with a question he did not want to answer, Jim Bob, as usual, danced. "Let's talk Thursday, when you get back to Dallas."

"Same place?" Rebelde cooled down and asked.

"Ramon, buddy, why don't we meet at the Derrick Club—then wheel over to The South-Country Inn, up on the hill in Dallas. It's one of my favorite places. Presidents even stay there. You can order whatever obscene amount you want. The world will be at your fingertips."

"OK, big spender. One o'clock? Bring your checkbook."

Akkre did not offer a concluding comment. He was already into his next issue. He did not ask Hilda to dial his next telephone number. It was known to possibly three other people in the United States.

"Cartoom Enterprises," the pleasant voice, with Spanish influences, answered.

"I would like to speak with Zatar," Akkre said.

"May I please have your name?" she asked.

"This is Jim Bob Akkre. Zatar knows me."

"Please, sir, will you allow me to request someone to return your call?"

"Thank you, Miss. I may visit your office soon. What is your name?"

"Sir, that is not allowed. Thank you sir." The line was dead.

22

The attendant on the small jet from the Twin Cities to Duluth understood the situation as they were boarding. Hands just stood without moving or speaking beside the regular aisle seat that he had been assigned. Something like "two pounds in a one pound bag" would have characterized the problem. After she consulted with the suited businessman sitting comfortably in the forward bulkhead seat, Hands added his looming presence. The suit did not like the idea, but he soon realized that it was the better part of peace and quiet to exchange seats. He earned a nod from Hands as he moved. The giant rested for the forty-minute flight, in spite of the penetrating stares of the accommodating attendant.

After landing in Duluth, Hands took a cab into town to the Ford dealership to rent a 4WD F150 pickup. Having used the morning for his visit with the blue-eyed waitress and the noon hour cabbing to O'Hare, he was starved. It was now nearly five o'clock.

The metabolism of a man like Hands required regular attention. When not fed on schedule, his generally peaceful nature could schiz into a malevolent *Mr. Hyde* at the slightest provocation.

Hands saw the *Sky Blue Tavern* sign as he drove north out of Duluth. Promising "Booze—Billiards—Barbecue," it fit his urgent needs completely. Three pickups—two of them monsters with jacked up suspensions and huge Wrangler off-road Goodyears—joined a few less ominous vehicles in the parking lot.

The tavern was one-story but looked like a steep mansard roof torn off of a three-story building and plopped down to ground level. The front cedar shingles were weathered nearly black and had a gouged ridge at bumper height running the width of the building. Three dormers in front accommodated a single green entry door in the center and fake windows on each side. Actually the "windows" were signboards—one proclaiming the "Booze—Billiards—Barbecue" and the other announcing Tuesday as "Ladies Nite (proof required)" and "Amateur Strip Show."

Hands parked his red Ford 150 Ranger alongside one of the monsters and opened the green entry door—to a pitch black hole. At least that is what the contrast from the bright sunlight did to anyone first entering.

After a few seconds of eyeball adjustment, the neon signs and recessed lights above the bar, on the left, stood out like white-hot horseshoes on a blacksmith's anvil. Then the rectangular lights, hanging over the two pool tables, came into view. They partially illuminated dark booths running along the right-hand wall.

Three mud-hued figures at one table and two at the other were barely visible until one of the apparitions bent down to use his cuestick as a ball buster. After the multiple "crack" sounds, the cue ball and fourteen numbered balls frenzied around the green felt. The macho force of the "break" propelled the fifteenth off the table toward the makeshift stage at the unlighted end of the large room. The hanging light cast a half shadow over the shooter's unshaven face that was punctuated with a cigarette dangling from under a bush mustache.

Four hotshots at the bar reacted in unison towards Hands as he did a somewhat exaggerated hunch to miss the top of the entry door frame. All but one of them jerked back immediately toward the suspendered bartender and began a heated mumbling, while leaning over their beers. The fourth, somewhat smallish barfly gaped with his beer mug frozen, in limbo, a foot and a half below his wide, open lips.

Hands moved over to the first booth to the right and squeezed in between the dark mahogany bench and the laminate-covered table. It was hinged to a wainscot board on the wall.

The tall, balding bartender smirked one more time to his bar patrons and raised the bar service counter. With obvious reluctance, he walked slowly toward the first booth. His thumbs, firmly hooked in his suspenders, drew his unbelted waistband one inch away from his beer barrel belly.

"What'll ya have, shorty?" Beer Belly had apparently experienced some success leading with a tough opener, especially in the view of nine regulars.

"Two Buds and barbecue," Hands said.

"No barbecue 'til six," Beer Belly said.

Hands gestured toward the front door and gruffed, "Sign says barbecue."

"Like I said, shorty—no barbecue 'til six!"

Hands, in one sweeping motion, grabbed both of the bartender's suspenders with his left hand, pulling him forward while rolling the beer belly over the edge of the table and bringing the balding head—eyes now bulging—to within six inches of Hands' face. A second later, he casually turned his left wrist to glimpse at his new watch. The motion brought his captive's left ear down solidly on the table.

"Two Buds—NOW—and large barbecue by 5:15 or I microwave them myself and you with 'em," Hands said to the head on the table. He then raised the beet-red face and shoved, propelling the sweating bartender back six feet.

The three pool players at the nearest table had halted their game and stood in a line, cues at the ready. When the bartender recovered his footing a distance away, the poolies moved in to stand shoulder-to-shoulder across the front of the booth. Hands looked up calmly.

One of the poolies said, "Nobody treats Big Mac like that. We're telling you to get out!"

Hands smiled and slowly placed his huge mitts palm down on the laminate table top.

The talker then made his second critical error—he

started to raise his cue stick. The non-talkers started to follow suit—but not nearly fast enough.

Hands flipped his giant paws and thrust them under the table near the hinge end. With a full-throated grunt for leverage, he ripped the top free of the hinges and in the same motion broadsided the three stick-holders with it. Two of them fell bass-ackwards onto the floor. The talker checked his fall and came up with his stick in a martial arts mode.

Hands picked up the top, which had started to break into the three boards under the laminate. He ripped off one board, raised it and came down between the talker's hands, splintering the hickory cue into a mess of pointed shivs. The other two started to move towards Hands, but the table board lashed an arc, inches short of their heads. They backed off.

The two pool players at the other table, used to talking more violence than acting it—other than against their girlfriends—took steps toward Hands. Another glance at the flashing table board, with the jagged, broken laminate, and they moved to the far end of their table. They began absently chalking their cue sticks.

Hands stepped through the scattering players and debris and moved to the bar. The perspiring bartender had neglected to start Hands' barbecue order and had just placed beers in front of two of the barflies. Hands grasped the two bottles, leaning over one guy's head. He looked at his watch and threw a stare at the bartender. "Twelve minutes—one large barbecue. I'll sit here."

The smallish barfly had seen enough. He slid off his stool and made fast tracks for the door.

By six o'clock, Hands was back in his pickup for a two-hour trip to his evening's destination. He smiled. His appetite was satisfied. His adrenaline was charged just enough for whatever might come.

* * *

George Heudak relaxed in the relative vastness of Ryker's

actually moderate-size log home. He grilled a large sirloin on their Weber, heated some Tater Tots and worked through a couple Miller Genuine Drafts. He was about asleep in front of a muted TV when he heard an engine.

He exited the back door and took the path through the pines to the construction yard, instead of the driveway. He saw the Ford pickup standing in front of the tool shack. At first he wondered if Joe had a new truck and had come back to check things out. In fact, the figure he saw was bent over, fooling with the door's locks. As he approached silently, he saw that the figure was about two of Joe and was dressed in a sport coat.

"What's up, buddy?" George said loud enough to cover the thirty feet between them. The giant of a man did not even look up, but said, "You Ryker?"

"You got the wrong guy and the wrong time. You can leave the way you came in."

"Where's Ryker?" Hands said, closing the distance between them.

George could see that his adversary had him by six to eight inches in height, fifty pounds, three inches in reach, and he had never seen hands like that—ever.

"I told you he's gone. He won't be back!" They were now six feet apart.

"Deal with you then," Hands said.

"What are you here for?"

"Tree-huggers need a lesson," Hands said and took another step toward George.

"Either get out or I'll get you out!" George said in a low voice. That appeared to end the talk.

Hands threw a punch that came so fast that George was only able to turn his head, directing the huge fist to his cheekbone and left ear. The force drove him back and he stumbled over a pile of eight-foot logs ready for trimming into landscape timbers.

George picked up one of the eighty-pound rough bark logs and hoisted it at the giant's head. In a disturbingly simple move, Hands boxed the ram away. The ex-SEAL picked up another log and this time put all his weight behind a two-hand shot-put directed at his enemy's head. This time, the force and momentum broke through Hands' barrier. Blood spurted and ran down into one eye.

George immediately clambered over the pile and ran toward the cab of the nearby log loader. The giant got into his pickup, no doubt intending to run George down.

Hands was now wiping blood out of both eyes. He didn't see George jump into the loader—he was busy trying to steer the pickup.

George levered open the giant jaws of the "clam" and wheeled the boom in the direction of the on-coming truck.

The wide-open clam banged down on the cab of the F150, crushing the top. He grabbed the clam-lever and the spiked claws compressed together, collapsing the pickup doors inward until Hands was centered in the cab. He was still holding the steering wheel, but it was now bent toward the center as well.

George cranked up the boom arm and lifted the entire F150 eight feet off the ground. The infuriated but trapped Hands jammed his fist through window glass and spoke more words than he had during the past week.

George got out of the loader, walked past the shattered window of the F150 hovering eight feet above him. "Don't know who you are, but you sure make a helluva first impression," he said to the imprisoned man who was twisting and turning like a caged animal.

* * *

George had to admit to himself that he had not been as shook since SEAL days. He made his way to the tool shack, unlocked the door, grabbed the phone and dialed the Nordland County Sheriff.

"'Lo, Dan, where'd I catch you? Out in your garage? What's the matter—mama tire you out? Oh, she *threw* you out. Well, some days are like that. Dan, you might be interested in this one. Had a little tussle with an intruder over at Rykers'. Yeah, I was sort of standing-in while

Buck and Casey are on an overnight at Marsh Lake. This guy's a tough one, but I have him cornered. Caged, actually. You might send someone over. You will find him a little up in the air. Better bring your stun gun and bear tranquilizer darts. You and three deputies would play hell getting cuffs on this guy."

23

The first morning of their canoe trip had been a disaster. However, by noon, Buck and Casey were reconciled, albeit somewhat on edge, given the slight possibility of continuing menace from across the lake. After a long campfire in the dark of evening, there had been nothing to do but make the most of their northwoods experience. The nylon, aluminum-pole tent served very well. The experiences required little space.

Paradise was contradicted abruptly, however, with the reality of Tuesday's three o'clock wake-up. Buck quietly gathered their belongings. Casey stirred, but gave no appearance of waking. He stowed the gear in the pack and carried it down to the shore—tested the hole patch and pulled the canoe down to a landing point between the boulders. The sky was black, the air deathly quiet. There was no sign yet of the unfriendlies on the opposite shore.

Buck crawled up to the campsite and opened the tent flap. He gazed at Casey.

"Morning, Miss Brown," he said crisply, mimicking her nurse's wake-up call at Olympia General. Her sleepy eyes opened with an innocence that poets write about.

"I hope you're my husband," she said.

* * *

The northern shore of Marsh Lake offered a microcosm of the boundary waters experience. Their early morning departure had brought them down-lake, well past the opposite campsite. The mist on the glassy water rose as the horizontal rays of the sun squeaked above the tree tops. They followed the shoreline closely to immerse themselves in the silent, wild sensations. The birch trees along the shoreline were fighting the pines for space. Wood ducks and mallards were gliding back and forth in the rushes, with no apparent motion, as if they were being operated by remote control. Occasionally, they would flurry up in a territorial squabble and then settle down again. A few turtles were moving among the boulders, intent on establishing positions for catching rays. The smell of the earth and water mix was standard but like nature's perfume—intoxicating.

There was no sound!

"OK, smart guy, you have sold me," Casey said, after an hour of no conversation. "If you promise me that no one will shoot at us, I think we should get out here more often."

"You're on—whenever I can take time away from the yard."

* * *

The two minds at peace in the wilderness were almost matched with LeYan's pleasure as she stepped out of the elevator into the high-ceiling luxury of Alactra International. Her expression was of instant peace. She was at home in her total world. Paulette was there behind her desk, backed by the continuing drama of the Chicago skyline and Lake Michigan shore. Ling was in his place at the marble slab front station. She knew that, in spite of his calm visage, he could easily dismantle any three intruders or charm any three Junior Leaguers asking for contributions.

"Paulette, Ling, I can't *tell* you how good it is to see you. Please tell me how *you* are."

Ling was brief but appreciative, "Miss LeYan, I am good." Paulette was more serious as LeYan approached her. "LeYan, Mr. Alactra has been quite nervous yesterday and today. Perhaps the lodge and the oil projects are unsettling him," she said.

"Thank you for telling me." LeYan gave Paulette a hug.

"Is Mr. Anderson in the office?" LeYan asked.

"He is in the conference room," Paulette said. Her blissful look, from the previous warm exchange, settled into a grim resignation, at the shift of attention to Anderson.

LeYan slowly opened half of the double door leading to the conference room. The sight of Bill Anderson, doing his thing, reviewing his Boundary Lodges presentation, gave her pause—and a smile of satisfaction.

"Hello, Bill. Hard at it, I see."

"Hi, LeYan. I'm just re-doing a few of the slides. Practice makes perfect."

"I think things are going well," she said. "As I said when I called from D.C., I don't think we have a problem with the two Representatives. We can get the bill introduced—or brought up as an amendment to some bigger bill. But even if we get the bill passed in the House, we need help in the Senate. I understand that there is a Wisconsin Senator who is very up on the wilderness idea. He may need some attention. I think his name is Wood."

"I have heard of him. He lives in Milwaukee. His name is Art Wood."

"That's it, Bill," she said. "Do you think you can get to him?"

"Could be. I'll work on it."

"One thorn in the side that keeps coming up is that we have to either keep the tree-huggers away from the politicos, or let Congress know how weird the locals really are—especially Mr. Ryker. I am confident that Hands took care of him last night. I hope to hear from Hands this morning."

"It was a good idea to send the Cousins in to sniff out the local action," he said. "From what I understand, they are presently out of trouble."

"If you call 'in jail' out of trouble." She made light of his compliment. "We *do* know more than if they had not gone there."

The scene was interrupted by a knock on the conference room door. LeYan opened it and Paulette stood there with an expression of dismay.

"Paulette, what is the problem?" LeYan asked.

"I just heard from Hands—indirectly, that is," Paulette said softly. "There was a call from the Nordland County Sheriff's office. Hands was apprehended in the Ryker yard and will remain in jail for several days during an investigation. They left a number and also reported that Benny and Luther were just released. The deputy giving me the message was quite a joker. He said that, since they were coming into their busy season, it would not be necessary for Alactra to send any more Chicago customers for their jail."

* * *

As shocking as the three o'clock wake-up had been out at Marsh Lake, it had gotten Buck and Casey home only a couple of hours after the yard crew had checked in. Casey moved directly, did not pass GO, to the shower and to bed.

Buck's adrenaline, plus the thought of the scene he loved, thrust him immediately out to the construction yard. His sensation was one of unencumbered opportunity. Like it was the first day of the rest of his life.

The home under construction was virtually complete, ready for Buck to inspect. The white, peeled logs were notched and stacked into a twenty-four foot by thirty-two foot building. The trusses in the center and at the gable ends were in place. Full-length logs were temporarily secured horizontally at the peak, at the lower end of the roof and midway, to accept roof boards that would be installed at the owner's site. All that remained was to tag each log with its numbered place in the structure, to guide in the re-assembly.

Buck worked steadily, along with Joe and the other three members of the crew. By 4:30, the structure was ready to take apart and be loaded onto trucks. Buck knew that George had already rented the semi that, in addition to his double-axle flatbed with a trailer, would take the entire home in one load. A call to George's cell phone rang three times.

"Heudak," the gravel voice answered.

"We're ready to roll, ol' buddy," Buck said. "Can you tear yourself away from all those loggers?"

"I've got the semi in my yard now."

"Great! Also, thanks for babysitting the place last night. Any problems?"

"You mean you didn't have a surprise waiting for you when you got there? Your guys didn't see anything?" George asked.

"No, nothing. What happened?"

"I can't believe that Dan got it hauled away already. When I went to bed last night, your log loader had an F150 in its clam, hoisted eight feet off the ground. The driver was still inside. He had come to visit you, without real friendly motives."

"My God, George, did he get to you?"

"Not much. Lucky the loader was where it was. I'll tell you more about it later...got to go."

"Hey, just a minute. Why don't you come over for supper and get a real meal, if you can stand steak again. I've got some mammoth T-bones. Bring your stuff and sleep over. I can drive you to your place in the morning to get the big rig. We can load as soon as the crew gets here."

"Can't fight all that planning. What time?"

"Five-thirty. The Sawbill can get along without you one night."

"I'd better call and warn 'em. They might come looking for me."

"See you about five-thirty." Buck hung up and went out to organize an early morning for the crew.

* * *

The sun streamed in the windows of the beamed living room. The wide-blade pine window blinds had been one of the few expensive house features that they had purchased in Duluth. Buck turned the rod that partially closed out the sun, burning in from the west. Casey was at work in the office alcove. They both smiled.

"I'm trying to make up for lost time, she said. "Well, actually not lost at all—it was marvelous!"

"*You're* marvelous!" he said. "By the way, you know that George is going to make the trip tomorrow with the semi. Joe and Gary will drive George's truck with the grappler on it. I thought it would be good to ask George over for supper tonight and we can go over details. I can cook steaks outside. OK?"

"Sounds good. I'll round up some salad and stuff."

"Any word from the clinic?" he asked.

"Zip. I suppose Betty called last night. I'll phone her tonight."

"You feel OK about it?"

"Like I just had a tumor successfully removed."

"That's over, then?"

"Way over," she said. *It better be!* she thought.

* * *

The Tuesday evening was old times: lots of laughing, except when George detailed his adventure of the previous night. Casey turned pale several times. Buck said he would check in with Sheriff Dan tomorrow. They talked about the truck trip to the suburb north of Minneapolis. George estimated six or seven hours to the owner's site.

"We should get a start laying down the lower logs before dark tomorrow, depending on how well the owner's contractor has done the foundation work. Should finish by dark Thursday and head back real early Friday morning," George said.

"That would be a fast turn around," Buck said.

"Want to get back for the meeting Friday night."

"You plan to make a speech?" Buck asked.

"Just want to keep the locals from getting too far out of line," George said with a smile.

"Seems to be a bit of a change in your thought," Buck said.

"Yeah, I suppose. Truck business is one thing. Future is another. There have been some strange decisions made to protect big logging companies. Like in Alaska's Tongass National Forest, where they've clear-cut seventy percent of the productive timber, resulting in erosion and a lot of silt in streams and bays. I might do this hauling thing for another twenty years. The trees go on for hundreds. If we cut down the trees and screw up the lakes, what's the use of people coming up here ... and what's the use of being here?"

"You said it better than I could," Buck said.

"I might have something to say at that meeting," Casey said with one of her wry looks. "I heard plenty about the preservationists trying to hang on to the natural course of the Colorado River. I could tell a couple of horror stories about how so-called development cost the government and taxpayers millions but never accomplished anything good for the future."

"Do it!" Buck said immediately. "If Senator Wood is there, I bet he can pick up on the Colorado issue and the whole water question. With you guys speaking up, we will keep Alactra back in the windy city."

* * *

Buck fried six eggs and a half-pound of bacon at 5:30 a.m. Wednesday. George watered the old, encrusted aluminum pot, dropped in a load of grounds and brewed some strong and black that even they shuddered at. "Should keep me awake for a while," George admitted. They left the house at six and were back at the yard by seven, with George driving the flatbed semi. Joe operated the log loader to hoist the ten-to-twelve-inch-thick logs carefully onto the bed of the eighteen-wheeler. And then they were gone!

Buck smiled. It was not like losing some happy-work, it was like gaining thirty grand! The phone rang in the shack. He hoped the house ring wouldn't wake Casey.

"Morning, Dan. I understand we sent you some heavy trouble. George gave us the whole play-by-play—right out of the movies! How's the giant doing now? Pretty rough, eh? Have you tried saltpeter in his Pablum—might soften him up a little? Good, I'm sure that the Alactra people were happy to hear that he's being well taken care of. Be sure to get him on a cattle car going south. We don't want him around here. But, Dan—thanks a bunch for handling the giant, as well as the two goons! Appreciate it a great deal."

* * *

Casey waved at Buck as she left for shopping in Fall River. As she drove past the Information Center parking lot, she saw one Chevrolet Caprice station wagon, loaded with gear and two kids in the back seat. She slowed as she approached the Center. Charlie walked out the door with the man and the lady from the Caprice. He recognized the old Subaru and waved excitedly for her to drive in.

"Casey, can you hold for a minute," he shouted as he closed the passenger door of his visitors' wagon. He walked over to her open window. "Need to talk to Buck. Could you ask him to call me here? Oh, how was your canoe trip?"

"It was good. Buck can tell you all about it. I'll ask him to call you." He walked into his official domain and she proceeded to Fall River.

* * *

Loaded cars, pickups pulling campers, SUV's and a few boxy travel homes filled the main road along the waterfront, but few cars visited the Valueline Superstore parking lot. It had been Casey's observation in recent years that most of the locals were cautious about their spending. They tried to hunt, fish and grow as much of their food as possible. Another taconite processor, lumber mill or fishing fleet would solve problems for some. Those businesses dependent upon tourists were grateful for it but found it to be competitive and seasonal. She realized that she and Buck did not contribute a great deal to the local economy, other than buying logs from George, employing four men and buying a few groceries. Two of Valueline's four checkout lanes were open to her when she had finished her tour of the store with slightly more than a half-full cart. *Time for me to be cautious also*, she thought. The idea of no clinic check and only moderate profits from their business did not create a picture of luxury. She packed the three bags of groceries into the back seat of the Subaru and drove out. "Damn," she said to the steering wheel, as she let an insidious notion steal into her consciousness: *that high-dollar job with Alactra would solve the money problems.* Buck had been totally dismissive—disdainful actually—when he hinted about their offer. She knew at the time that he was trying to convince himself as much as her that it was out of the question. She knew then that she wanted to kill the portage challenge as much as Buck. *It just wasn't right!* She knew that the two of them would go all out if it became necessary.

I could grow my own vegetables and raise chickens, she thought. And then a more logical thought occurred to her—that she could get a part time job at the county hospital in Fall River. Closer to home and not supremely focused on one arrogant MD.

* * *

The one location in town that was busy this Wednesday was the Serve-U convenience store. Nearly all twelve gas pumps were either in use or blocked. The pumps closest to the store opened up and Casey pulled in behind an SUV that no doubt was taking on enough fuel to at least make it home.

She sensed another customer entering the lane behind her. As she opened her door and glanced in the side mirror, she saw something she did not want to believe—a dark green Jaguar sedan. Another furtive glance confirmed her worst fears. The Jag's license plate read "MD-1."

She instinctively closed her door again, as if to block out the possibility of confronting Thacher. Then she realized that would be ridiculous.

She slowly opened her door again, eased back to the filler hose, and began the gassing process facing away from the crouching Jaguar. *Why did she always feel trapped when he was around?* Then the unavoidable happened.

"Casey! What a break seeing you here." The doc squeezed along the pumps, still carrying the window squeegee he had been using.

"Hello, Dr. Thacher," she said.

"It seems to me that's where we left off on Saturday. I think we know each other a little better than just doctor and nurse," he said.

Casey busied herself with the filler hose and said, "There is no need to. I won't be returning to the clinic."

"Yes, Betty showed me your note. Have you talked to her? She is quite confused," the doc said.

She isn't the only one, Casey thought, but said, "No, I haven't. I've been out of town. I will probably call her at home tonight."

"Well, it probably is a good idea for you to take some time off—with your homework demands and all. But we certainly—and I for sure—want to have you come back to the clinic."

"At this point, that is doubtful," she said as she immediately returned the hose to the pump before the tank was full.

After the drivers from the vehicles waiting in line finished eyeing Casey's shorts and the doc's Jag, they began grumbling about the holdup.

"I've got to get checked out," she said.

"At least stop in to see us—maybe Friday," he said. She made no comment and hurried in to the cash register.

* * *

Wednesday's late afternoon graying skies were the opposite of Buck's mood. He sat in the leather club chair with his feet up in front of the stone fireplace. It was alive with the crackling of dry birch logs. This was his first nothing-to-do relaxer in front of the fire since Christmas.

Dangerous, he thought. He could get used to this. Casey brought him a Leinie and deposited herself in his lap, holding a glass of wine.

"I saw Charlie today," she said.

"Wonderful." His irony was palpable.

"He seemed to be up-tight—wanted you to call him at the Center, but it is obviously too late. Maybe you can call him at home."

"Lately, his calls mean nothing but trouble," Buck mumbled into his beer.

"He must have some extra interest in this portage deal," Casey said.

"At times, it sure seems that way. I'll try to check that out when I call him."

"I have to ask you a question that you may not want to answer," Casey said softly.

"Stop teasing me. What is it?"

"If Alactra had given you a firm offer of multi-bucks, would you have considered their proposal?"

"You do get to the balls of an issue," he said with a serious smile. You know damn well I will never lie to you. Hell, yes, I'd *consider* it. What's the price of a man's convictions? Million bucks? Who knows? Maybe I would rationalize that I could put some of it back toward the environmental effort. But, I hope, even with a big offer, I would say no—because it's more important to keep the boundary area safe from development. Dumb, huh?"

"Not so dumb. I'd be happy if that would be your decision." There was a light kiss and Buck reacted in several directions. One of them was to lift Casey and carry her halfway to the telephone. "I'd better call Charlie before you con me right out of my jeans."

"Go ahead, the con can wait."

* * *

Charlie brought Lillian a cup of tea. He had rinsed their early supper dishes and stowed them in the portable dishwasher, hooked by rubber hoses to the kitchen sink.

"Charlie, you seem nervous again tonight," Lillian said. "I thought that you had been feeling better lately—since we had our little talk about the big company."

"Oh, I'm OK—I saw Casey this afternoon and asked her to give Buck a message. He may call tonight."

In about a half hour, the black, circa thirties, cradle telephone on his roll-top desk barely rang once before Charlie grabbed it. "Henstead home." He often answered as if it were a retirement home. "Buck...hello. I'm going to move to the kitchen phone. Lill's in the living room."

"I just wanted to tell you that I have been talking to this lady at Alactra since the first day," he blurted out.

"She's no lady," Buck interrupted.

"Well, she certainly *sounded* good, at first. She said that if I would keep her informed of local attitudes and plans, she...Alactra...would pay me considerable money...even an annuity into the future. I could not resist at the time, but now, I don't want to be involved. They want to push their plan over, regardless of how locals—or anyone else—feel about it. I don't want any part of that. Lil senses that it is wrong."

"I understand what you are saying, Charlie. But you've done OK. What we need to do now is to play along, without making any commitments."

"This afternoon I got a FedEx from them, with a check for one thousand dollars!"

"Not surprising. If you talk to them, don't turn it down. But DO NOT CASH IT! Hold it for evidence, but do not cash it. It will be like you never received it—except you signed for it. But you didn't know what was in the FedEx. So don't worry about it. We will work it out. Gotta leave now. I have a pressing engagement."

* * *

The next morning compensated for the previous day's weather insult and promised a northwoods wonderland. Shortly after dawn, Charlie fixed himself toast, Wheaties and instant coffee. He moved out the kitchen door to the redwood picnic table in the small brick patio. He sat quietly, took several deep breaths and gazed at the surrounding mix of trees and native shrubbery. He looked with pride on the half acre of grass he kept mowed. He was at peace, except for the nagging question of what to do about Alactra. He was glad he had unburdened himself to Buck. But he knew he could still play it both ways. Could he be that shifty? Will LeYan call?

The kitchen phone jarred his reverie. He wondered if LeYan had ESP. He answered as was his custom.

"Charlie, this is David." The surprise equaled his disappointment.

"David, it is only a little after six."

"I'm sorry. You know that it is 7:15 here. I had to call you before I left for the office. I got tied up last night—had to attend a fund-raiser."

"No problem, I was up anyway. It is just a wonderful morning."

"It's already hot here. Probably a ball-buster today, with heat and humidity. Anyway—I wanted to tell you about yesterday evening. As I was leaving, my guy, Representative Wayneson, had a visitor in his office, a Representative Saguaro—or something like that. I hung around because Wayneson had asked me to be available. So I was able to listen-in pretty well. They talked about a lunch they had with the Alactra company person. She must be something! They discussed her for several minutes. The upshot was this: they agree that the Alactra proposal is interesting, but they need to get some direct, local input. They sure are not going to visit the area themselves. They are asking the Alactra babe to get a BWCA local to appear at a preliminary sub-committee hearing this coming Tuesday, June 29. All I can say is that the two Congressmen seem to be open-minded about introducing the bill. They seemed to think that if they got good vibes from the local guy, it would stand a good chance of passage."

"David, this is very good information. Believe me,

we appreciate your help. All I can do is to report this to the people here who are most involved."

* * *

He had expected it. The black phone had become to him like the red "panic" phone in the Oval Office. It seemed to ring even louder than usual.

"Charlie, here," he said with conviction.

"Charlie, this is LeYan. I am sorry that we have missed connections lately. Did you receive the check?"

"Yes, I did."

LeYan filled the momentary conversation void. "We wanted to show our appreciation for your continued help. Have you spoken to Mr. Ryker recently?"

"No. He has been gone the past two or three days. Have not seen him." If he had been hooked to a polygraph, Charlie's reading would have zigged off the chart.

"I have an important message for him. You had better write this down, Charlie." He got a paper and pencil. The excitement built. He was alert and ready to hear more *insider* information.

"OK, please tell Mr. Ryker that United States Representatives Wayneson and Saguaro request that he appear at a preliminary meeting of the House of Representatives subcommittee next Tuesday at 10 AM. He will certainly receive an official confirmation of this request tomorrow."

"I will try to reach him, or at least leave a message."

"Thank you, Charlie. We owe you a great debt and you can be certain that we will repay that debt to both you *and* Lillian—one way or the other!"

24

Twelve hundred miles straight south of Charlie's conversation, three slender Texas beauties sashayed slowly among the booths and tables of Fort Worth's Derrick Club. While they were ostensibly modeling lingerie, available at local shops, they were never adverse to meeting new friends among the rich and not-so-famous.

Jim Bob Akkre arrived at 12:30. His regular booth was ready. The beauties paused a bit longer and smiled a bit brighter at him but stayed just beyond arm's reach. In fifteen minutes, Ramon Rebelde entered the Club like he owned it. He was not alone. A smallish man in a dark blue suit, white shirt and dark maroon tie followed him dutifully, almost as if he were a tag-along chimpanzee.

"Ramon, you're surprisingly on time—even early," Akkre said, remaining seated in the red leather circular booth.

"You need a surprise now and then. This is Thebold Themis. He knows everything about anything," Rebelde said, continuing immediately, "Now before we get into any details, my chart shows that you owe my company forty-six thousand dollars. Thebold here has the backup documentation."

"As you say, before we get into the details, where are the results" Akkre replied.

"Our contract did not specify results, only reports of findings," Rebelde said, eyeballs lasered on Akkre. "I've given you the preliminary reports. I have more with me. I need payment for time and expenses up to now!"

"Listen you, I could have you thrown out of here!" J.B. reacted to the demands.

"I could have you blown away within the next half hour," Rebelde said calmly.

"OK, I'm writing you a check! See—here's my checkbook, damn it!"

"Good start," Rebelde said.

"So, what do *you* give *me*?" Akkre insisted.

"Maybe a half billion in oil, copper, and nickel. Maybe a billion."

"Prove it!"

The readings I gave you before were just a start. We made other tests and the whole area is ripe! But you have to get the titles and the rights."

"That's being taken care of. Now, I promised you a big dinner at the South-Country Inn, and I'll do it. Give me your new readings and we'll move. Incidentally, Georgia and the other two ladies will be out again in a minute, now that their program is over. I'm sure that they would be happy to make your acquaintance. Anyone in my booth is a friend of theirs."

"You may have surpassed my expectations—but not by much," Rebelde said.

"Before we leave, I need to call the executive vice-president of Alactra. Order a round and enjoy the view." Jim Bob Akkre eased out and walked to one of the five commodious telephone booths. The floors, walls and ceilings were covered with deep red plush carpeting, making them soundproof and very comfortable for the Derrick's highrollers. He closed the booth door, sat on a small, upholstered chair and dialed the red phone on the miniature desk. The five booths had facilitated billions of dollars of transactions in the ten years since they had been installed.

LeYan Syn grabbed her cell phone and identified herself.

"Jim Bob Akkre here, LeYan, honey. I'm at the Derrick Club in Fort Worth—called to let you know that I just received a report from my exploration company. Potential in the sticks up north could be in the billions!"

"That is interesting, but not very," she said. "At this stage, the sticks, as you call it, is off limits. Unless we move a bill through Congress, there is no oil, no lodges and no fat fee for you."

"I thought you had the Congressmen going your way."

"I might have, but the whole deal could be wrecked if this local tree-hugger brings some kind of negative mandate to D.C. The Congressmen want to get local input at a preliminary hearing next week. I have managed to find out that the locals are meeting tomorrow night. I might be able to get a couple ears in there to determine what they are thinking."

"LeYan, I need to get back to my important guests here at the Club."

"Well, go then, it's your nickel. But think about this: we have to lose the Ryker guy. I have someone who can get to him if he comes to D.C. If that doesn't work, it will be your turn."

"Well, if you can't get him to roll over, I would be surprised. But if you can't, I may have to give him and his sweetie a taste of southern hospitality."

"If that has to happen, you'd better not get too rough. It could backfire on you and the project."

"Just rough enough, LeYan, my lovely. Just rough enough. But, if I take care of that little problem for you—you will owe me—big time."

Jim Bob's two *important* guests were languishing in Akkre's largesse. Thebold Themis was looking askew—tie loosened, cheeks flushed, glasses fogged, like they had been sprayed but not squeegeed. Georgia had extended her stay at the Club, courtesy of Rebelde's whispered promise of big bucks from Jim Bob. Her hand on Thebold's thigh had his eyes rolling. Rebelde was munching on a lobster appetizer and quaffing the Derrick Club's only over-the-top imported beer.

"I see that you gentlemen were not disturbed by my absence," Jim Bob said. He stood in front of the table with hands in a knuckle-cracking mode.

"When in Rome, do whatever the host will pay for,"

Rebelde slurred, through a swallow of lobster. It was apparent that he was enjoying this moment nearly as much as the forty-six thousand.

"Rebelde, I may give you a chance to add some value to those pieces of paper that I have over-paid you for. I may need to entertain some people out at your friend's Jambalaya Joint in the bayous. The entertainment may not be entirely to their liking."

"Relax, I've got you covered on that one," Rebelde replied. "Huge Henry and I can set it up. I'll call him before we leave here. Now, I think Georgia's got a friend coming. We can pour Thebold into a cab and really find out how *Jim Bob Does Dallas*, starting at the South-Country Inn."

* * *

Ramon Rebelde always opened one of his infrequent conversations with Huge Henry in the same manner: "Henry, just how huge are you?" Henry would always answer: "Ah'm so huge that you wouldn't believe it!" Usually, Rebelde would call to set up a crab and gumbo feast, for clients, at Henry's Jambalaya Joint in the bayou country south of Baton Rouge. The atmosphere was so beautifully menacing and the Cajun crawdads and gumbo so delicious that the Joint attracted a wild variety of adventurous folks from nearby, as well as New Orleans and even "Big D."

"Henry, we've got a little deal for you," Rebelde said.

"I'm not so sure about your deals," Henry said. "What's the gig?"

"An associate of mine may have some people coming in that he wants to impress."

"Who's the associate?" Henry asked.

"Jim Bob Akkre."

"Not my favorite," Henry said. "Last I recall, I didn't care if he lived or died."

"Know what you mean, but he's paying big money. And he's easy to con. Actually, my guys will take care of any influencing—just want you and Paradise to be the perfect host and hostess. We'll do the rest."

"The last time I saw your screwy bunch, I had to throw them out—actually broke my own record—threw one of them sixteen feet. They were trying to hit on Paradise. Good thing she didn't get near them. They probably wouldn't be of much use to you. Or, don't you need balls in your line of work?"

* * *

Every log home sold and delivered over the past six years had been an occasion for a minor Ryker celebration. Some had been elaborate, some just a bottle of good wine. This Thursday, Casey and Buck decided that a Sawbill lunch was right. They even took a table in the dining area. Casey ordered a vodka gimlet, which she usually had to describe in detail to the waitress. "I liked them in Colorado," she said. "Why not have one here?"

"Been a while since we have had lunch here," Buck said.

"Yes, it's been a while," Casey said slowly, with a glow that changed a lunch into a prom date.

Buck looked toward the door and then back to Casey with a frown. "That's all we don't need now—is Charlie," he said.

"Buck, Casey, I'm so glad to find you here," Charlie said.

"Charlie, sit down and have a drink. You look like you could use one." Buck waved the waitress over and pointed to Charlie. Charlie said "VO" and in what seemed like less than a minute, she was back with his VO and Seven-Up.

"You know that I would like to get out of this whole portage and Alactra deal," Charlie said, with some excitement. "It's bothering Lil and, let's face it, I'm too old for all this."

"What's the latest?" Buck asked.

"I got two phone calls this morning. One was from

David, bless his heart. He called at 6:15 to tell me that the Congressmen are leaning toward approval of the portage project but they want someone from this area to come to Washington to give input from the area citizens."

"And you're thinking..." Buck started.

"Buck, it's *got* to be *you*," Charlie interrupted.

"Can't do it! I'm not straying from the homestead—or the homemaker." He gave only a slight glance at Casey.

"You know, I could visit my favorite aunt, in Arlington," Casey said, her eyes rolling toward the ceiling and her lips pursing.

Buck looked surprised...pleased. "Charlie, sometimes I think I don't even know this girl! So, what is the plan?"

"After David called to warn me, I got a call from the Alactra lady...er, person. She confirmed what David said. She had already set up a place for you to stay Monday night—some townhouse in Georgetown. It seemed like she was sure that it would be you. We can talk about this at the meeting tomorrow night, but I am sure that the members will agree that you should represent us. Of course, all the expenses that Alactra doesn't pay will be paid by the county group."

"Not that the extra cost is a big deal, but I don't go anywhere without my new *Partner in Crime*." The "Partners" exchanged a smile. Both had watched the public television dramatizations of Agatha Christie's novel, *Partners in Crime*. Casey had read the book.

"I will assure you that the county will be totally supportive—or I will tell 'em what's what!" Charlie said as if he were pounding the table.

"Don't bet too much on total support," Buck said. "If we get over fifty percent that want to fight the development, I think we will be lucky. But OK, I guess you have our acceptance of the plan to tackle Washington. Now, on another subject, I am going to call Senator Wood this afternoon and offer to pick him up in Duluth tomorrow morning. Maybe he can help us get a mandate at the meeting."

* * *

Reaching a Senator's office is not difficult. Getting through his shield is something else. But it is possible.

"Mr. Ryker, the Senator will be with you in a few minutes," one of his secretaries or aides promised.

"Buck! How's it going?"

"Senator, just checking in for tomorrow. I will be happy to pick you up at the Northwest gate in Duluth. It is then about two hours to Fall River."

"I have been thinking about this trip," the Senator said. "Have a special request—if it's possible."

"You name it."

"It has been years since I have actually been out in a canoe in the BWCA. Do you suppose there is a way I could get a taste of it?"

"There is a way! We could drive from Duluth, through Fall River, straight to a boat access and put you in another world ten minutes from launching the canoe."

"That sounds fantastic! My secretary will give you my flight times and I will meet you in Duluth. This will be an unforgettable experience for me."

* * *

As soon as Buck hung up from speaking to the Senator, the phone rang and he picked it up in the office.

"Buck, this is George. Everything is moving along at the site. We are going to break at 5:30 for supper and let the contract carpenters get the plywood on the roof rafters. The local building center is due here in a couple hours to drop off the shingles and rolls of felt paper. They will probably have the bundles of shingles stacked on the roof peak before nightfall. We will come back after supper to clean up a few details. We'll take care of anything that's left tomorrow, early. Should be able to vamoose at least by nine-thirty or ten. We will be back in time for me to get to the meeting."

"That is great, George. The plot is thickening here. With any luck, Casey and I will be mounting an offensive against Chicago and Washington, D.C. within the next couple days. We won't need the boats or the helicopters, but our urban guerrilla tactics may come in handy."

25

The early morning trip to Duluth was getting old, for Buck. Then he remembered that the Senator would have to depart D.C. about 6 AM, fly to Minneapolis, and grab an Airlink flight about nine to get to Duluth by 10 AM. He realized that if the Senator was willing, he should be.

Senator Art Wood arrived on time, was well met and the two of them headed north.

"I cannot speak for everyone you will see tonight, but I greatly appreciate your interest and involvement in this controversial issue," Buck said.

"Like you, Buck, I have spent enough time visiting the northland to have a personal need to preserve it."

"Since you mention 'visiting'...that is one of the hot buttons. Some people who have lived around the BWCA over the years have come to...well...*resent* the visitors...that they visualize as coming from rich suburbs of Milwaukee, Chicago or Twin Cities. Even though they like the tourist dollars, the year'rounders often look at the two-weekers as intruders who want to keep the locals' backyards silent and wild."

"I can't blame them for that, I guess," the Senator said. "Maybe I would feel the same if I lived right next to the BWCA. But still, the situation is similar in most every tourist-oriented economy. Those who benefit have to deal with the influx for part of a year. Then the locals usually have a good share of the year when they have the area all to themselves."

"Each new law change is a precedent to take away more of the wilderness protection, I believe," Buck said. "The primitive nature of the area is in danger."

"I agree. But now what about this company that wants to construct buildings?"

"Alactra International, based in Chicago, is trying to convince Congress to pass a law, or change the law, to allow them to build tourist lodges on portages between BWCA lakes."

"Oh, a Voyageurs theme park?" the Senator mused, gazing out the window at Lake Superior.

"Exactly!" Buck said. "Can you imagine it?"

"Yes, I can imagine some folks wanting it. You would probably get a fifty-fifty vote on it being a good thing."

"But, how would they vote in ten years, when jet skis and high-powered motorboats were zipping all over the lakes and being hauled quickly from one to another?"

"Probably the same fifty-fifty, but the fifty against it would have given up and gone to northern Canada to feel the old individuality and quiet that they used to get in the BWCA." The two men had drawn scenarios that halted further thought for several minutes. Neither of them wanted to proclaim any further philosophy or guess at what might be the consequences.

"The information that we present to the county tonight is still sketchy," Buck finally said. "There will be members there who will not have given a thought to this portage matter until this meeting. This won't be a Senate caucus."

"Well, that is good news. At least, the opinions will be based on individual motivations, without outside influences."

They drove the North Shore highway and the Senator silently enjoyed the shoreline and the craggy, rock-edged rivers running to the big water. By the time they had finished Casey's great lunch basket, they were through Fall River and out to a BWCA landing.

Jake Sharker had his canoe in the water, ready to go. They strapped on life vests and shoved off into Eagle Lake. With three men paddling, they reached the Eagle Lake portage in less than an hour. They scrambled up the bank to stand at the highest point, from which they could view the lake on each side.

"Not room for a lodge on this portage," Senator Wood said.

"No, but there are a half dozen portages within a couple hours canoe time from here that could be possible," Jake said.

"Of course, water and sewer would be a problem, but it could be solved," Buck said. "I went out to High Portage last week—about three miles north of here. Good possibility that might be Alactra's first objective." They returned to the canoe and started back.

"Buck and Jake, this is a rare treat. I appreciate the trip—gives me a good reminder of the value of this wilderness and this silence. Of course, this hour or so is nothing like several days of canoeing, portaging and camping, but I have done that before and this trip brings the old feeling back to mind."

"Senator, we can head back to the landing, drive to my home for supper and get to the meeting by seven," Buck said.

"I am looking forward to hearing the opinions of your local folks," Art Wood said.

"Oh, you'll hear opinions, all right, Senator. I can guarantee you that!" Jake Sharker said, from his stern position in the canoe. He noticed that the Senator was doing his best to keep up the stroke. Jake continued, "One thing I've noticed at these meetings: fellas seem to like to say it big and hear themselves talk. What they actually do about it is something else. Buck, I think we need to draw the picture of the pros and cons straight and clear. Then ask the tough questions."

* * *

Casey woke early Friday morning and smiled in anticipation of spending the day doing some cleaning and business accounting. However, as soon as she settled at the computer, her thoughts strayed. *Jonas had said she should at least stop in Friday—a reasonable idea since she had not yet talked to Betty.* The more she thought, the more she rationalized. She could leave at 12:30, get to the clinic about one o'clock, and just stay a few minutes. She needed to buy a couple of items in Fall River before their D.C. trip anyway. She would still get home in time to get some work done.

That thinking shot the balance of the morning, most of which was spent in grooming and selecting the best casual outfit she had.

By 12:15 she was already wheeling out of the driveway. *Cool it*, she thought, *or you'll get there too early*. She marveled at the excitement generated by a trip she had made hundreds of times.

The miles from Fall River to the clinic seemed endless until the parking area and building she knew so well came into view. But there was not one car parked in front. *Maybe Betty and the others parked in back for some reason*, she thought. She stopped near the front entrance and approached, half expecting the door to be locked.

As soon as she entered, she saw that, while the front waiting area was lighted, the small window in the door to the back area was dark. There was light, however, in the small window in the swinging door to the employee lounge.

As she looked, the swinging door opened and Dr. Jonas Thacher strode through—as surprised as she was at the meeting. He seemed taller and tanner than usual in a brown suede jacket, white shirt, and fancy jeans.

The shock and electricity of seeing him momentarily precluded her breathing as well as her speaking. The doc, however, was able to rise to the occasion. "Casey, what a nice surprise."

"Where is everyone?" was all that she could utter.

"Oh, it's June 25th—my birthday—so I gave everyone the afternoon off. We thought that if you were coming you would be here by noon. So will you join me for a birthday lunch? You certainly look like you are ready for a little celebration."

Casey cursed herself for spending so much time trying to look her best. *What was she thinking?* "Doctor, I came to say goodbye to Betty and the others—not for a party."

Thacher stepped toward her—too close for her comfort, and she retreated two steps.

"I am beginning to think that you are afraid of me—of the way you feel about me."

That may be true, she thought, *but you'll never know it.* "Doctor, you can think what you want, but my time here at the clinic is over. I will call the clinic people at home and tell them of my decision."

"Well, as they say, 'we can still be friends,'" he said.

"We can be the same as we have always been—acquainted from work. Goodbye doctor." Casey pushed through the doorway and out to her better friend—the old, white Subaru.

* * *

Twenty-nine members of the Nordland County citizen's group filled the meeting room at the Nordland Bay Lodge, on the shores of Lake Superior. Most were already seated and jawing with each other. Senator Wood, Buck, Casey, George and Charlie filled their coffee cups at the side table and sat down.

Charlie stood up from his chair at one end of the table. Not an arresting figure, he used a firm projection of his voice to command attention.

"Fellow members, please—it is seven. Let's get to it." The jawing almost stopped and he continued, "First thing, I want to acknowledge United States Senator from Wisconsin, Arthur Wood. Thank you for taking time to be with us. I promise we won't ask you for a speech. You have expressed your interest in simply being a listener.

"As you all know, this is a special meeting to follow up last Friday's discussion of the proposal by Alactra International to build lodges on portages. To put this in perspective, I will ask Claude Tremayne to give us a brief history of the BWCA."

Claude did not stand. He looked calmly around the room, meeting, for a split second, nearly every eye. "I have never talked to a Senator before," he said, "I'd better watch my language." He paused for a brief chuckle from the crowd. "Now, I could start this brief history with the early 1800's, when Canada and the United States had opposing ideas about who should *own* all this land we are now sitting on. Or, I could start with 1854, when the treaty was signed by the Lake Superior Chippewa Nation to give up all entitlement to their native lands.

During the next century, people developed opposing ideas about how the land should be used. In 1964 the first Wilderness Act was signed. It allowed boat motors on some lakes and motorized boat carriers on some portages. In 1978, the Boundary Waters Wilderness Act added more land to the BWCA and applied more restrictions, with the intent to gradually reduce motor usage further. This Act was not fully implemented until a 1992 court ruling required it. It was also stated that further restrictions on motor usage would begin in 1999—six months ago. Before the last ruling could take effect, as you know, a compromise bill passed Congress last year to allow motorized vehicles to be used to transport boats and gear across the two main portages.

"That is about where we stand now. If last year's easing of restrictions will be a precedent for more activity or building on portages, no one knows." Claude was through.

Charlie spoke right up, "Claude, we appreciate your quick summary. That brings us to the current challenge— the idea of constructing vacation buildings, with water, sewer, motorboats and all that goes with it, in the midst of the wilderness that has been fought over for centuries."

"Charlie, you seem to have a strong point of view. Maybe everyone does not look at it as that bad," Jack Waidlow, area commissioner interjected.

Buck noticed that Charlie was taken aback by this abrupt challenge. "Jack, I don't really think Charlie said anything out of line. He simply said some facts. But we are each going to have points of view. We are here to express them."

Ernest Blyson, chairman of the Commercial Development Committee, spoke next. "Well, I think we are all making too much of this. So what if a couple of lodges are built? What's the big deal?"

"The big deal, Ernest," Coach Geoff Brush said quickly, "comes when you paddle—or even use your ten-horse motor—to visit the wild lakes and come up to a portage. If you find all kinds of activity like floating air mattresses, people jumping off docks, music playing, jet-skis circling—it's just like any other lake in the state. The peace and quiet of nature is gone. The boys and girls that come to our Scout Camp are looking for something different than they could find at their hometown lake."

Ernest countered, "You *know* it's never going to be like it was in 1854."

Janice Overbly, from the Forest Service, had to weigh-in on that comment. "I think you need to get out there. I was out two weeks ago and portaged into several lakes. There was not another person on those lakes at that time. There was not another sound! It was probably no different from 150 years ago."

Amos Nedderly owned the hardware store in Fall River. He said, "I have lived in Duluth and Minneapolis and I have lived right here for the past five years. I can now get in my pickup, with the canoe tied on, and be in total wilderness in a half hour or less. Naturally, a person around here begins to take that for granted. When I would come out here from Minneapolis, or even Duluth, it was an absolute thrilling experience! I wouldn't want that to be taken away—not from me, nor my kids—nor from anyone—from California to New Jersey."

"Why should we who live around here have to change our way of doing things for a bunch of people who only stop in for a couple weeks?" Ernest still hung in there.

"Just to put a practical note on it, Ernest, how many of us *could* still live here if we didn't have 200,000 or so visitors coming into the BWCA each year?" Jake Sharker said. "I know that the reason I get customers for canoe trips is that they want that special feeling of getting back to the quiet of nature."

Jack Waidlow insisted, "I would take my chances with all that in order to take my fishing boat and motor anywhere I wanted. I believe that a lot of people feel that way."

Charlie inserted a question for Jenny Alburton, a local leader of youth groups. "Jenny, what do your girls and boys say about the trips you take them on to the BWCA?"

"These kids are teens, mostly thirteen to sixteen, most from urban areas," she said. "At home, they are mostly impressed with the latest hip-hop, flashy MTV and adolescent sex. But when we get to the first BWCA lake, they invariably say, 'It's so *quiet*! I *love* it.' They immediately stop shouting at each other. They respect the quiet. They respect nature. They start to respect each other."

No one spoke for several moments after Jenny finished.

"All this is fine," began Jimmy Wheater, owner of a major Fall River restaurant, "but what does it have to do with Alactra lodges? It looks to me like they would bring in big bucks right away and for some time to come. After all, the development would be good for all of us."

Casey raised her hand at Charlie. He nodded to her and said, "I am sure you all know Casey Ryker."

"What I am going to say does not relate directly to the BWCA," Casey said. "In the late eighties and early nineties, I learned a lot in Colorado schools about the way that rivers and natural river basins were pushed around by politicians and bureaucrats. To put it bluntly, I can tell you that billions of taxpayer dollars were spent because Congress got manipulated into approving dams and irrigation projects. Many of the projects cost more per acre than the land was worth. They were approved by some in Congress so that they could get projects in their own states passed through. That may be the way things work, but my point is that we cannot rely on elected officials to save the future of our wilderness. If we as individuals don't fight to keep what little we have left, it will be taken for profit and politics." As Casey sat down, there were a number of affirmative nods and a few wondering looks at the Senator.

Senator Wood rose, probably as much as anything to stretch his legs. "As Charlie mentioned, I am only an observer here—basically to listen and learn. Casey, I am aware of the situations in Colorado, and other places in the west, where water resources have been bandied about with little value resulting. I will only make one comment and it happens to back up what you just said. Nothing is more powerful than a firm mandate from voters. Obtaining that clear mandate is the tricky part. But that process has to start right here, like you are doing. If an issue is left up in the air, at the local level, other influences will become dominant—such as government forces that have their own motives. If necessary compromises cannot be made by the citizens most involved, the compromises made later will likely be less satisfactory. In other words—Jake's words from this morning as a matter of fact—'ask the tough questions and come to firm conclusions.'"

It came time for George to have his say. He got the nod from Charlie and said, "Got to say a couple words about motives. Mine have gone all the way from protecting my business first to realizing that we have to take care of the future *now*. Buck and Casey have taken a lot of pressure these past two weeks—and they probably have the least to gain of anyone. They simply want to do what's right for the future." He got a couple of laughs when he confided, "I wouldn't normally say anything good about him so's he could hear it." Then he continued,

"My statement is this: I think it is more important to save the wild portages, and the silence, than to gain some temporary business or make the BWCA easier to use."

"George, I think that is clear enough," Charlie said. "I believe we would all be interested in hearing just what Buck and Casey *have* been going through."

Buck rose and said, "I am going to be brief. For one thing I will leave in a few minutes to return Senator Wood to Duluth. There is no need to go into details. It is clear that Alactra is pulling out all the stops to keep me and anyone else from saying anything negative about building on portages; George had quite a battle with one of them Monday night. Ask Sheriff Dan about that. We can handle that stuff, but it is an indication of how they can be tough. And, I don't expect it is over yet. Now, Senator, if you are ready, we can head south. Casey can stay and represent the Rykers. I think she's doing pretty good so far." All eyes turned to Casey and she blushed.

* * *

Both the Senator and Buck had been up since dawn. Neither looked forward to a trip from eight o'clock twilight to ten. Buck would have another two hours back, after he delivered Senator Wood at the Radisson overlooking the Duluth waterfront.

Charlie took the opportunity of Buck's departure to bring up the Washington, D.C. trip. When he mentioned that Casey would be going also, she felt she had to say something: "For some reason, he wants me to go along—protect him from the city girls, I guess." There were some good-humored laughs and elbow jabs from the gentlemen. Casey blushed again. There was no question that the members approved the representation by the "partners."

Mac Smalle was not a man to hide his thoughts. Also, he believed that he was good at summarizing. "One thing that I think is relevant is that over the years, elected officials have used the BWCA as a political football—siding with one group or another to gain votes. Sometimes they gained votes, sometimes lost—even lost elections because of the BWCA. That tells me that we need to do what the Senator says...make up our own minds based on what we think is right in the long run. If that takes some compromise, let's do it here."

Some members were stirring and pulling their chairs back before Smalle finished. Charlie quickly adjourned the meeting with the assurance that the results of the Rykers' trip would be promulgated.

* * *

George lightly apologized to Casey for his beat-up red truck. He cleared a raft of junk out of the front seat and helped her up onto the torn and sagging perch.

"If I had known you would be riding with me..." George started.

"You'd have done what? You don't own anything else," she smiled.

"Don't have much need for a fancy vehicle," he said.

"That reminds me, George," she turned to him, "it's about time you find yourself a dream girl."

There was a slight pause and he said quietly, "She's already taken."

"*George*,", Casey tried to be brusk, through a lump in her throat, "you are not supposed to *say* things like that!"

"You are right! I didn't say it! You didn't hear it! Like a sound in the forest. If you don't hear it, it wasn't there. Oh, one other thing," he hurried, "Sunday night, I got a call from an old girl friend of mine...well, she's not old...and not really a girl friend. She is from Texas. Her daddy is filthy rich. I went to Aspen once to see how the other half lives. She was there skiing. We had a good time. Told her I'd call her...didn't. Sent her a birthday card once, after we had all gotten here. So she knew how to reach me. She wants me to visit her some time...out on the big ranch...practically a whole county. I said maybe this fall. She tried to pin me down, but that's dangerous, you know...could get trapped."

26

Both relief and latent anxiety flushed through Charlie's mind on Saturday, as he called the Alactra lady, collect, on her private number. He knew he was on the verge of cutting himself away from any further Alactra association. However, Buck had said to hang in there long enough to learn LeYan's plan. So now, ironically, he was becoming a double spy—or double agent—or whatever they called it in the espionage movies.

"LeYan here," she answered.

"Hello, this is Charlie. We had a meeting of our citizen's group last night and everyone agreed that Mr. Ryker should accept the invitation to appear at the subcommittee meeting."

"Charlie, slow down." LeYan interrupted. You seem to be almost out of breath."

"I believe you said that the Congress meeting would be Tuesday at ten. Will you please tell me again where he should stay Monday night and what time he will be picked up for the meeting. I will write it down."

"OK, Charlie, here's the plan." She gave him the Georgetown address of the townhouse borrowed for the night from a large investor and political friend of Alasom's. "Ryker should arrive after three in the afternoon and take his gear with him in the morning. Our hired limousine will pick him up at 9:15. Mrs. Kontz will prepare his dinner when he gets there and attend to any other needs, before she leaves at seven. "One more thing Charlie—are you certain that Mr. Ryker will be alone?"

Charlie swallowed hard through his lie and realized he was getting better at it. "I am certain."

"Also, Charlie, and you had better write this down,

too, his appearance at the sub-committee has already been leaked to the press—these politicians, you know. There will be a high-ranking reporter calling Ryker late afternoon to get an appointment to interview him in the evening. It may be late, nine or ten, when they can get together. Be sure he understands that this will give him an opportunity to establish his position."

"I will pass all this along to Buck today. Thank you for all your help." Charlie had not only developed the ability to lie, but also to schmooze.

* * *

Gracie Fielding was feeling better by noon on Saturday in her large Washington D.C. apartment. The Friday evening call from LeYan Syn, offering her five hundred dollars for a proposition, had been enough reason to celebrate. Now, at noon, she soaked in her large-enough-for-two whirlpool tub. Then an almost-cold shower in the separate travertine marble enclosure. A couple cups of coffee, interspersed with a Bloody Mary, brought her back to her twenty-eight-year-old self, instead of the old crone she felt like when the ocean sounds had begun on her cassette-radio alarm. Gracie Fielding was, of course, a far cry from Janette Bloskie from rural Ontario. Her grandfather's stories about WWII, the White Cliffs of Dover, the bombings and the courage of Britain's civilians, led on by patriotic entertainers like the songbird, Gracie Fields, convinced her to select a Gracie name, when she entered into a field of *entertainment* along a much different line. When she had returned last year for her 10-year class reunion, she had to be careful not to describe the fact that she lived in a two-level flat that had been professionally decorated and installed with heavy-duty locks, visual warning systems and an audio/visual intercom.

Gracie had played many roles—some she wanted to forget. LeYan had positioned the scam "a high-ranking reporter"—a first for Gracie. At least, in this project, she could wear regular, or provocative, clothes. And then an address in Georgetown that any entertainer would fight for. She knew that she had to get up for it...eat, don't drink...well maybe a small tumbler of vodka. After all, she was only supposed to lead him astray. And the gig wasn't until Monday.

* * *

Jake Sharker and Mac Smalle were early for their never-to-be-missed Saturday nooner at the Sawbill. Charlie walked in with an unusual degree of pensive going on in his expression. He didn't even acknowledge his buddies but blurted out, "It's getting heavy, gents. I hope Buck can handle it. I called him to join us, but he said he had to do double-time today to get business done before he leaves for D.C. this afternoon."

"It's good Casey is going along. He's been getting a lot of lady-pressure lately from these trips—well, I guess only one time so far," Mac said.

"You're right! And I'm not so sure this trip is going to be different," Charlie said. "The company lady wanted to be certain that he was going to be alone. No telling what they might be thinking and planning—seems to be a game they play—trap 'em like a muskrat and then put 'em on TV—or in the newspaper."

* * *

The best thing in the world is to have another order to start, after you ship one out, Buck thought, late Saturday morning. Well, not the best thing—the best thing was to have Casey practically attack him when he got home from Duluth at midnight Friday. He wondered if something at the meeting or during the day had turned her on. He shook his head at her recent mysterious behavior.

But, this new order was going to be a big one—main building plus two side structures. He could see the forty-five grand slipping right into their available capital. A new saw complex could increase their efficiency by fifty percent. Casey would factor that into their business program and tell him the precise value of the capital addition. In his head, he knew what it meant.

They decided to take the old Subaru to Duluth in the afternoon. No one would be interested in sabotaging that antique. No North Star Motel this time. Nothing but the Radisson and dinner in the Harbor Room.

The 6:40 AM flight to Minneapolis Sunday morning was a terrible time. Get up at 5:30 to get to the Duluth airport by 6:15. Casey moaned all the way. He could not blame her.

After a quick flight to Minneapolis and another to D.C., they descended into Dulles International. The Northwest pilot warned them. "It's going to be hot, folks. You just left seventy degrees in Minneapolis, now you have ninety-two and equal humidity here in our nation's capital. It is one-o-five eastern daylight time."

Casey and Buck moved directly to the sidewalk by the baggage area. With only carryon luggage, they were able to beat the throngs somewhat. Aunt Miriam soon acknowledged their waves and pulled up to the curb.

"Casey, Buck, it's been years. So glad to see you."

"Miriam, I wish we were just dropping in for a casual visit," Buck said. "That's what we would *like* to do."

"Well, what *are* you up to?" Miriam asked.

"As unaccustomed as we are to political dealings, I am supposed to appear at a sub-committee meeting. And I think they are trying to pick me off. One way or another, I think only Casey can save me," Buck said.

"I'm ready to put my money on you two," Miriam said.

The early afternoon ride to Arlington was easy, but not a breeze. They parked in the carport and walked in the clematis-edged doorway. "Now for a glass of iced tea in an air-conditioned porch," Miriam said. "In April it would be a nice breezy natural-air porch."

Miriam's small but comfortable condominium provided a perfect calm before the storm.

* * *

A light breakfast out on Miriam's porch was a tease. No way that the rest of the day could be as pleasant.

Buck cabbed downtown for lunch with Senator Arthur Wood. He had an iced tea. Buck had one Heineken. They reprised their boundary waters trip, like two boys years ago would have talked about their agates and marble shooters. The gleams in the eyes told more than the words. The Senator had not uncovered much about the bill to be introduced in the House of Representatives. He was aware of the "leak" that identified Buck as a back-woods logger who was going to lurch into the sub-committee meeting Tuesday morning. His appearance was already positioned as a freak-out, not to be considered worth committee time.

"Buck, none of us in Washington, D.C. takes this crap seriously, to say nothing of believing it. The media just sucks it up and spits it out to justify their being there. What you say in the meeting tomorrow will be respected, unless some committee member has got a reason to give you trouble about it. Stick to facts that you know and no one can touch you."

The Senator said that he was not a close friend of either of the Representatives who were involved with the subcommittee session. However, he believed that they both were men of good reputation. Buck knew that it was going to be every man for himself. He would take the Senator's advice and tell it like he saw it. He wondered if he should invoke some Teddy Roosevelt philosophy about preserving natural resources. *No*, he thought, *not his game, philosophy. Just the facts, man.*

He asked the cabby to drive over to the Capitol and then past the Mall on the way out to Georgetown. It was more inspiring than he thought it would be. The man George Washington hired to establish the original design for the city encountered severe challenges from those who had little vision. Fortunately L'Enfant persisted in doing what was right, and with the President's support, left a legacy that instills pride, over two hundred years later.

Buck knew that he was far from a George Washington, or the engineer, L'Enfant, for that matter. But he could still do what *he* knew was right.

The cab driver had been impressed when Buck gave him the address. "That's some high-priced real estate around there," he said. They stopped in front of a tall, narrow building that immediately abutted the structures on either side. *Not what I would call home*, Buck thought.

The fancy doorbell got results. After what seemed like multiple locks being overcome, the *vault* door opened to the cheery presence of Mrs. Kontz. She welcomed him and directed him into the first floor parlor. The entry was not large, but did house a stairway *and* an elevator. *That's how they do it*, he thought. The parlor scene was in a word, traditional. Another word was comfortable. The pillowed sofa faced multi-paned French doors that led out to a small patio. Some expensive-looking wrought iron outdoor furniture occupied most of the patio. It was defined by a seven-foot red brick wall at the side and ends. At the moment, the daylight from the French doors kept the room from darkness. An adjoining room held a mahogany dining set.

"Mr. Ryker, I can turn up the lights, if you wish. Here is the rheostat switch. This cabinet opens to provide most every kind of liquor. There is a small kitchen in here," she explained as she held out her arm to suggest that he look. The kitchen reminded him of the galley of a luxury yacht he had visited while at the Coronado Amphibious Base. A navy captain had given his platoon a "thank you" trip one afternoon. That captain had resources way beyond his four-striper pay. Mrs. Kontz informed Buck that she would prepare a steak for him if he wished. Or, there was a variety of sandwich material or pizza in the refrigerator. She could stay until seven, if he wanted to dine about six.

"Thank you, Mrs. Kontz. I really don't need much for supper," he said, using the local-Minnesota 'supper' instead of 'dinner.' "There certainly is plenty in the refrigerator for me. In fact, I can just make myself something later. If you will show me the sleeping area, you can take off." They made use of the elevator to the third floor. She informed him that the second floor was the owner's private office and bedroom suite. The elevator opened into a small sitting area, beyond which stood a king-size bed with dark mahogany headboard. A padded bench in front of the window and a large chest of drawers matched the aged, heavy-wood look. Buck asked about the fourth floor, so they went up: another entry/sitting area and bedroom/bath suite, similar to "his" suite, but done in pickled-white finish over heavy pine. He had in mind a use for this country-look layout.

Mrs. Kontz left after explaining the system of locks and alarms. He visualized his platoon attempting a break-in—not easy. As he walked back into the parlor, the phone rang. Before he picked it up, a contradiction occurred to him: with all the heavy-duty security for the front door, the French doors seemed strangely vulnerable.

* * *

"Buck Ryker."

"Hello, Buck Ryker," a somewhat slurred, sexy voice said. "This is Gracie Fielding...from Associated Press."

"Hello Gracie, what's up?"

"Well, I hope *you're* up...for a little visit this evening. In talking with LeYan Syn about their Boundary Lodge project, she told me you would be appearing at the subcommittee meeting tomorrow..."

"That's why I am here."

"This is...an important...issue. We would like to...get your side of the story. Is there a chance I could come over this evening?"

It seemed to Buck that the voice was trying to read from a script. "Could be," he said.

"I have some...commitments early—how about 9:30? I do have your address," Gracie said.

"Ring the bell a few times. I may be asleep in front of the TV."

A feeling of confidence and control filled Buck's thoughts—with one exception: for complete satisfaction, he needed his partner. *Five-thirty*, he thought. *They're probably talking a blue streak and getting ready for an evening meal.* He visualized the pickled pine suite and made a call.

"Hi, Miriam, how are you—oh, things are good here. I've got an entire Georgetown mansion to myself. Is Casey handy?"

After a minute Casey came on the line. "You're sure that you are by yourself—some of those mansions come complete with live-in Barbie dolls.".

"There is only one Barbie doll I'm thinking about. I bet you would like to see this place."

"You mean, come there *tonight*?"

"Why not, it's probably only fifteen, twenty minutes away at about eight-thirty. Miriam could bring you over after you eat."

"Well, OK...it feels kind of strange...like I'm a call-girl." Her voice sounded small.

"Funny you should mention that...but we can talk about that later," he said.

"You sound awfully sure of yourself," she said.

"When you're a big man on the Beltway, that happens," he said. "I believe I gave you the address—OK, I'll see you then—about 8:30—not much later—I've got a reason—actually a couple of reasons."

Buck took full advantage of the goodies in the refrigerator but only *looked* at the liquor cabinet. The wide range of bourbons, scotches, rums and vodkas, with vermouths and other mixes could float a heavy-duty cocktail party. Another unexpected phone call interrupted his bountiful buffet.

"Buck Ryker."

"Mr. Ryker, this is LeYan Syn. Just checking to see if you made it. How are your accommodations? Is Mrs.

Kontz fixing you dinner...you are doing your own...aren't you handy. Have you received a call from the reporter, Gracie Fielding? Oh, she's coming over at 9:30? That's good. And our driver will be at your door tomorrow morning at 9:15 to take you to the Congress meeting. Good luck." Not the languorous LeYan from the Alactra passion pit. This was the all-business LeYan—and soon to be monkey business, he guessed.

* * *

The Lounge was a well-known Georgetown watering hole with just enough Beltway biggies and legal hangers-on, abusing their expense accounts, to make it a favorite of more-or-less social ladies on the way up—or down. The ratio on this Monday evening was about right: two-and-one-half men to every woman. The half was not interested, leaving two potential payers for each lively lady.

In spite of her attractiveness, verging on glamorous, Gracie Fielding did not cause immediate head-turning. She selected a small table away from the crowd. She had promised herself that she would just have a drink...not more than two...to fortify herself for her evening's assignment. It was unusual for her to have a first appointment with a man, without some previous recommendations. But five hundred was five hundred, and since this LeYan knew the owner of the Georgetown place, it couldn't be all bad. Still, all this reporter-make-believe made her a little nervous.

A couple of vodkas, added to several touches before she left home, would make her seem more at ease. She looked up to see two suits moving toward her table like sharks toward a piece of red meat. She knew the lines so well. First there would be their variation of "What's a girl like you doing in a place like this?" They would identify themselves with doubtful names but impressive credentials. She knew for certain that the drinks would come...and they *were* both quite good-looking and interesting. If she were not already engaged, she might consider turning off the meter. She cautioned herself to take care of business first; she could not screw up the Alactra gig. Her second trip to the ladies room was more difficult than the first and she had to excuse herself a few times for bumping people and almost lurching into a table.

* * *

The traffic from Arlington had been heavier than Buck had guessed. It was nearly nine as Miriam and Casey entered Georgetown. Casey was visibly nervous but did not try to interrupt Miriam's chit-chat. They arrived at the townhouse at straight-up nine. Casey ran up the steps and was about to ring the bell when Buck opened the door.

"Buck, I'm sorry we're late. Miriam does not drive quite as fast as we do."

"No problem, it's just good to see you. Now I will have to do some things that will seem strange to you, but please bear with me. I will explain them all to you in an hour or so. In the meantime, I have a place for you to relax that I think you will like." They took the elevator to the fourth floor and stepped into the sitting area of the Pickled Pine Suite.

* * *

"Fellas, I really have to go...maybe one last...one..." Gracie finally traded her phone number for their help in loading her into a cab. She gulped deep breaths of the humid night air, through the wide open window.

The cabby recognized that it was the better part of valor, or something—getting rid of her in exchange for a large tip. He helped her up the steps at the Georgetown address and steadied her hand as she pressed the doorbell numerous times.

She finally seemed able to stand without hanging onto the door handle. Buck went through the unlocking routine and opened the door to see a beautiful, if slightly fuzzy, young lady. "Come in, Gracie," he said. The fact that he immediately took her arm did not appear unusual at all to Miss Gracie Fielding *from the Associated Press.*

Buck had been watching baseball and enjoying a Tuborg beer—a brand that he had vaguely heard of but never had paid for. He sat her down at one end of the pillowy sofa. She seemed to sink into the softness like into a dream.

"Would you care for a drink?" he asked. "We seem to have everything here: scotch, bourbon, vodka."

"Yes, that...would...be...nice." She lifted her head and smiled more sweetly than probably was her custom. Buck realized that it would be the server's choice. He poured her a highball glass of vodka, with a touch of tonic, that would certainly test her consciousness.

Gracie accepted the glass of vodka like she had just crawled over the desert into an oasis. The contents could just as well have been cool, clear water the way she absorbed nearly four more ounces of the booze. No more comments were forthcoming. Buck tried a question: "Do you like your job, Gracie?"

After a few moments of thought, she answered slowly, as if each word were a struggle. "Oh, most of the johns...are OK...but some nights...you really get...some we-i-r-d..."

"How about the Associated Press?" he asked. The question appeared to place a large burden on her. As she laid her head back against the soft sofa, Buck was able to catch the highball glass that was about to slip out of her hand.

He watched her for five minutes. She really was a pretty girl. Then her mouth opened and the sounds began. No one can look very good in that condition. He went out to the entry and took the elevator to the fourth floor.

Casey was busy reading one of the current magazines in the sitting area, as he knocked and stepped in. "Do you have company?" she asked without looking up.

"I did have, but my company is either extremely bored or she has passed out." He briefly explained, to Casey's amazement, what he thought was going on. His plan now was to give Gracie a rest in the third floor suite. He explained the lengths to which the Dragon Lady would go to assuage the insult of his rebuff in the Chicago penthouse. With Casey's nurse-like guidance as to the accepted methods of moving a dead-weight body, they got Gracie tucked into the huge mahogany bed. They quietly descended to the main floor parlor and then Buck started over again:

"Would you care for a drink?" he asked. "We seem to have everything here: scotch, bourbon, vodka."

"Don't try that on me, sailor. I would accept a glass of wine—whatever color you have," she said with authority. "What did you give *her*?"

"She was gliding on thin air when she got here. The cabby had to practically carry her to the door. When I was sure I understood her mission, I did help things along with a glass of vodka. Too bad, somewhere in her is probably a good person."

"Oh, yes, I have heard of those ladies with hearts of gold—usually someone else's gold," she said.

Buck handed Casey her white wine and sat down beside her on the sofa. One dim patio light on the brick wall outside shone through the French doors to provide the only illumination. "Does a sailor get rewarded for staving off this wild woman and returning to his true love?" he asked.

No sooner had they begun to sample the full length of the comfortable sofa than Buck reluctantly raised his head. "What's wrong?" Casey reacted to his distraction.

"Unless I miss my guess we are about to be interrupted," he said. "But don't move. Just act natural."

"Are you kidding? Buck, get off!"

They didn't get a chance to act one way or another. The bright flash momentarily blinded them and illuminated the entire room—especially the love bench. After rubbing the bright sparks out of his eyes, Buck tried to peer through the doors.

Casey rolled back and forth to get Buck's near-200 pounds off of her body. He could barely make out two men standing right outside the glass-paneled doors. It looked like they both were in the ugly-American uniform: Bermuda shorts and wildly figured shirts hanging over tremendous girth.

The flash hit them again and the ugly bodies retreated. Buck got up slowly, walked out into the patio and looked down toward the end wall. The heavy wood, curved-top door was standing half open. He thought, *they had to know the door would be left open.*

The couple rode up to the third floor and checked on their guest. She had not moved since they placed her there. "Unless her bladder wakes her up," Buck said, "she'll be there when we leave in the morning."

"What will happen then?" she asked.

"We will be picked up at 9:15."

"We?"

"Of course! I will need you by my side for moral support."

After a couple of glasses of wine, a night in the garden of Georgetown was far from a total loss.

* * *

Benny and Luther roared away in great spirits. "I have to admit," Luther said, "I think it would be hotter'n hell in our suits. This D.C. place is not fit for regular people. Can't wait to get back to Chicago and that lake breeze."

"How about that hot action that we photographed!" Benny bragged. "That babe LeYan hired sure knew how to squirm around like she was enjoying it. If Ryker sees those pictures, he'll do what ever LeYan wants, rather than let the nurse see them. Look for a telephone booth. I gotta call LeYan right away." They soon located an outside booth near a convenience store.

"LeYan, Benny here. Yeah we got two great flash shots and then left. Like you said, that back door to the patio was unlocked. We walked right up to the French doors and took the pictures. They were going at it hot and heavy. No...no one could see us with the bright flash going on. Did you say that girl was a redhead...she looked darker than that, but except for the flash, we couldn't see anything."

"Now, Benny I want you to take the film to the all-night photo place and order twenty prints of each," LeYan said. "This is very important. You must insist that they are ready by 9 AM tomorrow. Then bring them to J.B. Akkre at that Congress building—the one to which you have the map. Meet him no later than 9:30!"

"It will be done. Those pics should get Ryker in plenty trouble...yes, we did get the summer clothes...should fit right in here in D.C.," Benny assured her.

27

Jim Bob complained, "LeYan, honey, what an ungodly time to call—it's not even eight o'clock. Oh, I've got plenty of time. The meeting's not until ten!—Yes, I remember—your guys are supposed to have incriminating evidence about Ryker that I show to the Congressmen. Hopefully they will withdraw their concerns about locals and press for immediate passage of the portage bill.

"How do I know these guys? Dressed in what? We'll be lucky if the gay-bashers don't pick them up first. OK, 9:30 in front of the House Office Building on Independence. Yes, I know it well. The Longworth Building."

* * *

Benny had to practically beat Luther to get him up after their wild night terrorizing the nation's capital. Benny and Luther hustled out of the motel at 8:45.

"Get a move on, Luther. LeYan said we had to pick the prints up at nine or else." They hurried out to the 1986 Cadillac. Luther had finally prevailed and they had picked out an Eldorado at Rent-A-Wreck. They raced to the twenty-four-hour-service photo shop just off Pennsylvania Avenue. Benny had to ring the bell on the counter three times to rouse the clerk.

"Where are our prints?" Benny demanded of the wiry, curly-headed fellow, as if the shop existed solely to service him.

"When did you bring them in?" the clerk asked with little enthusiasm. He did not even look at Benny.

"We brought the film in about 10:30 last night. The guy guaranteed they would be done by nine this morning."

"Yeah, well he quit after last night also. We don't give no guarantees, mister!"

"Listen, buster, we need those prints NOW! It's an emergency. They're for a Congress meeting—going on in less than an hour!"

"Hang on to it. I'll see what I can do."

* * *

The black limousine eased to a stop in front of the Georgetown residence at exactly 9:15. Buck had left the townhouse door stand open to facilitate their departure through the security system. Also, he expected Mrs. Kontz, the house lady, any minute. She arrived, almost simultaneously with the limo.

As the Rykers walked out, Buck introduced Casey to Mrs. Kontz. They exchanged pleasant smiles. "Thank you for getting me settled last night," Buck said. "Oh, by the way, you will find an extra guest in the third floor suite. I believe she is a friend of LeYan Syn. We did not get a chance to talk much. She needed a good night's sleep."

Buck introduced himself to Carlos, the young driver, officially dressed in black suit, white shirt and black tie. The limo pulled away and Buck said, "Incidentally, Carlos, where are you taking us?"

"To the House of Representatives Office Building," Carlos answered.

"Where do you go after you drop us off?"

"I hover—and wait for you to come back out."

"You mean you would be available to give us a tour later?"

"Anywhere you say, sir."

"That is very nice of someone."

"I believe that it is Alactra International that has engaged the limousine."

"Well, well, how sweet of LeYan," Buck said softly to Casey. He checked his watch. "Do you think we can make it there in thirty-five minutes?" he asked Carlos.

"We should arrive in front of the building right about 9:50, sir."

* * *

Benny was becoming distraught. Luther had remained in his Caddy and was hanging on lovingly to the padded steering wheel. Benny couldn't stand it any longer and hollered into the back room, "It's nine 9:35, goddamn it! I've got to have those prints NOW!" As he finished his demand, the clerk walked out and began methodically inserting them into various papers and envelopes.

"Here, gimme those," Benny screeched. He grabbed the prints out of the clerk's hands and threw a twenty on the counter.

"Get us to that building on the map, Luther—Longworth or something. We're late already!" They both peered frantically at the street signs, trying to follow the tiny map sketched on the fax that LeYan had sent them. Benny was also trying to figure out the description that was typed on the paper. "This guy's name is Jim Bob Akkre. He's supposed to be 190 pounds, good six feet, wavy brown hair, blue blazer, light blue shirt and red tie—sounds like one of those news anchor smoothies on TV," Benny calculated.

* * *

It was exactly 9:50 as Luther jammed in front of a black limousine that was attempting a smooth positioning at the curb in front of the Longworth Building. It was the center structure of the three House of Representatives office buildings, situated adjacent to the Capitol Building.

"Geez, Luther, you just about creamed that limo! Now, you see any 190-pound, wavy-haired smooth guy in a blue blazer?"

"There's only one guy out there, standing on the steps," Luther advised, pointing in his direction.

"No way that bozo is 190. He goes at least 230 or

240. And he's s'posed to have brown hair. What little *he's got*, it's half gray." Benny was hyper.

"He's the only one out there. Better try it," Luther said, hanging on the Caddy steering wheel with an obvious display of proprietorship. In a minute, he noticed that an extremely animated discussion ensued between the two sweating heavyweights.

"Where the hell you bin—the damn meeting starts in less than ten minutes," Akkre growled.

"Photo shop was late. Besides, you don't look none like the description I got," Benny said.

"You're not exactly a pretty picture yourself. Where'd you come from—Coney Island? Now, where are the prints?"

* * *

The uniformed Carlos opened the limo door, glancing with disdain at the old Cadillac that had just cut him off at the pass. Casey slowly and gracefully emerged, followed by Buck. Carlos' glance away had shielded him from the unavoidable raising of Casey's fashionably short skirt, as she slid out the door. She smiled, catching Buck's long stare. They were both unused to her in a skirt. Buck shook Carlos' hand and said a few words, while noticing the confrontation between the bulging blazer and the ugly American in the shorts and Hawaiian shirt. Ugly looked somewhat familiar, but Buck had not seen a Hawaiian shirt since Panama.

* * *

Benny and Jim Bob looked at the prints together, both for the first time. The world stopped for a moment. Benny could not believe what he saw. Then he looked, with panic, at J.B. Akkre.

"That's not the right broad! That's the nurse...the Ryker broad...and there she is...by that limo with Ryker!"

Jim Bob moved faster than he had for years. He left

Benny standing there and ran up the steps, two per stride, until he caught the Rykers.

"I'll bet you are the Rykers," he said, trying to parlay his puffing into puffery. "I am Jim Bob Akkre, a representative of Alactra International."

"Hello," Buck said. "This is Mrs. Ryker and I am Buck."

Jim Bob took them both by the arm and led them the remaining steps, up to the Longworth Building entrance. "I am so glad I caught you here. There has been a delay in the proceedings. Will you please wait here for a few moments while I make a telephone call?" He walked part way into the building while punching numbers into his cell phone.

"Hello, LeYan. This is Akkre. I only have a second. Your boys blew it. They got pictures of Ryker and *his wife* wrestling on the sofa. We can't show those to Wayneson and Saguaro. We'd get laughed out of town!...right! I'll run in and talk to the two Reps...tell them to get to the Chair and tell him that the Rykers couldn't make it...postpone the hearing for a couple weeks, 'till after the Fourth. OK, I'm gone!"

Akkre waved at Buck and Casey and hollered, "I'll be out in a minute or two. Just checking things out. Please wait here."

"Things seem to be heating up a little early this morning," Buck said. Casey was busy viewing the magnificent sight of the Capitol and other imposing buildings. Looking further she could see the Washington Monument and, in the distance, the Lincoln Memorial.

* * *

Benny stood in dazed disbelief for a few minutes and then walked slowly to the Eldorado, where Luther was no doubt dreaming about wheeling down Chicago's State Street, commanding the envy of the crowd who would be watching.

* * *

Jim Bob was lucky. He caught Representatives

Wayneson and Saguaro before they had ascended to their chairs on the raised level in the front of the committee room.

"That is unfortunate," Wayneson said. "I hope Mr. Ryker is not seriously ill. I will inform the Committee Chairman and he will undoubtedly postpone the subject on today's agenda."

"It won't be a problem," Saguaro added, "We have plenty to cover this week, before the Fourth-of-July break."

Jim Bob took out his handkerchief as he left the room, wiped his entire face and breathed to himself, "That was close!"

Buck and Casey were still standing just inside the building entrance. Jim Bob, in a gesture of personal warmth and gratitude, put a hand on the shoulder of each of the young, cool, vigorous-looking people. "Thank you for your patience. The Chairman of the sub-committee had to postpone the subject of the portages. They are so jammed this week—you know, the week before they break for the Fourth. He sends his sincere apology and promises that your testimony will be valued when they can reschedule.

"Now, I understand that LeYan Syn has reserved the limousine for your use throughout the day. Unless you have to leave Washington immediately, I suggest that you be my guest for a lovely luncheon at the Bombay Club—one of Washington's finest. Your driver can give you an interesting tour prior to that."

Buck mentally grimaced at the thought of wasting a lunch with this guy around—until Akkre relieved them by saying, "Just give the Maitre d' my card. He'll put the lunch on my bill." He presented his "BMOB" card to Buck and guided them down to the limo, where Carlos appeared and opened the door. As a parting gesture, Jim Bob offered to procure accommodations for the night or provide return tickets.

"Thank you, we will stay at a friend's house tonight and we have our tickets for departure tomorrow."

"Would it be possible to have the telephone number where you are staying? There may be some news from the meeting that I could give you this evening." Casey accepted another BMOB and wrote the number for him.

"Well, so much for our day in the political spotlight," Buck said, after Jim Bob had left.

* * *

Benny got up enough courage to call LeYan after lunch.

"LeYan, we couldn't help it. We took the pictures...it just wasn't the right people." Benny looked sad. "Should we come back to Chicago?...Oh, a vacation...that would be nice...Oh, Hands will be on vacation too? Are you sure that you can get along OK without our help?...Oh, OK. Well, good-bye, then."

LeYan was not having a good Tuesday afternoon. Her Gracie Fielding plan had backfired. It was a relief to get Benny and Luther away on vacation. She needed brains, not buffoons. Hands was still in the Nordland County pokey. He could have been a pleasant diversion at this time. She knew that Alasom was becoming uptight. He did not say anything, but she understood his reluctance to communicate, hoping it would all go away. She made a phone call from her penthouse apartment.

"Hello, Paulette. How are you? Oh, I'm not real thrilled at the moment. I just thought you might be able to help me smooth over the edges. Would you like to drop over after work? I could fix something for a snack. We could have a few drinks and have a nice evening. Oh, good! I'll see you then—whenever you choose. Oh, Paulette, would you ask Bill to confirm the arrangements for Thursday's meeting in D.C.?" She started to hang up and then, on second thought, she took the receiver off the hook and placed the telephone under a pillow.

* * *

Carlos proved to be an excellent tour guide, calling attention to the many points of interest and providing a good historical background. It was obvious that he was proud of his wonderful new country. He and his parents had recently become citizens.

Most of the tour was drive-by—the White House; Bureau of Engraving, where U.S. currency is printed; National Museum of American History; Library of Congress; Supreme Court building; and the Smithsonian. When they got to the Lincoln Memorial, Casey wanted to walk up the majestic steps to the impressive statue. They also visited the Jefferson Memorial. The Washington Monument was so central and ever-present that they merely observed it from the streets skirting the beautiful mall. Buck and Casey both got up close and personal at the Vietnam Veterans' Memorial.

Buck invited Carlos to join them for lunch at the impressive Bombay Club. He declined very politely, saying that he had to stay with the limo, to be sure it would not be borrowed, either in the whole or in parts. As they returned to Arlington, Virginia, they drove past the huge National Cemetery, on the way back to Miriam's home.

It was a pleasure to return to her cool townhouse and have supper on the porch, with some real-people talk. Everyone planned to retire early to be prepared for a 6:30 wake-up. Their flight was at 8:45 AM.

At 9:30 PM, however, Miriam answered the phone and said, "Buck, it's for you." He answered "Yes," guessing correctly who it might be.

"Buck, this is Jim Bob." Buck had not realized that they had achieved that degree of familiarity, but he supposed, *That's what the lunch was for.*

"Hello, Akkre what's new—oh yes, the lunch was great—had a fine tour."

"I was thinking that, with your interest in the environment, you might like to see how we do it in the south. I happen to be returning to Dallas tomorrow. Would like you two to be my guests for a few days? You could come down Thursday morning or early afternoon and stay at the South-Country Inn—it's so comfortably fancy that you won't want to leave—swimming pool, terrace— anything you want. I'll take you to a place for dinner that made Texas steaks famous! Next day we can take my plane down to Lafayette and then drive around the bayou country—whole different world among those Cajuns."

"Akkre, this *is* a surprise. We'll have to talk about that some. Why don't I call you back in an hour. Oh, yes, we have your number all right."

Buck outlined Jim Bob's offer to Casey and Miriam. Miriam thought it would be just wonderful—probably thinking that any place other than D.C. in late June would be a blessing. He continued, "It might be kind of fun if George were down there with us. Maybe he would reconsider that offer of Mindy's and we could all get together."

"Oh, I think he is already considering Mindy," Casey said with a far-away look that Buck did not try to figure.

"I will call him right now." Since it was well past the Sawbill cocktail hour, George was in the middle of a Twins game. Buck explained the scenario and George replied:

"I don't know if she'll have me, but I'll give it a try. I will call you right back."

The early-to-bed idea was put off indefinitely. Casey agreed that it could be fun to get away from their place— the crew was on a long Fourth weekend anyway.

George called back in fifteen minutes. "It's a go! Mindy was wild about the idea. She said you two could stay at her place after you got tired of Akkre. I'll probably take the afternoon flight out of Duluth, though. Got to take care of some matters here. Probably get to Dallas about nine. Mindy will pick me up. I'll give you Mindy's number at home in case you want to check in. She may even fly her plane, from the ranch, into one of the fields in Dallas. Or else she will fly in low in her souped-up Mustang. She says she averages a hundred across country. One way or another, we should be at her place by 10 or 10:30."

"OK. I'll call this Akkre guy and say we're coming."

Jim Bob Akkre was delighted and said he would make

all the arrangements. "Check in the South-Country Inn any time during the day. Just charge everything to the room. Use the pool. Have a ball."

* * *

"Rebelde, this is J.B. Akkre. Remember, I talked to you about a couple visitors I wanted you to help me with? Now is the time for you to show me how good you are. I have invited them to come to Dallas, day after tomorrow. The Jambalaya Joint scene will be that evening. You can tell your man Huge Henry that they will show Thursday night. Maybe Paradise could pick them up at the Lafayette airfield about seven."

"Oh, one other thing. I got a call from Cartoom—yeah, Zatar himself. They are really pushing me to get an oil connection made so that they can get the laundry going. They've got so much drug cash, they don't know what to do with it. Of course some of it was that forty-six grand you conned me out of...OK, OK, you earned it. Talk to ya."

28

George called the Rykers at home Wednesday evening, June 30. "So you are really going to do this Dallas trip? From what we said about Akkre being in cahoots with Alactra, he could be involved with the oil characters as well. Not a good bunch to pal around with."

Buck replied, "We will just sponge off him for a couple days and then accept Mindy's invitation for over the Fourth. Should be a good break. We can get a 9:20 out of Minneapolis—arrive Dallas at about noon—be in the pool by one! Of course we will have to catch the eight o'clock from Duluth to make the 9:20. After all this is over, I'm not getting on another aer-eo-plane for a year." Buck hollered at Casey who was in the kitchen, "Honey, do you want to sleep over in Duluth tonight or get up at 5:30 tomorrow?"

Casey had been examining the schedule pamphlet also and replied, "Honey," she mimicked, "how about we get up at *6:30*, catch the *9:15* from Duluth, the *11:15* out of Minneapolis and get in the pool at *three* o'clock?"

"I was afraid you'd say some smart-ass thing like that! OK, that's what we will do." Talking back to George, Buck asked, "So Mindy is OK about all this?"

"Oh, she thinks it's great! She said all she had going for the Fourth was the local Rodeo Blast-off. 'Probably party too much anyway!" she said.

"I'll call you tomorrow night at her place, then." Buck said. "Probably be about ten."

* * *

Northwest Airlines flight 403 departed Minneapolis nearly on time at 11:25 AM., Thursday, July 1. Buck had convinced Casey to travel light, so they had their world in two carryons. Casey had worn her do-everything light gray pants suit, with the matching short skirt packed in her carryon for social emergencies. Very few people in northern Minnesota had seen her wear a skirt. At the clinic, she opted for the white slacks version of her nurse's uniform. She and Buck lived in jeans at home and for dinner "dates" at the Nordland Bay Lodge and the Sawbill. She had only worn "the skirt" once a year—at the county group Christmas party. The effect on the local members had been devastating and on their wives, even worse. Each year, Casey vowed not to "show off" again, but each year Buck proudly talked her into strutting her stuff a little.

Buck enjoyed jet travel when the flights lasted longer than Chicago to Milwaukee. He and Casey settled into 24A and B and he was totally relaxed. It was as if he were suspended in life, as if he were in a situation over which he had absolutely no control and therefore was forced to submit. He could not recall any other time in his life when he was not keyed up to anticipate or react to what the world might throw at him. Of course the SEAL training and experience made that happen. He remembered, however, that even during his high school days, he maintained a wary attitude. There were some "cool hand Luke" remarks made by the high school girls, but Buck did not go to movies much and thus missed the point.

The fact was, sitting in 24B next to Casey, he felt about as high as they actually were, at forty thousand feet. At the moment, there were just the two of them—babbling about what a crazy trip this was, forgetting about their cash flow, Nordland county, everything serious. In a 1930's movie, they would have crash-landed on a desert island, lived a wild couple years and returned to a ticker tape parade in New York City.

"What do you really think this Akkre guy wants?" Casey finally introduced reality.

"I'm not sure," Buck replied, realizing that the euphoria was growing thin. "I know that he is not part of the

Dallas Welcome Wagon. He either wants to sell me something, or he's hoping to get you in a corner. I am sure there is a connection here with the Boundary Lodge group. George thinks he is probably in cahoots with the oil boys also. In any event, let's go with it. If things start to get tight, we'll worry about it then. In the meantime, I love you." Heads turned in 24C-D-E and smiled nervously as a brief passionate kiss, seldom seen in real life at forty thousand feet, unsettled the atmosphere in the forward compartment of flight 403.

* * *

As Casey and Buck were relaxing, LeYan Syn and her token Scandinavian, Bill Anderson, were arriving at Dulles in D.C. They cabbed directly to the scene of LeYan's disaster two days earlier.

"Bill, I know that you are well aware of the importance of convincing Wayneson and Saguaro of the value of our project. I think that our meeting in the House Office Building conference room will give you an opportunity to use your fine visuals to emphasize how valuable the Boundary Lodges will be."

"We will make it happen!" Bill smiled.

"We have to assume that there will be no significant negative input from the locals—namely Ryker. I believe that J.B. Akkre will convince him and his wife that they should no longer interfere," LeYan said.

"Do you really believe that this Akkre is doing us any good?"

"Good question. I don't like him! I don't like his methods! If he mishandles the situation in Dallas—or wherever—I will have to recommend to Mr. Alactra that we drop him."

* * *

The view of Dallas through the window showed a surprisingly green landscape. They landed and proceeded to the arrival gate waiting area. One look was enough to locate a large sign, hand-lettered "Welcome Casey and Buck." It was held by a fellow of indeterminate origin, in full chauffeur's uniform. While somewhat scruffy and ill fitting, the uniform did give him reasonable legitimacy.

"Mr. and Mrs. Ryker," he announced loudly, not realizing that they had already spotted him. Buck waved his hand overhead and they made the connection. They proceeded through the terminal to the baggage area and out to the curb, where another uniformed original was standing just inside the open driver's door of a silver-gray limo that sported too much gold-colored trim.

"Where are we off to?" Buck asked as they were directed into the commodious rear seating area.

"The South-Country Inn," original number one answered. It was expected that anyone in the United States and certain South American countries should know that name. A thirty-minute trip down LBJ to Stemmons, across Oak Lawn, and finally up Foxhill Road, brought them to the hilltop location of South-Country Inn.

South-Country appeared to be a fine and venerable establishment. The countryside look was at the same time a culture shift from the modern high-rise city and a little of what one would hope Dallas had to offer—an urban "Southfork." It was probably Jim Bob's only touch of class. The meticulously landscaped grounds brought to mind tea parties and weddings rather than barbecue brouhahas. The chauffeur led them through the quiet, dignified lobby area as far as the front desk and then, with a word to the distinguished desk manager, disappeared. The mention of Jim Bob Akkre seemed to work magic. With much finger snapping and no check-in procedure, Buck and Casey were escorted to the fourth floor terrace suite. The bellman, having little luggage to carry, took Buck's tip as a bribe to leave immediately.

Casey looked at Buck and said, "Not *too* bad," (their favorite understated praise).

"Jim Bob knows how to treat his guests," Buck had to concede.

A few minutes of checking out the huge bedroom with oval bed (thankfully no ceiling mirror), opulent bath and luxurious living room area, the inevitable question arose: "What do we do now?" they said together.

"Well, it's almost three. Do you want lunch?" Buck asked.

"I'm not really hungry yet. Where's the pool? I'd love to do a few laps and catch some sun," Casey answered with a girlish enthusiasm that Buck had not seen for quite a while. He opened the curtains wide and stepped out onto the small balcony overlooking a large pool.

"You could make quite a splash right from here," he said. "It looks like they've got room for a couple of tourists down there."

"Last one in the pool gets to dance with Jim Bob," Casey threw out as she grabbed her bag and jumped for the bath. She showered and was out in a few minutes. He showered, and tried on his boxer trunks that had not seen use for a year. Once at the pool, they established two lounge chairs and dived immediately into the totally vacant deep end of the Olympic-size pool. The middle and shallow end, however, were filled to near capacity with a variety of ages and equipment. Absent completely was any sign of actual swimming. Buck did four laps and vaulted out at the deep end. Casey continued for another dozen laps.

As Casey emerged, shaking the water out of her short, dark hair, Buck said, "How about some lunch out here at one of the tables? No telling when we will eat dinner."

"You got it, big spender," Casey answered, and they both sat at one of the umbrella-covered tables in the sun. A young man in a sharp white shirt, black tie, black trousers and a modest earring quickly appeared.

"Wide receiver?" Buck guessed to the waiter, observing his sturdy, six-foot-two athletic build.

"Trying out for rookie free safety with the Cowboys," he answered with no further comment.

"Good luck," Buck continued, giving up further pleasantries. "Two Bacardi white rum and tonics," please. Then we'll order lunch." Casey took this news with raised eyebrows.

"You haven't ordered a rum and tonic since we used to go to the lounge in Colorado Springs," she said, after the free safety had left.

"I guess my past is showing," Buck said. "We used to hit the rum pretty hard when George and I were in the Canal Zone. I started to do the tonic then to keep from mainlining the stuff like a lot of the guys did."

The Cowboy returned with the drinks and stood waiting with some impatience as they each took a sip and did the cliché glass touch.

"Perfect blend," Buck said, attempting to justify the pause that refreshed. Casey had grabbed the menu and began studying it with voracious interest. Buck let the menu be and placed his order:

"I'll bet you folks make a great Eggs Benedict."

"Yes, sir, I'm sure we do," the waiter responded. "What would you like to accompany the eggs, sir? Hash browns?"

Buck let this somewhat supercilious attitude pass. After all, he thought, the kid had to have *some* fringies. Semi-insulting the non-Texans could be one of them.

"No hash browns, thank you. How about a little artichoke salad. And be sure the hollandaise on the eggs is not too sweet." Buck had never ordered artichoke before but thought this would be a good time to give it a shot. Whether or not hollandaise could be more or less sweet was another wild guess.

"And the lady" the waiter asked.

"What looks good to you?" Buck asked.

"Well, aren't you going to order for me?" she asked, raising one eye and managing a smile.

"Not unless you have a mental block," Buck replied.

"I'll have the Shrimp Louis salad, please," Casey said. "And I'll have another Bacardi rum and tonic. The gentleman will have another one also." The waiter left the table shaking his head slowly, followed by a burst of laughter from the Rykers.

"You certainly are a smooth talker," Buck said. "Do you do anything else as well?"

"Wouldn't you like to know," was all that Casey could come up with at the moment.

"Let's find out," Buck said as he stood up, leaned over the table and kissed her up-turned face. Aside from hitting his head on the metal table umbrella as he sat down, he thought he was doing one of his best Cary Grant acts. The drinks came, followed by well-served salads, a beautiful Eggs Benedict and no more conversation from the free safety. They settled into the warm ambiance while other guests used the pool as it "should" be used—for jumping around and floating on fancy air mattresses.

The main fascination for the two of them seemed mutual. It was as if they had just discovered each other. The penetrating glances gradually developed into unspoken consensus about what would follow lunch. Buck signed the check and showed his Terrace Suite key to the waiter, who was pleasantly startled at the size of the tip, courtesy of Jim Bob Akkre.

* * *

The elevator trip to the fourth floor was quick and the swimmers were back in the Terrace Suite. The gas fireplace was lit, competing with the air-conditioning to maintain a temperature that was not warm, not cool. Buck turned the fire off. The style of the South-Country Inn suite was enhanced by comfortable Early American furnishings.

"Why don't you take your shower first," Casey said. "You're always so quick."

"It's a deal," Buck agreed. After he emerged from the shower in the "his" version of the terry cloth robes that were folded neatly in the bathroom, he settled into the oversize chair near the fireplace. This being the first time since early morning that he really had time to think, the inevitable weight of realistic considerations began to sink in. This whole problem of hustlers trying to invade the boundary waters with tourist resort hotels and now maybe oil exploration was becoming more involved and rotten at every turn. First the Alactra episode in Chicago. Then the Congressional subcommittee fiasco, leading to this strange association with Akkre—what next?

The immediate "next" blew all his other thoughts away. Casey walked slowly out of the bath—not in the "hers" terry cloth robe, but in her bathing suit "coverup" which never really covered up anything. This time, the tank suit had been left behind.

Buck was pleased that, after six years, the sight of Casey could stir him this intensely. As she stood in front of a decorator mirror twenty feet from his chair, combing her hair, he realized that she was performing for him.

"You look good..." he started to say.

"Don't talk about it," she interrupted—"just do it."

That was all he could handle without action. He was behind her in an instant, with the "his" left halfway between the chair and her position in front of the mirror. He kissed her neck and slowly ran his hands over the coverup and beyond. He picked her up, strode through the semi-darkened room and gently laid her in the middle of the oval bed. He stood there for a moment. And then they were together. In their immediate world, all problems had been solved, all questions answered. And then they slept.

* * *

Ring...ring...ring. Buck could not believe that he had become zonked in a half hour. Usually, the slightest sound pulled his trigger and brought him to full alert.

"Terrace Suite," he said.

After a pause, the voice said, "Can I speak to Mr. Buck Ryker?"

"This is Buck."

"Sir, this is Jacob, calling for Mr. Akkre."

"Oh...where is he?"

More pause..."He...he is not here at this time and he wants to invite you to dinner tonight."

"What time tonight?"

"His car will pick you up at 5:45."

Buck glanced at his watch. It was 5:30 and he looked at Casey, who had just roused. "We can make it by six," he said.

"Mr. Akkre said 5:45."

"Make it six," Buck said.

"Thank you sir."

The South-Country Inn set the mood. Their total togetherness wrote the script. They dressed slowly and gradually let the world enter their scene.

* * *

No limo this time—only a Mercedes 600. One of the afternoon's drivers had changed into more of a film noir waterfront Blackie—but with his stereotypical chauffeur's cap. He held the door for them to enter...*the trap*, Buck wondered.

"Where are we off to?" Buck asked.

"Mr. Akkre say, 'surprise'."

"What if I don't like surprises?"

"Mr. Akkre say cocktails at 30,000 feet. We go to airfield...I think we make quick fly to Lafayette."

Realizing that the poor fellow had gone beyond his authorized disclosures, Buck said, "Thanks buddy. How long to the airfield?"

"Twelve minutes, sir."

"Can't get *too* bad in twelve minutes," Buck assured Casey.

The Lear Jet was waiting, with its tail facing the setting sun. The small airfield was one of several in the Dallas-Fort Worth area that catered to private aircraft. As they drove out on the tarmac, Buck could see the uniformed pilot—bright white Bermuda-length shorts and short sleeve white shirt, open at the neck. Two gold stripes on the shoulders and gold "scrambled eggs" on the black visor of his white military-style cap, proclaimed his proficiency. Buck wondered if this was a paid-for charter or if Jim Bob really owned this five million dollar aircraft.

"Welcome Mr. And Mrs. Ryker," the pilot said. "Welcome aboard!" He took Casey's hand and got her started on the short stairs into the plane. Buck followed.

"What is our destination, pilot?" Buck asked.

"Mr. Akkre asked me to keep it a surprise, but actually we go as far as the private field in Lafayette—under four hundred miles. Should be there shortly after seven."

"Then what?" Buck asked.

"That's as far as our orders go, sir."

* * *

Jim Bob Akkre looked out from an unlikely perch on the top floor of a two-story white frame building, on the outskirts of Lafayette, Louisiana. He owned the building, but leased the lower level to a one-man body shop. The small neon sign—Cajun Collision—was visible as J.B. used two fingers to separate the closed window blinds and peer into the street. He reached his hideaway by an open stairway on the east side of his south-facing building. The interior included a narrow plywood table, supported by three saw horses—all painted white. A daybed in one corner and a couple of two-by-eight-foot plywood shelves, supported by four double-drawer file cabinets completed the furnishings. Strangely, a camcorder on a five-foot tripod was positioned near the narrow bed. Apparently, Jim Bob did have a guest occasionally. The back corner was walled off to contain a shower, pedestal sink, and stool. The main decorative feature of the room was a display of centerfolds from at least the past twelve issues of *Playboy*. The functional features, however, included a fax machine, a portable typewriter, two telephones, a Compaq computer/printer, a VCR and a twenty-five inch Panasonic television set. It was obvious that Akkre's home away from home was intended for concentrated conspiracy. The small peephole in the steel door and the heavy-duty dead bolt provided security.

He answered one of his phones shortly after seven. "Yes," he said, knowing that only three people knew the number assigned to the red phone.

"Sir, this is Steve, the pilot. Your guests have arrived and were just picked up by a six-foot black beauty in a white Eldorado convertible."

"Thank you Steve. Oh, Steve—who am I?"

"I haven't the slightest idea—and I have already forgotten this number. Your chauffeur gave me a quite satisfactory envelope."

Akkre turned to the blue telephone and dialed a Fort Worth number. Ramon Rebelde answered.

"Ramon, this is Akkre. As we speak, the two northwoods types are on their way from the airfield to the Jambalaya Joint. Are your people ready?"

"They are there at the bar. By the time they take action, they should be damn willing and able."

"Tell 'em not to get *too* rough."

"You tell 'em. From now on it's your scene."

"Have you heard from Zatar at Cartoom Enterprises?"

"Called me this afternoon. Wants to meet me off shore tonight—wants to see the oil results he's been paying for. That should be your job—to keep him happy. I'll go, but I don't like it. If I don't show up soon, you'll know where I am—fifty feet below the water line."

* * *

The white Eldorado convertible raced smoothly along the narrow blacktop. The two passengers in the back seat were happily enjoying the balmy breeze and the start of a starry night. The friendly charisma displayed immediately by Paradise, the statuesque black lady chauffeur, gave them a semi-secure feeling as they once again launched into the unknown. They crossed a number of bridges over narrow rivers that the driver referred to as bayous. After twenty minutes, Paradise wheeled the big Caddy sharply onto a dirt and gravel road. The car-wide path barely cut through between luxuriant vegetation, which was outranked by tall cypress trees. The hanging Spanish Beard shut out all the remaining twilight. They were in darkness, penetrated only by the Eldorado's high beams.

Buck, recalling other jungle scenes he had known, asked Paradise if they didn't get things dropping into an open car like this.

"Oh yeah. We just throw 'em back out," she said.

They could hear the music a half of a mile before they saw any lights. Then the aggressive-looking trees and bushes parted, and a ten-acre clearing opened up to them.

"This place is even more remote than our place," Buck said to Casey.

"It's out-of-touch all right." Paradise had overheard.

At first, it seemed that all the action was going on out on a vast open-air front porch. Two brown-skin young men, with red bandannas, ala "Neon Dion" were vigorously strumming guitars. Twenty or so people joined the strummers in the lively song. "That's a Dewey Balfia number," Casey said.

Paradise drove up to the front porch, precluding an inconspicuous entrance. Adding to the flurry of their arrival, a well-built black man of medium height came down the steps and opened the door for Paradise. He looked cool in pressed white cotton trousers and a light beige batiste shirt, unbuttoned to the center of his hairless, well-developed chest. His bare arms bulged with smooth muscles. A broad grin was as bright as his trousers.

He gave Paradise a very public kiss on the lips. She said to the emerging Casey and Buck, "Casey, Buck, please meet Huge Henry."

* * *

LeYan was surprised to hear the phone ring in her penthouse apartment. Her private number was known to very few. She and Paulette had returned to the penthouse after work and were enjoying some camaraderie.

"Hello, Alasom. So nice to have you call."

"LeYan, have you heard anything from that Akkre in Dallas?" Alasom Alactra asked.

"No, sir, I have not spoken to him since Tuesday. I rather expected him to call me yesterday afternoon." Paulette, hearing the conversation, rolled her eyes, pointed to LeYan and herself.

"Perhaps my phone was accidentally off the hook for a while," she continued.

"Yes, I will, Mr. Alactra. I will start trying to reach him immediately. I agree that he should be monitored closely. I will call you as soon as I reach him. Oh, one other thing: Bill and I had a very good meeting with the two Congressmen. We even talked about language that could go into the bill. I believe they are ready to go our way—without any local citizen testimony.

"Thank you sir. Goodnight." LeYan mimed a hand wiping a brow and said to Paulette, "He's really getting nervous." She immediately dialed the BMOB phone number and got a recorded message.

* * *

Jim Bob sat watching HBO in the near darkness of his Spartan hideaway. With no one to observe him and no confrontations planned, he was letting it all hang out—a liter of Dewar's was diminishing rapidly.

He reached for his blue phone and dialed his message machine in D.C. The first message was from his secretary, Hilda.

"Mr. Akkre I just wanted to remind you that I will be taking off the day tomorrow, Friday, July 2. I will be home most of the day, however. Please call if you need anything."

He smiled. The next message started, "Akkre, this is LeYan Syn. I need to talk to you immediately. It is now eight o'clock Thursday night. Call me ASAP!"

"No way, babe," he said to himself. "I'll call you when I have something to tell you."

29

The jumpin' Jambalaya Joint porch scene was a Sunday School picnic compared with the goings-on inside. As Casey and Buck walked in, escorted by Huge Henry, the first impression was wall-to-wall and body-to-body people. They were people of all shades, all styles from long dresses, white suits, Panamas—to practically nothing. Buck's outfit about matched Henry's except in reverse—white shirt and tan Dockers. Casey was about in the middle of the pack of women's apparel—sort-of-short gray skirt and open-but-not-plunging blouse.

She looked delicious, and a gaggle of ganders at the bar were clicking their bills. Buck tightened his arm around her shoulders.

Henry was glad-handed by everyone they walked past, on the way to a table for four. It was nearly in the corner, on the other side of the large room from the band. The six-piece wild group, consisting of accordion, violin, two guitars, clarinet and drums, was dispensing decibels like they were trying to blast the water moccasins out of the swamp. The Cajun foot-stomp ruled and twenty couples tried to survive on the too-small wood-plank dance floor.

Paradise walked past the bar, nearly getting groped but always maintaining the upper hand—or lower hand, if she really had to put some local swarthy in his place. Three sailors, no doubt in from a ship docked in New Orleans, looked at the whole scene with wide eyes. Paradise gave them each a light punch in the chest. One of them got a kiss on the cheek. She made his day. After completing her review of the bar troops, she walked through a dozen tables and joined Henry, Casey and Buck.

Buck had described to Henry how he had happened to meet Akkre and why he and Casey had been in Washington. They compared the bayou country with the boundary water wilderness, arriving at consensus about the need to preserve both from development or destruction.

"Some people from the north are leery of our swamps and wild animals and such—not really a problem, once you get used to it and know what you're doin'," Henry said. "Only one thing though. I've learned to stay away from the water moccasin. Some call 'em cottonmouth. Either way, they're deadly. Some local guys around here pick 'em up in back of the head, but I've seen those guys get bit too—and it ain't nice."

Buck could see Casey trying to block out what she was hearing. Other than a couple garter snakes in her garden, she hadn't seen a real snake since hiking around Denver—and then she was twenty feet away.

"Well, Henry, there aren't any snakes in here," Buck said pleasantly.

"Only the ones like at the bar." He nodded at three roughly dressed, and not-too-shaven characters chugging beer.

Attempting to steer the conversation to a different subject, Buck said, "Henry, I don't consider myself too big, but I'm at least your size. How come they call you *Huge* Henry?"

"You know, Buck, I really don't know. I guess it started a couple weeks after I met Paradise here. She started callin' me Huge Henry. I don't know exactly why." Paradise gave Henry a substantial punch on the shoulder. Casey laughed nervously. Buck just grinned.

"Now, Casey, how about a dance?" Henry said. Buck wasn't sure of his dancing anyway, but doing "the stomp" with this woman who would give the model, Iman, a run for her money—and who could probably toss him a time or two—was a challenge. But he took a deep breath, turned to Paradise, who was patiently waiting for him to make up his mind, and said, "Ma'am, it would be my

Parad...it would be my pleasure." She smiled and they moved to the dance floor, as six or seven at the bar burned visual holes in them, one-by-one.

As they returned from the dance floor, Buck noticed that the bar-snakes' stares at Casey were not only lecherous—but mean-lecherous.

They ordered bisque, gumbo, clam cakes and crawdads. Buck excused himself to go to the men's room. Casey looked up surprised. He could usually hold nearly as much as a camel.

"A popular place," Buck said when he returned, after a long ten minutes. Then he said, "I wonder what happened to our so-called host—Jim Bob Akkre. Not that we need him, but he looked like a guy who would like to party."

"Buck," Paradise said, "he sometimes runs with a bad crowd—like those three up there from Baton Rouge and their boss, from Fort Worth. We're not missin' anything by not having him here. We'll take care a'ya all right."

Buck stomped with Casey and Casey danced with Paradise. "How'd it go, with Paradise?" Buck asked.

"Better than a lot of *guys* I've danced with," she said.

"Call for Buck Ryker," hollered a large lady who walked out from the kitchen.

Buck jogged to the outstretched phone and answered.

"This is George. They said you called. What's the caper?"

"No time to explain," Buck said. "Can you get Mindy to fly you out here? Maybe her plane to Lafayette and copter out to the Jambalaya Joint, about fifteen minutes east of Lafayette. Everybody knows this place. I wouldn't ask you if I didn't think it was serious. It's now twenty to nine. Make it as fast as you can!"

"Bucko, you sure you're not a tad paranoid?"

"George, if we learned anything, it was to trust our own instincts."

"Roger." The line was dead.

"Who was that?" Casey asked when Buck returned with a serious look on his face.

"George called from Dallas. He has decided to come out to join us."

"That's quite a trip. You guys sure move fast," Henry said.

"We do what we have to do," Buck said and managed a smile.

Casey asked Paradise about the ladies room. "You don't want to go in *there*," Paradise said. "We've got a room and a bath in the back of this building. I'll show you where the door is." They walked together past the bar. The groping was restricted to grunts and groans. Casey looked fiercely straight ahead. "We shouldn't let those three bastards in here," Paradise said.

Buck glanced at his watch. "Eight forty-five," he said quietly, to himself.

"Expecting someone?" Henry asked, overhearing him.

"Just trying to guess when George would get here," Buck said.

Casey used the key that Paradise gave her to enter a cozy combination living room and bedroom. She hurried directly to the bathroom, in back, off the main room.

Henry, Paradise and Buck were discussing the inroads that had been made on the bayou environment when Buck saw the three Baton Rouge snakes get off their stools and head toward the back of the building. Not wanting to believe what his instincts told him, he tried to continue conversation until Henry said, "What's wrong, Buck?"

"Casey's been gone a while and the three snakes have left the bar. I don't like it," Buck said.

"Let's go," Henry said. All three moved immediately to the back area where Paradise had brought Casey. She grabbed the doorknob.

"It's open! I told her to be sure to lock it!" They burst in and saw the answer in one look. The back casement window was wide open. CASEY WAS GONE!

* * *

The bag over Casey's head was filthy with dirt and fish smell. They had bound her hands and thrown her in the back of a pickup. Her whole life seemed as if it had ended. She tried to keep away the thoughts of what might happen to her.

* * *

"We'll go after them," Henry shouted, as they ran outside.

"Henry, I'm not sure that you and I and Paradise can handle this. I have some help coming. Do you have a Jeep? Can you guess where they would take her? Do you have a gun?"

"Yes to all those," Henry said. I am going to call my right-hand Cajun, Muskrat-Man. He knows the ins and outs of this area better than anyone. I am sure he can be here in twenty minutes."

* * *

"Where you gonna take her?" Snake-Two asked. He was already chugging on a bottle of cheap rum.

"To that old hunt-shack we used to use. It's got to be out here somewhere. Ease up on that stuff so you can help me find it."

Snake-Two looked at his other seatmate, next to the window. "Old Clinker is out of it. He was pouring 'em down in the bar."

"If I was you, I'd stay sober. That broad will be fun to toy with," Snake-One cautioned.

"Rebelde said to not get too rough."

"Who said rough? I bet she'll enjoy it. Now where is that old road we used to take?"

"That was two years ago," Snake-Two said. "You shoulda picked a better place."

* * *

Mindy met George at the arrival gate. After a hug and a few words, he got serious.

"Mindy, where is your plane? Can we take off immediately for Lafayette?" He explained the urgent call from Buck.

"George you are nothing, if not exciting. Haven't seen you for years; not more than a card once in a while. Now you want me to fly off to save someone's ass." Mindy was pushed, but nevertheless amused.

"Hey, Mindy, what are friends for?" George said.

"You're damn lucky I spend my free time schmoozing these aircraft types. Flying is one of my get-off's," Mindy said, as they climbed into the Lear Jet on the fringe of the D-FW International Airport. "When we get up, I'll radio to Lafayette and get a chopper to meet us to get to Jambalaya in ten minutes. I've been there. Great place! Huge Henry. Paradise. Love 'em!"

"Some little toy you've got here," George said.

"Actually, the pilot is a friend who is trying to sell the Lear to my daddy," she said. "Anyway, George, what's money for?"

* * *

Muskrat screeched to a stop near the Jambalaya Joint in an ancient Chevrolet El Camino. The robes in the back truck-bed looked innocuous but contained enough firepower to make a stand at the levee.

"Muskrat, we've got a problem," Henry said. "You know those three cockroaches from the Rouge who show up once in a while? They've kidnapped my friend's wife and hauled her into the bush! We have to figure where they would go and then go after them. I called my son to bring the Humvee from our house. He should be here in about ten minutes. Buck here has got some help coming in by 'copter. We know that time is short. Those guys would do anything."

Muskrat spoke: "I know where they go. I happy to catch them and string them up. They no good!"

* * *

"It can't be far from here," Snake-One said. "I remember

these trees. Find it—I got to watch where the hell I'm going. These ruts and stumps are killing the truck. How's the broad in back?"

"She's gettin' bounced around like hell—should be ready to come across when we untie her."

"*If* we untie her."

* * *

The Humvee arrived in twenty minutes. It was driven by a younger version of Henry. Junior explained that he had been in the middle of rotating tires when he got the call.

They were ready except Buck's reinforcements—then they heard it from a distance. The chop-chop-chop was unmistakable—then they saw it.

The 'copter hovered until its powerful spotlight zeroed in on them and the open landing patch. It sat down. George jumped out and ran up to Buck.

"The bastards took Casey!" Buck shouted, above the chopper noise.

"Buck, we'll get 'em. Hold it together," George hollered back.

Mindy talked to the pilot for a minute, then jogged over to Paradise, standing by the edge of the front porch. The two guitar players were still singing their songs on the porch, but most of the patrons' eyes were focused on the helicopter.

"This is rotten!" Mindy said.

"It sure is," Paradise answered. "You're Mindy, right? Your group had a very good time here a couple years ago."

"Yeah, we did. I've toned down a little since then. Not a lot, but a little."

Muskrat, Buck and George crowded into the Humvee, along with Muskrat's firepower. Young Henry took off like a drag racer in the direction Muskrat dictated.

"I remember those bastards," Muskrat said. "They hunt when no one else can hunt. They used to stay in a shack out along the bayou. They sometimes bring women out there. They all bad!"

* * *

In ten minutes, Muskrat said, "See, fresh tire tracks—*got* to be them!"

"Let me tell you, Muskrat. If you get us there before they hurt my wife, you got yourself a brand new truck," Buck said.

"Don't like new trucks! Thanks anyway. We get there!"

After another fifteen minutes of rut-to-rut, damaging terrain, Muskrat said, "Stop!" They all peered hopelessly through the lampblack-darkness—at nothing.

Then Muskrat said, "The hut is up there three hundred yards—barely make out their truck."

* * *

Casey kept her eyes closed. She could not believe what was happening to her. Snakes One and Two were still semi-sober, but getting drunker by the minute. They started a new bottle of rum and were passing it back and forth while they tried to decide what to do. They *knew* what they *wanted* to do.

"Listen, babe, you do what we want and we'll let you go. OK," Snake-One said and started to slide his hand inside her blouse. She lurched away, almost knocking over the chair to which she was tied.

"It's time to bring out the persuader," Snake-Two said. He walked over to a cardboard box, put on a leather glove, reached in and brought out a wriggling three-foot cottonmouth.

"Now, Missy, have a look at this fella. I bet he'd like to give you a kiss." He waved the head of the spitting reptile within six inches of her face. She turned her head violently, but did not make a sound. "I think you'd rather kiss us nice guys instead of this little 'ole cottonmouth, wouldn't you?"

* * *

George and Buck approached the hut stealthily, not making a sound. George moved to the pickup, reached in the open door and grabbed the passed-out Snake-Three around the neck. He woke up, but was immobilized. George pulled him out of the truck, ripped off the Snake's shirt, twisted it into a rope and tied it through his mouth and around his head. George took the rope they had brought from the Humvee, circled the captive's hands around his back, and hog-tied his ankles and wrists.

Buck crawled the distance to the hut and cautiously looked through the dirty window. Casey's eyes were wide with terror. Snake Two was moving the cottonmouth toward her. Buck was ready to smash through the window and take what came. But George was there and put a hand on Buck's shoulder.

Using SEAL sign language, George indicated that he would go in the door while Buck would break through the window, gun drawn. George's 230 pounds disintegrated the rotten door and brought him halfway into the small cabin. Snake-Two, holding the cottonmouth, turned with his eyes wide open and then jumped wildly as the three-foot reptile took its vengeance on his uncovered arm.

Buck burst through the old double-hung window and made it to the other character in two steps. Buck grasped him with one arm around his neck and the other arm closed around his head. Buck gave the closed arm a vicious jerk and the man went limp. Buck threw him aside like a rag doll.

"Casey, Casey, Casey, it's OK now! It's OK!" He first held her for a second and then began cutting her bindings. As Buck held her, Casey cried softly, releasing the terrible tension. George walked out to meet the Humvee with young Henry and Muskrat aboard.

Muskrat got out. Buck led Casey out to the Humvee. They got in and he held her as young Henry drove the two of them back to the Jambalaya Joint.

"What you want to do with these bastards?" Muskrat asked George.

George said, "I *know* what I'm going to do—leave

those two in the hut and tie this guy to a tree. The guy that got bit is nearly done for already, and the other has a broken neck. I'll get his keys and we'll take his pickup back to the Joint."

"There won't be much left of any of them by morning," Muskrat said. "The animals will get 'em."

"The less, the better," George said. "I've got to do one thing before you and I leave in the pickup." George took a pail from the shack and drew repeated fills of water from the nearby swamp, splashing each directly on the drunken captive's face. After the third pail, as George was about to heave another, the semi-sober man said, "Stop! Stop!"

"Now that we have your attention, scumbag, you're going to tell us who hired you," George said. The man hung his head and made no sound.

"Hold on a minute, Muskrat. I'll be right back." George entered the hut, saw the cottonmouth slithering off to the wall. He grabbed a burlap bag and threw it over the reptile's raised, probing head, that was searching for escape. George grabbed it five inches back of the head. As he held the snake aloft, the burlap fell back, uncovering the angry tongue and fang.

George carried the snake out to the shaking captive. His bleary eyes widened to the maximum, as George brought the flicking tongue within inches of the man's nose.

"Listen, you sonofabitch," George said. "I don't care if you get poisoned or if you stay out here tied to this tree forever. But I think you know what it's like to die from a cottonmouth bite. Now answer the question. Who hired you?"

"Don't let it hit me man, I'll tell. It was Rebelde and Akkre."

"What was their game?"

"*Oil*, man, *oil*! They wanted to launder cash from some Colombia outfit—I don't know who—maybe Cartoom."

"Where is Akkre?"

"He's in Lafayette, man—above the Cajun Collision body shop. We're s'posed to call him tonight."

"OK, 'man'—have a nice time—you and the bugs and the eyes in the night. If we remember, we'll tell the cops you are out here."

* * *

Buck comforted Casey in the back seat of the Eldorado. When George returned, Buck got out and Mindy took over, sitting with Casey. George told Buck about the interview with the drunk-turned-informant.

"Akkre is holed up above this body shop in Lafayette. We can get him—make him confess to all this crap," George said. "Remember, SEALs always say, 'Don't get mad. Get even'!" A few minutes between the two and the strategy was set.

Huge Henry got Buck aside and said, "Don't worry about the two dead guys in the hut. The cottonmouth bite speaks for itself and the one with the broken neck would be self-defense—at least around here."

The four of them bade a quick good-bye to Huge Henry and Paradise. Buck told Muskrat that he wanted him to come to the northwoods so that he could visit some of Minnesota's "bayous."

"Oh," Buck added, "can we borrow those two silenced .45's? We'll get them right back to you."

Muskrat's eyes lit up with the idea of gun action. "Let me know the worst of it!" he asked with a fervor.

* * *

The helicopter made fast work of the trip to Lafayette airfield, dropping down within fifteen minutes. Mindy schmoozed the pilot into borrowing his car. The foursome found a respectable-looking Spanish Beard Motel four blocks from Cajun Collision. Buck checked in and Mindy gave Casey a Valium out of a prescription bottle. Buck had an idea and asked for six more tablets. Mindy drove George and Buck to the nearby body shop and returned to comfort Casey.

* * *

It was almost midnight in the garden of Cajun Collision. Humidity hung on the body like a damp towel. Bright stars tried to improve the ambience, but failed. Spanish Moss, aka "Spanish Beard" clung to surrounding cypress trees like anticipatory shrouds.

George and Buck moved soundlessly up the creaking 2 x 8 wood steps, by placing their feet out to the far sides of the stairway, instead of stepping in the center of the well-worn tread. They arrived at the top landing and looked at the steel door with the heavy-duty deadbolt. Buck took out the silenced .45 and pointed to the deadbolt. He looked at George as if to ask, "Ready?" George nodded. Buck angled the gun along the wall to avoid accidentally blasting the inside occupant.

The .45 blew away the deadbolt and doorknob. The door swung open simultaneously with the big mouth of Jim Bob Akkre. He was seated at the equipment counter, having just inserted a paper in the fax machine. He started to get up, but George sat him back down, hard. Buck strode to the fax and pushed the "off" button. He retrieved the original out of the roller. It read, "From: J.B. Akkre To: LeYan Syn: Have taken care of your problem and..." Buck didn't even read the rest. He grabbed a blank sheet of paper, wrote: "Cancel previous message. Wait for new message." He punched in LeYan's private fax number and inserted the handwritten note.

Buck turned to Akkre, who had not recovered enough to object, and said, "Now, you slob, here's what you are going to do." He eyed Akkre's tripod and camcorder by the small bed and then he walked over to the portable typewriter on the plywood counter. He inserted a sheet of paper and quickly hunt-and-pecked a statement in which Akkre confessed to being an agent of Cartoom Enterprises. It defined his objective as providing illegal entry of drug money into the United States, in order to purchase shares of a mineral production company with rights and resources in the BWCA of Minnesota. The statement also confirmed a contractual relationship with Alactra International, as represented by Alasom Alactra and LeYan Syn. The statement was dated July 2, 1999, with a line for Jim Bob's signature.

Buck rewound the camcorder two minutes back and pressed "play." The video showed a heavyset, naked woman entertaining Akkre. Jim Bob was shown making a few special moves—including a wave—for the camera.

"Now won't that be a nice intro to the presentation?" Buck said. Akkre tried to lurch off the chair, but George held him in a grasp of steel.

"Now listen hard, Akkre. If you give us a moment's hesitation or if you try to screw up your big role here, we have ways to encourage you to give your best performance. That lamp cord, for example." Buck held the base of a lamp in his left hand, and with his right he yanked the cord out of the cheap bulb socket. With the cord still plugged into the wall receptacle, he touched the copper shreds of the electric wire to the back nerve center of the Compaq computer and Fourth of July came early. In one brilliant flash, the cathode ray tube exploded toward Akkre. He was paralyzed with fear and sat up very straight.

Buck gave Akkre a clipboard, with a blank piece of paper on it, and told him to practice signing. He did and the production began. After a few minutes' running time, Buck had him repeat the signature—and then one more time. The last time was a "take." Buck shut off the camcorder and extracted the tape cassette.

"I'll do you a favor, Jim Bob, and not show it back to you," Buck said. "Now, you're probably tired after all that acting—we've got something to take away the pain."

George handed Akkre four of Mindy's Valium tablets while Buck poured a full tumbler of scotch. He added a dash of soda, just for class. "Take those big aspirins and chug that scotch and you'll forget any of this happened, Jim Bob," Buck said. "Now for nighty-night." They hauled him over to his fun-couch, laid him out and tethered him by all fours. "Just so you won't talk in your sleep," George said, as he found yet another use for duct tape. As George and Buck prepared to leave, they could see that the shock, the Valium and the booze had taken over. Jim Bob was nowhere.

Buck typed out a short note to LeYan: "Re: Akkre's recent fax: the next page is what he *really* wanted to say." He signed it, "The Tree-hugger." "P.S. Stand by for a phone call tomorrow at 10 AM Chicago time. I will talk only to Alasom Alactra!" The ominous note, followed by Akkre's "confession," transmitted July 2, 12:30 AM.

* * *

George and Buck walked the four blocks back to the motel. Mindy was sitting in the car. "Casey's asleep in the room," she said. "The Valium really took over. She must not be used to it."

"Never has used it," Buck said.

"Now what, squad leader?" George said.

Buck smiled and put a hand on each friend's shoulder. "You guys have been the best. I can't begin…"

"Don't. We're just glad we got there in time," George said.

"I think we'll drive back to the Lafayette field and take the Lear to the ranch," Mindy said. "I'll bet you could use some rest, Buck. There are two double beds in there. Here is the key."

Mindy gave Buck an 'ole-buddy bear hug. George and Buck did a brief handshake.

Buck entered the motel, gazed at sleeping Casey and joined her, in spirit, on the other bed. At the moment, the boundary wilderness seemed much more than twelve hundred miles away.

30

LeYan Syn, executive vice-president, arrived at her office Friday morning, at 7:45, only to realize there was nothing she could do until it was time to call Alasom Alactra, president and chairman of the board of the billion-dollar conglomerate.

Paulette arrived promptly at 8:15. LeYan was almost teary as she nervously explained the fax action of the previous night.

"You never did think much of Akkre, did you?" Paulette said to console her.

LeYan leaned over and gave her a kiss on the cheek and said, "Paulette, I don't know what I'd do without you."

Ling stepped out of the elevator with a cheery, "Good morning, Ladies." He did not deserve the grumpy looks he received.

At 8:30 sharp, LeYan pushed the button to automatically dial Alasom Alactra.

"Sir, a situation has come up that I believe should have your attention. Will you be in the office before ten o'clock?

"Oh, you're leaving right now. Good. Thank you, sir.

"He'll be here in forty-five minutes," she said to Paulette. " I'll be able to put the fax on his desk now and explain to him before we get *the phone call*."

* * *

Room 120 in the Spanish Beard Motel was already warming up at 9:15. Buck had turned off the air-conditioning before he got in bed so that it would not awaken them. He stirred in his heavy sleep and let one eye open toward the radio alarm clock. He jarred himself awake and immediately glanced at Casey. She was still out. *I wonder if Mindy gave her two of those Valium*, he thought. He turned off the alarm, before it came on at the set 9:30. He had to compose his thoughts for the ten o'clock call to Alactra. *That should at least queer the exploration deal*, he thought. Maybe it would scare Alactra out of the portage project. Maybe it wouldn't. They would probably believe that he had the videotape. Also, he had an earlier faxed memo from LeYan to Akkre's Lafayette hideaway. He could get a copy of the camcorder tape and send it to them, but he doubted that would be necessary.

He called Lafayette Regional Airport and found out how they could get out of there. They would be able to get to Dallas in time to catch the 3:10 to Minneapolis and the 6:40 to Duluth. *Damn! It will be eleven tonight before I can get this little lady back home*, he thought.

* * *

Alasom Alactra called Paulette from his private office suite on the forty-first floor.

"I am here. Please ask LeYan to join me."

LeYan got off the elevator at the forty-first floor, walked into a small entry area and pushed the square panel that brought a soft, full gong, about which Buddha would have been proud.

A muted light panel came alive above the door and LeYan was able to press the tiger's head latch to open the massive, pearl-inlayed door.

If the main office, conference room and penthouse had been softly luxurious, the ultimate ruler's "holy of holies" was hard (slate-tile floors) and Spartan (no art, no fireplace, no bar). His desk was a somewhat rounded, forty square feet of stainless steel, inlaid in ebony. There were no drawers obstructing the two ebony supports. The only thing occupying the spacious top was a telephone console, that included a visual monitor—and a brief "confessional" from J.B. Akkre.

"LeYan, please enter," he said. She obeyed and soundlessly moved to one of the two upholstered chairs in front of the desk.

"I will accept the call from Mr. Ryker on the speaker phone. Do you have anything to say prior to his call?"

"Mr. Alactra...I am sorry that..."

"LeYan, *please* do not excuse yourself. We need *facts*, not *excuses*."

"The only fact that I know of, sir, is that Akkre's people cannot help us."

The phone rang. LeYan jumped inwardly. Alasom was the essence of calmness as he answered the phone and pressed the "speaker" button.

"Yes," he said. His answer sounded like it came from a well.

"This is Buck Ryker. You have my message and J.B. Akkre's confession. I have a videotape of his capitulation. I have a copy of your executive vice-president's recent fax to Akkre. Your involvement is unquestionable."

"Mr. Ryker, please, what is your point?"

"My point is that with this evidence I can incriminate your company in fraud and criminal activity."

"What criminal activity?"

"Listen, Alactra, if you had witnessed what those hired bastards did to my wife, you would know what *criminal* is. Now, before I get specific about what *I* can do to each and every one of *you* there in your tower, here is what *you will* do! I am sure that your little playmate is listening. Have her write this down:

I, Alasom Alactra, Chairman and President of Alactra International, hereby acknowledge our involvement with one J.B. Akkre and his agent, Ramon Rebelde. While we do not condone their methods, we agree that we conspired in plans to make illegal explorations in restricted areas of Minnesota, namely the Boundary Waters Canoe Area. All such conspiracy will cease as of 10 AM CDT, July 2, 1999."

"Mr. Ryker..." Alasom began.

"Don't interrupt," Buck said quickly. "There is nothing you need to say. Sign the statement and fax it to me at the number I sent you, within the next fifty minutes. I warn you, do not change a word! If I do not receive it by 11 AM, I will immediately FedEx video tape recordings of Akkre's confession to Representatives Wayneson and Saguaro, also to Floyd Noyes, chairman of the subcommittee, and to Cartoom Enterprises." Buck hung up and grasped the phone with both hands, until his adrenalin stopped pumping. Then he looked at his wife. *Casey, I believe I have partly gotten revenge for what these people did to you*, he thought. Casey slept.

* * *

"It seems we have underestimated Mr. Ryker, the *treehugger*," Alasom said. "LeYan, send the fax to him—exactly like he read it!" Then he mused aloud, "Cartoom Enterprises—how does he know about them? That is the *last* thing we want to do—get *them* excited! They had my brother killed, you know, because he said the name of the boss at a cocktail party."

* * *

That Friday morning, Congressman Wayneson called his assistant, David, into the expansive office. "David, would you please take this rough and prepare it for my review when I return from the holiday break. I have visited with Congressman Saguaro about this and we want to introduce it into legislation as soon as the issue can be scheduled in subcommittee."

David took the sheet of rough typing, with pencil edits, and returned to his office.

In a minute, Wayneson appeared at his assistant's door and said, "I am going to get a head start today, David. Mrs. Wayneson and I are flying to Toronto and driving north to a lodge on a small lake out in the woods—got to get away from the hustle and bustle once in a while, you know. This lodge is great—not a soul within view. See you on the sixth—probably late afternoon."

David smiled at the irony of the Congressman's need to get next to nature and began slowly re-typing the words that he found hard to believe. He had never before intercepted information from his boss and passed it to someone else. Now, he said to himself, "Charlie has got to see this!" The one-page fax went over the wire immediately to Mr. Charles Henstead, Nordland County Tourist Information Center.

* * *

When Buck checked out of Spanish Beard Motel at 10:45, Friday, July 2, Alactra's fax was waiting. A quick scan told him that Alactra had followed instructions to the letter. He asked the clerk to call a cab for eleven. He also gave the clerk a small, heavy box and said, "This will be picked up soon by a Cajun called Muskrat Man. He needs this back today." Buck thought that Muskrat Man would enjoy the note about how the guns had been used.

Casey had disappeared into the bathroom as soon as she woke up. Neither had said a word. When he came back from the motel office, she was dressed and ready.

"Casey..." Buck started.

"Buck, I love you. I understand what happened. I can get over it. Can we go home now?"

They caught the 3:10 from Dallas to Minneapolis, and the residual Valium took over again.

* * *

Charlie first saw David's fax message about the Congressman's proposal at three Friday afternoon. It had arrived at ten o'clock, but they were so busy with tourists, two days before the Fourth, that he just ignored it, propped up in the Center's fax machine carriage. Even then, he assumed it was some information from the Forest Service about a BWCA entry permit. There was a lull about 4:30 and he read it. He immediately walked to the round table in the map corner of the paneled Info Center, and sat down hard. Lillian was pouring herself a cup of coffee. "Charlie, what's that you have?"

It took a minute for him to answer. He looked dazed.

"They've done it. They've got the two Congressmen to support the bill," he said softly to himself.

"What did you say?" she said.

Charlie shook himself and decided to save the news for Buck. *No use worrying Lillian.* "Oh, just some confirmation from the Forest Service."

He called Buck as soon as Lillian was busy: answering machine. Same thing an hour later. *I'll call tomorrow*, he thought.

* * *

LeYan did not try to talk to Alasom again until late afternoon, when she requested an audience.

"Mr. Alactra, as unfortunate as this morning was, I don't believe it necessarily affects our plans. The meeting Bill and I had with the Congressmen indicated that they were favorably impressed and would proceed. I plan to contact Wayneson's aide to see if he has any information."

"Very well, LeYan. We'll see," he said.

She left well enough alone and returned to her office, where she put through a call to Wayneson.

"Congressman Wayneson's office," David said.

"Hello, David. This is LeYan Syn from Alactra International. Can you tell me if there is any definitive action on the portages project"

"Ms. Syn, you know I cannot divulge information before it is officially promulgated. But I can say that the last I heard, the proposal was being considered positively."

"Thank you, David, we will wait for more information after the Fourth."

"Good-bye, Ms. Syn."

* * *

When they landed in Duluth at eight o'clock, Casey said,

"I wonder what we'll have waiting for us here? But whatever it is, we'll handle it."

"That's my girl," Buck said as they got up from the seats. He took her in his arms long enough to get some eager suits nervous in the rear of the aisle. "Probably nothing waiting but an old rusty Subaru," he said as they moved to the front of the plane.

"That's the Subaru that I love," she said.

As they walked into the gate area, the Northwest agent proclaimed over the loudspeaker, "Northwest flight 3013 is boarding now for immediate departure for the Twin Cities."

As they left the area, they glanced toward the group seated by the gate. One man rose slowly—and kept on rising, until he reached a full height of nearly seven feet. He towered over a U.S. Marshall standing next to him.

"Look at the hands on that guy," Casey said. The giant's hands were joined at the wrist with handcuffs.

* * *

KDAL-FM, on the way north from Duluth, started out soft rock and became smooth sentimental. They held hands and sang along until Fall River.

"You need anything at the Serve-U store?" Buck asked.

"Maybe a jug of milk," she said. As he walked into the convenience store, Buck saw Sheriff Dan's squad car pull up. He waited, and they walked in together.

"Been pretty calm around here since you left," Dan kidded. "Got the black suit boys out last Saturday and the Marshall took the giant on the plane tonight."

"They seem to stick to me," Buck said. "I think I saw the black suits—but wearing Hawaiian shirts—in D.C. Then tonight, I think the giant got on the plane we just got off of. Anyway—good riddance."

Another half-hour and the Rykers were where they wanted to be—a rustic log cabin in the woods.

***

"SNAP! POP! POP! POP! BOOM!"

Buck woke with a start. He listened during a pause. Then he recognized another series of noises. *Yeah! It's July 3. The kids are starting Independence Day early.* He was surprised that the sound carried the mile from his nearest neighbor family. He eased out of bed and saw Casey stir. He stood motionless for a minute then padded downstairs to use the first floor bathroom. He felt like firing up the whole bacon and eggs scene, but remembered that he had been eating too much. So he grabbed a piece of toast and made coffee out in the tool shack. A few jolts of his own black and strong would get him moving.

Saturday morning, with the crew gone, left him alone in his real world. Whatever happened outside of his twelve acres was now outside his area of duty. He and Casey had given other concerns a fair shot. Now it was time to take care of the home front.

He took a visual inventory of his home-building logs. He would need more shortly after the crew started on the new order. He also had to finish the construction prints before they start on Tuesday the sixth. The thought of more logs led to George and then to George and Mindy—probably having a great time on her ranch. George used to like horses a lot; but, in recent years, only had time to run the 150 horses in his old flatbed truck. Buck bet that Mindy would be game for a BWCA canoe trip. On the other hand, Nordland County was a long way from Neiman-Marcus and the Dallas Symphony Orchestra. He thought of George's urgent visit three weeks ago that started the amazing portage fiasco. Then the phone rang.

Ryker Log Homes," he answered.

"This is Charlie. Buck, I have something you have to see. Can I come over right now?"

"Any time, Charlie. I'm not leaving."

When Buck heard the car in the driveway, it was hard for him to believe that Charlie would push his old LeSabre to get there that fast. Charlie stopped in front of the shack and jumped out with a paper fluttering in his hand. Buck noticed that the usually meticulous Charlie had not yet shaved this morning and his shirt, hanging outside his pants, was buttoned out of line.

"What you got, Charlie?"

"I tried to reach you all afternoon yesterday, after this fax came from David. It sounds like Congressman Wayneson is ready to introduce the bill about the portages."

Buck read it:

MEASURE:	HR82694
SPONSOR:	Wayneson (D-NJ) and Saguaro (R-NM)
BRIEF TITLE:	A bill to provide for construction of tourist lodges on selected portages within the BWCA of Minnesota

HR 82694 would allow Alactra International a ninety-nine year lease on selected portages within the Boundary Waters Canoe Area Wilderness. It would further allow construction of lodge buildings near these portages. In view of the significant economic value to northeastern Minnesota and the facilitation of the wilderness experience to more Americans, it is proposed that Congress approve such leases and construction. There will be no less than eight and no more than twelve such portages approved. The locations must be approved individually by the United States Forest Service.

Buck was long past getting excited or surprised by the decisions made by the masters of conventional wisdom. He also realized that there were the usual loopholes: the fact that the Forest Service was left holding the approval stamp was in itself a harbinger of battles to come—*if* the rest of Congress rolled over for the proposal.

"What do you think, Buck?" Charlie was very agitated.

"At this stage, I don't 'think'."

"What can we do?"

"Now we will have to involve our Minnesota Congressmen and Senators. And that is where Senator Wood can help us."

"Will you do that, Buck?"

"No, Charlie, I won't. This has been a one-man show long enough. Our county group should write to our legislators and state our consensus. You may want to get nominations from members and elect an official representative. Incidentally, that will not be me."

"But you *will* come to this meeting?"

"I will attend."

Charlie departed and Buck walked slowly to the log home—his home and Casey's home. As he neared the "T" that then branched toward his home, Charlie came driving back—much too fast for Charlie. He screeched on his brakes and hollered out the passenger window, "Buck..."

Buck walked over and put his hands on the edge of the downed window.

"Yes, Charlie."

"Does this mean that I should send back the checks to LeYan?"

"It's up to you; but I would not *cash* them, whether you send them back or not. Maybe you should just pretend that they got lost in the mail. That old wood mailbox you have is not too reliable, is it? But I don't think you want to be connected with Alactra—possible collusion, you know."

Charlie drove away slowly. He was happy he had not cashed the checks. This was all too scary. He would not tell Lillian.

Entering the front door dissolved any concerns that Buck might have had about the recent news. He paused in the entry. He could hear Casey humming along with Mozart—not too closely on key—but enthusiastically. He banged the door closed to avoid a sudden appearance—she had experienced enough of that recently.

"Hi, honey. How about a cup of tea?" he said. They met and had a hug in the middle of the living room—Casey with a dust cloth in her hand. Her cut-off tank top and shorts outfit commanded Buck's full attention.

"You *are* loose," she said. "Tea at ten o'clock? What will the neighbors say?" Buck served tea at the dining room table.

"OK, Mr. Smooth, what are you selling me *today*?" she asked with a perfectly business-like countenance.

"You know, Case, if I were to tell you that I had won the lottery, I think you would know it before I said it."

"What are wives for?"

"OK, here's the deal." He showed her the fax and gave her the same rationale he gave Charlie.

"So, how do you feel?" she asked.

"Yesterday we won one. Today, we may have lost one. But fifty-fifty ain't bad."

Twenty minutes later, Buck hollered at Casey, who had gone in for a shower. She stuck her head out the bathroom door and said, "Will you *please* hold it until I come out?"

While he waited, Buck put in a call to Jake Sharker, who he knew had set up the trip for Jenny Alburton and her youth group. "Oh, out to Buckskin and Quicksilver lakes—yeah, they will probably camp near the Pine Portage."

Casey emerged with enough towels around her to forestall any intrusion. Buck looked, but she said, "Don't even *think* about it." He gave her an open-arm shrug and did a shower.

As they dressed, Buck decided to open a new subject. "You know, Jenny Alburton and her youth group are going to take off from the Buckskin point in three canoes tomorrow. It would be fun to canoe out there tomorrow morning—give 'em some support—maybe bring them a few goodies. I'm sure they are traveling pretty sparse."

"That's a good idea. I have always respected Jenny's work. If there were about ten of her, all the state schools would benefit."

They spent the day working on the design and specifications for the big new home for which they had received a five thousand dollar advance and signed contract.

"You know, Buck, the month of June was kind of a disaster in some ways," Casey said, as she turned off the desk lamp. "But it certainly was interesting."

"Somehow, babe, I'm not sure that the 'interesting' part is over yet," he said.

31

July 4, 1999 started hot and got hotter. An early sixty degrees in the northland was unusual. Buck loaded the canoe on the rack and placed the large cooler in the truck box. He filled the cooler with ice and a variety of sodas. He thought how the kids would die for a cold pop, where none would otherwise be available. No need to take a Duluth pack. He and Casey were only going out for a short day-trip—should be like a stroll in the park.

Casey pushed out through the screen door with an apple carton of stuff. "I have enough goodies in here to make them think they are back at the mall," she said.

Buck looked around the inside of his large garage and selected a number of items (including his standby 100-foot coil of half-inch line) to have available "just in case." He threw in a couple extra life preservers.

The early morning hot wind—some would probably call it a Chinook—gradually diminished. Strange sort of day, he thought. The clouds were building up in the west. Casey closed her truck door and they left with a slight sense of foreboding.

"We will make this a quick trip," Buck said. I don't like the looks of the weather."

They zoomed out to the big highway, then proceeded southwest and turned off on a two-car-wide gravel road. Casey gave him an up-eyebrow look.

"One of my mysteries, babe," Buck said. "This is a little-known cut-off to the pavement going west. It's rough, but it gets us there."

"We'll see," she said.

After a mile of good gravel, they turned off onto a questionable dirt road that would have required meeting-vehicles to touch the tundra on either side. They finally found relief—like an oasis in the desert. The state road offered a paved, but wavy route, all the way to the end of its sixty miles from the North Shore to their destination.

"For a few minutes there, buddy, I had my doubts," Casey said.

"For a few minutes, you weren't the only one."

"With all that bouncing around, I have to ask where is the next pit stop?" she said.

"You can pick your pit anytime along the road. Just watch out for the poison ivy. Otherwise, we get to the landing in about forty-five minutes."

"I'll wait."

A cities-type person, who for the first time has driven the super highway to Duluth, the North Shore highway and then this final state highway, is immediately put in another world. Within a few miles from the North Shore highway, the adventurer is in a wilderness. At times, there might be the challenge of a deer or moose crossing the road; however, the big challenge is whether to drive the speed limit or to slow down and experience the aroma and freshness of northwoods atmosphere blowing in the window. Within a few miles, a driver, whether in a compact or a gas-guzzler can turn off on a crushed rock road and approach a trophy lake. Once there, the first knowledge is that you are totally alone. Then you realize that all sound has been turned off—as if by some giant hand in the sky. You look again and there *is* something there! Two canoes, each silently paddled by two people, are gliding along the shoreline of the pine-fringed lake. They make virtually no sound. They are the guests. The pristine lake and its green- and white-dappled border are hosts to the visitors.

Casey breathed deeply from her wide-open window. "Have to admit—this is a great thing to do on Independence Day," she said. "The only thing that we might be dependent on is Mother Nature."

They stopped for a few minutes at a public campground and asked if Jenny's group had come by. "Oh, they were here last night, all right! We finally got them quieted down about one o'clock. Jenny was embarrassed, but we knew that kids would be kids," the camp supervisor said. "They were heading north toward Quicksilver Lake. I'm not sure I would try to cross that mile and a half of Buckskin Lake to get to Quicksilver. We're supposed to get some serious wind."

Buck turned on a scratchy, fading local radio station and heard more about "windy conditions imminent." They proceeded to the turnoff for the Buckskin Lake public landing. Two groups were standing around, considering their options. One of the canoe group said, "Yes, three canoes and six young people left here about an hour ago. We had just arrived. The wind was not a factor at that point." Another said, "They planned to hug the shore to the nearest point to Quicksilver Lake, and then push for it."

"How do you figure this weather?" Buck asked.

"I've been out here many times," the man said. "Today seems different. The water is still relatively calm, but it's hotter than it should be. I look for the wind to pick up. Might rain later—even storm."

"The hair on the back of my neck tells me that we have a problem coming up," Buck said. Casey had heard all the conversation and said, "It's your call."

"I'm concerned about those three canoes of kids trying to make it in open water over to Quicksilver. Look to the west. It's starting to cloud up—and they are not fun clouds! They might even make it over there, but they would be stuck. They certainly could not make it back if the wind came up."

"So what do we do?" Casey asked.

"We do what we planned, but faster. Let's try to catch them and help them get back here." Casey did not speak. She went directly to the truck and began untying the canoe. They lifted it off the rack and placed it in the well-worn launch groove at the shoreline. They left the cooler in the truck but took the apple carton of goodies. "Good luck!" one of the onlookers said.

* * *

"What if they are halfway across Buckskin?" Casey asked, after they had paddled a short distance.

"We will try to get close and then wave and shout like hell to get their attention. Then turn them around. This is one time when halfway back is better than going the other half to the far side."

They paddled hard and steadily at an angle between a shoreline route and directly across. They wanted to be able to see them if their canoes had turned back toward shore already. After a half-hour of fierce paddling among increasing whitecaps, they caught a glimpse of three specks, nearly halfway across.

"We're in it, partner! Got to turn them around pronto! Water's choppy," Buck shouted. Casey made no reply, but developed a determined look.

They both waved their paddles, as soon as they came into range. The heavy, ominous clouds were even greener and were approaching rapidly from the west. As they got farther out into the open lake, the waves were deeper. Buck could imagine that at least two of the canoes, with the inexperienced paddlers, were scenes of near-terror.

"I'm worried," Casey hollered. "Let's do it and get back."

They could see that the five teenagers were paddling frantically, but to no avail. Panic had set in, as the Ryker canoe came alongside Jenny's.

"Got to go back," Buck shouted. "Take this rope. Tie it to one of the other canoes. Then pull toward shore—at the closest point. Follow me, I'll tow the other one." Buck had cut the hundred-foot rope in two. He fastened his rope as far forward as possible in the kids' canoe and as far astern as he could in his canoe. "Don't worry," he hollered to the two kids, "just paddle steady—we'll make it just fine!" He could see that Jenny was following his lead. The last thing she did was to scream, "Tie those life preservers on tight!"

The waves were now nearly two feet, and growing. Whitecaps were everywhere. The gun-powder-color clouds were thick overhead and darkening. The strong breeze was almost pleasant in a warm, humid way. Both of the towed canoes—especially the one behind Jenny—were tossing on the waves. If they had not been supported by the towline, they would have foundered.

Buck kept looking back. Casey just kept plowing away, pulling deep, full strokes out of the lapping waves. Buck once delivered a very obvious thrust forward with his right arm, to encourage a gung ho resolve among his followers.

It was now one o'clock and there was no doubt about what Mother Nature had in mind. But no one knew how disturbed that she was really going to get!

* * *

News of the storm raging over 500 miles away had not reached Chicago, as LeYan Syn telephoned Alasom Alactra from her penthouse apartment. "Sir, I am sorry to bother you on the Fourth of July. I hope you and Mrs. Alactra are having a pleasant day. I thought you would want to know that I received word from a House of Representatives intern today. I believe it is good news. When Bill and I were there Friday, I gave the intern some encouragement to advise me if there was any news about Wayneson or Saguaro or the portage project. Today she called me, on her holiday, to say that she had seen a paper lying on the copy machine, next to Wayneson's office. In it, the two Representatives had written a preliminary bill proposal, recommending a ninety-nine year lease and approval for construction on eight to twelve portages."

"That is good, LeYan. Is there anything else?" he said.

"No sir. Not at this time." LeYan was devastated by Alasom's ambivalence. She turned and walked over to a very large man in dark chinos and gray, long-sleeved shirt, with cuffs rolled up. He wore no watch. As she offered him a highball, his huge hand totally covered the ten-ounce glass.

* * *

The strung-out water caravan of four canoes paddled for their lives as the wind became fierce. The shore now was closer—but less inviting. The firs and birches were waving back and forth, but many of them stayed bent toward the east.

The four canoes neared the roaring surf at the shoreline and then turned with the wind at their backs toward the landing. Two of the canoe people at the landing had stayed to watch the action. They helped Buck and Casey pull the three canoes, in Jenny's party, up safely onto shore.

"Weather Service says 'storm warning—unusually high velocity straight-line winds predicted,'" one of the men said.

"OK, folks," Buck said to Jenny and the kids, let's circle the wagons. We can't count on driving out of here at the peak of the storm. Jenny, move your two vehicles twelve feet from my truck and we'll put all the canoes and gear in the center. If the wind gets too tough and the trees start to go, we'll all squeeze under the vehicles."

"Ick," one of the two girls commented. Jenny put a hand on a shoulder of each.

By mid-afternoon, the storm was at a fury, with straight-line winds from 80 to 100 miles per hour. Huge trees snapped in the middle. Ferocious waves rolled into the landing, nearly reaching the three vehicles. There was a deluge of rain wherever they looked through their truck windows. One of the nearby campers had packed away his tent and was attempting to photograph the wild winds. He could not capture the all-consuming devastation. The hurricane-force gale escalated for nearly forty minutes. Then it stopped. The silence was deadly.

After Buck and Casey helped Jenny and her brood get packed up, Casey parceled out her goodies and the cans of soda, so that the kids' day was not a total loss. In fact they were, by that time, exhilarated with the adventure they had been through. Not exhilarated, however, were hundreds of travelers and resort-owners left with the aftermath. The trip back east, on the state road, was a scene reminiscent of a war zone. Trees of all sizes were broken off and left lying in one direction like matchsticks. Many spots in the paved road were covered with trunks and limbs, requiring motorists to remove them before they could proceed.

The hardest hit section of the boundary waters area extended about thirty miles west, with a swath about twelve miles wide. Storm accounts were dramatized on major radio and television networks.

* * *

It was early evening before the day-trippers returned to Ryker Log Homes.

"Looks like we dodged the bullet this time," Buck said, surveying the intact construction yard.

"But the wilderness is set back about fifty years," Casey said.

As soon as they entered the peace and quiet of their home, the phone rang. "It's George," Buck said to Casey, with his hand over the receiver.

"How do things look there?" George asked. "The Dallas stations have you at the top of the news."

"No problem right here, but we just came back from the Buckskin Lake area. The damage there and further west is too much to describe. There's more timber down in that thirty-mile by twelve-mile swath than your tree-cutters could take in twenty years."

"Say, I've got some news for you!" George said, with unusual excitement. "I casually mentioned a few good things about the northwoods and hit a nerve. Mindy's dad is ready for you to build him one of your log palaces on a nice lake. Says he wants to get away from the Texas heat. And Mindy wants to look into buying out and taking over the Sawbill."

"George, we've got to send you out more," Casey said on the kitchen phone.

"Well, Buddy, don't hurry back," Buck added. I'll check your phone calls for a few days. Probably run your business better than if you were here,"

"Well, Mindy and I are going to take a dip in the pool. Eat your heart out."

32

Bill Anderson called LeYan away from the giant distraction in her penthouse. "Did you hear about the storm? It's all over the six o'clock news," he said.

"I just heard the last part—that the storm will impact nearly half of the BWCA for decades. Doesn't sound good, but you *could* say that it is now even *more* important for tourists to have good places to go in what's left," she said.

"LeYan, I *do* admire your conviction!"

"I can't imagine how Alasom will react," she said. "He will probably call me. I will let you know."

Hands' usefulness had now been concluded. He left while she was on the phone. LeYan's next phone call was from Paulette.

"LeYan, Alactra wants a meeting tomorrow morning at eight. He did not give me a clue."

* * *

The steel and slate office mausoleum was more austere than ever when LeYan and her sidekick responded to their summons. They sat in two of the three upholstered chairs before the vast stainless steel and ebony desk. Stainless steel and ebony could also describe the look of Alasom Alactra. LeYan Syn and Bill Anderson knew that they were in for a pronouncement from the master.

Then it began:

"For the past two weeks, I have been reading about the region called Boundary Waters Canoe Area. I have read about men who tried seventy-five years ago to develop these waterways and portages for their own profit. I have read about men like Ernest Oberholtzer, who spent most of his life with no other motive than doing what he thought was right. He and others *stopped* developers. Then I think of our project with its motives. When we get close to fruition, an individual man calls me in my office and tells me that I have to do this or that because 'it is right' and that he is going to make it happen. He even threatens me with vengeance from Cartoom. And this is from his own will—in spite of whatever power we think we have—and even after we have offered him substantial enticement to go our way.

"Then there is this historic storm. If we had built in that area, everything we established would be gone. The overwhelming forces of nature would have risen up against us—a sign that what we were planning is not to be—that it is against nature.

"LeYan, I have written here what I want to do. Please take care of it for me. Now I must go."

The beauty and the prom king were left with nothing further to say.

* * *

Charlie did not expect much action in the Information Center on July 5. He was doing some housekeeping when the fax machine began running. He hurried to read it as it came through "From the Office of Representative Wayneson" but with a "Hi Charlie" in David's handwriting at the top. Charlie did not even wait for it to finish printing before he called Buck. "Buck I would like to meet you and Casey for lunch at the Sawbill. Can you make it early? I believe you will find it interesting. Ok, 11:30!"

* * *

As they drove to the Sawbill, Buck and Casey exhausted all lines of reasoning in an attempt to guess what Charlie had up his sleeve. "He was absolutely mysterious about it!" Buck said.

Charlie sat at a table by the bar, with his hands folded—no beer, no water, only an almost totally worn out place mat showing a couple "Hamm's Bears" cavorting in the woods. If anyone had remembered these brewery icons of the 1950's, it would have been stolen for historic, or trading value.

"Charlie, this is the first time I have ever actually seen anyone who looked like 'the cat that swallowed the canary'," Buck said. "Before we do anything else," he continued, waving away the waitress, "you must tell."

"Casey, Buck, I can't even tell it right. Just look at this." He spread the fax from David out on the table. It read:

> *To Congressmen Wayneson and Saguaro:*
> *In view of our study of the timeless treasure represented by the Boundary Waters Canoe Area Wilderness, Alactra International requests the withdrawal of our proposal to develop buildings on portages. We believe that such a project would violate the unique natural gift that is now available to all.*
> *Signed: Alasom Alactra, President*
> *Alactra International*

After a moment of silence, Casey said, "Gentlemen, I am buying,"

33

Charlie was just as mysterious when he called an emergency meeting at Nordland Bay Lodge. Only half the usual group was available on this short notice, but Charlie didn't mind. He was so ebullient, when he left home for the meeting at seven o'clock, that Lillian asked him if he had been in the cooking sherry. Buck attended the meeting, Casey declined.

When Buck returned home, Casey expressed immediate interest.

"How did it go, Buck?"

"After Charlie had read the fax to them, they had a dozen questions about what you and I had done in D.C., Dallas, and anyplace else. Of course, I was quite general. I don't even want to think about the details."

"Well, there were *some* details I don't mind remembering," she said.

Buck shook his head and continued his thoughts about the meeting: "Some of those guys actually seemed *disappointed* that the project was dead. They started wondering if it would be possible to dig canals in the portages to allow excursion launches from lake to lake."

"Will it ever end?" Casey asked. "Will the boundary waters ever stay silent and wild?"

Buck paused and then replied, "Claude said that the U.S. became the *owner* of the area over 150 years ago—but people are still arguing about how to use it. Will it ever end? I doubt it. I believe we'll all have to keep up the fight—to keep the wilderness as it is.

"Now, partner, what say we get back to the *log home* business?"

THE END

AUTHOR'S NOTE

On July 4, 1999, gale force winds of up to 100 miles per hour did actually devastate a thirty-mile by twelve mile section of the Boundary Waters Canoe Area, along the Minnesota-Ontario border. The United States Forest Service is cautiously tending the miles and miles of downed trees, to avoid further destruction by fire. Through careful administration, however, continued access is available to those who would experience the silent wilderness lakes.

As noted on the reverse of the title page, *SILENT WILD* is a book of fiction. All the personal names, with the exception of Sigurd Olson, Ernest Oberholtzer, Howard Selover, William Jardine, and Edward Backus, are fictitious. The lakes mentioned (except Superior) have been given fictitious names to avoid involving any actual inhabitants of the general areas in the story. While Fall River does not exist in northeastern Minnesota as implied, Duluth and Two Harbors are real, thriving cities, approximately twenty-six miles apart. "Grandma's Marathon" is the registered name for the famous event that is run every June. The scenic rivers mentioned, that course to the vast Lake Superior, are real, as are Gooseberry Falls and Split Rock Lighthouse.

The most genuine and heartfelt objective of *SILENT WILD* is the attempt to present the indefinable, soul-satisfying experience of being a part of a beautiful area that is the same as it was thousands of years ago. But the condition of this wilderness is frail. A few laws changed, a few near-sighted decisions made, and a treasure of nature could be GONE FOREVER.

Lloyd Rice

Give *SILENT WILD* to a friend.
Help expand the awareness of our precious legacy: the pristine wilderness.

YES, I want _____ copies at the special Mail Order Price of $12.50 each ($13.75 regular price).

Include $2.25 Shipping & Handling for one book. See below for multiple book order S&H.

Book total: _____ copies @ $12.50.......................$_____

S&H (1 book $2.25, 2 books $3.00,
3 books $4.00, 4 or more books $5.00................... _____

Minnesota resident Sales Tax (6 1/2%)................. _____
(See reverse side for order and sales tax calculation)

Order Total ....$_____

My check or Money Order for $_____ is enclosed.
(Remit to Pine Publishing, Inc. in U.S. funds. Do not send cash.)

Please charge my: ___ Visa   ___ MasterCard

Name _____

Address _____

City/State/Zip_____

Card #_____Exp. Date_____

Signature _____

Phone _____ E-mail _____

PLEASE ALLOW UP TO FOUR WEEKS DELIVERY. MAIL TO:
PINE PUBLISHING, INC.
P.O. BOX 999   PINE ISLAND, MINNESOTA   55963

ORDER CALCULATION

Number Of Books Ordered	Total Books Plus S & H Only	Sales Tax (MN only) 6.5%	Total MN Order (Incl. Sales Tax)
1	$14.75	$ .96	$15.71
2	28.00	1.82	29.82
3	41.50	2.70	44.20
4	55.00	3.58	58.58
5	67.50	4.39	71.89
6	80.00	5.20	85.20
7	92.50	6.01	98.51

For orders of more than seven books, please use this calculation method:

No. of books _____ X $12.50 Plus $5 S&H = Total $

Minnesota Residents: Add the above total to .065 multiplied times that total. (Example: 10 books would be $125.00 plus $5.00 = $130.00 plus $8.45 for an order total of $138.45.

Note: If you use a separate paper as an order form, please be sure to include all information requested.

NORMANDALE COMMUNITY COLLEGE
LIBRARY
9700 FRANCE AVENUE SOUTH
BLOOMINGTON, MN 55431-4399